THE CAMBRIDGE LIST

BY ROBERT CLEAR

Published by Robert Clear
Copyright © Robert Clear 2011

ISBN: 978-0-9571503-0-0

A cold wind whipped ac
little city of Cambridge. It has
long before the spires of churches and the turrets of towers
pierced the vast East Anglian sky. It will continue to journey
here long after grass has covered the untilled earth and the
square-cut stones are buried deep beneath. On this cold
morning the wind brought with it droplets of rain. Landing
across the city they covered it in a fine film, imparting a
fluidic, slippery beauty to the ancient colleges and narrow
streets.

Bollocks, thought James Connor. *This place is fucking
miserable when the rain gets up.*

In his tiny room on the top floor of Elite Learners
English Language School the only source of light was the
grime-encrusted roof window, inches from his head. The view
offered little more than a few branches of a neighbouring tree
(the only few that it had left, in fact). As far as he was
concerned the glass was a thin membrane separating him from
the infinite grey abyss beyond.

He was into the second hour of the working day, though
it felt like the twelfth, and his latest student was horrendous.
When he had taken the job at the school he had been told that
his role would be to teach academic English to advanced
international learners.

"We're considered one of the posher schools," his boss,
Abigail, had told him during the interview. James had
summoned all the strength his facial muscles could muster to
avoid grimacing at this, though the task was made harder by
her teeth-clenchingly nasal voice.

The truth had been apparent from day one, when he had
been lumbered with two teenage students, neither of whom
could scrounge together a word of English. They had set an
unbreakable precedent for his time there.

3

As he tried to ignore the incessant tapping of the branches on the glass James glanced at his latest student. Mischka, the nineteen year-old Russian, had been stumbling through an ancient and battered English language textbook, and was now on 'Chapter Three: A Typical Workplace Dialogue.'

"Can you direct me to the Photostat machine?" she asked to thin air, in the guise of Mrs Smith, the hypothetical secretary at the fictional cement works. "Yes of course," she replied as Mr Brown, the firm's director. "It's the first room on the right, straight down the hall."

My God, this is boring, thought James. He had lost count of the number of times he had heard this script, and now his skull ached at the tedium.

"What is 'Photostat machine'?" asked Mischka.

James sighed.

"Oh, er, it's a very old photocopier."

Mischka looked mildly suspicious, but hesitantly resumed the script.

"How many secretaries are there in the typing pool?" she asked as Mr Wilkins, accountant at the cement works.

James cringed inwardly. *For God's sake. Why can't Elite Learners afford text-books that were made this century? What next, 'Where is the nearest air-raid shelter?'*

"What is 'typing pool'?" asked Mischka.

"It's a large body of secretaries who… well it's a very old-fashioned term that…" He could see her drifting off. "Just carry on."

"There are seventeen secretaries in the typing pool," she said, once again as Mr Brown.

I'm not sure how many more times I can stand this, thought James in an increasingly frustrated internal monologue that he had repeated as often as he had heard the turgid script. *Oh bollocks, Mischka's looking at me in that*

weird way again. I'd better look interested or I'll end up
mumbling to myself. God, that was embarrassing last time.
Mischka paused and arched an eyebrow.
"What is 'bollocks'?" she asked.

*****

Two floors below, Abigail Price was stirring skimmed
milk into her weak, urine-coloured tea as she cast her mind to
James. Her newest recruit was such a sullen boy. If she hadn't
been so hard-up for staff she would never even have
considered him. She wasn't one to be nasty, but he really was
about as wet as a patch of frogspawn, and with about half the
personality.

At this point James walked into the student common
room, which doubled as Abigail's office. With an effort to
disguise her thoughts she turned to him and smiled.

"How was your lesson?"

"Oh, very good thanks," he said absently. This ritual
occurred at the end of every day and was invariably followed
by a few words about the next week's intake. But not today.

"James," said Abigail, her false smile metamorphosing
into a frown. "I want to talk to you about your work. Now I
haven't exactly had any complaints about your teaching but
everyone has been noticing how… well… how miserable you
look. It's beginning to affect your rapport with the students.
You've been late more than once in the past few weeks too. Is
everything okay?"

The concern in her voice was so artificial as to render
the words almost meaningless, and James was in two minds as
to whether the question was rhetorical.

"Er… well…" he stuttered. For a moment he was almost
tempted to tell Abigail the truth. "I'm fine," he said. "Some
problems at home, but they've cleared up now."

The 'personal issues' lie was a classic, and he felt sure it would get the old cow off his back for the time being. But it wouldn't keep him in the clear forever.

Abigail let out a small, exasperated sigh.

"Fine. See you tomorrow. Try to be in on time."

Zoning out whilst Abigail made inane chat was usually easy. Having to avoid explaining that something was wrong, however, was not. Over the last two months he had become used to disguising his depression with the appearance of mere sullenness, and avoiding contact with others during periods when his anxiety attacks were more frequent. Now, though, his mask was beginning to slip, and having the fact pointed out by someone else jarred him.

He left the school and walked home down Park Road. The wind whipped up the leaves around him but he didn't notice. People passed him by, huddled against the chill, but they were unreal. Nothing beyond his body had substance, but was hollow and without form.

*****

James lived in a large house in the leafy surroundings of Jesus Green. It was owned by his old college, Midsummer, whose notoriously slow administration had failed to turf him out even though he had finished at Cambridge over two months ago. His housemates were all still engaged in their studies.

Dumping his coat and bag in the hallway he made his way upstairs to his bedroom. It was a pigsty and had been so for a long time. During the last two months he had neglected all domestic chores, and his clothes lay strewn in towering piles. His appearance too had become ever more dishevelled, unnoticed by himself but increasingly apparent to those he lived with. Jumping onto the bed he eased backwards on aching muscles, but as soon as his head touched the pillow a knock at the door made him flinch.

"Who the hell is that?" he muttered under his breath.

"Jimmy are you there? I heard you come in."

"Er... yeah come in, mate," said James. He tried his best to clear the irritation from his voice and appear friendly.

The door opened and in came Rasheed Arash, known to all, even his fellow PhD researchers at the biotech labs, as 'Bumrash.'

"Hey Jimmy," he said with a tentatively light-hearted note. "I haven't seen you for over a week. Why are you keeping yourself to yourself these days?"

"Oh, no reason, I've just got a lot on my mind," said James. As soon as he registered a note of concern in Bumrash's voice he found it more difficult to maintain the façade.

"Have you been applying for any more jobs?"

"Yeah but nothing's come back. That bitch at the language school has been on my case about looking sullen, and I know she won't think twice about letting me go."

"That's rough, man. I can't believe you still can't find a job. It's like the fates are conspiring against you or something. Everyone else I know from your year is working, and one or two have really landed on their feet. David Slaker's started off on forty grand, and they pay his...."

"Bloody hell, Bumrash, you're not making me feel any better. These last few months have been the worst of my life."

"I know, they really screwed you over. I thought that after they stitched you up you'd at least be able to find a job in town."

"That's the worst of it. I was torn up at what those bastards did."

"I know, I know. Although if you think about it, failing your degree is sort of a mark of distinction. You know, 'street cred' and all that. Years from now, when you're fixed up with

7

a career and a place of your own, you'll look back on this and laugh."

"I thought I'd get over it straight away if I could just find a proper job and put it all behind me. Instead I've ended up at that shit-hole of a language school. My prospects are well and truly crap. I don't want to sound self-pitying, but…"

"No, no, mate, I completely understand. To be honest we've all been worried about you, especially over the last few weeks. You've become really distant with everyone, and we're supposed to be your friends. Did you go to the doctor like I suggested?

"Yeah I went a couple of days ago. He told me my anxiety attacks were stress–related and that I should make 'lifestyle changes.'"

"No surprise there," said Bumrash. "That's why I decided to take things into my own hands."

A cunning look entered his eyes.

"What do you mean? What have you been up to?"

"Well you know what happened with my research, don't you?"

"Er… no. I'm sorry, I haven't been paying much attention to anything lately. Remind me."

Bumrash gave a sigh of mock exasperation. "Jimmy you're useless," he grinned. "We'd been working on a new drug called Flanoxiride. Studies were pretty far advanced, almost at the human trial stage, but then the private sponsors pulled the funding and the whole project folded."

"I see," said James with only a vague sense of recollection.

"Well Flanoxiride had a number of different applications, but the most promising was as a new type of anti-depressant. In the lab tests the results were amazing. In rats whose brain chemistry had been altered to inhibit serotonin levels the drug returned them to a state of neurological stability almost immediately."

"So what are you suggesting? It sounds pretty amazing but you've only tested it on rats. And in any case the project has been scrapped."

"Yeah those bastards pulled the money after two whole years of labour. It worked out all right for me in the end. I got transferred to the Mex-Gen project. But I still wish we'd have been allowed to go through to the human testing stage."

The expression of intent was unmistakable and he leaned forwards conspiratorially.

"Bummers, you're not suggesting…"

"I want to test the pills on you."

"What? You want to use me as a human guinea pig for your failed experiment?"

"It's not failed," said Bumrash. "Just stalled. Honestly I wouldn't be suggesting this if I didn't think it was safe and that it could help you. Like I said, we're all worried, and if your boss has noticed then things must be bad."

He made a good point but James was highly dubious.

"But how would you even get hold of the Flanoxiride? You said the experiment finished a while ago. Surely all the samples were disposed of?"

Now the look of cunning became one of triumph.

"Not quite," he said. "I took a stash when they cleared out the lab. I couldn't bear to part with it, and something told me that I might be able to make use of it."

"Bumhole, I couldn't…"

"It's safe, man. Trust me, I'm a qualified doctor and I'll monitor your progress. I'm not gonna be breathing down your neck or anything, what with all the time I'm spending in the lab, but I promise it'll be okay. A couple of months is all I'm asking."

James sighed. He had nothing to lose. A glance at tomorrow's timetable lying crumpled on his desk was enough to persuade him.

"Fuck it. I'll do it."

CHAPTER TWO

At first she only hummed. It was a sweet tune that had initially alarmed but then fascinated James. It came from nowhere, and had happened the very first day after taking Flanoxiride. When he started to hear the female voice in his head he assumed it was a side-effect of the drug.

"I'll tell Bumrash about this as soon as I get home," he had thought.

But as the hours passed he had allowed himself to be swept away by the beauty of the melody. It certainly beat listening to students stumbling through passive verbs. Her voice was stunning, its fluctuations in tone and pitch incredibly complex. He seemed not to be experiencing any other symptoms so at the end of the first day he had decided to sleep on it and see if it had cleared up by the following morning.

The next day he woke in a state of blissful relaxation, but within seconds he registered the voice.

"Jesus," he thought. "What the hell's going on?"

Today, however, it was different. There were indistinct suggestions of words here and there, as if the singer were absent-mindedly expanding her repertoire of sounds, adding new textures to the harmonic tapestry. Though yesterday it had been beautiful to hear, now James was amazed at being able to feel the tune as well. Each change in tone and pitch created a sensation of pleasure that rippled across his body.

"I should really tell Bumrash about this. But I wouldn't mind listening for just a while longer. Maybe after work."

Days passed, however, and the song continued to evolve as words gradually replaced the humming. They began as unintelligible utterings, mysterious and difficult to grasp. Soon, though, they formed language and James listened with increasing awe.

On the fourth day the physical sensations stimulated by the voice started to intensify. What had begun as feelings of warmth and pleasure deep inside his body became a broad scale of impulses that raced through every part of him. Nouns were played out across the skin on his back whilst sharp, crystalline prepositions were droplets of warmth deep in his shoulders.

The voice also began to tell a story, and its subject, like the song, rapidly gained in complexity. She sang of existence itself: stories of the stars and galaxies of the universe; the atomic and subatomic, and all the life contained upon the Earth. Human history was spun out like a giant web, and men, women, empires and nations were garnered upon it like dew, glistening and bright.

On the tenth day James lay in his bed blinking at the ceiling. He woke with what had now become a customary sense of peace, and listened as the song told of an as yet unknown species of fish whose eyes glowed purple and which stored its young in a sack above its head. The words and sensations seemed to dissolve the connection between his mind and body, creating the impression of a beautiful waking dream. The smooth melody of the voice drifted across the…

"Shut the fuck up!"

A new voice blasted through his mind, causing him to leap involuntarily out of bed and fall to the floor. It too had been female, though its volume and force were horrific. The singing immediately ceased.

"What… who…?" He was shaking and painfully aware that the shock had rendered his thoughts confused and stumbling. Nevertheless it now occurred to him that all this time he had, without realising it, considered the singing voice to be something external; not part of his own mind but of someone else's.

"Is… Is someone there?" he attempted.

11

"Silence, shit-face!" said the new voice, with
  devastating force.

"Sorry, sorry" he mumbled instinctively. "Er, who… no,
what… no, sorry, *who* am I speaking to?"

"I am Hera, Queen of the Gods," said the voice.

"Oh, I see," said James, confusion making him sound
more resigned than he felt. "Er… What can I do for you?" He
winced at this, knowing how flippant it sounded (how could a
voice contain such authority as to make him feel like an errant
school-boy?).

"Wait a minute," said Hera. Her voice then seemed to
direct its focus elsewhere (in as much as a sound with no point
of origin, and which fills all available space, may be redirected
at all). "Stop hassling me Athena, I don't give a shit if you've
prepared a script." The attention focused once more on James,
"My subordinate is rather keen on forward planning."

"Subordinate?" This was a third female voice. Its sense
of surprise was palpable, although James noted that it did not
have quite the paint-stripping power of Hera's.

The original voice that had sung that beautiful song had
gone. Whoever it belonged to had obviously departed at the
first sign of trouble, as James himself now urgently wished he
could.

"That's right Athena. Can you deny it? Can you? Don't
make me box your ears!"

"You're right of course. Awfully sorry, Hera. Got rather
carried away with it all." The feeling of embarrassment was
pronounced.

"Good. Now back to this mortal…"

"Me?" said James.

"Yes you. Listen carefully because I do not repeat
myself. We are the Olympian gods and we've taken great
interest in your affairs of late."

"How do you mean?"

"I mean your undergraduate thesis. It showed an appreciation of the divine that hasn't been displayed for centuries. We were outraged by…"

"The way they treated me?" James piped up despite himself.

"Silence, you unwiped arse-crack! I don't give a toss about how they treated you. It's the snub to the all-powerful gods that we're concerned with. Such things are unacceptable from those who purport to study the very civilisation we crafted."

"Y-Yes, I see," he stuttered.

"You will be given a list of those who have wronged us and you will exterminate every one of them."

"What? You mean kill people? I… I couldn't…"

"If you don't we'll kill you in their place." This time there was no outburst. Her voice was calm.

"Yeah!"

"Shut up Athena you idiotic little lap-dog," spat Hera. "Think about it mortal," she said again to James.

Then, for the first time in days, his mind was left in silence.

*****

The Sceptre was one of the most popular pubs in Cambridge. Every evening its many rooms were packed with students, lending its quaint interior a lively air. Over the course of its three hundred years the exploits of its more notable regulars had entered the annals of Cambridge folk-tale, and in its most recent nod to the morbid interest of future generations Tim, the long-suffering barman, had heroically preserved the dislocated prosthetic limb of Peg-Leg Sue, the local prostitute. It hangs in an inconspicuous corner as a reminder of an unusually tragic incident. On a rainy Thursday evening three years ago, young Billy West, a fresh-faced engineering student, had pulled up a chair in a quiet alcove to meet Peg-Leg for a quick drink followed by a mighty rogering session back in his room in Emmanuel College. Little did he realise that she had double-booked that night, having prematurely finished off a quickie with her previous client in order to get in a bit of overtime with young Billy himself.

This would have been unremarkable except that on this occasion Billy's supervisor, Dr Burton, had been seated on the table round the corner, out of sight but well within earshot. The doctor was a lousy academic but a first-rate pimp, and Peg-Leg was one of his most lucrative assets (perhaps indicative of the average Cambridge student's low sexual standards). Having heard Billy's boyish voice in concert with Peg-Leg's throaty, forty-a-day growl he had put two and two together and made four (one of the more successful attempts at numeracy in his mathematical career). Enraged at the thought of one of his escorts getting in some unauthorised overtime he had leapt from his seat, charged round the corner and grabbed Billy by the scruff of the neck. Peggers, enraged at the prospect of losing a lucrative shag, had slapped Burton in the face. He had reciprocated in kind, at which point Peg-Leg removed her appendage and began beating him about the head with it.

In a move that was half self-defence and half retaliation Burton had lashed out, undercut Peg's good leg and sent her toppling like a felled tree into the roaring fire. She had gone up like a log, consumed in the inferno. The gallant barman Tim, having seen the whole thing, had jumped over the bar and flung himself into the fray. Ignoring danger he had rushed to Peggers' aid, scooping her up and dousing the flames that had consumed her hair, skin and clothes, whilst Billy and Burton looked on.

Tragically, however, she expired in the searing heat, and barman Tim's heroism came to nothing. All that remained of her was her plastic peg-leg, which now hangs in the same alcove where she met her last punter.

Today, experiencing its late afternoon lull in custom, the Sceptre was subdued. A low murmur of conversation pervaded, mingling with the clink of glasses and the occasional jangling of the cash register. James entered with a sense of purpose on his face and a sure tread in his step. Passing through one room after another he reached the back bar, where he occupied a single, worryingly rickety and cushionless chair at a table near the fireplace (he had always had a strange, rodent-like compulsion to seek-out the most inconspicuous dark corners in pubs and restaurants).

As he lowered himself into his seat a mental reflex approximating the inner ear told him that more than just the chair was unbalanced. It took only a moment for him to realise that he could not remember where he had been before coming here. Had he been at home? In a shop? At work? Travelling only a little further along this avenue of thought he found that he was also unable to recall what had compelled him to make the journey itself. Searching for a point of reference from which to trace the lapse he found that beyond the last two minutes everything was a haze. Generally when one realises that a significant series of memories is unaccountably missing the natural reaction is to flail and thrash about in a sea of thought. Searching becomes a desperate struggle as it does for a child who, having learnt to swim his first strokes, realises that the bottom is suddenly far below. As the feeling gripped him James looked quickly about, and disorientation washed over him.

"Oh God, perhaps I'm not really here," he thought. "Perhaps this is just a dream." Almost in response the colours of the room, the noises and the smells, struck him with a sudden, heady clarity. Everything seemed to draw itself more sharply into focus insisting that 'all is just so, there is no need to worry.' To his relief the sense of panic subsided as he took

15

in the familiar scene. Everything seemed to be just as it ought: the smell of stale beer, the dirty carpet, the cackling of old men in the other room. They were all too immediate, too vital, not to be real.

Then, like a barrister delivering a last eloquent statement that leaves the case for the defence in tatters, the beautiful female voice resumed its ode.

The muscles in James's stomach involuntarily tightened. He could not recall how long the voice had been absent, or indeed why it had ever ceased, but now it was as if she had never stopped singing, as though the time that he had been without her was a mere pause for breath. But something was different. The sensations that the song had created inside him were now gone and all he was left with were the words. But what words they were: a beautiful elegy to fish and chips. Succulent white flesh encased within golden crunchy batter was evoked in hot, steaming glory, the tastes and smells summoned before him in exquisite detail.

He had been wrong, his body was indeed experiencing sensational harmony with the song. This however was not a symphony of pleasure but of powerful, biting hunger. As adjectives of heat and nouns of grease joined in union, so ravenousness became one with desire. After a few minutes he could stand it no more.

"Blow this," he said to himself. "She's making me famished!" The confusion about how he had come to be in the Sceptre, or why, evaporated. He leapt from his chair, almost breaking it in the process, and slipped round the corner to the food counter. As he did so the tune gathered pace. Now the fish mutated from a haddock into a skate and the batter was enriched with Belgian Trappist beer. Standing in the queue he could barely contain himself, and he shifted from one foot to the other. Annoyingly there was an old woman in front of him, taking her time to order. She was wearing a lurid green scarf and seemed to be in a state of profound indecision. Matters

16

weren't being helped by the inept-looking girl behind the counter, whose fingernails were individually decorated with what looked like Maori death symbols, rendered in fluorescent, vomit-coloured shades. They were so talon-like that her attempts to jab the correct keys on the till were mostly unsuccessful, though whether this wasn't more to do with limited motor functions was anybody's guess.

"Do you do toad in the hole?" asked the woman.

"Yeeaah," drawled the girl.

"Can you make it… vegetarian?"

"Dunno."

"Hmmm, maybe I'll go for the toad in the hole…"

"Okaaaaay."

"Or… maybe… I'll… go… for… the… chicken…"

As time itself seemed to slow down, James's pulse began to race.

"If you two vultures have finished picking over that conversational carcass, I'd like to order some frigging food!" he said, more loudly than he had intended. The pair turned and stared at him, the woman in outrage, the girl in passive idiocy.

"Mind your manners young man!" said the woman.

"Eh?" said the girl.

James groaned. "Sorry, sorry. I'm just *really* hungry."

The two eventually drew the transaction to an ambling conclusion. Meanwhile the singer was torturing James with the prospect of a fried rainbow trout battered in a golden, champagne-flavoured crust. He could have screamed with frustration by the time the girl behind the counter waved a talon, beckoning him forward.

"Yeah?" she said.

"Do you do fish and chips?" asked James, fine beads of sweat peppering his forehead.

"Yeah," she replied.

"I'll have that, then. I'm on table five." He handed over his money. "Thanks."

"Yeeeaaahhhh," she said again. She drew the syllable out for a couple of seconds, giving it all the form, if not the contemplative quality, of a mantra.

James returned to his rickety seat and began his impatient wait. In the meantime the song's volume slowly intensified, its notes sharpening. He could block out neither the words nor the melody, both compounding the effects of his hunger. After ten minutes of irritably checking his watch and glancing at the kitchen door, however, he suddenly registered a change. It was as if the voice, formerly echoing as if in a cathedral, had been transported into a small room with plaster walls and wooden floors. It no longer reverberated around the recesses of his mind but skimmed the walls and furniture of the pub. It had a source and she was approaching.

From around the corner came a girl of about nineteen. Her hair was highlighted to the point of ridiculousness and tied back with a fluorescent scrunchy. She wore a scruffy pair of trainers and sported a huge pair of hoop earrings that might have seen better days wielded by gymnasts in a Russian circus. Her makeup was applied copiously and in the style of a wax mask: tarantula-leg eyelashes jostled for attention on heavily shadowed eyelids, whilst layers of foundation sat, plaster-like, on youthful skin. She was a chav. Yet the song, that beautiful, entrancing sound that James had heard for two weeks fell freely from her cheaply glossed lips.

He was agog.

As she stepped up to the table and awkwardly laid the plate before him, she gracefully rounded off a closing note. James's hunger died.

"Who are you?" he gasped.

"I'm the Muse." Her voice was beautiful and possessed a strong East London twang. "I've been singing for you, James."

"But… How is that possible?" he stuttered.

18

"Because I'm an Olympian, like the ones who visited you. Remember?"

The word was like a blow to the head, memory pouring in and saturating the neurons beneath. He recalled everything: Hera, Athena, a list. His mission…

"Oh god!" he whispered.

"Gods," corrected the Muse a little testily.

"I remember! You're one of them? You want me to kill the people on a list!"

"Yes that's right."

"But you can't be serious. I can't just murder innocent people!"

"Oh they're innocent are they? I don't call insulting the gods innocent."

"How can you possibly mean that? Countless individuals have insulted the Greek gods over the centuries. No one even believes in you anymore! Christ, I don't even believe in you! And, anyway, if the gods are real why don't they kill the lecturers themselves?"

"Oh come on," sighed the Muse. "You've read enough Greek literature to know the answer to that. The gods have always carried out revenge through human agents. It's what makes it all worthwhile. They illustrate the futility of mortality through the use of mortals themselves, combining divine wrath and with a heavy dose of irony. It's an essential characteristic of the immortal psyche. I call it 'divirony,'" she said, chuckling smugly at her turn of phrase.

"But this is ridiculous! I can't believe I'm even entertaining the idea that this is real!"

"But you *are* entertaining the idea," said the Muse. She sat down next to him, her delicate, overdone face a model of patience. "You know you are and I know it too."

"But… it doesn't make sense!"

"Irrelevant."

"N-No!" he stammered. He felt giddy now. "The past twenty-four hours have been the worst of my life," he thought.

"Well it's going to get worse before it gets better," said the Muse, in response to his unspoken words.

"What the Hell?? How did you…?"

"I told you, I'm a god. And not just your run-of-the-mill god either. I'm the daughter of Zeus, King of the Gods, and when I was born Daddy endowed me with the power to see the past, present and future, and to inspire mortals with poetry and song about all three."

"Well… okay, just for a moment let's say I'm prepared to accept what you're saying. You're telling me that you are responsible for Homer? For the greatest masterpieces of literature?"

She started nodding.

"The *Iliad*?" (nod) "The *Odyssey*?" (nod) "Macbeth?" (two nods). "And you know everything? You're omniscient?"

"Put it this way, I know a hell of a lot more than all the professors in Cambridge put together."

"Then, if you don't mind my asking, why do you look like…well… a chav?" He winced a little at this, half expecting her to slap him. But she did not.

"Well James," she said calmly, "things were okay between me and Daddy at first, but then my bitch of a step-mother, Hera, moved onto the scene. She's hated me from the word go. Once they were married and she'd been recognised as Queen of the Gods all the other women in Daddy's life were chased away."

"You mean your dad ran away with a slag and left you high and dry?"

"Pretty much. I had to raise myself, so in the circumstances I've not turned out too badly"

"That's tough. Sorry to hear that."

Unexpectedly she smiled at these words and cocked her head to one side, letting her cheap, acrylic-looking hair splay across her shoulder.

"Thanks. You know, you're not so bad. Daddy could've chosen a worse mortal to be the instrument of our divine anger."

"Well I'm not sure how comfortable I am being your instrument. I mean you're asking me to murder people in cold blood. I can't do that. Besides, whatever I may think about them they have families, loved ones."

As he said this, the Muse adopted a sly, knowing air. She leant forward.

"Are you saying you *can't* kill them?"

"Well not exactly. Any human being is *capable* of murdering another, but…"

"So you mean you don't want to?"

"Of course I don't!"

"Really?"

"Yes!"

"But really?"

"Well… y-yes!"

The Muse, paused for a moment, and looked deeply into his eyes.

"I saw what they did to you James," she said calmly. "I know what happened after they screwed you over."

"But… that doesn't mean they deserve to die," he said desperately.

"That wasn't what I asked, James. I asked if you wanted to kill them."

"I…"

"Did you?"

"Well…yes. I did." James winced as he recalled the weeks of sleepless nights, of lying in bed despairing.

"And now? Have you forgiven them?"

He exhaled slowly.

"No."

"We are the Olympians, James, the most powerful forces in the universe. The people on our list have offended us and must be subject to divine wrath. You are to be the vessel of that wrath. Whether you understand the whys and the wherefores is irrelevant."

"But how can I follow what I don't understand."

"You must simply accept that you cannot understand our will."

Her voice lilted melodically as the words slipped from her lips like steam from a hot bath. Her rhetoric somehow seemed to derive all the more force from her beautiful voice being so incongruous with her scruffy demeanour.

"I know you want to kill them, James."

"But it's wrong!"

"Within your limited conception of things perhaps, but it's their fate. And yours. You'll only find peace when you submit to fate. It's the only way that mortals, whose destiny it is to know nothing, can cope with being alive."

"And all because you tell me so?"

"No. All this is so and I'm telling you. Accept your fate and seal theirs."

James leaned back in his chair, which screamed in protest to deaf ears. He was beaten, drained. Everything she had said had struck a chord deep within him. He no longer had the strength to enact resistance.

The Muse registered these psychological machinations as clearly as if they were displayed on a television screen. She nodded in acknowledgment as James whispered, "yes."

At that moment the front door of the Sceptre burst open, the presence of the entrant filling the building and creating the same light-headedness in its occupants as a plane descending from thirty thousand feet. Each footstep seemed somehow to echo on the floor like the drum-roll of a funeral dirge. James looked towards the Muse, who was now backing away from the table. Her face had hardened but otherwise remained inscrutable.

A woman swept into the room. She was magnificently beautiful, her blonde hair cascading in gentle waves down her wonderfully proportioned shoulders, her pale blue dress clinging to her body.

The Muse took a small step forward again before announcing with a slight hesitancy in her voice, "James, this is Hera."

"He knows who I am," came the savage reply. It was true, James had somehow known the moment he had heard her enter. But what did this mean? Were the gods now appearing before him physically as well?

"Silence!" commanded Hera, apparently hearing his thoughts as clearly as the Muse had done.

"Sorry, sorry," jabbered James. He lowered his eyes, as one would do before a schoolmistress. "What's going on?" he mumbled.

"I can see that this little vaginal wall-scraping has been repeating the instructions we gave you not an hour ago," she said, before addressing the Muse. "I suppose you created this place to put his mind at ease whilst you reiterated the urgency of his mission?" Her voice was heavy with disgust as she swept the room and its contents with her blistering gaze. "As if what we had told him to do wasn't clear enough you took it upon yourself to translate for us?"

James was confused. She seemed to be suggesting that the Sceptre was not real. And had he really heard her voice only an hour ago? It seemed like days.

"I wanted to spare him the trouble of finding out the hard way how serious you are," said the Muse, her voice tinged with fear. "We spoke about it and he accepts what he has to do. Please don't be hard on him, Hera. I brought him here, it wasn't his fault." She was scared and her shrinking posture showed it.

"You stupid little bitch," spat Hera, advancing menacingly.

The Muse began to back away until she reached the wall of the fireplace and could go no further.

"How dare you take it upon yourself to meddle in my affairs."

"But… But Hera, Zeus convened the Olympians and said we all had joint responsibility for the plan and its execution. I'm just doing my bit." She was visibly shaking now.

"Well you've bitten off more than you can chew this time, you piece of pond-scum."

Hera raised a tightly clenched, milky-white fist and slammed it into the Muse's jaw. The sound was sickening: a stomach-turning crunch that could be heard across the room. The Muse was thrown with an ear-splitting crack against the wall, which crumbled under the impact. Dust was thrown up, as bricks and lumps of cement were scattered before settling as a dense pile of rubble on top of the Muse's crumpled form.

James leapt from his chair aghast.

"Bloody hell!"

Hera turned menacingly towards him. The authority she exuded was clearly backed-up by terrifying power.

"Now then, mortal, since you obviously didn't understand me before I'll make things nice and easy. Everything you see here is a mental construction, a dream." She inclined her head towards the devastated wall.

"That little piece of crap conjured it up in order to have a private word with you before things get underway. She's always been a human-loving meddler and I can only suppose she thought that she could evade detection. But she underestimated me. Don't make the same mistake. If I catch the two of you cavorting together again I'll snuff you both out. Understand?"

"Y-Y-Yes," stammered James.

"Your work begins tomorrow. When the sun rises you are to begin exterminating the people on the Cambridge List. We'll tell you exactly who you're killing and what you need to do as-and-when."

"I... I... Okay, I'll..." He could barely spit the words out. "I'll do it."

"That's right. And if you should fail in your task…" She paused, turned and stooped to pick up a large, bowling-ball sized lump of brick and cement. Brandishing it in her hand she took a single step towards him. Without a word she raised it aloft and brought it crashing down on his skull. He could not even yell out. Pain wracked his body as he fell to the floor. Through the agony and sickening shock he felt lakes of blood rapidly pooling behind his eyes, and in the far corner of his fast-fading vision he could just observe the Queen of the Gods stepping over him, holding the weapon above her head and letting it drop with a gory crunch upon his skull.

*****

James woke gasping for breath, arms flailing. His left hand instinctively went straight for his head where he had felt the impact, whilst his right lashed out, grabbing for the stool. But there was no stool, no beer-stained carpet. He was lying on his bed, fully clothed and drenched in perspiration. He gulped down a couple of breaths. So it *had* been a dream! As he wiped his hand across his face any sense of relief he might otherwise have felt was quickly crushed. When he drew back his fingers he found them covered in blood.

Jumping out of bed, he ran over to the small mirror above the sink. The lower half of his face was a red mess, the gore still pouring from his nose. With trembling hands he ran a basin of water and made a shaky attempt to clean himself up.

There was no questioning what had happened now. With his head pounding he went to his desk. There on a sheet of paper, written in a hand that was not his own, were five names: Harriet Mason, Penton Wildencrust, Alan Tanning, Elliot Norther and Paul Fringe.

The Cambridge List.

CHAPTER THREE

An hour later and James had instinctively turned to the English cure-all for stressful situations: a cup of tea. As it sat steaming on his desk, however, it offered little comfort.

"How the hell can this be happening?" he thought as he leant forward in his chair. He cast his mind back two weeks ago to when he had been depressed, unable to sleep and experiencing almost daily panic attacks about a future that seemed endlessly grey. Now everything was black and sinister, but it was undeniably exciting.

"Don't worry, my darling, black really is the most flattering colour. Grey looks so draining on you anyway."

At this point James was hardly shocked to hear another female voice. In fact, all things considered, he had rather expected it. This, though, was a duskier, smokier intonation than the authoritative boom of Hera or the lyrical warmth of the Muse. It left the hairs on his head and, more disconcertingly, those around his groin standing on end.

"Er, thank you. I think," he said. "May I ask who I'm speaking to?" It seemed that one of the most distracting things about disembodied voices, other than their existence, was that you were never sure which way to turn to address them. As instinct compelled him to look about in search of the incorporeal source he began to sympathise with Jonny the Jester, the resident beggar of the park round the corner. Jonny would look slyly from side to side and swivel his head as he listened to the pigeons, who apparently told him all the latest gossip from the coop.

"I am Aphrodite, Goddess of Desire," came the reply. "My reputation precedes me of course." Her voice was saturated with a self-command that made it compelling. Having heard only a few words James found himself desperate to hear more.

"Yes of course," he said. For some reason he felt sheepish. It was like being thirteen all over again and speaking to his teenage crush, Amy Cavendish, except that Aphrodite's voice made Amy's sound like a cat being beaten to death with a pair of bagpipes.

"James, I'm here to inform you whom you'll be terminating first."

When she spoke his name he could feel a distinct rustling in his underwear.

"Oh God, I mustn't get a hard-on mid-conversation. The embarrassment!" he thought. He tried to concentrate his energies on suppressing it, but his rather feeble efforts were swiftly quashed by the goddess.

"Stop thinking about your schlong! Focus on my voice."

"Sorry, sorry. I forgot that you're inside my head," he said aloud. It occurred to him that this might be true in more senses than one as his erection breached the elasticated perimeter of his boxers and poked its own head over the parapet.

"Listen," she purred. "I have come to inform you that the first victim of our divine wrath will be Harriet Mason." James looked down at the list and pencilled an asterisk by her name.

"Sit tight, my darling, and await further instructions."

*****

Fatty Mason had been James's supervisor, the lecturer personally responsible for overseeing his academic work. Her role as academic mentor included setting him weekly essays, helping him with his final year dissertation and advising him on his Master's degree application. Ever the mighty bitch, she was hideously obnoxious in person and equally rude via email. Towards James himself she had been particularly vile: he, the lone male supervisee amongst an otherwise female cohort. Her most notable physical characteristic was her vast, corpulent bulk. Seeing her waddle into the Faculty each morning was akin to watching an oil tanker docking in a fishing pond. The door at the front entrance was scarcely designed for a being of her circumference, and she was forced each day to slide in sideways. The wheezing that issued forth from her lungs during this complex feat of manoeuvring was enough to make innocent passers-by wince.

Having spent a year suffering essay titles such as 'Why Are Men the Scourge of Greek Literature?' and 'Wasn't Hercules a Total Bastard?' James had learnt to dread his supervisions. Tightly squeezed into the two-seater sofa in her rubbish-tip of an office, she would carry out hour-long tirades about anything and everything, just as long as it had nothing to do with Classics. She would grunt like a pig as she handed back his essays, expressing only the mildest, most reluctant praise at even his best work.

The undergraduate dissertation was the largest and most important assignment of his degree: a ten thousand-word piece about any classical topic he wished. He could set his own title, carry out the work as he liked and it would be evaluated based on its originality and quality of research. Many students dreaded it and it loomed over their final year like a dark cloud on the horizon. James, however, had taken to the work immediately. He had chosen the title, 'A Re-Examination of the Gods: The Nature of the Divine in Ancient Greece.' It proposed that the modern understanding of the Greek gods was flawed, and that a radical new approach was needed. Ambitious though it was, he was certain that his ideas had potential. Unexpectedly even Fatty had eyed his proposal with interest. Most of her students could be relied upon to churn out the usual old dross each year but here was something different. His ideas had been original and the methodology of his approach flawless.

"Shame he isn't a woman," she had thought, "then it might almost be worth taking seriously." She had offered him no support, and James's attempts to prod her into action were as futile as a one-man mission to lever a beached whale back into the sea.

Despite this he had diligently submitted drafts of his work to Fatty regularly. She would, however, read them without comment, and after a while he had given up asking her for feedback.

From his earliest undergraduate days he had aimed to carve-out a career in academia. What had begun as a natural wish to avoid gainful employment had become, by the time he undertook his dissertation, a genuine scholarly interest. Looking ahead to beyond his undergraduate studies James knew that the essential next step on this path was post-graduate research, and he had little doubt that a Master's degree from Cambridge was the surest way forward. There was, however, a strictly limited number of places on the Classics Master's course, and it was common knowledge that most of the supervisors would select only their personal favourites from amongst the applicants. James had always seen this as grossly unfair, but the fact that none of Fatty's other students had intended to apply, combined with the quality of his work, had buoyed his hopes.

Towards the end of term, however, in one of his last supervisions, the first sign of trouble had made itself known.

James recalled that day vividly. Cambridge had been grey, drizzly but otherwise unassuming. In Dr Harriet Mason's office, however, the atmosphere was charged.

Crammed into her throne-like sofa, Fatty gave the appearance of holding court amongst the empty pizza boxes and chocolate bar wrappers that littered the floor.

"What did you think of my essay?" James asked, after gingerly finding a spot amongst the crisp packets and sweet wrappers on the sofa opposite.

"What essay?" Fatty snorted.

"The one you set me last week. 'Were Ancient Greek Men as Ludicrous as their Modern Day Counterparts?' Remember?"

"Oh, yes," she grunted, swallowing a mouthful of food. "Very good, I suppose. You can't have it back though. I binned it."

"Oh. Any other comments?"

Fatty had now shifted her attention away from him and was attempting to unwrap a chocolate ice cream. Naturally her sausage-fingers were not endowed with much dexterity, and the treat was proving to be a slippery prey indeed.

"Hmmm? Oh no, nothing much…" she muttered. "Things have been a bit topsy-turvy what with the ambassador's son wanting to come here for the Master's, but it looks like everything's been taken care of…" She trailed off as the wrapper finally split to reveal the chocolatey goodness beneath.

But James's ears had pricked. For here she had let an interesting fact slip. Very little of what went into Fatty's mouth ever made a return journey, but like a little sardine that slips the jaws of a dolphin and swims to safety, this little fact had darted out from behind her sharp teeth before she could swallow it back down.

"But I'm still on for making the grades though?" he said.

"Yes, of course."

"Okay. Because you know how hard I've been working towards this. All the other places have already been assigned, so there's only one space left. You told me it was assured, but if there's anything else I should know…"

"Don't be so pathetic, Connor, it's in the bag. Christ, you're so wet you must have algae growing up your back."

Her words were about as reassuring as they could be for Fatty, but something was wrong. He excused himself as soon

31

as politely possible and practically ran out of the Faculty building into the drizzle.

"So now there's another applicant, and the son of an ambassador at that," he thought. On the face of it there was nothing to worry about. If the last place was going to James, the ambassador's son would simply be forwarded to the new round of applications next year. Something, however, sat uneasily with him. It might have been Fatty's body language or the conspiratorial sense that had been conveyed by the words 'everything's been taken care of.' Whatever it was he paced up and down the little court outside her office for fifteen minutes, working himself up until anxiety got the better of him.

"I have to know what's going on here," he said to himself eventually, before rushing back inside. As he approached her office he slowed his pace and tried to appear nonchalant.

"What could my excuse be for returning? Oh screw it, I'll just have to blag it."

His knocks received no reply. He tried the handle and, to his surprise, the door was unlocked. What was more a cautious peep revealed the room to be empty of Fatty's gargantuan presence. He had never done anything like this before, and as he snuck across the debris the thought that she might waddle back in at any moment gave him a giddy rush of adrenaline.

"What the hell am I looking for?" he thought desperately. "If she finds me here she'll eat me alive."

Then something caught his eye. There was nothing overtly conspicuous about the note, it was scrunched-up and dirty like everything else there, but he picked it up and read it anyway.

"Dear Harriet, thanks for the favour re Sir Malcolm's boy. Nobbling Connor shouldn't be too much trouble. The plan should work a charm. Thanks again, I owe you a pint. All the best. Fringe."

James's face went white as he read it. Professor Paul Fringe was the Faculty Secretary, sitting atop the academic pecking-order and responsible for admissions and general academic affairs. As the words of the note sank in their meaning became painfully clear.

"He's asked that fat bitch to sabotage my work in order to make a space for the ambassador's boy! And she's agreed!" he gasped. "What am I supposed to do now? I can't confront her or she'll know I've been through her stuff, and then I'll really be screwed! Fuck!"

He had begun spluttering with shock when suddenly he heard feet in the corridor outside. These were not the ordinary footsteps of a passer-by but the heavy thumping of too great a weight upon unreinforced floorboards. Fatty had returned, and with her chubby fingers fumbling at the door handle James's outrage turned to terror. If she caught him here she would have all the excuse she needed to have him expelled. Looking around in desperation he saw that the only place to hide was behind the sofa.

Ignoring the threat of E. Coli and rat bites he darted across the room at lightning speed and dived behind it just as the door opened to reveal Fatty's bulk. Like a great ship she bore down upon the couch at full-steam-ahead and began scoffing the pastries that she had purchased from Mrs Jacob's Patisserie across the street. In mounting discomfort James was forced to listen to fifteen minutes of stomach-wrenching chomping and lip-smacking as the cakes were devoured. It was only when the ogre had finished gorging and fell asleep where she sat that he was able to venture an escape, the foghorn blast of her snores covering the sound of his footsteps.

After James discovered the plot, events unravelled with the certainty of fate itself. Since Fringe, the highest person in the Faculty, was obviously the prime instigator of a conspiracy against him there was no one he could turn to for help. Instead, he pinned his hopes on making his work so good that

33

they would have no choice but to accept him onto the Master's course. All his future plans depended on it.

A month later, after his thesis was handed in and his exams were over, he received a curt letter from one of the administrators. It informed him in terse, administrative tones that his work had not been properly bound, that some of the pages had been lost and that this had had a profoundly negative effect on his final marks. In addition, the three markers, Penton Wildencrust, Allan Tanning and Elliot Norther, had found the ideas too radical for an undergraduate dissertation and had reduced the score to less than a pass. It was decided that, in the final analysis, his marks were not sufficient for him to be awarded a degree.

As far as the academics at the Classics Faculty were concerned, that was the last they would ever see of James Connor.

*****

Aphrodite's instructions had been clear. Obviously things were about to kick-off in earnest and James just had to sit tight until then. He looked up from the list and saw that his bed-sheets were spattered with the blood that had poured from his nose minutes before. Gathering them up he went downstairs to the kitchen where, irritatingly, the washing machine was in use and still had almost half an hour to go. Never mind, he would wait.

Dropping his load into the empty laundry basket he stalked off to the toilet, though upon his return he found that his other housemates, Greg and Maisy, had adjourned in the kitchen. Greg had spotted the bloodied sheets and now brandished them in a disconcertingly triumphant manner.

"Hey James. Whose are these gore-rags?" he asked, grinning.

He was the most friendly and engaging of all James's housemates, and his propensity to get hammered every weekend had rendered him numb to the implications of clothes stained with bodily fluids.

"Er, search me," replied James. His tone of voice was perfectly dissimulating, but his face had involuntarily adopted the same expression it always did whenever he lied or experienced chronic diarrhoea.

"Bloody hell, check these out, Maisy," he said, brandishing the sheets like a war trophy.

"Ha ha! Manky!" Her cackle was witch-like and teeth-clenchingly loud. She was also universally popular and, had it not been for her petite physique and pretty face, her rough-and-ready sense of humour might have rendered her a tomboy.

As James watched, Greg threw the bloody sheets over his own head and adopted the mannerisms of a ghost.

"Wooaaahhh!" he moaned, bobbing up and down in front of Maisy's face. "Maisy, I am the ghost of Virginity Past. Your sheets are covered in blood! Why have you not kept your chastity?"

"Ha ha. I'm so sorry. I tried my best but I was at the grocers the other day and I didn't have enough change for a loaf of bread. I had to pay the shopkeeper somehow!"

"You little slag. I shall show you a vision of your future. Behold!"

Greg took a step over to the kitchen counter and deftly switched on the small television. The screen flickered brightly into focus and a familiar voice issued forth.

"Hello and welcome to the Malcolm Anderson show. Today we're speaking to kids with kids. It's the teenage mum special!"

Maisy burst into a fit of cackles and even James couldn't resist a smile. Greg was nothing if not smooth.

"No, anything but that! Ha ha! I repent, I repent!" guffawed Maisy in mock horror.

"It is too late for you, you brazen hussy," said the ghost of Virginity Past in a moan that conveyed a mischievous note. "Now you must be punished!"

He and Maisy instantly descended into fits of laughter as he playfully tackled her and they began scuffling on the floor. James wryly wondered how long it would be before the pair were paid a visit by the ghost of Pregnancy Present. Turning his attention away from them he looked absent-mindedly at the TV.

"Our first guest today is a young lady from Cambridge. She has four children, all by different fathers, despite being only a teenager herself. Ladies and Gentlemen please welcome the Muse."

James's jaw dropped. There she was onstage, cheap trackie and scuffed trainers complimenting the soiled scrunchy and brutally applied eye-shadow to create a perfectly coherent impression of cheapness. She was real, her face identical in every respect to its appearance in his dream. How the hell could this be happening? James's head began to spin, and he sat down on the kitchen stool, gripping the counter-top to prevent himself from falling. Through the giddiness one thought formed clearly: even though in the dream he had accepted the gods and their mission, there was still a part of him that had hoped all this had really been caused by the Flanoxiride. Now that hope had been dashed and the immediacy of the sounds and images flowing from the screen made his stomach lurch.

"So tell us about yourself, Muse," said Anderson.

"This is messed up!" thought James, incredulously. "This is insane! And doesn't that dolt at least think it's odd that she's called the Muse?"

His question was almost answered.

"Well Malcolm," she said, her voice edgy with a chavvy twang. "I'm a young single mother from Cambridge, and after the fathers of my four kids left I had to turn to part-time

36

rapping in local clubs to make ends meet. In fact I prefer to be called 'Muesli.' It's my street name."

At this she stood and turned round to reveal the word itself emblazoned in huge gold letters across the back of her tracksuit top. It was rendered in graffiti-like bubble writing, each letter surrounded by a thick, black outline that created an effect remarkably close to that achieved by her jet-coloured eyeliner.

"And how much do you earn a night, Muesli?"

"About ten quid," she said, tossing back her straggly, bleached hair with fingers that were tipped with garishly painted false nails.

"So your children are all by different fathers? What's the story with your latest man?"

"The latest one's called James Connor. To be fair he's been seeing me more and more lately, even though I know he doesn't want to."

This was met with murmurs from the audience.

"How could he not want to see the mother of his own child?" muttered some.

"I wouldn't wanna touch that minger with a bargepole," whispered others.

"I know he's got issues right now though," she continued.

"What sort of issues?" asked Malcolm Anderson with an insincere facsimile of sympathy. "God, these little skanks are all the same," he thought. Sometimes entire weeks would fly by in a whirl of fake blonde hair and near-identical sob stories.

"Well he's been popping pills every day," said Muesli to the sound of canned disapproval from the audience. "Also he's living cheek-by-jowl with a lot of unwelcome guests at the moment."

Anderson had been nodding automatically when suddenly he adopted an air of focused concern.

"Muesli, you'd like to address this guy, wouldn't you?"

37

"Everything's wrong with this bloody scenario," thought James. "Don't the idiots in the audience find it wrong?"

The camera shot to a close-up, and Muesli turned into it.

"That's right, Malcolm. James, I know you're watching this now. I want to tell you that you're gonna be seeing a lot more of me. It's just that Hera..."

"Is that the woman he ran away with?" interrupted Anderson, whom she ignored. The audience gasped.

"She mustn't know that we're in contact, or you know what'll happen. I just wanted to tell you that she and Aphrodite..."

"Oooohh, so there are *two* others?" Anderson interjected again.

"... have both got some serious beef. They're having a bust-up, or at least they will do, and there's gonna be collateral damage. Hera's gonna be visiting you very soon too. I can't be any more specific because she'll find out, but don't worry babe, I'm gonna help you as much as I can."

The audience were clapping now.

"Right on cue," thought Anderson.

"What a brave young woman," murmured the spectators, as one. "She's doing everything she can to keep it straight with her boyfriend for the sake of her kids. What a decent mother."

"I just wanted to let you know that I'm still here and still thinking about you. I'm not like the others. I really want to help," said Muesli.

The TV suddenly went dead and James's heart skipped a beat. By comparison his encounter with Aphrodite earlier in the afternoon had been easy, for he had braced himself for more visitations from the gods. To see the Muse (or 'Muesli,' apparently) talking to Malcolm Anderson, however, had been a slap in the face. She had been interacting with real people; millions of viewers had seen her on their screens. For a moment the idea, the hope, once again entered his mind that he might have been transposing ridiculous thoughts onto otherwise innocuous talk-show babble. But the likelihood was too remote to be entertained. She *had* addressed him through the television, there could be no doubt.

James took a gulp of air and swallowed hard. Ignoring the feeling of exhaustion that suddenly gnawed at him he left the kitchen. On his way to the door he gingerly stepped over Greg and Maisy who were still covered by the sheets, and from whom a different, markedly less disembodied, moaning was emanating. With each step towards his bedroom the beating of his heart made itself felt in his ears, and when he locked his door behind him the sharp clink of the latch made him wince.

Shattered, he walked over to the bed and stretched his legs across the mattress. No sooner had his head touched the pillow, however, than a now hideously familiar voice struck him like a blow to the temple.

"Get up you lazy bastard, you've got work to do."

James sat bolt upright and instinctively suppressed a despairing groan.

"Oh, hello again. How nice to see you... I... I mean hear you." He tried to sound congenial but his own tone of voice made him cringe.

Hera was not impressed.

"If you've finished trying to ram your nose up my perfectly proportioned arse I've got your instructions for the first killing."

"Oh yes, Harriet Mason isn't it?" Again he tried to sound blasé, but hearing his own voice he had to admit he actually sounded a bit of a dolt.

"You know damn well it is, maggot. Now listen carefully. That lard bucket is going to die eating, which was always bound to be the case considering how corpulent she is. We've decided the best way to proceed with her is simply to speed up the process."

"Er… okay. What do you want me to do?" James could only envisage tying Fatty up in a cellar and force-feeding her lumps of beef until she burst, though surely for her that would be more like foreplay than torture.

"You're going to go to Mrs Jacob's Patisserie and buy a job lot of doughnuts. Make sure they're jam-filled because if you buy those ring ones you'll cock up the plan."

"Okay, jam doughnuts. Check," said James.

"Then you're going to give them to her as a present for all the help she's given you with your degree."

"But isn't the point that she helped to wreck my degree?"

"Don't be so fucking simple you little dipstick!" bellowed Hera. "You're going to put poison in them first. Bloody hell, did you think that a little present and a pat on the head constitutes Olympian wrath?"

"I'm sorry, I'm sorry," said James, shaken at the sudden force of Hera's outburst. "Where do I get the poison from?"

"You're going to make it yourself," she said. "Those pills that you've been taking are rather powerful drugs. By coincidence they contain several of the key ingredients to the heart tablets that Fatty was prescribed only two weeks ago. You're going to grind up your pills into a fine powder, mix it into a pot of hot jam and use a baster to insert the mixture into the centre of each doughnut."

It occurred to James that he should have thought it would run along those lines. After all, where else could he acquire poison? Then something struck him.

"If you don't mind my asking, won't it be an open and shut case for the police? Surely they'll have no trouble pinning the blame on me?"

"I should have thought you'd be able to figure that one out on your own. If your pills and her heart medicine have several of the same chemical compounds she'll die of an overdose, not as a result of some other toxin that can be

40

identified through an autopsy. They'll think that she's taken too many pills or been given the wrong prescription."

"But… But won't they be able to identify my pills in her system based on the other chemical compounds that couldn't otherwise be accounted for?" James knew he was skating on thin ice by asking these questions, but he had to know.

"Oh for gods' sake!" Hera's wafer-thin patience was obviously beginning to fray at the edges. "Your little friend prescribed you a drug that hadn't been fully developed. It was scrapped before it even reached the human testing stage. The coroner will never have heard of Flanoxiride, so there's no way he could identify it based on the existence of its other constituent compounds. He'll just assume that she had been taking other medicine alongside the heart tablets."

Despite Hera's foghorn-like voice pounding against the inside of his head James could not help but smile. Her plan was certainly a good one. It eliminated Fatty and got him off scot-free.

"That sounds like a pretty decent plan," he ventured.

"If I want a running commentary I'll supply one myself, you piece of excrement," she spat. "Now shut up and start grinding those pills. And as soon as you've finished get down to Mrs Jacob's." Then the force of her near-palpable presence vanished, and James knew to his relief that he was alone again.

*****

Grinding the pills took the best part of an hour. Afterwards his desk was covered in fine powder, and he with sweat, but he had obtained a neat little pile of innocuous-looking white dust. He then snuck down to the kitchen, from which Greg and Maisy had absented themselves, and spirited a jar of jam from the cupboard. After heating it in the microwave he went back upstairs to finish producing the

41

deadly mixture. With that done, all that remained was to buy the doughnuts and fill them with the poison.

"Easy," he thought.

James grabbed his coat and headed out the front door. It took him twenty minutes to walk to Mrs Jacob's, and on the way he felt successive waves of adrenaline course through his veins. Each street with its inevitable assortment of languid, shuffling fatties brought his murderous actions closer to the fore. He turned the corner onto Silver Street and approached the patisserie, from which the smell of freshly baked bread and cakes, normally so enticing, was now the olfactory equivalent of poison gas. He flinched as it hit his nostrils, and when he opened the door to the tinkle of a little bell he almost grimaced. He knew for whom it tolled. His anxiety rose as he stepped to back of the queue.

He had resigned himself to his fate after the encounter with Muesli and Hera in the phantasmal Sceptre, and once he had begun to act on it by mixing the poison he had allowed himself to be caught up in the preparations, distracted from the burden of thinking. Now, as he looked forward at the queue, he saw only three people standing between the mere prospect of murder and the cold fact of its execution. The sense of immediacy made him shiver as his doubts began to resurface.

Suddenly his phone vibrated with a message from an unknown number.

"hey babe its muesli. don't worry, everything's ok, just proceed as planned. i know u can do it- u're just worried cos things r startin 2 get hot. it's just nerves. i believe in u."

Having read the message twice he furtively deleted it. Why the hell did she keep popping up like this? Was she deliberately trying to make him jump out of his skin? Then he remembered what she had said on the Malcolm Anderson Show: Hera was watching and would unleash her wrath if Muesli communicated with him openly. Perhaps contacting him in this way was a means of preventing the other

Olympians from knowing? In his dream he had watched Hera punch Muesli through a brick wall, and he wasn't eager to be caught out in the waking world. She was right: like it or not, for the moment he was a mere instrument of the gods, and failing to proceed would bring lethal consequences. This thought gave him a certain peace of mind in a way that he would have found unthinkable only forty eight hours before. He was damned if he did and damned if he didn't, so why not just get on with it? He looked ahead again and saw that there were now only two people in front. It wouldn't be long before the deadly doughnuts were in his hands.

Suddenly a pressure rose in his skull. He flinched and instinctively swallowed to make his ears pop. It was no good though. A couple of futile, fish-like gulps were enough to tell him what was about to happen.

"What the hell is going on here then?"

The silky intonation of Aphrodite echoed through his mind. She was angry, and her voice contained a note that was at once dangerous and arousing. James immediately felt his elastic parapet being encroached again. She sounded exactly as he remembered her, and even though he didn't want to be seen with a gigantic boner in the middle of the bakery, part of him (a large and growing part) wanted to hear more. This was not the best day to have worn skinny jeans.

"What are you talking about, Aphrodite?"

It was Hera. Her now familiar boom was witheringly powerful, and whilst it would otherwise have been enough to deflate a hard-on, this time the schlong tower held firm. Despite her natural authority her tone contained a sense of forced aggression, like the teacher caught sneaking a cigarette in the toilets, who attempts to bellow her way out of embarrassment.

"You know bloody well what I mean!" yelled Aphrodite. "The mortal's buying doughnuts and he's going to fill them with poison. That was your stupid idea. At the last strategy meeting we all agreed that we'd be running with my plan!"

"Your plan was idiotic," retorted Hera. "You can't kill someone by having them eaten by a pack of rabid guinea pigs."

"Well Zeus consented to it and he has the final say," Aphrodite hissed. "We agreed to make your plan the backup in case the mortal wasn't able to train the guinea pigs fast enough. How dare you!"

"Oh shut up, Aphrodite. We all know that you only managed to trick Zeus into giving the nod to your brain-dead scheme because you sucked him off minutes before the meeting."

"That's legitimate practice, Hera, and you know it! Besides, how else did you get him to change his mind so fucking quickly?"

"I blew him so hard he didn't know Monday from Sunday," yelled Hera.

"You bitch! I'm surprised that even worked," spat Aphrodite. "He must get more satisfaction from flossing his teeth than one of your pissy blow jobs."

"You little shite! Just you come over here and say that to my face!"

"I bloody well will!"

James was reeling. The pair of them yelling at each other felt like a series of explosions inside his skull, and he grabbed the counter for support. The customer who had been at the head of the queue was now walking out the shop and giving him a puzzled look on her way past. The pale-faced boy at the back of the line had a suspicious lump in his trousers, a desperate look in his eyes and he didn't appear to be too steady on his feet. Bloody students. All over-sexed and under-nourished.

"Fucking whore!" yelled Hera.

At that moment James's phone buzzed again.

44

"babe u beta b careful! get the doughnuts sharpish cos there's gonna b a bust-up between hera and aphro any minute."

"Tell me something I don't know," thought James.

"ok then, try this: hera inhabits the pre-frontal cortex of your brain, whereas aphro lives in the hippocampus. if they have an argy-bargy at hera's place there'll b hell 2 pay. get it?"

"Er, not really," James whispered under his breath. Judging by what she was saying it seemed that the gods didn't actually exist as disembodied voices at all. If he had understood correctly they occupied different physical portions of his brain. But why was this dangerous for him? He couldn't work it out.

"for gods sake, didn't u pay attention in biology? the pre-frontal cortex regulates ya rectum. if they have a bust-up there u won't be able to control your own arse-hole!"

"Oh my God!" thought James, as cold panic sloshed over him.

"gods" the little vibrating handset reminded him.

"You call yourself a goddess?!" yelled Aphrodite.

There wasn't much time. Though only one person remained in front of him, James registered with horror that it was a pregnant mother.

"Oh no," he thought. "Look at the size of her! She could be here for hours trying to satisfy her bloody cravings!"

Her bump was indeed mountainous, and the pregnancy clothes appeared to be fighting a losing battle to contain it.

"She must be eating for at least seven!" he said to himself.

The woman was busy scanning the cakes and sandwiches beneath the counter, and continually jabbing at the glass. Dancing to this percussive tune were the two serving girls, each labouring furiously to wrap the mountain of pastries and stuff them into bulging carrier bags.

Another vibration.

"watch out, aphro's about to strike. she means business!"

Suddenly James felt a violent clenching in his bowels, before a gusty fart blasted noisily from between his buttocks. The exodus of pastries from the cabinet was instantly halted, and the women, along with the two sweating shop girls, turned in disgust.

"You bitch! You hit me!" cried Hera in outrage.

"There's plenty more where that came from!" retorted Aphrodite.

"How rude!" said the woman.

"Aaargh, don't pull my hair!!" screamed Aphrodite, whose cry was concurrent with another gut-wrenching bowel rumble and a second, louder, fart.

James had doubled over and now looked up, his face expressing a combination of mortified embarrassment and pained awareness of what was to follow.

"You dirty bastard!" said the woman.

Another vibration.

"babe, u've nearly run out of air in there. the next thing to come out won't b gas! Hurry!"

James crossed his legs, hobbled forward beside the pregnant woman and looked up pleadingly to the nearest shop girl.

"I… I need to buy some doughnuts. Quickly… Not much time!"

"You'll have to wait till I've finished paying," said the pregnant woman, who was slowly counting change into the hand of the shop assistant. "There, that's it." She fumbled to put away her purse before looking at James with severe disapproval.

"You oughta show more manners in public, mate."

Words of wisdom, but they were a bluff. With a fourteen pound baby pressing against her bowels she had sneakily

46

taken the opportunity to let loose a gastric tempest of her own at the same time as James's second colossal fart. The trumpeting sound had been the perfect mask for her own rampant incontinence. "You wanna get down to the pharmacist and buy…"

"My boob!!" yelled Aphrodite. The sound caused James to bend double as another impact clenched his stomach. "You hit my beautiful boob! How could you?!"

"I'm just getting warmed up!" shouted Hera.

Suddenly another spasm within his innards, and a spluttering fart was followed immediately by a pronounced squelch.

"Yaaarrrr!" roared Hera.

"Oh god! No!" whimpered James.

Another vibration, and this time not from his anus.

"babe i think that's the last of it. get the doughnuts, quick!"

Indeed the pressure in his skull seemed to subside, and the clamour appeared to have ended. Hera had apparently prevailed.

He looked up at the shop girls, who were standing horrified. The closest one suddenly raised her hand to her nose and took a step back.

"Fucking hell, Trish," she said to her colleague without looking away from James. "He's shat himself!"

"Kat, I'm gonna hurl!" said the other. "Get him out of here!"

At this point James interjected.

"One box of doughnuts please."

"Not likely, mate. Oh my God, the stench!" The girl backed away from the counter and retreated behind the door that led to the stock room.

"Please, you don't understand," he said, hobbling forward a pace. Unfortunately his entreaty was not helped by the slopping sound that came from his trousers as he moved.

47

When he looked down at his skinny jeans (for the first time, in fact, since the fight had broken out) he saw such huge slicks of faeces staining his thighs that, had they been oil, they would have prompted an environmental clean-up operation.

Heroically he persevered. "Please, just one box of doughnuts. That's all I'm asking."

"Fuck off you bleeding tramp! We're calling the manager." Her reply was not encouraging.

Suddenly another text message.

"this is getting ridiculous. tell her you'll crap yourself again if she doesn't co-operate."

The stench rising from James's nether-regions was sickening. He looked up at the horrified shop girls.

"Look, just give me the doughnuts, or… or…"

The girl peeping round the door went green, as her friend, who could contain herself no longer, vomited over the counter. James looked on in horror as the puke splattered the Chelsea buns, sausage rolls and Eccles cakes, and a thick glacier of bile rolled towards the loaves of bread.

"Oh God, please don't let it touch the doughnuts!" he thought.

His luck held, and the vomit flow was halted by a pile of Belgian buns.

"Fucking hell, Trish!" yelled her friend. "You okay?" She rushed to her stricken comrade's side as the latter grasped the counter and began dry-heaving.

"Look," said James desperately. "If you don't give me those doughnuts right this minute I'll… I'll…"

"You'll what?" said the girl, shooting him a look of hatred.

"I'll shit again!" He felt rotten for having made such a threat. Bowel warfare was indefensible but needs must.

The girl gasped. "No, don't shit again! Look, just take the fucking doughnuts and get out!" She grabbed a box and slid it across the counter.

He took it and ran.

CHAPTER FOUR

Later that afternoon, having undergone a lengthy cleanup procedure, James made his way to his old college, Midsummer, where Fatty had her office. The liquidation of the first name on the list was now well and truly afoot. He had placed his phone on silent, so as to avoid Muesli, and packed an extra pair of clean y-fronts in his back-pack just in case Aphrodite decided to have another run-in with Hera. Walking through the gilded gates and past the miserable porters, he entered the Great Court.

The noble institution of Midsummer College was founded in 1392 by Lady Maxima Lupa, who had begun life as a prostitute working the streets of Norwich and had eventually married the Earl of Spede, who happened to be her favourite client. Her husband, despite having been a tearaway in his youth, had soon settled down to a marriage of godly contemplation and pious charity. Lady Maxima's most pious act was to send him through the pearly gates to heaven, where she felt he would be much happier. His journey to the afterlife was lubricated by means of a poisoned apple, the image of which now adorns the college crest (along with Adam and Eve, *sans* fig-leaves). It wasn't a quick death, and the sheer quantity of diarrhoea had threatened to reduce the effectiveness of the toxin, but it worked in the end. On the 12th of February 1385, at half past four in the afternoon, Lord Spede was declared dead by his priest, and at one fell swoop Lady Maxima acquired his lands, money and enemies. The latter unfortunately proved somewhat difficult to overcome, the most formidable being Lord Spede's mother, the dowager Countess. The old bag sought vengeance for her son's death (which had eerie connotations of her own rise to power) through every court in the land. After years of outmanoeuvring her, Lady Maxima concocted a plan that would allow her to secure her fortune legally and prevent any further attempts on it by the dowager. She sold all her worldly possessions, including the ancestral home, and founded Midsummer College on the Cambridge common of the same name. Since the college was an independent legal entity in its own right it was untouchable, and having declared herself master she was free to run it as she pleased.

Centuries later it remains a beautifully endowed place, with a handsome set of medieval buildings and spacious lawns. The chapel is the only one in the country to have a fully naked statue of Christ above the altar. From the congregation's perspective, however, his modesty is preserved by the fact that when the dean kneels to pray his head is exactly level with Christ's manhood. Lady Maxima not only commissioned the sculpture herself, but also made the history books by becoming the first female dean in the University's history. The image of the great lady herself is preserved in one of the stained glass windows of the east transept. It bears a scene in which she is wrapping the body of Christ. She is deeply absorbed in her work, and though it may look like she is salivating, art-historians insist that the tears, which should of course be springing from her eyes, have been worn away over time. This explains why they now issue from the corners of her mouth instead. Pure coincidence they say.

Midsummer is a place of long-established rituals and ceremonies, many of which were founded by Lady Maxima herself. One of the most characteristically archaic occurs on Dowager's Day. This takes place every year on the winter full moon, when, after a vast and sumptuous formal meal, an effigy of an old woman is lowered from the ceiling of the Great Hall. It is then ceremonially beaten with poles by the fellows of the college. This gory practice was started by Lady Maxima, and the effigy is said to represent her mother-in-law, the dowager. Legend has it that when the latter had taken up residence in Cambridge, late in her nineties, the old crone had a stroke. Never one to miss a trick, Lady Maxima gathered the townspeople together and publicly condemned her as a witch. Having been persuaded by a combination of rhetoric, bribery and the spasmodic twitches that now afflicted the dowager down the left half of her body, the townspeople agreed that she should undergo trial by ordeal. Lady Maxima graciously concurred, and after some subtle mental construction formulated a plan whereby the dowager would be hung by a rope from a beam in the Great Hall and beaten by the fellows of Midsummer. If she should survive, her innocence would be proven. If not, then both trial and execution would have been amalgamated in elegant economy. Suffice to say she did not live, though the tradition that she reluctantly helped to establish still does.

It was through this ancient setting that James now walked. Every passageway and window was a piece of history, not just of Cambridge but of himself and the three formative years that he had spent there. Striding through the entrance to Second Court he could see the doorway that led to the set of offices where Fatty made her lair.

"Where do you think you're going?" came a voice from behind him.

He turned to see Martin Wetherblaine, the head porter, and grimaced. Wethers had always been a colossal arse to both students and fellows alike. His oft-repeated life-story was typical of a Cambridge porter: twenty years on the police force before dedicating the rest of his life to the tedium of porterhood. The job description was remarkably similar to that of a turkey: gobble in outrage at anyone whom you come into contact with; strut around college grounds, preening, and make your nest in the porter's lodge with your fellow turkeys.

James sighed.

"It's me, James Connor. I've just come back to pay a visit to my old Supervisor, Fatty... I mean Harriet Mason."

Wetherblaine wore the face of one who has received a roundhouse punch to the groin, which was his standard expression of disapproval.

"I see," he drawled, nasally. "Well I hope you'll be on your way soon enough. I assume you'll want to be getting on with finding a job."

His comment stung, as it was intended to, and James repressed an irritated flinch. Such snipes had been typical of Wetherblaine since the day James had come up to Cambridge.

"I'll sort you out soon enough," he muttered under his breath, as he turned and walked away towards Fatty's den.

*****

Fifty yards away Fatty Mason was firmly ensconced in her office upon a huge, over-stuffed sofa that creaked under her colossal weight. Perched meekly on the chair opposite was a timid first-year, whose essay for this week was entitled "Why was Agamemnon such a Twat?"

Harriet Mason was not happy.

"No, no, no! This is all wrong!" she yelled. "How can you bring this crap to me and expect me to give you a good mark? You're looking at a 3rd for this piece of shite, my girl!"

"But… But Dr Mason," stuttered the timid first-year. "I tried my best. I did exactly as you asked."

"I told you to bring me something amazing. This hardly cuts mustard. In fact I barely detected any mustard on it at all!"

"I swear to you I put mustard all over it, and tomato sauce and mayonnaise just as you told me."

"Liar! I've never tasted anything so bland! It's the poorest excuse for burger I've ever eaten!"

The first-year was on the verge of tears now.

"I'm so sorry. I asked for the Mega-Whopper Cow-Slayer Burger and I told them it was for you. It cost me nearly £12!"

But Fatty was not to be persuaded.

"I told you to bring me a decent-sized burger and you couldn't even manage that. I said as clear as anything that you couldn't expect me to mark an essay on an empty stomach but it obviously went in one ear and out the other! I'm giving you a 3rd for this, you dimwit! Take it and go!"

With that she grabbed a handful of papers and threw them in the poor girl's direction.

"But this isn't my work!" she whimpered as she knelt down and scooped them off the floor. "It's a set of invoices from the butchers!"

"Just get out of my sight!"

The girl took the papers and fled the office in floods of tears. James was walking down the corridor when she tore past him, and he didn't need to look twice to guess what had happened. Fatty was horrific when she was having hunger pangs. During his degree he had dreaded them, though now they would work to his advantage.

He knocked on the door, and from inside heard a faint stirring. He knocked again but was only able to elicit a loud grunt.

"Screw this," he thought, and pushed the door open. Inside it looked as if a bomb had exploded. Every surface, including the floor, was covered with debris. Most of this was the remains of food containers and wrappings, but there was the odd piece of paper that might suggest her time was occasionally punctuated by periods of academic work. Over on the sofa lay the beast. She was propped up on one arm, snoring. James had found her like this on numerous occasions. Several times she had even drifted into unconsciousness halfway through supervisions.

"Christ, she looks like a beached whale," he thought. "Actually she looks more like a whale that's eaten several other whales before beaching itself."

Shaking her would involve physical contact, so James stepped over the debris and held the box of doughnuts under her nose. The effect was akin to that of smelling salts. Fatty jolted and her eyes flickered open.

"What the...? Where...? Huh?" she grunted, disorientated.

James summoned his strength.

"Here we go."

"What's going on?" asked Fatty, still dazed.

"It's me, Dr Mason. James Connor."

"Eh? Oh you. What the devil are you doing here?" she said, finally registering her surroundings.

"I just wanted to give you a present. There was a bit of unpleasantness over the whole degree business but I wanted to make sure there was no ill feeling between us."

"Present? What present?"

"Well, it's not much really, just a box of..."

"Gimme!" She grabbed the doughnuts and raised them to her nose. Her little nostrils quested the air for a few seconds before she tore open the lid.

"Doughnuts!" she exclaimed.

"Yes, well I know how much you like them and, as I said, I don't want any unpleasantness..."

At this a perceptible look of discomfort flickered across her face.

"Er, well yes there's nothing you can do about that now, so if you've come looking to try to change what's been done..."

"No, no, I'm over it now. It's like you said the last time we met, 'life will screw you over anyway so you might as well get used to it.'" It was one of Fatty's favourite catchphrases and was trotted out whenever she did something particularly horrible to any of her students.

"Yes, quite right," she barked.

Now that he had delivered the cargo James suddenly felt the need to distance himself from what would soon (very soon, considering Fatty's appetite) become a crime scene.

"Okay then, I suppose I'll be out of your way."

"Good. Get down to the job centre."

He flinched as he closed the door behind him.

CHAPTER FIVE

Mrs Taylor's doughnuts were fantastic.

"Just what the doctor ordered," thought Fatty, an arsenal of saliva waiting to form an opening salvo down her chin.

In fact doughnuts were specifically not what the doctor had ordered. When a female patient complaining of chest pains and breathlessness had entered Dr Smith's office three weeks ago he had been staggered to observe the bipedal equivalent of a sea cow heaving itself into the rickety swivel chair opposite his desk. Self-diagnosis was something he vehemently discouraged, but in her case how could it be avoided? Perhaps the full extent of her condition was lost on her, given the fact that the average mirror was not wide enough to display her full girth? Still, the toffee apple that she had been eating when she had entered had made him wince, each bite seeming to bring her one waddling step closer to oblivion. The doctor had informed her in no uncertain terms that if she continued as she did she would soon have a heart attack. Despite his entreaties to reform she hadn't seemed very convinced by his exercise regimen. Couldn't she just have pills? Well insulin shots would probably be more in order. But pills would be preferred, thank you. Chewy ones. Strawberry flavour if possible.

She had left with little time on her hands.

Three of the four doughnuts were scoffed down and now the fourth was about to meet its fate. She bit into it, tearing away the freshly baked dough and crunching against the generous covering of sugar. Rich, red, strawberry jam burst out as the golden crust was penetrated, and as innards were ripped out it oozed freely. The pleasure she took in the tactile sensations and glorious taste were beyond sexual for Fatty. As the jam spilled onto her fingers and over her lips she felt an ecstatic pang of desire.

"This tastes bloody gorgeous," she said aloud. "I don't know what Mrs Taylor puts in these things but she's a genius."

Waves of satisfaction stimulated waves of desire, and she exercised no restraint in vocalising the experience. Kitchen walls had felt her moans rebound as the bedroom never had and now a cacophony of pleasure echoed down the hall. There was an intense delight in allowing the jam to spread itself on her skin, and in the knowledge that every molecule of it would end up sliding down her throat. Each finger was mechanically licked clean after each doughnut had been finished, in a process that was as swift and automatic as a car assembly line.

"Phew, all this chewing is making me hungrier. How many are left?" She glanced down. "Just one? I must be on starvation rations or something."

In it went and the great, toothed maw began the process of grinding and gnashing. Now she lay back in her chair and really began to savour it. Even the chomping slowed down as the sense of relaxation and completeness overcame her.

But something was wrong. She opened her eyes and let out a little pig-like grunt. There was a tightness under her jaw that was spreading across her face.

"Crikey, I must have worn myself out with all that chewing. Who said exercise was good for you?"

She raised her sausage fingers and wiped her brow, which had become beaded with perspiration.

Suddenly a jolt of pain ricocheted up her back and into her neck. She gasped and staggered to her feet, but as she did so a wave of cramp swept over her body and knocked her to the ground. It felt like the impact of a hammer over every inch of her skin, an agonising reverberation that echoed in her blood vessels.

"Shit! What's happening?"

She scrabbled to get up, but as she did so her nerves crackled, every point of contact with her skin becoming a conflagration of pain. Her clothes, her shoes, even her hair, all screeched in agonising symphony. She wanted to scream, to call out. The instinct to make a noise of any kind became a sudden and overwhelming compulsion.

But she could not. Her throat was closing up and she could hardly force down air. Her breath came in rasping starts concurrent with the pounding waves of pain that shuddered from the top of her head, through her body and into her legs.

"What the hell?!"

The words formed in her mind, a weak whisper against the deafening rush that now filled her ears.

"How can this…? What can…?" Though she felt the chilling touch of delirium encroach the perimeter of her mind she was lucid enough to know what was before her. It was happening in mere moments, but left no room for misinterpretation.

"Oh God. Oh God this is really it. I'm going to die!"

The instinct for self-preservation is one with the ability to identify death when it approaches. Her blood vessels were beginning to rupture, and as they did so great patches of her skin were turning black.

"How can this be? What in the world can have…? The doughnut! It was something in the doughnut! But who was responsible? Mrs Taylor? Surely not! It must have been…the boy! James Connor!"

Her hair was falling from her head in clumps, and thick rivulets of blood ran from her eyes and ears. All was pain, but this dark realisation seemed to give her a furious, momentary strength.

"That bastard! That twisted bastard! He's embittered by what had happened with his degree. The scumbag! He'll pay for this! But no… now it's impossible… If only I had time enough for revenge and, to a lesser extent, to say goodbye to my family!"

But then something caught her eye. On the corner of the table was a large globule of jam. It had fallen from the last doughnut during the feeding frenzy, evading detection like a solitary blade of grass whose five billion comrades have been devoured by a ravenous swarm of locusts.

"I may be a gonner but that little shit can get flushed!" thought Fatty, the sudden lust for vengeance momentarily overcoming the furious pain.

The inferno that seemed to engulf her was not enough to stop her reaching out.

"Okay, Harriet, you've got one chance at this. If I dip my finger into the jam I can write Connor's name across that sheet of paper on the floor. But I've got to hurry!"

As she leant over the side of the desk and pressed her blubber against the wood nausea clawed at her stomach.

"Oh Jesus!" she gasped. "No. I have to do this. On the plus side at least I'll make a beautiful corpse."

She reached out for the jam and dunked her finger into the little pool of deep red. The moment seemed to pass in slow-motion as she retracted her arm and prepared to scribble her gory testament. With her chubby finger passing before her eyes the blackness in her vision thickened. Then, through the horror of death, she had an epiphany.

It was incredible: a dancing, pulsating beacon of light, indescribably beautiful; a glowing bubble of energy, beaming divine radiance. It seemed to her to come from a place beyond the mortal world.

She was transfixed.

"Heaven! I always knew I'd make it there. I hope none of the other bastards from the Faculty are stinking up the joint. I have to reach it!"

And so she plunged, head first.

60

The light she saw was indeed unearthly. It originated in the sun and had travelled through the void of the solar system, penetrating the Earth's atmosphere and gliding through the windows of Fatty's study. The beautiful beacon through which it beamed was made of sugar, the little bubbles of energy being complex carbohydrate molecules. In fact the heavenly creation that mesmerised the near-deceased lecturer was the very dollop of jam that she had gleaned from her own desk, and when she moved towards it she did indeed embrace heaven... with a slurp.

Divine as it tasted, it was gone in an instant. Her lungs were collapsing now, and her skin shed itself upon the floor. But she no longer convulsed. For a split second she stopped cold.

"I've licked my finger. I've licked my bloody finger!"

She had succumbed to her greed at the point of death, as she had done throughout life. She did not attempt to cry out or curse her failing, though. Instead she lurched sideways and caught side of the empty doughnut box, which contained the last remaining granules of sugar stuck to the inside.

"Well if I'm a gonner I'm at least popping my clogs with sugar in my mouth!"

And so she lunged forward, arms outstretched and tongue slobbering with blood and froth. She had only moments until she expired and Harriet Mason wanted to use them well.

She wanted to eat.

CHAPTER SIX

Deep in the recesses of James's brain a debate was taking place, though he, being only a mortal, was not invited. The Olympians had set up their headquarters in his hippocampus, and from here they had been plotting the demise of the unfortunates on the Cambridge List. Now they were assembled in council, dozens of them, all members of the great celestial family convened within James's synaptic pathways to discuss matters of cosmic significance.

"My left boob hasn't stopped aching since you punched it, Hera," moaned Aphrodite. "It was foul play and I shall never forgive you, you bloody bitch."

"Oh shut up, Aphrodite. My ears have been aching since we pitched up camp inside this human. All I can hear is your whingeing voice ricocheting off the walls of his skull," came the booming retort.

"Yeah your complaints are giving us all a headache. Hera's absolutely right, as always," piped-up Athena, casting obsequious, sidelong glances at her idol.

Hera didn't need anyone to tell her how great she was, and would usually have slapped down such blatant brown-nosing. For once, though, she held her tongue. Athena was the favourite daughter of Zeus, ruler of the gods, and having been in awe of her step-mother for millennia took every opportunity to ingratiate herself. Though Hera was normally scathing of such practice, circumstances had changed. The mission to destroy the lecturers on the Cambridge List, on the face of it such a simple task, had divided the gods, and allies were now a much-needed resource.

Within the Olympian family the traditional means of asserting dominance was to express authority in the council, which usually entailed a combination of brashness, coercion and bullying. That the dynamics of the school playground formed the basis of the divine order would doubtless distress theoretical physicists and astronomers the world over. Goat-like political rutting, however, was a long-accepted practice amongst the Olympians. The strife that often occurs in families was constant amongst the gods, but when one's relatives are both immortal and vastly powerful the ordinary rules of family conflict cannot apply. Battles for power took place in public, where egos were built up or knocked down for all to see and the subsequent gain or loss of standing was measured by influence in council.

Though all the gods were in full agreement that the mortals on the Cambridge List should be destroyed, there had been deep discord regarding the methods to be used. If Hera could dominate the proceedings and force the others to agree to her own plans for divine retribution, her position at the top of the food chain would be consolidated.

The obstacle to this noble plan, and indeed all the plans she had ever made, was Aphrodite. She was one of the most ancient and indisputably the most beautiful of the goddesses, making her a serious contender for the position of alpha female. Though the relationship between the two had been strained since the dawn of time (and, some would argue, long before), it had turned irreversibly sour after the Judgment of Paris. There, in a much-hyped divine beauty pageant, one of Ancient Greece's foremost warriors had chosen Aphrodite over Hera and Athena as the most desirable of the Olympians. Hera, never one to ignore a snub, had taken her anger out on humanity by starting the Trojan War. Throughout that epic conflict she and Aphrodite had naturally taken opposing sides. Hera had been adamant that the Trojans, and Paris in particular, be destroyed and had eventually managed to secure a Greek victory. Aphrodite had supported the Trojans, and even though she had known that the writing was on the wall for Troy from the start she had proven a formidable sparring partner against the Queen of the Gods.

Now, over three thousand years later, the Olympians had received a collective snub from the Classics Faculty at Cambridge via the rejection of James's flattering thesis. On the face of it their united resolve to seek lethal retribution should have drawn them together, but amongst the omnipotents nothing could be so simple. The deity who dominated proceedings in the council, which would have to agree on the methods of killing, would achieve pre-eminence amongst the gods until the next squabble. It was a tempting prize but a dangerous one. Invulnerability was the mother of political invention, and there was no limit to the deviousness that each player was willing to employ in exploiting the perceived weakness in an opponent.

"Athena makes a very good point, Aphrodite. I *am* always right," said Hera as her sidekick beamed at the unexpected compliment.

"Now, now, you two," said Dionysos. "Let's not get bogged down in useless arguments."

"My boob is a highly relevant topic at any meeting," said Aphrodite, with an exaggerated air of effrontery.

"That's only because they hang out all over the place," sniped Hera.

"At least mine aren't hairy!"

"Yours point in different directions!"

"Ladies, please!" yelled Dionysos over the top of what was becoming a divine slanging match. "Since Zeus has decided to absent himself from these meetings and leave it to the rest of us to see the mission through I think we should at least give the pretence of concord."

"I still don't understand why Zeus chose not to participate," said Aphrodite, settling down again.

"Well he's the King of the Gods so I guess it's his prerogative," shrugged Dionysos. "All I know is that we need to delegate a messenger to update him on developments here and to pass his input back to us."

"I nominate Athena," said Hera, quick as a flash.

"Shit," thought Aphrodite. "She doesn't want to go herself because she and Zeus have been fighting like cat and dog. Come to think of it that must be the reason he's not attending the meetings. Either way, if his beloved Athena gets to be the go-between the little brown-nose will be able to convince him to assent to whatever Hera wants."

"Seconded!" yelled Athena gleefully.

"Do you wish to contest, Aphrodite?" asked Dionysos. Having drawn the short straw the God of Wine was playing the role of Chairman in lieu of his father, Zeus. Supervising the cosmic soapbox required the same degree of delicacy as successfully pirouetting over a field of landmines, though amongst the Olympians he was considered to be one of the more tactful when the occasion required.

Aphrodite could hardly nominate herself against Athena. The filthy suck-up would simply run off to daddy, who would of course insist on his little princess. Another tactic would have to be adopted, and she knew exactly which.

"No Dionysos, let Athena be the go-between," she said, smiling sweetly and nodding politely towards Athena.

"What can she be up to?" thought Hera at this incongruous display of good grace.

"Are there any dissenting voices?" Dionysos enquired, addressing the extended family of assembled deities. The latter merely murmured amongst themselves. No one was willing to step into the middle of a power struggle between the two most formidable goddesses, especially if Zeus himself was involved, even if indirectly.

"Very well. Athena, daughter of Zeus, shall convey messages between the Olympians and her father. Let the council meeting on the destruction of the second victim from the Cambridge List commence."

*****

65

James strode across Market Square.

Returning home the previous day, having deposited his cargo of doughnuts, he had collapsed onto his bed and fallen into a long, uninterrupted sleep, the first in longer than he could remember. When he had woken this morning, however, the events of the yesterday surged into his mind on a wave of adrenaline. The local radio had been on when he came into the kitchen, and the presenter's voice, bright and chirpy, left him cold. As the details of the crime scene and a biography of Fatty were reeled off he had found himself panicking. The tone of the newsreader was so normal, so measured and familiar. He had felt that it should somehow be different, altered to reflect the horror of what he had done. Surely everything couldn't be as it was before? He couldn't just listen to the radio as normal from the safety of his kitchen, as if it wasn't telling him how he had taken a life. The presenter's voice was like a rupture in the side of a diving bell. His actions in the outside world had filled the room like a rush of seawater, breaching the divide between the public realm of law and order and the safe, comfortable world of home. They left him gasping for air.

He had grabbed his coat and hurried out of the house before anyone else decided to come downstairs.

As he paced across Market Square his mind churned. There were not many people around but anyone who happened to pass by provoked a flurry of speculation. He wondered what their reaction was when they had heard the news; whether they had stopped what they were doing and paid special attention; whether they had told their friends and neighbours. These questions were torturous, and as panic started to rise up in him he felt giddy. He closed his eyes and began to stumble. The air suddenly felt cold against his skin and a gust of wind cast his hair about. He wanted to be inside now, to sit down, and he staggered to the nearest doorway. He didn't care what shop it was, he just had to be in off the streets.

Keeping his eyes screwed shut he pushed at the glass and heard the tinkle of a little bell overhead.

"Morning love," came a salutation. "Don't you look cold?"

The voice was now all too familiar, though as he opened his eyes he hoped he was mistaken. He found that he was standing in the Silver Spoon, a dingy little café opposite Caius College that was famed for the greasiness of its breakfasts and the industrial strength of its coffee. It was open round the clock and was a popular haunt for students who had early supervisions, or those who had been partying hard the night before and were yet to return to their rooms (although amongst the various species at Cambridge the former far outnumber the latter). The place was almost empty, but standing conspicuously behind the bar was a waitress whose harshly bleached hair was tied back with a dirty, shocking-pink scrunchy, revealing dark roots that a three hundred year-old oak would be proud of.

"Table for one, darling? Well go on then, pull up a chair. No need for a reservation, we ain't the Ritz, you know," said Muesli with a wink, before turning and walking off through the door to the kitchen.

"Oh Jesus Christ," sighed James, slumping down at the nearest table. Opposite him, next to the till, sat two girls from Trinity. Both were blonde, pretty and petite, and wore their hair in that artfully scruffy fashion that their mothers had taught them. Their slightly horsey accents weren't hard to hear over the radio.

"Have you heard about the…"

"Yah, everyone has, it's simply…"

"Oh isn't it though!"

"I heard she was found naked."

"Oh Clarissa that's foul! Hilarious to think though."

"I suppose they'll have to have the wall taken out to

remove her."

"But they couldn't though. You can't go blasting holes into the side of Midsummer. They'll just have to brick up the office and make it her tomb!"

"Did you ever see her?"

"No, but Toby's a classicist and she supervised him for a term last year. He said she's just awful. She used to make him bring her sausage rolls, and if he ever forgot she'd fail his essays."

"What a bitch! No loss by the sounds."

The pair looked at each other and giggled. James was agog.

"They know, and yet they're joking about it. They're fucking joking about it!" he thought with a mounting feeling of mirth. "They don't give a shit. I'm sitting right here and they don't know a bloody thing." The smile that was beginning to tug at the corners of his mouth, however, was aborted when the Muse materialised next to him, pen and pad in hand.

"Take your order, darling?" she said, nonchalantly.

"But... Muesli you know it's me, right?"

"Yes James, I know," she said in a hushed voice.

"Then why are you pretending to be... well...." He indicated to her dirty apron. "Can't you sit down?"

"I'm not pretending to be anything. And I can't sit down. I'd be in serious trouble if I was caught. The boss doesn't want me socialising, especially not with you, as you well know."

"The boss? But surely he can't..."

"She."

Then came the realisation.

"You don't mean? You mean you're doing this because of Hera?"

"She's the Queen. I have to be surreptitious."

"Oh, I see. Are we in danger?"

68

"Yes, always. So make with the order," she whispered through gritted teeth.

James almost smiled at the prospect of going along with the pantomime.

"You may find this funny," she said in response to his thoughts, "but remember she's the most powerful bitch in the universe. Think about what happened before."

The memory of Muesli being punched through the wall in the Sceptre flashed across his mind. He winced as he recalled the sound of the impact and the gritty smell of crumbled cement.

"Sorry, of course I'll go along with it," he said shamefacedly. He didn't even need to look at the dog-eared, laminated menu.

"I'll have the full English."

"Good choice. Now I'll fill you in, but I'll have to do it in stages so as not to arouse suspicion. I'll be back with your grub in a few minutes but just to let you know, the gods are convened in council in your hippocampus to decide the fate of the second victim from the list."

She paused, and for a second looked vacantly at the space above his head. "They've just decided it's to be Wildencrust."

With that she turned away and trotted back into the kitchen, leaving James's pulse to quicken.

CHAPTER SEVEN

With Athena relaying messages to and from Zeus, and being firmly under Hera's thumb all the while, the Queen of the Gods wore a confident smirk that left no illusions as to her clear tactical advantage. She and Zeus may have been arguing more ferociously than usual lately, and his decision to forgo the council meetings had certainly unnerved her, but perhaps his absence would turn out to be a blessing in disguise. The fact that the King of the Gods was sulking in his royal chambers in James's pre-frontal cortex might otherwise have been regarded by the other deities as a sign of disfavour towards his wife, and thus have weakened her standing in council significantly. With his snivelling little daughter willing to endorse whatever she said, however, Hera felt secure. Aphrodite was the only deity with enough gumption to challenge her these days anyway, but by pulling the strings on her pathetic husband and his ingratiating progeny Hera could become the council's sole puppeteer. Consolidating her position and rendering impotent that genital-obsessed bitch was a prospect that gave Hera an almost sexual degree of excitement.

Across the hippocampus Aphrodite sat observing Hera's smirk, and replied with a dignified smile. She knew that alone she could not hope to muster enough force to mount a head-on challenge to Zeus's wife and her lackey. Instead she would have to find her own powerful ally on the council, and Dionysos was the obvious choice.

The God of Wine was the brother of Athena. Like her he had had a somewhat unusual upbringing, as a result of which he had earned the nickname 'Twice-Born.' His mother, Semele, had been a particularly beautiful mortal who, like so many others, had caught the wandering eye of Zeus. The King of Olympus had yearned to have his way with such a seductive creature, and made plans for a jolly outing of rape and pillage. Date rape drugs had yet to be invented, and were in any case superfluous as far as the omnipotents were concerned. For Zeus had only to cast a deep sleep upon the girl to furnish himself with a pliant victim. Materialising before the unconscious Semele he had subjected her body to a level of depravity that only a god could hope to achieve, and the next morning an aching vagina and an absent memory were her only clues as to anything untoward.

Thus, over the coming months, and unaware of the ravishing that had taken place that night, the girl began to put on weight and started to experience sickness in the mornings. One day she gazed at her swollen form in the mirror and realised with horror the true nature of her situation. She, a poor, unmarried maiden had been cruelly ravished by an unknown assailant, and would now surely be an outcast in the village. Though a problem shared is usually a problem halved, tragically for Semele as she stood in her bedroom, wailing and tearing at her hair, her cries were heard by only one other: Hera.

Naturally Zeus's wife did not take kindly to her husband's philandering, but she was hardly in a position to smite the King of the Gods. Later she would spread malicious and detrimental gossip about why Semele couldn't remember a thing the morning after ("didn't even touch the sides" was the mantra that spread across Olympus, like wild fire), but for the moment revenge would have to be exacted on the girl herself.

Therefore, having discovered the deed, Hera appeared before Semele in her bedroom. The girl was terrified at first but the goddess soon soothed her with kind words. Consoling the wretch on her condition she promised that she was there to help. Shame and abomination were not her fate, the Queen of the Gods said, because the one who had left her with child was none other than the great and glorious Zeus himself. The girl could hardly believe her ears, and exclaimed that such a thing couldn't possibly be true. Hera, charming and sweet, urged her to see for herself and to invoke the god in person. There had been a natural hesitancy on Semele's part, for it wasn't normally the done thing to call upon the ruler of the universe whilst standing in one's knickers and with an appalling case of morning breath. Hera, however, had persisted, and eventually Semele, mad with curiosity, had called upon the rapist to show himself in his true form. Knowing that Hera could only be pushed so far Zeus had reluctantly appeared, divested of human appearance and in the closest state to true divinity that a god can assume: a bolt of lightning.

For any villagers who happened to be passing by the house, Semele's death happened literally in a flash. Hera, however, being unbound by the mortal passage of time had been able to enjoy the sight of the girl's eyes bursting out over cauterising flesh before both were vaporised, whilst bones, teeth and fingernails crumbled to dust.

The child in the girl's womb fortunately fared rather better. Despite his cruel mistreatment of the mother, Zeus took a shine to the foetus and snatched it away milliseconds before the human bonfire could claim an unborn victim. He decided that the baby should be allowed to live, and so, doing what any concerned parent would do, he sowed the infant Dionysos into his left thigh, thus allowing the pregnancy to run its natural course. Sure enough, several months later Dionysos sprang forth, and Zeus became the proud mother of a healthy baby god. The King of Olympus never doted on his son as he did Athena but he nonetheless respected Dionysos, and it was this respect that drew Aphrodite to him as a prospective pawn in her war with Hera.

If she could persuade Twice-Born Dionysos to support her unconditionally Aphrodite would be able to mount a credible threat to her enemy's ambitions. She could not, however, risk revealing her hand. Thus she decided to wait and to use this session of the council to parry Hera's political thrusts by more subtle means. If she could comprehensively water-down the latter's proposals for Wildencrust's death and make them as vague as possible, she could then privately arrange for the don's destruction before Hera had a chance to act. By doing so she would gain all the glory at the next assembly of the council without appearing to have defied its decision. The prospect of getting one up on Hera made her tingle all over.

"Well, now that we've decided that Wildencrust is to die next there's no reason to labour over the details. I'm sure all of you have your own ideas about how he should be dispatched, but mine are obviously better," boomed Hera, casting a sidelong glance at the Goddess of Desire.

"You'll be smirking on the other side of your face soon, you bitch," thought Aphrodite, clothing her thoughts in a sweet smile.

"May I take it that you have a proposal to hand, Hera?" Dionysos enquired.

"Yes. I believe that there's no better way for this particular specimen of humanity to die than by having his brains beaten out upon the desk in his study."

There were murmurs of approval from the assembled deities. Her plan was a delicious blend of sharp brutality and goriness, making it the ideal paradigm of old-style Olympian wrath.

Sensing the positive mood, Hera continued.

"The added pleasure that we the almighty gods would receive from such a method of execution is obvious. His desk, the place from which he contrived to dismiss the thesis that flattered our glory so wonderfully, shall be the implement of his own destruction."

The other gods and goddesses were openly applauding her now. In the council of death she had caught perfectly the mood for blood and theatre, and was striking a winning note.

Hera rammed home her advantage.

"Furthermore," she crowed theatrically over mounting applause, "the pounding of his skull upon the desk will form the wretched mortal's own funeral dirge!"

The crowd went wild.

"His brains will be beaten out and spilled upon the carpet for all to see! Let the blood run forth!"

A surge of excitement swept through the assembled deities, who were whipped into a frenzy around the unmoving Aphrodite.

"Hail Hera! What a plan!" cried Ares, God of War.

"Blood and Death! Glory to the Olympians!" yelled Demeter, Goddess of Natural Fertility. She was not normally one to be caught up by such rhetoric but even she could not resist the electrified atmosphere.

Hera was riding the wave now, and nudged Athena.

"Prepare yourself, little one. Prepare to go to your father's bedchamber and give him the news." Then, turning to the others and with a sweeping gesture she declared, "For the Olympians are decided upon the mode of the second death!"

Athena could hardly contain herself. Only in Hera's most exultant moments would she have uttered anything approaching a term of endearment, and even then it was usually to lull one into a false sense of security before delivering a cosmic kick to the teeth.

"Oh Hera, you're just super! What a speech! I'll go and tell Daddy at once…"

"Wait a moment, Athena," commanded Dionysos above the roar. "This has yet to be formally decided. If there are any dissenting voices they're entitled to be heard before the vote."

A hush descended across the hippocampus. All eyes were on Aphrodite. Throughout, the goddess had been a picture of composure. Now the stage was hers and for a moment her smouldering gaze caught that of every other Olympian simultaneously, holding them fast.

"What an excellent suggestion, Hera," she said slowly and with a heavy sense of earnest. "To have the don's brains beaten from his head is an idea worthy of epic."

The other gods nodded and murmured amongst themselves.

"However," she continued, "don't you think it would be best to have Athena put it a little more tactfully to Zeus?"

Hera's eyebrows arched in suspicion.

"After all, Athena herself sprang from her father's skull after he devoured poor Metis, his first wife. It didn't take much for dear old Metty to anger him, and once his temper was hot he crammed her down his divine gullet like a reticulated python. Why I believe I was there just in time to witness her pretty little sandaled feet sliding down last."

Hera's face hardened at the memory. Zeus and Metis had been the power couple of Olympus in the early days, before the creation of humanity. Not far into her pregnancy with his first child a vicious prophecy had begun to circulate that she was destined to give birth to a son whose strength would be even greater than his. As soon as Zeus got wind of this he devoured Metis without a second thought, cannibalism being used in lieu of marriage counselling. Months later the King of the Gods began to suffer a severe and unrelenting headache. Eventually, at the point when the pain became too much to bear, his skull cracked open and the child that Metis was carrying when she had been swallowed sprang forth from Zeus's head. Athena was born.

"If your skull-shattering plan were to remind him of the bad old days," continued Aphrodite, "and the way he used to deal with quarrelsome partners then he might start getting ideas. I don't of course mean to suggest that you and he have been on bad terms lately…"

"Er, well, yes," Hera stammered. She was more flustered than she cared to reveal. "Of course he and I have been a picture of marital harmony, as usual, but I wouldn't

75

want to evoke memories of his acrimonious first marriage. I think perhaps we should change the proposal slightly. Purely out of sympathy for Zeus of course."

The other gods and goddesses were looking at each other and whispering with surprise.

"Very well," beamed Aphrodite. "I would, of course have endorsed your suggestion, but as I said I would probably make it something a little less contentious. Perhaps instead of 'having his head beaten open against his desk,' I might suggest 'bloody and torturous demise'?"

This was clearly less rhetorically impressive than the original idea, but Hera gritted her teeth and swallowed it. Though Aphrodite seemed to be stealing a march on her moment of glory she was willing to let it slide. For all her showmanship Hera certainly did not want Zeus to be flossing the remnants of her gown from his teeth tomorrow morning.

"Very well, 'grim and torturous demise' it is," she said with a clipped note of frustration.

The assembled gods were baffled. It was almost unheard of that Hera and Aphrodite should reach agreement in council. Aphrodite had knocked the air out of Hera's sails but why not take the opportunity to press home the advantage? And why didn't Hera put up more of a fight for her wonderful plan? It was all very strange, but now the sense of anticlimax seemed to have put paid to the possibility of any further excitement.

"Well… okay then," said Dionysos. He was no less surprised than the others. "I don't suppose anyone wants to argue with that?"

There was silence.

"Very well. Professor Penton Wildencrust, second on the Cambridge List, shall be subject to a 'grim and torturous demise' by the order of the council of Olympus. Athena, you may now inform your divine father of our collective decision. This meeting is over."

Aphrodite left the Hippocampus with a sly smile.

"Time now to set the ball in motion," she said to herself.

CHAPTER EIGHT

The news reports hadn't been favourable. The death of Dr Harriet Mason, University Lecturer in Ancient Greek, had predictably received full-scale coverage in the local press. Despite the sense of shock that a killer might be on the loose, such was the extent of Fatty's foul reputation that the gory details of her demise had elicited morbid fascination rather than grief. The local editors didn't miss a trick.

"SHE-WHALE SLAIN IN HER OWN STUDY. CAPTAIN AHAB SUSPECTED," ran one headline.

"ONE DOUGHNUT TOO FAR FOR GLUTTONOUS GREEK DON," smirked another.

Penton Wildencrust had laid the offensive rags on his desk and was casting his eye over them with a look of cold disgust.

"The plebeians. It's highly disrespectful," he spluttered.

"I know that you and Mason were close, Wildencrust, but we just have to get on with things. Dwelling on it is a luxury we can't afford," said Paul Fringe.

The pair had convened in Wildencrust's study for an early morning meeting. Outside, a light mist covered the Great Court at Midsummer, lending the place an air of tranquillity. Within, the atmosphere was charged.

"When did you hear?" asked Wildencrust.

"At the same time as you, I suspect. I turned on the television at about 7pm and there it was all over the local news."

"I'm surprised you even watch the local news."

"Well one likes to see what the plebs are up to. It's so much cheaper than a trip to the zoo, don't you think?"

But Wildencrust was lost in thought. "Murder," he murmured thoughtfully. "Can it really be the case?"

"Oh I hardly think it likely," said Fringe with a scoff.

"No, just before I arrived I telephoned the Chief Inspector, who happens to be a close family friend. He told me that there was no obvious sign of a struggle and that it's more likely she had some sort of reaction to her heart pills. Bloody fool to be taking the things, if you ask me."

"Well, quite. Modern medicine does more harm than good by all accounts," agreed Wildencrust. "I haven't been to a doctor in years."

This much was true. In fact Wildencrust hadn't patronised any sort of hygiene or grooming specialist since the late eighties, including dentists, opticians and hairdressers. As a result he looked like the love-child of a yeti and a gorilla, with a mighty beard that spilled half-way down his chest. Over the course of twenty years it had become a repository for bits of old food, and consequently he smelt like an open tomb. Despite the milk-curdling horror that the prospect of kissing such a creature would induce in any normal person, however, Wildencrust was rumoured to be something of a stud. From his private set of rooms in Midsummer he was said to have seduced at least one undergraduate per year, and even a certain female Faculty member.

Sitting opposite him, Fringe eyed Wildencrust with his usual withering glare. Any casual observer would have been struck by the contrast between the pair. If Wildencrust really had been a yeti then Fringe could quite plausibly have been his publicist, there to advise on negotiating tactics for tabloid photo shoots. His stiff, formal clothes and shrewd eyes gave him an air of meanness and authority.

"You realise that the police may want to question us about our professional relationships with Harriet Mason. They may be interested in yours in particular," said Fringe with distain. He arched his eyebrows suggestively, and a note of disapproval rang clear in his voice.

"Fringe, that was nothing. Rumours, nothing but rumours," said Wildencrust, nervously.

"Don't take me for a fool," said Fringe with quiet force. "I never said anything until now because it all seemed perfectly harmless, but if the police find some sort of love interest connected with Mason they'll have all the excuse they need to start digging. I needn't remind you that when I was shortlisted to succeed to the position of Vice Chancellor of the University it was largely on the basis that I would represent Cambridge to the rest of the academic world. It was on the assumption that I was sound. Mason's death is troublesome enough, but if it turns out that I head a Faculty associated with sleaze... Well it'll be disastrous for me."

Fringe's selfless consideration for others was hardly legendary, though his self-assurance was such that he spoke without the slightest hint of embarrassment. Wildencrust began to squirm, knowing that reticence was not an option.

"Yes... I can see what you mean, but honestly..."

"Is it true?"

"Well, there are elements of truth..."

"Wildencrust, I'm warning you..."

"Oh, very well, it's true. But it was just two people who happened to enjoy each other's company. I swear there was nothing in it that would arouse suspicion."

"Considering the state of Mason I'm surprised there was anything arousing about the situation at all," grimaced Fringe.

"Oh I know she was no looker, but believe me some of the saucy things she would do..."

"Stop!" said Fringe, wincing. "I don't need to know the gory, personal details. Just give me the abridged version. When did it start?"

"Last year."

"Specifically?"

"Well it was during the summer. Do you remember when I was treated for a cracked rib?"

"Yes, your climbing injury."

"Well I suppose it was a climbing injury, but I wasn't

actually the one doing the climbing."

"Explain."

"We had just started seeing each other and… well, she wanted to go on top."

"Oh dear god! Your mean she rode you? Isn't that rather like a shire horse riding a gerbil?" spluttered Fringe in disgust.

"Well… I…" stammered Wildencrust in embarrassment. "We only did it the once…"

"On the advise of your physiotherapist I assume. Dear God, what a horrible image." Fringe shuddered and looked about the room with emphatic distaste, though within moments he had regained his composure.

"When did it finish?"

Wildencrust looked sheepish.

"It did finish, didn't it?"

"Well… it has now."

"Wildencrust! You were still seeing each other when she died?"

"Yes, yes we were."

Fringe drew his hands across his brow.

"You know what will happen if the police find out about this? We don't need that kind of attention here!" As he spoke his voice became increasingly shrill, and the veins in his temples began to bulge. "You bloody idiot!"

"Fringe, I'm so sorry but…"

"No buts! Now listen to me: you are not to speak about this to anyone. If someone asks you what your relationship was with Harriet Mason you tell them that you were just colleagues."

"Of course, of course, you can rely on me. But what if they… you know."

"What?"

"Well what if they bring up… you know, the rumours? I know they were spread around; I saw the graffiti in the Faculty toilets." Wildencrust looked sheepish, and beneath the undergrowth of beard he turned red at the memory of the whale humping a gorilla, doodled in biro by a bored classicist.

"Just tell them that you were shagging an undergrad. In fact tell them whatever the hell you like, just don't breathe a word of the truth. I should have thought that shame alone would seal your lips."

"Yes, yes, of course," said Wildencrust, looking sullenly down at his hands.

With that, Fringe rose from his chair and swept out of the room, leaving Wildencrust to ponder the grim turn of events. After hearing the door slam shut he shuffled dejectedly over to the drinks cabinet and poured himself a large brandy.

"Oh Harriet, why did you have to take those wretched heart pills?" he said to his reflection in the dirty little mirror hanging inches from his face. "Oh God how I miss your curvaceous body! The things we used to do! If only you could come back, just for a single moment."

Memories overcame him, and he began weeping silently to himself.

*****

Fringe, having returned to his office, was irritably drumming his fingers on his desk. The phone had been pressed against his ear for nearly five minutes now, and the interminable music being played down the line was a dirge to his mounting blood pressure. There were very few people for whom he would have tolerated being placed on hold but Sir Malcolm Ruffles was one of them. As one of the highest-ranking ambassadors in Her Majesty's service he was a very important figure. As one whose influence at the University was legendary he was barely less than divine, at least in the estimation of the socially ambitious Fringe. The pair of them had a working relationship that went back many years, though Fringe had never felt anything more than a spectral shadow cast in the brilliance of Sir Malcolm's limelight.

82

All this would soon change, though. As he drummed his fingers against the desk, subconsciously providing a counter-beat to the awful music that issued from the phone, Fringe mused on their relationship. It had been nearly thirteen years since they had first met at a dreary University party held by a wealthy donor. At that time Fringe, having languished for years as Senior Lecturer in Early Roman Wall Graffiti, had recently been promoted to the position of treasurer of the Classics Faculty. He had thus been given sole responsibility for overseeing the distribution of the Faculty's considerable annual income. It hadn't taken long for Fringe to discover that oversight at the archaic Faculty was virtually non-existent, and that scrutiny of his annual reports to the governing committee (chaired at that time by the decrepit Arnold Lathebone, Professor in Etruscan Voting Practices) did not take place at all. During the first six months he had taken on his role as treasurer with relative diligence. Soon, however, lack of supervision and the large sums of money that passed through his office became too much to resist.

At the dreary party for the wealthy donor he had been introduced to Sir Malcolm, who had recently been knighted for his commendable duty as Britain's representative to an energy-rich African nation. During that high-flying tour of duty the ambassador had cultivated a highly developed nose for opportunity. In dealing with the vilest dictators in the most exploited regions of Africa he had turned the combination of corruption, natural wealth and appalling infrastructure to his advantage wherever he encountered it. To his delight Sir Malcolm found this same combination of qualities in the Classics Faculty and its treasurer. Before long the pair had struck up a productive and mutually beneficial working relationship. Sir Malcolm, though not formerly part of the University, was one of its unofficial links with central government, and his influence in both academia and at Whitehall relied on his status as an old-school political patron.

He would act as mentor to those on the first rung of the career ladder, an ever-neutral mediator in factions between friends and, most importantly, a lender to the politically well-endowed but financially destitute. Shortly after meeting Sir Malcolm, and finding that he was in every way a 'sound' man, Fringe, in his first move towards what would become a career in politicking and corruption, began siphoning money away from the Faculty funds and into the shady bank accounts of Sir Malcolm's shadow companies and offshore holdings. Within a year Fringe was appointed to the coveted position of Professor of Roman Map-Making, whilst diligently agreeing to continue in his capacity as treasurer. A year later, after the decrepit Professor Lathebone was mysteriously forced out by an obscure order from the University authorities, he was elevated to head of the Faculty.

From here Fringe had swiftly consolidated his position. Carefully selecting the most corrupt, contemptible and all-round good sorts that he could find, he surrounded himself with an inner circle of followers. Each of them agreed to partake in Fringe's corruption, facilitating it and making sure it was never discovered, and each in turn received their reward of senior positions at the Faculty. Thus within a few years Fringe reigned supreme in the world of classics at Cambridge. His hold on the Faculty was unchallengeable, his relationship with the ruling body of the University greased by the patronage of Sir Malcolm, to whom money was diverted in ever-greater quantities and through ever more elaborate means.

Tapping his fingers on his desk Fringe fidgeted with irritation, and was about to replace the receiver when a couple of rings interrupted the music and a sharp voice shot down the line.

"Ruffles," it said crisply. "Who is this?"

"Sir Malcolm, it's me, Paul."

"Fringe? What on earth are you calling me now for? You know full well I don't do Cambridge business whilst in Bermuda. Got a lot of big things going on here. Can't be bothered with all that academic fluff at the moment." His voice was cut-glass, his tone brooking no nonsense.

Fringe hardly ever used his Christian name, and would promptly have slapped down any classicist who dared refer to him by it. Calling himself by the slightly alien 'Paul', however, was an attempt to create a sense of at least nominal equality, though he would never have gone so far as to omit the 'Sir' from his address to the ambassador. That he had been slapped back so casually was, as ever, teeth-gratingly annoying.

"Oh I know, Sir Malcolm, I do apologise. It's just that there have been some significant developments here and I think you ought to be brought up to speed."

Sir Malcolm gave a small grunt of irritation.

"Very well."

"I know it comes completely out of the blue, but Harriet Mason is dead."

"My condolences. Who the hell was she?"

"You secured a senior lectureship for her a few years back, remember? She had been working very closely with me on the Classics Outreach Fund."

"Oh yes the Outreach Fund. Yes, I recall now. Involved with that was she? Well then it really is a sad loss. I was hoping that would be up and running in the next month. After all, I secured your nomination to the Vice Chancellorship on the basis of such long and devoted friendship to me and, well, the Outreach Fund was to be the cherry on the cake, so to speak. Ultimate proof of loyalty and all that. How disappointing." His voice was calm, but there was a distinct hint of something threatening in its tone.

Fringe shuddered. He was acutely aware of the dangers of provoking disappointment in Sir Malcolm. If the

85

ambassador revoked his patronage it would be disastrous for his career. He knew that reassurance was necessary, or even with his nomination secured he could wave goodbye to his dream of becoming Vice Chancellor.

"Oh, no, no, it okay, Sir Malcolm, it's all absolutely fine. Nothing to worry about," he stuttered desperately. "The Outreach Fund is so close to completion that I expect the money will be ready for transfer into your Bermuda account within ten days."

This was a hugely ambitious promise, but one that Fringe knew he had no choice but to fulfil. The Fund was the most substantial amount of money that he had ever organised for Sir Malcolm. On the pretext of voluntary budget cuts, in line with government recommendations, he had siphoned off fully half of the last two years' worth of the Faculty's budget into a Swiss numbered account in preparation for payment to one of the ambassador's shady fronting companies. It was a ruse fraught with danger, and had until now depended on the compliance of Mason, Wildencrust, Alan Tanning and Elliot Norther who, as his loyal cronies, had each played their part in pushing his proposals for phantom budgetary constraints through at the Faculty's quarterly meetings. Even this task, however, had not been quite enough for Sir Malcolm to feel that the ultimate prize, the Vice Chancellorship, was worth expending political effort for to secure for Fringe. Thus at the end of the previous academic year Fringe had carried out one more favour for his patron.

"That reminds me, Fringe," said Sir Malcolm. "How are things going with that boy of mine? Did you manage to get him in?"

"Oh, er, yes Sir Malcolm," said Fringe, surprised and relieved that the subject had been changed. "He's been settling in well. Hasn't he told you?"

"Hardly. I never answer his calls. Even talking to him reminds me of my bloody wife."

"How is Lady Ruffles?" enquired Fringe, more out of politeness than real interest.

"Same as ever. Fucking harpy. She's in France at this time of year, and good riddance. I hope that useless boy of mine is on course not to get kicked out."

"Oh no, Sir Malcolm, he's doing really... er, oh, let's just say he's doing frightfully adequately," said Fringe, wincing at such a considerable overstatement of the young man's academic progress.

"I'd be very surprised if he is," Sir Malcolm drawled, sceptically.

"Well it took quite a concerted effort on our part. Indeed, getting him onto the Master's degree was made rather more of a challenge by the fact that he doesn't even have a GCSE to his name," said Fringe.

"Oh I agree the boy's thick. But for some reason that I've given-up trying to fathom he's his mother's pride and joy. After she caught me having a romp with that secretary the only non-financial term she imposed for her not seeking a divorce was to get the dunce into Cambridge or, failing that, Oxford. Seemed like the only way to quell the beast and stop her from causing social ripples. Tricky things, ripples."

"Well, I'm glad we could help. It involved bumping off another student who was set for taking up the place now occupied by your son, but that was relatively easy."

"Bribed him, did you?"

"Failed him," said Fringe, matter-of-factly.

"Delightful." The ambassador's tone now betrayed an element of boredom. "Look I want to wrap things up. Lots to do, you know. All I want to know is whether or not the Fund will be ready on time."

"It will," said Fringe. "And can I count on no delays, blocks or unforeseen obstacles over my promotion to the Vice Chancellorship?"

"None."

"Wonderful," exhaled Fringe, with relief. "In that case I'll tell Wildencrust, Tanning and Norther that they can expect promotions imminently, assuming that you can arrange professorships for each of them?"

"Yes, yes, that's fine. Don't bother me with the details, just get on with it. You'll have everything you need. Goodbye."

Fringe replaced the receiver with great reassurance.

*****

As the council of the Olympians adjourned and the age-old deities began to disperse across James's synaptic network, Aphrodite saw her chance and collared Dionysos.

"My darling," she said, sweetly. "I thought you did terribly well back there. You really handled yourself with dignity in what could've turned into quite a nasty situation."

"Thank you Aphro," said Dionysos, a little warily.

They had always been civil to each other, though they moved in rather different circles. He was the God of Wine and Levity which, at least in the old days, had been an exclusively male affair, whilst she was the archetypal divinity of all things feminine.

"Yes, I was rather taken with your commanding stance. You really are your father's son."

"Well that's very good of you. I was a little nervous, what with it being my first time and all."

"Darling I had forgotten all about that," she feigned. "Why, I'd say you were as expert at handing that divine rabble as anyone could wish."

Dionysos blushed.

"Well I suppose it was an honour to be chosen, though I can't think why me in particular. Poseidon could just have easily have done the job. Or if Zeus was after another youngster he could've chosen Apollo.

"Oh pish. Poseidon would never stomach being given the job because it would be tantamount to acknowledging his inferiority to Zeus, and as for your brother, he's sunning himself with the Hyperboreans," said Aphrodite. The Ancient Greeks knew well enough that every winter Apollo visited his favourite race of people in a mysterious area of Europe that modern cartographers have never quite managed to chart.

"I suppose so. Anyway, is there something I can help you with?"

"Oh no it's nothing. I was just wondering when you were going to tell the mortal about his new mission, that's all."

"*Me* tell him? I thought one of the others would…"

"Surely not, darling? As Chairman of the council it's your responsibility. If you were to stand by whilst one of the others informed him it would make a mockery of your authority. An authority that Zeus himself bestowed upon you."

"Hmmm, I see what you mean I suppose,"

"Excellent," thought Aphrodite with wile. "Zeus is turning out to be a bit of a trump card these days. The old bastard should throw marital paddies more often."

"Although," continued Dionysos, "didn't Hera inform him of the first mission?"

"Er… oh yes, she did. Well surely that's all the more reason to assert your authority now. You don't want her to think that she can walk all over you."

"I guess not. Okay then, thanks Aphro, I'll inform him myself," he said, smiling.

"Better make it quick, my darling, else Hera will whip the chance right out from under your little nose."

"Will do. See you later then." And off he went, spurred by Aphrodite's carefully chosen words.

"Right, time to get this show on the road," said the goddess to herself, as she summoned her powers. "Dionysos," she whispered deeply to the absent god. "When you see the mortal boy you will feel my hand upon your heart. When you look upon him Zeus's bolt might never have lit up the sky. It will be as nothing to the force of what you'll feel when you see that human form. Let all the gods in heaven see the power that I have over the passions of life."

The spell was cast, and with it the die.

CHAPTER NINE

James's full English was greasier than a Jaguar salesman around a lottery winner. Every bite felt like an assault on his arteries but was nonetheless vastly satisfying. Muesli had gone to and from the kitchen throughout the meal, periodically returning to deliver a new piece of gossip about the unfolding debate. As events had gathered pace James had begun to feel slightly more secure in the knowledge that this time he would be able to anticipate what was next in store. Presently the Muse reappeared at his side, but now she wore a look of mild concern on her over-painted face.

"What's wrong," asked James through a mouthful of sweaty bacon.

"Er, nothing really, babe. It's just that…"

"What?"

"Well the meeting finished a couple of minutes ago and Aphro and Dionysos have started talking privately."

"So?"

"The thing is I can't hear what they're saying."

"I thought you could hear everything?"

"No, as long as the gods reside in your brain my omniscience is constrained. I have an enhanced perception of events but I don't know everything."

"Well what can we…"

"Oh shit, ssshhhh, don't speak to me, Dionysos is on his way!"

"What, here?"

"Ssshhh, yes! He mustn't see me talking to you!"

"Oh bloody hell, Muesli! Can't you just disappear?"

"Bollocks, it's too late, he'll sense something's up."

"Well get into the kitchen, quick!"

"Miss? Excuse me, may I order some food please?"

It was one of the Trinity girls on the other table. They

had both turned and were looking expectantly at the Muse, who winced.

"It's as good a cover as any," she whispered to James through clenched teeth before trotting over to their table.

At that moment the door opened and a gust of air was cast in from the icy streets. All inside turned at once, gaping at the figure who followed. The individual in question was devastatingly good-looking, and the Trinity girls let out an involuntary gasp in girlish harmony.

"Bloody hell, Clarissa," breathed Jessica. "What a dish."

But her friend was wide-eyed and mute.

James was hardly blind to the god's appearance, and could well have appreciated his aesthetic appeal just as he might a piece of fine classical sculpture, but the knowledge that Dionysos was an Olympian tempered him. Any being that swung from the branches of Hera's family tree was to be treated with caution of the highest order.

"Steel yourself, James," he thought. "This guy has the look of the queen bitch about him. At least this time I can brace for the storm."

He half winced as he waited for the deluge.

Silence.

The Trinity girls were rapt; Muesli made not a peep, and James himself hardly dared to draw breath. Slowly the god's mouth opened, and the chilled calm of the café was braced for the first clap of thunder.

"Cor!" breathed Dionysos, throatily.

"Erm...I... I'm sorry, but are you talking to me?" asked James, hesitantly glancing behind him.

"Yeeeaaaahhh..." came the languid drawl, giving voice to the glazed stare. James was reminded of the girl behind the till in the dream Sceptre. Perhaps examples of Olympian perfection were running at a surplus in the Fens.

"Well... is there something I can do for you?" James's initial anxiety was fast ripening into confusion.

"You... are..." drawled the god.

"Yes," thought James angrily. "I know I'm feeble, and mortal, and pathetic, and whatever. Do they have to tell me at every turn? Okay, fine, so I just so happen to have been born..."

"Beautiful!" gasped the god.

"Excuse me?" spluttered James.

"Typical," said Clarissa.

"What a waste," sighed Jessica.

"Fuck me," muttered the Muse, under her breath. "This must be what mortals call 'surprise.'" Blessed with divine foresight, she had had so few opportunities to experience the sensation that she was almost willing to stand and relish the moment. The Trinity girls, however, could not be allowed to witness the next five minutes, regardless of what transpired. She leaned down and whispered into Jessica's ear.

"Excuse me miss, but it's nearly ten o'clock. Oughtn't you be getting to supervision?"

"Hmmm?" said Jessica. She was still distracted, wondering if the beautiful stranger wasn't one of those charmingly old-fashioned sorts who called everyone beautiful. If so then he could well be straight, and if she should 'accidentally' bump into him on the way out then she might just slip her number into his...

"Miss?"

"Sorry? Oh yes, I suppose it is getting on. Could we have the bill please."

"It's on the house."

"Really? But..."

"No really. You're regulars," said the Muse with a nearly perceptible degree of irritation.

"Oh okay. Well thanks. Come on Clarissa, I suppose we'd better head off."

"Really is such a shame," said her friend, as she rose, trance-like, from her chair.

93

Then they were gone. The Muse turned to find Dionysos staring down at James, who glanced across at her with fear and confusion embellished on his forehead. There was nothing for it, she'd have to go over there. The fact that the god hadn't detected her presence beforehand was a sure enough sign that he wasn't fully *compos mentis*. She removed the apron from her skinny frame, flicked her dirty fingers across her straggly locks and marched over.

"Hello Dionysos," she said, in the manner of a passenger announcement at a train station.

"What?" mumbled the god, without taking his eyes off James.

"Oh bloody hell," sighed the Muse. Was she invisible to everyone today? She leaned forward and snapped her violet fingernails in his face. "Wake up you great lug!"

Dionysos blinked.

"What? Who's... Oh it's you, Muse. What are you doing here?"

"Oh... I'm, er, seeing how the other half live. I assume you've come to inform James of the next victim?"

"Have I?" he said dreamily. "I was just coming into this wretched little place when I saw... him!"

"Well now that you're here you can just get on with..."

"This mortal is the most beautiful specimen of blood and guts I've ever seen."

"Now look here, er... your majesty," said James self-consciously. "I know I'm not a bad looking chap, but I really don't..."

"Shut up, James!" whispered Muesli raspingly. "I'll handle this." She then raised herself up as high as her scuffed trainers would allow and plumped out her A-cup chest. "Now listen here, Dionysos. I don't know what your game is but don't even think about it. We're strictly to have nothing to do with mortals. Remember what Zeus said?" She took a great gulp of air, and when she spoke it was with the booming

94

intonation and baritone voice of the god-king himself. "None of the divine shall sully the Olympian name through excessive contact with the mortal vessel of our wrath. Nor shall the plan be carried out but through that vessel." She exhaled and her voice returned to its usual twang. "Remember?"

"But he's…" he said, taking a step forward.

"Hold it right there, Dionysos," snapped the Muse. "You absolutely have to tell him what needs to be said."

"But I…" trailed the Olympian. He hadn't taken his eyes off James throughout, and was speaking as if through a veil.

"No buts. Tell him who the next victim will be."

"Erm… er…."

"W, it begins with W."

"Wibble…."

"No, Wildencrust. Say it: *Wildencrust*." Her patience was fraying now. "Something bloody dramatic must have happened between Dionysos and Aphro," she thought. "The one time I can't hear what's going on and everything goes pear-shaped. Typical."

"Oh yes, er, Wildencrust," blubbered Dionysos. "He's the next victim."

"I see," said James, shrinking back in his seat. "Well I suppose I should get onto it straight away, shouldn't I?" He had never used organised killing as a conversational escape route before, but if there was ever a time to start, it was now.

"Yes, that's… er. Maybe, yes," drawled the god. "Did I mention how beautiful you are?"

With this he took anther step forward and reached out, but the Muse was too fast. She darted forward and stood in front of James.

"Stop that Dionysos, right this second. Get back to headquarters immediately."

Now, at last, Dionysos's countenance changed. As soon as the Muse placed herself between him and James, his face became dark and anger flashed in his eyes.

"You can't tell me what to do. I'm the Chair of the council of the Olympians, appointed by Zeus himself, and if I want to have this mortal then so I shall."

"And how long do you think you'll last when Zeus hears that you've breached his non-interference order?"

This was the clincher. Even in a fit of passion Dionysos was clear-headed enough to know that angering the King of Olympus was about as serious as it could get. He cast a smouldering glare at the Muse and slowly stepped back.

"Yes that's right Dionysos. It's nothing personal, and I'm sure no one would begrudge you any other mortal. But not this one. I'm saying this for your sake as much as anything." She spoke with as much confidence as she dared, knowing that there was little she could do if the god decided to push ahead.

"I suppose so. But while we're on the subject of grassing, I'm sure Hera would be interested to know how closely involved you are in the mortal's affairs."

The Muse couldn't prevent worry from freezing her face, though her voice remained calm.

"Fine, Dionysos. I'll keep quiet if you do."

"Agreed," he said. Then he cast a strange look upon James, which seemed to convey an emotion the latter could not easily interpret, before turning and sweeping out onto the street.

Muesli and James were alone in the café now, as the rain spattered against the windows and the wind decanted itself through the crack under the draughty door.

CHAPTER TEN

Back in James's neural network Dionysos made his way straight to Aphrodite's chambers. The mortal vessel was certainly one of the most ravishing creatures he had ever laid eyes on, and relinquishing it for the sake of a stuffy old set of orders from the King of the Gods was not something he could bear to contemplate. Had such a scenario presented itself in the good old days (as they did with divinely ordained frequency), he would simply have had his fill of whatever it was that took his fancy: man, woman or animal. In present conditions he couldn't force himself on the mortal without encroaching upon his father's authority. If the boy were to offer himself of his own accord, however, what was a red-blooded god to do but *carpe* the very *diem* with due diligence? Only Aphrodite had the power to make it happen, and he was determined to use every ounce of his charm to persuade her to do so.

Thus, heady with lust, he invited himself into her boudoir and she was delighted to receive him. There he put his case with all the subtle eloquence that he could muster. His words of 'match made in the heavens' and 'a meeting of two destinies' fell upon a warm and understanding face. The goddess smiled beautifully as he explained how he had felt the very moment he first caught sight of the mortal, a beacon of almost divine beauty in a fetid pit of mortality. Surely she, good and dear friend as she was, could grant him a favour and make the object of his desire reciprocate?

"Absolutely not my darling. Fuck off," purred Aphrodite.

"But Aphro, please!"

"Nope."

"But I really…"

"Nope."

"But why? I mean it's not so much to ask that you do me this one little favour."

"Dearest it's a huge thing to ask. If I go interfering then Zeus will have my guts for garters," simpered Aphrodite.

"Not at all! You wouldn't be directly intervening in his actions. You'd simply be giving him a nudge in the right direction."

"It would risk the very mission itself. It took a talking to from Hera to persuade the little bugger to carry out the mission in the first place. After being told that he had to murder a mere five people his gut reaction was to refuse. Now that's hardly a reasonable response is it? If I were to go altering the delicate electro-chemical balance of his brain to make him fall in love with you it would make *you* his prime objective."

"Yes exactly, that's precisely what I want."

"Indeed, but his prime objective must be the mission. By making him lust after you I'd be breaking Zeus's rule myself. Don't you see?"

Dionysos assumed the face of a toddler who has had its new toy taken away.

"Oh for fuck's sake, Aphro! Well yes I do see what you mean, actually, but it really is too bad. Is there nothing you can do for me? Please, I'd be eternally grateful."

"Eternally grateful? You mean you'd do me a favour in return?"

"Yes of course, anything, anything!" said Dionysos excitedly. He had sensed a glimmer of hope and was willing to claw at it.

"Well perhaps I might be willing to bend the rules a little…"

"Oh Aphro, you're the best! I'll always remember this. I'll never forget what..."

"The condition of my helping you is that you support me in council."

"Of course, of course."

"When the time comes you will give me priority of the floor and, most crucially, restrict the chance that Hera has to put her case."

"Yes, yes, no problem. So when can you get to work?"

"After Wildencrust is dead."

"What?" he said, his face suddenly sinking. "But I want it now!"

"Tough. I want to be sure that you'll do as I ask. A fool in love is as changeable as anything and I don't want to be caught with my neck on the line."

"Oh but I can't wait that long. I simply can't!" said Dionysos, squirming in the manner of a hooked fish.

"You'll have to, my dear. Otherwise it's a firm 'no.'"

"But... oh very well. Agreed," he said stroppily.

"You won't regret this my sweet," beamed Aphrodite. "Fabulous," she thought. "This idiot has played the part like a pro, and soon I'll get to watch Madam Bitch dance to the same tune."

*****

Back in his room James paced. He knew who the next victim was, and that the wretch was ordained to die as soon as possible, but beyond that there wasn't much of a plan. The Muse had absented herself after Dionysos had left, and without her it was difficult to know how to proceed. Was he to grab the nearest meat cleaver and stalk through the town looking for bearded males of a certain age? The poison trick had been orchestrated from on high and was unlikely to work a second time without landing him in hot water with the police.

He walked over to the mirror above the sink in the corner and took a long, hard look at himself. The face he saw wasn't bad for someone who was acting as a medium for divine retribution. The initial strain that had shown around his mouth when he had woken from the deathly vision of the Sceptre seemed to have disappeared. His eyes were shining and his skin was clear, neither betraying the stress that brutal murder would exhibit on a normal, well-adjusted man. The only blemish he noticed was on his forehead, just below the hairline. He moved closer to the mirror, and as he did so it vanished, revealing itself to be an imperfection in the glass. As he withdrew again he noticed another, just below his chin, and another above his right eye. It had never struck him how warped the glass was but now it seemed that there were distortions across its entire surface. Through the window a black cloud swept across an already overcast sky, shifting the light in the room and instantly throwing up a host of shimmering waves. James caught his breath, for the glass itself seemed to be moving. Ripples glided across its surface, one striking another and causing a cascade of peaks and troughs across its silicate structure. Bubbles appeared. Breaking against the air they formed tiny clusters around the edges near the frame, but were soon as large as marbles, great bursting pockets of heat.

James stepped back to shield his eyes from the steam that leapt from the boiling mirror, but before he could cast his weight upon his back foot an arm reached out from the molten pool and grabbed his collar, pulling him beneath the liquid glass.

In he plunged and the agony was indescribable, the heat so intense around his eyes and face that shards of cold pain shot through his nerves. Within, the mirror was not fluid but simply heat and light. He tried desperately to wrench himself back through the barrier of boiling glass and into the cool air again, but the hand held him fast, and from out of the brightness a face drew close to his own.

"Don't bother crying out, mortal," said the Queen of the Gods.

"Hera? What's happening? Why have you…"

"Silence! I don't have time for idle conversation. I'm here to tell you who the next victim is."

"It's… It's Wildencrust," spluttered James. The pain was so extreme that he didn't think twice about trying to cut the experience short.

"What?" exclaimed Hera with irritation. "Who told you that? Has that little cock, the Muse, been talking to you again? I'll cut her up like a…"

"No, no it wasn't her, it was Dionysos."

"He came here and told you that?! Of all the presumptuous little…"

"Aaarrrgh, please, please Hera. I can't stand…"

"Shut up! What did he tell you to do?"

"He said… he told me… oh Jesus Christ!"

"Speak!"

"To kill Wildencrust as soon as possible!" spluttered James. Tears streamed down his face and glistened like crystals across Hera's slender fingers.

"Fine. But you listen to me. When you kill Wildencrust you must intone very loudly and clearly 'All glory to Hera.' I want you to stamp this piece of handiwork with my name for every divinity in the cosmos to hear. Understand?"

"Yes, yes, I understand! Please let me go! Please, I can't take any more!"

"Then say it!"

"All glory to Hera!"

"Again!"

"All glory to Hera… Hera, please!"

The boiling glass around his neck seethed, and in the light around him black and red spots began to form, growing and moving across each other. He trembled in the heat, convulsing against the iron grip that bound him fast inside the mirror. Then, as blackness covered his eyes, a sharp jolt cast him backwards. He landed hard on the bedroom floor and lay prone. The carpet was cool and wet against his skin, as the tap in the sink had been running all the while.

CHAPTER ELEVEN

Evening, and Midsummer College was a beautiful sight. In the light of the full winter moon spectral shadows were cast across the Great Court, an assemblage of phantoms that danced as the wind rustled the ancient trees. The greater part of the archaic pile was still, though one area glowed with light and life. In the Great Hall festivities had been underway since late afternoon. Drinks were flowing freely, and course after course was placed before worthy fellows in black gowns. Dowager's Day was the most raucous event in the college's calendar, and had been so for the last six hundred years. Having been established by the institution's founder, Lady Maxima Lupa, it involved a long day's eating, drinking and debauchery, culminating in the ceremonial beating of an effigy of the founder's mother-in-law, the dowager. Tradition stated that this venerable ritual should take place in the dining hall before all the fellows, who would raise three cheers for the demise of the old crone before forming a loud and drunken procession to drag the battered effigy through the courts of the college.

On this particular night of the year undergraduates were confined to their rooms, though many abandoned college altogether, scurrying off to assignations of their own. The lights in the windows in Great Court were dark and the fellows' laughter and cheering echoed down empty corridors.

The window of one set of rooms was lit bright, however, and inside Wildencrust paced. This was the first Dowager's Day feast he had missed since his election to the fellowship twenty years ago.

Harriet Mason's death had been a dead weight upon him. Formerly they had enjoyed the festivities together, each sitting on separate tables and exchanging their own secret signals across the sea of silver throughout the course of the evening. Virtually all the fellows had known what was going on between the pair, and the majority had disapproved of the college's most abrasive members seeking pleasure in each other. To face the academic rabble now would be intolerable, so Wildencrust had decided to exchange an evening of whispered gossip for one of silent loneliness in his rooms.

Over on the desk lay an Ancient Greek text, Pindar's victory odes, alongside a large and neglected pile of second-year essays. These were to be his company tonight. He was too restless to sleep, but if he could immerse himself in work then the whole wretched evening would be over and done with in a flash. Plans such as these have been carried out ever since men have possessed desks to brood at, and with varying degrees of success; but not tonight. Now, from the depths of the connective nerve tissue inside the skull of a young man came forth a being of indescribable beauty and power, her mission singular. She would enter the don's chambers whilst he was alive and leave when he was dead. None of her illustrious family would know of her dealings, and so glory in council would be hers. She who controlled the love and lusts of all living things approached the chambers of the don, clothed in all that was beautiful to him, wrapped in the flesh and bone and blood of that which he could not refuse.

A knock at the door.

"Piss off."

Another knock; firmer this time.

"I said fuck off. I'm not unlocking it, whoever it is. I'm not going to the feast, I don't care about fucking college statutes."

No knock this time, but a clink as the handle turned and the latch fell uselessly away.

"What the hell? Who do you think…"

"Shhh. Don't say another word, my darling."

There in the doorway stood Harriet Mason: vast, corpulent and naked. Against the stark light cast by the desk lamp she resembled some unspeakable marine life form, scooped from the lightless depths of a deep ocean trench, her flesh quivering and translucent.

In his own fish-like manner Wildencrust's mouth flapped open and shut wordlessly, and his eyes bulged in their sockets. Mason turned and gently closed the door, the soft click of the latch sending the same ripple across the bare flesh of her stomach as a bubble bursting in a pot of boiling porridge.

"How can this be? You're… I mean for God's sake, how can this possibly be?"

"It just is, my sweet. Don't try to understand. All you need to know is that I can't be without you. I need you one last time. Tonight."

"You… You need me? Oh mercy God, what the hell is going on? This isn't possible!"

Mason walked closer to him, each waddling step sending the precarious balance of her flab-mounds out of kilter, giving her a wobbling, tottering gait. Despite his shock Wildencrust's nether-regions stirred at the sight, and the breathless pant that walking induced in his beloved's lungs exacerbated his sudden urgency.

"I don't understand," he stammered.

"Don't bother trying. Just accept that stranger things happen in life than fiction, that tonight will be our final farewell… and our greatest coming together," breathed Fatty.

*****

Two floors below, in a darkened room, James waited with dying patience. The corridor outside led to the Great Hall, and just across it was the flight of stairs that would take him to Wildencrust's rooms. People were still scurrying up and down in preparation for the effigy-beating ritual in half an hour's time. The room in which he sheltered contained a large

105

table, and laid on top were all the components that would be used to recreate the old dowager, most notably a hideous purple frock that was to be stuffed with pebbles and hay. James knew that it would only be a short while before the rowing team would assemble here to begin work and that he would have to make a move before then. He glanced around at the shelves that lined the walls. Each was heaving with bottles of wine. These were to be quaffed by the fellows after the ceremony, and had gathered dust there for the entire year solely in preparation for this night.

Suddenly James sensed a presence across the room and felt himself jump. Surely someone couldn't have been in here when he walked in? If so he would have a tough time explaining himself.

"Who's there?" he ventured. "Come on, speak up."

From out of the shadows stepped the last person that James wished to see, and he felt himself tense as the figure came into the light.

"Oh, Dionysos. I didn't see you there. Is... er... is everything okay?" James was nervous, and rightly so.

"Oh yes everything's fine. I just came to wish you luck, that's all," said the god in a gentle but calculating voice.

"Well thank you very much. Yes I'm just on the point of going up there and doing the job now," said James warily.

"Good, good. Now I don't suppose you've changed your mind at all about you-know-what?" he said, taking a step closer.

"Er... no, I'm afraid not," said James, slightly fearful now as Dionysos crept closer still.

"Oh I thought not," he said with an air of grace, the smile remaining on his lips. "No matter. No matter at all." Suddenly he took a step back again, his body language softening.

James felt palpably relieved at this. He knew that it would be no good calling for the Muse's help here, and he would have been powerless if Dionysos had wanted to take things into his own hands.

"You must be terribly nervous about the killing, James," said Dionysos, with apparent sympathy in his voice. "Here, have a glass of wine to take your mind off things. I think you can trust the God of Wine that it's an excellent vintage."

The god reached out and took one of the bottles from the shelf behind him, deftly uncorked it and poured it into one of the glasses lined up on the sideboard. As he did so Dionysos looked intently at the liquid. He perceived the complex molecular structure of the alcohol and the power over the life and fortunes of men that it contained within it. These intoxicating molecules were his to command, and with his mind he reached out and imparted to them the spark of divinity. In that instant every drop in every bottle in the room was charged with power. Any mortal who tasted even a mouthful would be swept away by the force of the liquid, experiencing the kind of intoxication that brings humans close to the divine.

The god handed the glass to James, who tentatively accepted it.

"Just have a little sip," said Dionysos. "There's time, and you'll feel much better about your mission. I promise."

"Yes perhaps you're right, I could do with a drink," replied James nervously. He didn't know what Dionysos was up to, though there seemed little harm in playing along with the pleasantries.

He raised the glass to his lips and Dionysos stared expectantly. The mortal would barely know his left hand from his right if he were to drink it, and then the god could have his fill.

Suddenly a noise erupted from the end of the corridor, and James knew immediately that the fifth and final course was starting. Time was running out.

"I'm sorry Dionysos, I have to go or it'll be too late," he

said, absently placing the glass down on the table. Before the god could say another word James had run into the corridor and up the stairs. The God of Wine scowled at the near miss.

"Never mind, mortal. You'll be mine soon enough," he murmured to himself in the darkness.

*****

Wildencrust had unconsciously backed himself against the rear wall as his dead lover moved in closer to him and her small, pig-like nose brushed gently against his own. In such sexual proximity her stomach, thighs and mountainous breasts smothered his hapless body.

"Oh Harriet. There's just… There's nothing I can say. I don't care what this is, I have to have you now!"

"Yes, my love! Yes, on the bed, throw me down!"

Engulfed by passion Wildencrust summoned all the strength in his limbs and grabbed Mason's vast body. She moved not an inch, but merely stood salivating. A further heave proved equally futile so he tenderly took her hand and led her to his bed in the other room, where she willingly collapsed in a heap of gasping flesh.

"Now fuck me hard, Wildenthrust!" she panted, opening her legs to reveal a valley of congealed flesh and red-raw sores.

He wasted no time and pounced. Never before had he managed to disentangle himself from his clothes at such a rate. Never had he thrust himself upon her with such force or felt himself as hard as he did now. If this was a dream then he never wanted to wake, he would rather sleep forever and let the world canter past.

"Harder! Faster!" cried Mason, arching her back in a way that he had never seen.

"Oh dear God I'm close!" yelled Wildencrust, speeding up.

"I'm not!" retorted Mason.

Seconds later Wildencrust delivered the payload. When she had been alive this was always the point at which sex would end. He was not as young as he used to be and his lover was hideously obese. Even walking up stairs used to drain her reserves of stamina.

This time, however, she was different. At the first trace of a reduced thrust Mason reached over and touched her lover's temple, sending pulses of sexual energy through his body. He looked down and gasped at the mass of blubber beneath him, overwhelmed with desire. His energy seemed to increase rather than diminish. Something in her eyes unsettled him, urging him further almost against his will. Thrust after thrust saw them fly briefly into his field of vision and there, for a mere moment each time, they held him. Their vitality was not merely unnatural but blinding. So strong was the force of life that shone from them that they bore the sharp glint of madness, of wild urgency.

On and on he went. The minutes passed, and the energy that possessed him showed no signs of abating, though now mental and physical exhaustion clawed closer in from the edges, like a ravenous wolf circling the campfire. How much longer could he keep this up? Mason seemed so thoroughly in control of his passion and body that he felt his movements were no longer his own. He simply couldn't stop.

Suddenly she arched her back again, sending a wave of pleasure cascading across his spine. But now something was wrong. His heart spluttered against the exertion. He simply couldn't force enough air into his burning lungs no matter how hard he breathed. A stabbing pain shot across his arm, knocking him sidewards, but still he couldn't stop. Mason grabbed his hair in her fat fist and yet another surge of energy clattered through his burning frame, forcing him onwards, bankrupting him.

"Please my love. I can't... I can't..." he pleaded.

"You will! You… will…"

"It's… It's killing me! Please!"

But on he went. She arched her back yet again and sent another burning volley across the length of him. He could only thrust harder, chained in his own movement. Though raw and beaten he could not cease.

Suddenly a new, colder pain shot through his arm and a crushing pressure in his chest nearly knocked him from the bed. But still he could not stop. The tightening above his ribcage became a burning that spread across his back. He felt his breath fail.

"My… My heart…. It's…"

But there was no need for explanation. Aphrodite, beneath the innumerable pounds of Harriet Mason's flesh, could see exactly what was happening inside his pulmonary system and she smiled to herself.

"Don't concern yourself, mortal," she said with the dead woman's voice. "It happens to most of you eventually."

Now Wildencrust tumbled onto the floor and writhed in agony as cardiac arrest took hold. He felt convulsions of pain rack his form, and with horror sensed his mind reel across the memories of his life in preparation for its departure.

Aphrodite began to cackle gently to herself.

"You know it really is quite splendid to watch one's lover perish on the floor beside the bed. Makes one feel rather like a spider who kills her mate after copulation. Not that those poor creatures experience love or desire." Then she crouched and leaned close to the face of the collapsed, gasping don, and in the voice, manner and nearly the soul of Harriet Mason she whispered, "But then neither did I."

A quite different agony flashed across the face of the lecturer as the words sank beneath his skin, but at that moment there was a fumbling at the door. Aphrodite glanced up, angry that her relish should be cut short. But this was as it should be. The boy had arrived to carry out his task, and through his eyes the others would be watching. Behind the wood she could perceive James wondering how to contend with the lock without compromising a stealthy entry, so silently she waddled over to the door and released the latch, before retreating invisibly into the cranium of the intruder.

A moment later James carefully opened the door and took in the room with a cautious air. The study appeared to be empty, the papers on the desk tidy and untouched.

"Brilliant," he thought. "He must be taking a nap. It's always easier to finish someone off if you can take them by surprise. At least I assume so anyway."

As quietly as a mouse he pattered into the bedroom and poked his head round the door. The bed was a mess, with the pillows lying at either end and the covers tossed onto the floor. There next to them, however, lying in silent contortion was the still form of Penton Wildencrust.

"What the hell? He's already dead? He can't bloody well have died on the same night that I was supposed to do him in. Oh Jesus Christ." But then it occurred to him that not having to beat another man to death might have its perks. "Well I suppose at least that's one less body on my conscience," he said to himself. "Oh shit, wait, what about Hera and her 'all glory' routine?"

He knelt down beside the body and ruminated on the possibility of picking it up and bashing it against the bedpost a few times whilst reciting the mantra. Surely the old hag would accept that? He gazed down at the body, looking deeply into the pained face. He had hated the man for a long time now. The part he had played in making James so miserable was not something he would have forgiven easily. As he stared at the don's features he recalled the faces of his friends, of Rasheed, Greg and Maisy, after he had received the awful news about his results. 'So it was a fail,' they had all said, 'you'll get past it in the end. It won't hold you up' Their sympathy had endured for a long time, but as the weeks had passed and he had become increasingly depressed their attitude towards him had become one of concern, of pity. He cringed as the word formed in his head. *Pity.* After all, millions of young people were in the same boat. If the people he cared about knew that he had resorted to murder as a form of resolution they would be aghast. Yet, worse than that, he knew that they would probably not have hated him, but pitied him all the more. He felt sick at the thought. Sick, not at the act of murder, but at the idea that the closest relationship he would be able to build with another human being, should another know what he had done, would be built on pity.

He leaned in closer to Wildencrust, almost to the point where the great mass of beard touched his chin.

"Well," he whispered. "I'd better get on with it."

Standing again he hauled the body up like a sack of potatoes. It was heavier than James had expected, and he clumsily hobbled backwards towards the bed. Taking the academic's head firmly in his hands he positioned it over the nearest bed post and raised it up.

"All glory to…"

"Aaarrggghhh!!"

Wildencrust sprang to life and lashed out at James, catching him completely off guard and striking him in the stomach. James fell backwards, the wind knocked out of him, and sank to the floor.

"What the… What the fuck?" he groaned.

But Wildencrust staggered up and raced for the door, which he flung open and flew through at unnatural speed. James could only tenderly claw himself to his feet and lurch after him on hobbling legs as the don ran naked down the flight of stairs.

"Murderer!!" he screamed, and the mad, piecing cry echoed on the empty landings as he went.

*****

Minutes earlier in the room where James had hidden before stalking up to Wildencrust's chambers, the rowing team had assembled. They were in high spirits as it was a singular honour to participate in the Dowager's Day ceremony. Indeed, they had all spent these past weeks creating practice effigies in preparation for the event.

Boris Jonkers, standing at the foot of the table where the great purple frock was lying open at the seams, had decided to give a rousing speech. He was rather good at rousing speeches and had presented them every year at school at the annual Jenks Cup, awarded to the house of greatest sporting merit. His voicebox was so significant that even as a ten year-old his boom would carry from one end of the school cricket ground to the other. In short, he was not a man with whom to have a whispered conversation. Here, however, he stood before his team-mates, inhaling deeply in full preparation for a hearty speech, and yet none of them winced or jammed tissues into their ears. Neither did they give him the focused attention appropriate to such an occasion. In fact Jonkers himself, along with the cox and several other rowers, positively swayed on their feet. The reason for this behaviour was that upon entering the room they had seized three bottles of wine, which were glugged down in mere moments. Instantly the charm that Dionysos had set upon those bottles, meant for James, had bewitched them all and they became more heavily inebriated than any of them had ever been before.

"I just want to say to all of you on the football team..." slurred Jonkers.

"We're not the football team, Jonkers! We're the... er... the something or other," bumbled another. "But it's definitely not football!"

"Yeah Jonkers, he's right. We're... We're cricket or something."

"No we're rowing!"

113

"Yes that's it, rowing!" exclaimed Jonkers as though it were a revelation. "Well then, to all of you on the rowing team. It's an honour to be here this morning…"

"It's not morning!"

"Isn't it? Well when is it?" His swaying was becoming more pronounced now, even if his words were not.

"It's… er… 4pm," slurred Wilcott

"No it's 10pm. And twenty six seconds," bumbled Willis.

"I say forty seven seconds!" contended Makepeace.

"Well I say seventy two seconds," said Bishop

"There are only seventy one seconds in a minute, Bishop!"

"Gentlemen please!" bellowed Jonkers, flapping his arms. "I don't know who we are, or what time it is, or what subject I'm studying, but I do know that wrapping the old dowager is a great honour that we all…"

Suddenly Jonkers' rousing speech was interrupted by the naked form of Wildencrust, who burst through the door, slammed it behind him and launched himself into the room. His eyes were wild with terror and confusion, his skin pale and bruised.

"Don't just stand there, all of you," he blustered, looking frantically about. "You've got to help me!"

There was a split second of silence, when all eyes focused on his beaten frame. This was followed by a collective scream of terrific volume.

"The dowager!" cried Jenkins.

"She's back from the dead!!" yelled Jonkers.

"She's hideous! Hideous!!" yelled two or three others as one.

"Look, she's trying to get away. Do your duty… your duty, everyone!" yelled Jonkers, commandingly, as he swayed yet more in the confusion.

"No, no, you idiots! I'm not the… I'm… Get your hands

off me! Help! Help!!"

But it was too late to restrain such a rabble. Together the rowing team rushed upon him and, seizing him by his arms and legs, threw him onto the table.

"What are you doing?! Desist! Desist I say!"

"What's she saying?" cried Bishop.

"Don't listen to her, chaps! She's trying to confuse us," yelled Jonkers.

"Gag her. Quickly!" said Jenkins.

No sooner was it said than done. One of the more enterprising rowers had found an old rag that had been used to dust off the bottles lying in the corner, and the wretched thing was duly plunged into the lecturer's mouth, much to his detriment. For now he could no longer cry out as they tied his hands and feet. Try though he might he could make not a sound as they clumsily sewed him into the purple dress, pricking his sides as they bound him in.

Within minutes it was done. The dowager lay on the table with the rowing team standing around admiring their handiwork. Suddenly a gong echoed from down the corridor, signalling the beginning of the great event.

"Right men," said Jonkers. "This is it. Everyone grab a limb and heave ho!"

They did as they were told, and for a drunken rabble they did it surprisingly well. Each man dutifully and silently took hold of what he could get and lifted the dreadful load. So focused were they that none of them noticed the blood on their fingertips. The dark hairs that had been pulled from his beard lay scattered about the table unseen, and no one was troubled by the great weight of the effigy. They simply carried the dowager out of the room and down the passage, just as every honoured team of men had done for six hundred years.

*****

115

In the Great Hall the celebrations were reaching a climax. It was *de rigueur* to be drunk at this noble event, and everyone had followed tradition with great seriousness. Professor Alderthwain, Chair of Social Anthropology, had spilled the contents of each of the five courses down his front and now resembled a cubist portrait. Dr Preen, Senior Lecturer in Theoretical Physics, had slithered under the table after the port, and his snoring provided an almost soothing ambience to the lurid conversations exchanged across the silver-loaded surfaces above.

Now, however, as the ceremonial knocks on the door were heard there was a moment of silence. The dean of the college, Professor Whipsclyde, strode purposefully down across the hall, puffed up his chest, and in his most pronounced, thespian intonations piped up.

"Who goes there? Who dares to impose upon the feast of the fellows on this sacred night?"

"Oh worshipful dean it is we, the cricket team."

The dean was suddenly deflated.

"The what team? Don't you mean…?"

"Oh, oh yes, I mean the swimming team! No, sorry, er, the…"

The dean re-inflated himself, determined not to let six hundred years of theatre be scuffed by drunken rowers.

"Oh yes the ROWING team, is it?" he said, rather overcompensating.

"Yes that's the one. We're that thing you just said."

"Then enter, and bring with you she who would wish us harm!"

The doors were slowly opened and the prone form of the dowager was solemnly processed down the body of the great chamber. The fellows looked on, hushed with awe. Such was the power and antiquity of the ritual that all felt the gravity of the moment.

Eventually the rowing team reached the platform that

had been erected at the end of the room. They were carrying the grotesque, bound effigy upon their shoulders like pall-bearers, and now they lifted it up, drawing it vertical. A rope hung down from the ceiling, set up beforehand especially for the occasion. It was tied at the top to one of the gilded rafters, its bare, sinewy length tapering downwards and ending in a large noose.

Wildencrust's eyes could barely see through the wrappings that encased his head, and it was all he could do to draw fitful breaths. But through the pin-pricks that had been left about his facial bindings he could just gather the image of the rope, and his blood ran cold.

"Oh dear God!" he thought. "This can't be happening. Surely someone will realise. Oh God!"

His eyes ran tears at the nightmare that was unfolding before him. Suddenly a figure drifted into his field of vision.

"Whipsclyde!" he thought, a faint glimmer of hope flogging his heart to a gallop. "He'll see what's happening. Yes, he'll figure it out. He always was a dolt but now here's his chance to redeem himself. Why I might even be tempted to buy him a drink after all this is."

"Excellent work, chaps!" exclaimed Whipsclyde, to the swaying Jonkers. "You really have gone to town on this one. She's absolutely hideous."

"Thank you, Dean," slurred the rower.

"No you buffoon!" screamed Wildencrust inwardly.

"Yes it'll be a pleasure to give this old thing her comeuppance. I've presided over the last fifteen of them and I can honestly say that this is the best yet."

At this the hall erupted into applause, and a deviant group of anthropology lecturers in the corner started a chant.

"Hang! Hang! Hang! Hang!"

Whipsclyde turned and smiled as it gathered pace and began to encompass the room. Even the straight-laced mathematicians joined in.

"Well we'd better give the fellows what they want," he chuckled. "Almost a perfect turnout. I haven't seen Gilders this evening," he said, squinting into the crowd. "Nevertheless I'm sure he's here in spirit."

"Yes I'm here! I'm right here!" Wildencrust knew it was futile, that he could not possibly hope to make his identity known now that Whipsclyde had been fooled, but instinct made him yell inside his mind.

"Very well chaps," said Whipsclyde to the rowing team. "Noose her up and haul away. Make sure she's a good ten feet from the ground. We don't want the fellows to hit each other with the poles do we?"

"Heaven forefend," slurred Jonkers. "Alright lads, lets get this old bag strung up."

He inserted Wildencrust's neck into the noose and took the rope in his hands. The twitching coming from under the bindings was lost on him. The tremour that mounted from within the brutally stitched dress was of no concern.

"Right now, Bishop, you come round this side, Smyth, you on the other. Now, on the count of three. Remember, backs straight. One!" he bellowed.

"Oh please, dear God, no!" cried Wildencrust.

"Two!"

"No, not like this, no!"

"Three!"

In an instant, the pent-up strength of the three drunken rowers was unleashed. Wildencrust was wrenched upwards at a terrific rate, the floor flying away from his feet as his torso span and jolted towards the rafters. His life began to ebb from the first moment. This was the climax of the greatest tradition of the college; the act that was about to end his life the very same that preserved forever the vitality of the long-dead dowager.

As he dangled from the ceiling the tightness that he had felt all around his neck vanished and his body suddenly felt cold. As the rope throttled him and he vainly tried to force air through his throat he became contemplative.

"Perhaps this isn't such a bad way to go. I can feel the cold spreading through me. When it reaches my head I'll be gone. Soon I'll be with Harriet again. Just be patient, Penton. Just let yourself go to sleep."

As seconds that felt like hours passed, this meditative state was maintained with some degree of success. He allowed his mind to drift off, to detach itself from his body. If he could just release himself from his surroundings then slipping away would just be a matter of...

Thwack!

Pain rocketed through his prone form.

"What the fuck!? What the fucking hell was that!?"

He had forgotten about the poles, the beating. As his eyes roved desperately within his constricted field of vision he caught a glimpse of the assembled mass below. There were over fifty of them, all the fellows of the college standing in ranks just beneath his dangling feet. Each brandished a sixteen foot punting pole.

"Now, fellows," bellowed Whipscylde. "Let's give the dowager what for!" Nice and orderly now, one at a time."

With that he turned on his heels and gave Wildencrust a mighty wallop with the pole. It impacted on his pelvic bone and a mighty crunch echoed around the Great Hall, drowned out immediately by raucous cheers.

"My turn now!" yelled Dr Ethel Braith, Lecturer in Mathematics. She stomped up in her sensible shoes, brandished her weapon in a no-nonsense manner and pounded the dowager's crotch.

"Let me at her!" growled Dr Damien Mordcowl, Reader in Biochemistry. He limped up to the effigy (for he had never regained full movement in his left leg after a rugby accident in his youth) and smashed his pole into Wildencrust's right thigh, shattering the bone and ripping a gash in the skirt.

"Out of my way!" snarled Professor Jonathan Hunter, Chair of Modern History. With his pole gripped in both hands he bludgeoned Wildencrust's chest.

Now the skin on his body had become lacerated and the flesh beneath was pulped and torn. Lumps of muscle and fat were ripped away and, lubricated by blood, burst out through the gashes in the dress, spilling down into the hall below like discharge from a storm drain. Lumps of gore splattered onto the floor and the murderers themselves.

Still they continued. Pounding and pounding away, they hammered his body. The cheers from the fellows sitting on the benches were deafening, the light from a thousand candles fierce and the battle cries of the warriors terrifying. Two hundred livers cannot metabolise the alcohol of six hundred bottles of wine, and the toxin coursed freely though the arteries and into the brain of every fellow there. Every fellow except Wildencrust. For him the torture was more than he could bear. He had not passed away as quickly as he had hoped, and though his form and flesh had been pulverised, his consciousness remained woefully intact. In fact his eyes, just beyond the reach of most of the poles, had remained relatively undamaged and he could still survey the hall.

As he looked out across the ranks of executioners amidst the agony and the blood, he saw that the door of the great hall open was open. Standing there, having crept in unnoticed, was a familiar figure: James Connor. As his eyes met those of the boy, seventy feet away, a look of pained recognition crossed the latter's face and electrified the mind of the doomed lecturer.

"That bastard! That little bastard! He was behind this all along. If he hadn't come into my room I'd still be there! Harriet would still be there! Oh Lord above!"

Across the hall James stared aghast at the stricken don.

"Oh my God! How the bloody hell can this have happened?" he muttered to himself. His hand involuntarily reached for his head as he felt his stomach wrench at the sight. Wildencrust was there dressed as the dowager and being beaten to death by a pack of his colleagues. The pieces of innards that were falling downwards only seemed to spark further frenzy amongst the pole-bearers.

"What a job the rowing team did!" cried a voice from the crowd.

"Stuffing the dowager with tripe, what ingenuity!" yelled another.

"They don't know," James muttered, horrified. "They haven't got a clue." He looked down and in his left hand saw the large Ancient Greek dictionary that he had grabbed as he chased Wildencrust out of his study. He had intended to use it as a bludgeon but now it seemed that fate had saved him the potential muscle strain. Disgusted as he was at what he saw he couldn't help but feel a tingle of relief that the burden of guilt would now lie with the fellows of the college rather than with him. His awareness at the favourable implications of the situation simultaneously caused him a pang of guilt but this was easily suppressed. He reasoned that since bumping off Fatty he was too deeply involved to maintain the illusion that a guilt-free existence was any longer in prospect.

As the final blows were being dealt, Wildencrust willed death to arrive. He cast one last glance across the hall where he had spent so much of his adult life. He recalled the college formals and banquets that he had attended there as an undergraduate and the thrill of taking dinner at high table when he was elected a fellow. The face of the people beating him to death from below were those of savage animals, although that in itself aptly reflected his abiding impression of his academic colleagues.

Then something caught his eye. He had not wanted to cast another glance at James Connor but something had drawn his eyes to the door once more. There was that wretched boy standing awkwardly, fiddling with his mobile phone. But who were those people behind him? They seemed to be out of focus, not fully there. His mind was reeling now, and after several hits to the head his consciousness wavered. But out of the gloom that was beginning to envelope him he could make out a large group of individuals. They were extraordinary. Though they were gathered around Connor the dolt seemed not to be aware of their presence. None of them spoke but all looked up directly into his eyes. Each of them was only just within his focus but together they seemed to glow in the long shadows of the hall. At the forefront of the group was a tall and extraordinarily beautiful woman, with long blonde hair cascading down exquisite shoulders. Her face was twisted into a grimace of disdain and some other emotion that was not quite clear. Perhaps dissatisfaction.

Fascinated though he was, his curiosity was not to be piqued. A well-aimed blow to the temple by a junior history fellow dispatched him, though the pummelling of his corpse continued for some time after.

Over at the door James was absorbed with the thought of criminal responsibility, and had taken his eyes off of Wildencrust. At that moment his phone buzzed and as he read the text message he felt a pang of relief,

"job dun… kinda." wrote the Muse.

CHAPTER TWELVE

Martin Wetherblaine, head porter of Midsummer, was gobbling to himself. He had never seen such a commotion in college in all his years as Prime Turkey.

That night he had been woken from his slumbers by a frenzied phone call from his colleague on duty.

"Mr Wetherblaine, something's happening. Hurry, you've got to come quickly!"

"Mr Wilscote? What in Heaven can be so important that it justifies calling at 2am? I'm a very busy and important man, and if I don't get sufficient sleep it'll mean…"

"No time to explain. Hurry!"

Having scrambled into his porter's uniform, he had cycled round to Midsummer as fast as he could peddle. He had expected one of the common sorts of commotion as he walked through the grand entrance into Great Court. Kids from the town had probably got drunk and broken into college grounds, and Wilscote had never been any good with confrontation.

The entrance, however, had been calm, and from the street outside it would have been impossible to guess the scene contained within the ancient walls. When he entered the court Wetherblaine had seen at once a large crowd of fellows dispersed across the grass, which was otherwise pristine due to its status as a social exclusion-zone (at Midsummer even fellows are forbidden to walk on it). The various exalted academics had still been in their gowns from the evening's celebrations which, Wetherblaine had noted as he checked his watch, should have wound down some time before. Indeed, it was not the fact that they had congregated on the lawn like a murder of crows on a freshly sown field that had aroused his curiosity, but their behaviour. As Wetherblaine had walked farther down the path that approached the grass of the glittering Great Court, still resplendently decorated in honour of the feast, he noticed that the dons were distributed in odd groups of two or three, with stragglers staggering between them. One or two were standing by themselves or sitting on the grass, or even lying on it.

It was immediately obvious to the experienced college servant that this was no ordinary post-feast gathering. After all, there was not a flute of champagne to be seen, nor a hint of a smile on a single face. Now, as Wetherblaine peered closer, he noticed that several individuals were openly crying, some were pale and silent whilst others stuttered in some non-language of their own.

Gobbling quietly, Wetherblaine surveyed the chaotic scene. Suddenly something clawed at his arm.

"Thrice round the city! Thrice round the city they dragged him!" cried Dr Palic, College Lecturer in Ancient Greek Mythology. He was on the floor, his legs having apparently buckled beneath him. His gown was torn and his eyes were wild with desperation. Wetherblaine instinctively recoiled at the sight. He could not, however, kick the man aside as he would have done a tramp in the street (despite the lecturer's strikingly tramp-like appearance). Dr Palic was a fellow of the college, and protocol demanded that his rantings be listened to.

"What are you saying, Dr Palic, I don't…"

"Hector!" screamed the fellow, visibly shaking. "Hector! Dragged thrice round the walls of Troy after death. After Achilles slew him, his corpse was dragged round and round the doomed city by a team of horses."

"What are you talking about, sir? Who are Achilles and Hector? Are they undergraduates?"

The look of madness was now accompanied by a frenzied grabbing of Wetherblaine's sleeve.

"Achilles are we. We are Achilles, and the horses, the horses too!"

"I don't understand you, sir," said the porter, exacerbated. Dr Palic's frenzy seemed to be increasing. He hadn't succeeded in raising himself from the ground and he was beginning to froth at the mouth. In all his years on the force Wethers had never been any good at dialogue with maniacs, and fortunately his role as head porter required no communication skills whatsoever. In this case, however, he had no choice but to maintain the façade of politeness and hope that the man would start to make sense.

"I see, sir," he said through clenched teeth. "So who is Hector then, sir?" "Hector is Wildencrust. Don't you see? It's Wildencrust!"

At this, Wetherblaine flinched. Though he could not be sure what this cryptic remark meant, he sensed something sinister in these words.

"Sir," he said. "Where is Dr Wildencrust?"

Dr Palic looked up at him pleadingly, tears forming in his eyes.

"Sir, I need you to tell me where Dr Wildencrust is," said Wetherblaine, shaking the man's arm as a rising sense of danger made the hairs on the back of his neck stand on end.

The lecturer slumped down onto the stone path, dejected. His mouth opened and closed but only vague, half-gulped words found their way out.

"Sir, I need to know right now!" said the porter in a raised voice.

Dr Palic lifted a trembling hand and pointed to the far side of the court. It was almost pitch black, and as Wetherblaine scanned the darkened area in vain his sense of panic heightened. Something about that corner of Great Court, away from the path that led to any major rooms or staircases, was forbidding. The fellows, staggering and swaying with little coherence, were still scattered across the lawn. Now that in his mind he knew there was something special about that dark corner, Wetherblaine noticed that although the fellows looked as if they were randomly spread across the grass, and though none of them were talking to each other, each had positioned themselves in one way or another relative to that corner of the court. Some were sitting close to it, staring into its depths, faces fearful. Others were standing farther away and looked at it only fleetingly, their eyes darkened with disbelief.

Wetherblaine jumped into action. His instinct told him to rush over as soon as possible and make a thorough inspection. Knee-jerk reactions, however, were as nothing to his respect for college by-laws, and thus marching across the grass was out of the question. Instead he skirted the path that ran down the side of the well-manicured lawn.

This was a much lengthier route than simply walking straight across the grass, but as his brisk, porterly stride gathered pace he felt much more himself. Advancing down the path, the spectre-like dons seemed farther and farther behind him, and through the gloom he began to make out the features of the chapel's east wall. The familiarity of his daytime beat now bred a mild contempt for the darkness.

"Oh it's all a lot of fuss, really," he said to himself with an assured gobble. "I imagine Wildencrust got carried away at last night's jolly-up and now he's flat on his face. Being naughty with some undergraduate again, I'll be bound." Now the gobble was of a haughtier kind, such as only the heftiest of turkeys could muster. "Well if that's the case it'll be a sending-down for whoever the girl is: expulsion. Ex-Sergeant Wetherblaine doesn't stand for that sort of filthy sleaze, oh no. She'll be getting a piece of my mind. People have got to realise that this is my college and my rules. As for Dr Wildencrust... well, sir will certainly be getting a distinctly arched eyebrow, and possibly even a quiet tut."

Wetherblaine had finally reached the end of the path, and was now surrounded by the gloom. He seemed cut off from the rest of the court, enclosed by a shroud of darkness.

126

Looking across the grass, his once sharp eyes could at first make out nothing. Suddenly he caught sight of a shape some distance away. It looked like a large pile of clothes bundled together on the lawn, though it was too far away for him to be sure.

There was nothing else for it, he would have to invoke his porter's prerogative and make contact with the turf.

"What on earth is it?" he whispered to himself as he crept forwards. "I suppose it must be either Wildencrust or a…"

A sudden breeze swept across the open space of the lawn. It blew for barely a moment, though a brief rustling of the clothes was all that Wetherblaine needed.

"There now, it's a female!" he squawked quietly, now only yards away. "She's wearing a purple frock. What a filthy whore-bag, passed out there on the grass. I can't tell who it is though. Fat old thing. She looks like a great sack of wet cement. I'll bet it's that heifer of a second year geographer. The disrespectful beast!"

He had reached his target now, and as he leaned over to roll the beast face-upwards he launched into his disciplinary script.

"Right then, youngster, let's get a look at you. My God, you're a big girl. Nothing dainty about you is there? Ooof!" he heaved. "Cor blimey, you're not making this easy for…"

At that moment the offending woman was rolled over, and Wetherblaine's blood ran cold. It might have mingled seamlessly with that which splattered the woman's dress, for that too was cold and congealed. The porter's stomach turned at the sight of the woman's, which lay open and exposed to the air, strewn outside her body. All across the bare skin and covering the flesh beneath the torn dress a thousand pricks were there, marked by gore that had been pumped out by the heart whilst it still beat. Whatever force had torn the garment apart, whatever terrible impact had shredded it, had been

127

exerted against the woman's face and head too. Only one of her eyes remained, the other had left its socket.

She might have been the dowager herself for all the lines etched across her face, though they were done not by age but by terrible implements.

She might even have been a woman, were it not for the beard that clung in tufts to the battered flesh of a male jaw.

CHAPTER THIRTEEN

"FEMI-DON KILLED AT MIDSUMMER! GREATER PROTECTION NEEDED AT CAMBRIDGE!" screamed the front page of The Cambridge Clarion.

"GRUESOME DEATH FOR CROSS-DRESSER-PROFESSOR!" was The Chronicle's chosen cry.

"PORTER WALKS ON GRASS... AT MIDSUMMER!" gasped The Echo, before launching into a highly speculative reconstruction of Wetherblaine's route to the corpse.

Professor Paul Fringe eyed the offending rags as they lay across the table in the cavernous meeting room at the Classics Faculty, barely a quarter of a mile from the death scene. He then eyed the dozen or so senior members of the Faculty who sat around it. They looked timidly up at him, waiting for him to break the awkward silence. But he did not.

"Look at those rags," he thought to himself as he cast an eye on the horrendous outfit that Dr Glynys Leverton had dressed herself in that morning. The hideous felt skirt and bedraggled top that the toothy Roman historian was sporting did indeed cast her in the worst possible light. She caught Fringe's gaze and quickly averted her own, preferring to fix her attention on her shoes (noticing as she did so that they did not match).

"What a hideous specimen," thought Fringe as he looked her up and down. "Even Wildencrust must have looked better in a dress than her. And even after the beating. God, I'd love to tell her. I'm just in the mood to tell old Gormless Glynys what a state she looks."

Then, straining to lever his mouth into the appropriate manoeuvre, he smiled. It was as rare as it was chilling, and the timid lecturers were taken aback.

"Don't look so distraught, my… my dear," he strained, through clenched teeth. As he spoke his inner voice was growling to itself: "Should I call her 'dear'? She's such a shite I can barely manage it. But needs must. If I can maintain Faculty-wide calm until my inauguration as Vice Chancellor I'll be home dry. Just a week, just a week, just a…"

"Oh yah, er, well… yah, thanks, Professor Fringe," stuttered Glynys, plummy and nervous. "I, er… well, I. Er… Yah."

"Not at all," he said. "We're all shocked by what happened at Midsummer last night. But we have to keep our heads." Inwardly he was balking. "Frankly I'm shocked that it didn't happen sooner," he thought. "God, I hate this drivel."

Fringe winced as he strained not to speak his thoughts aloud.

"That's true, Professor Fringe, we're all shocked and saddened that a second member of the faculty should meet such a terrible end. And both within forty-eight hours of each other," piped up Dr McVerne, Senior Lecturer in Greek Vase Painting. He had been emboldened by the sudden and unprecedented softening of Fringe's usual, malevolent demeanour.

"Thank you, Dr McVerne, that was very well put," said Fringe, nodding sagely. "My God, you're an obsequious little turd," he thought.

The others nodded too now, collectively amazed at the incongruously pleasant and caring demeanour of their leader. Usually meetings with Fringe were to be dreaded. Since he had assumed his position as head of the Classics Faculty all those years ago he had developed an iron grip on what had become his personal fiefdom. Running the show with the help of a small clique of cronies, his preferred method of rule was to shout down potential rivals. Meetings such as this had become mere formalities, and were used as a means of publicly humiliating the other senior members of staff who weren't members of the inner core.

Today, however, it seemed to this weak and submissive group that Professor Fringe was treating the sad occasion with respect.

"Dr Wildencrust deserved to die with so much more dignity," intoned Ronald Levine, Professor of Archaic Greek Poetry. Having seen Glynys avoid a savaging, despite catching the eye of Fringe, he too was attempting to jump onto the bandwagon.

Hearing his words, Fringe's demeanour almost cracked. He couldn't bring himself to respond to such pathetic sentiment, and simply nodded in false agreement. "This wretched oaf has must have lost his wits," he thought, acidly. "Wildencrust got more dignity than he ever deserved. I don't know what he was thinking, allowing himself to be murdered. I specifically told him not to make waves before my inauguration! I told him after Harriet died that all eyes would be on the Faculty! On me! And then he gets himself trannied-up and beaten to death! What a stupid, lousy, idiotic…"

Suddenly Fringe realised that he had started to drift down an avenue of angry internal dialogue, and that he had been nodding in total silence, and with increasing aggression, for almost a minute. He quickly cut himself short.

"So true, Professor Levine," he said. "So very true."

Despite the general perplexity at the fact that Fringe appeared to be acting so pleasantly, the atmosphere amongst the senior classicists was exactly as he had wanted it. Feeling that the inner beast could not be contained for much longer, Fringe decided to cut to the point.

"Now everyone," he said, allowing himself to assume a slightly more august tone. "The deaths of Harriet Mason and Penton Wildencrust, which have come so suddenly and tragically, are truly a blow to the Faculty, and I fully intend to arrange a memorial lecture in their honour in due course. For the moment, though, we must remain calm and carry on with our jobs as best we can. The students' exams are coming up in a few months, and we don't want to allow this terrible incident to derail a good year's worth of work."

The others murmured in agreement.

"Do they have any idea who might have been responsible?" ventured Dr Smollen, Lecturer in Roman Funerary Practices.

Fringe shrugged. "Considering they were both at the same college I can only imagine it was a deranged undergraduate. Frankly it's Midsummer's problem," he said, a little more bluntly than he had intended.

The others looked at each other awkwardly.

"Er, what I mean," Fringe quickly added, "is that it would be futile, not to mention highly inappropriate, for us to speculate on who might be responsible. The most we can do is extend our sympathies to Midsummer and hope that the authorities catch the killer as quickly as possible." He wanted to cut this wretched mothers-meeting short now. He had plans to make.

"That's very true, Professor Fringe," piped up Dr Herzig, the venerable but doddery Lecturer in Late Roman Aqueducts. "And furthermore…"

"Yes, yes, alright Herzig!" snapped Fringe in a familiar tone that instantly set the group's teeth on edge.

Dr Herzig was visibly taken aback, and several of his chins wobbled in surprised embarrassment.

Fringe winced. He had to keep the members of the Faculty from descending into open speculation about the deaths of Mason and Wildencrust. Whoever had done it would surely be caught in due course, and until then Fringe didn't want a lot of idle talk that might draw the attention of the police or, God forbid, the newspapers to his Faculty.

"My apologies, Dr Herzig," he muttered through clenched teeth and the closest approximation of a humble smile that he could muster. "Perhaps I'm more affected by this double tragedy than I realise. Let us all keep a united front in these troubled times and carry on with the professionalism and dedication that Dr Wildencrust and Dr Mason would have wanted."

This seemed to do the trick, and the nodding and murmuring that followed the senior Faculty members as they filed out of the room left Fringe reassured that things were under control. After a few moments he got up and walked to his office, one floor below.

Passing the office of Miss Nelson, the Faculty secretary, which was adjacent to his own, he had but one stern command,

"Get me Dr Tanning and Dr Norther. Now!"

Miss Nelson nodded and immediately picked up the telephone.

"At once Professor Fringe," came her standard, nasal acquiescence.

"And if anyone comes knocking, send them away with some choice words."

"Yes Professor Fringe. Will there be anything else for you?"

The slamming of his office door was all the reply she needed.

*****

In the dilapidated offices of The Cambridge Clarion, at the grottier end of St Andrew's Street, reporter Wendy Pipford was attempting not to cringe.

"That's a good question, young lady, and I'm going to give you a long and interesting answer in return," gobbled Martin Wetherblaine in response to Wendy's enquiry about his previous career with the Cambridgeshire Constabulary.

Wendy smiled patiently and prepared herself for the long haul. Her editor, David Blithe, had snapped up the exclusive to the Wildencrust killing, cocking a snook at The Clarion's rival, The Echo. Now he was determined to rinse the story for all it was worth, and had assigned Wendy, the office's up-and-coming young reporter, to the case.

These were tough times and Cambridge needed a hero, he had argued. Wendy, having met Wetherblaine on a previous occasion, knew that there were few people less suitable for the role. Besides which, Wetherblaine hadn't actually done anything heroic.

Blithe had not been convinced. Hadn't Wetherblaine cycled down in the dead of night through the rain and fog, determined to get to the bottom of this terrible business?

Wendy had pointed out that it had been a clear night, that Wetherblaine only lived round the corner from college and that, in any case, he hadn't even known that there was anything seriously wrong until he arrived.

It was all in vain, though. Blithe had wrenched up his trousers (as he was wont to do in times when a bit of authority was required) and pulled rank. Wendy was to interview the porter, and by golly if she didn't build him into a hero she'd be sent packing back down to London, or whichever "posh hole" she came from.

Wendy was in fact from Bath, and seven years at St Swithin's Boarding School for Girls had rendered her politely spoken rather than posh. Her parents, a barrister and a teacher, were highly critical of their daughter's decision to enter the 'not really that respectable, is it dear?' world of journalism. Defiant to the last, however, Wendy had had her own way. Now, as she sat listening to the life story of the most obnoxious porter in Cambridge, mummy and daddy's endless nagging seemed, for the first time, to ring true.

"… and after that particular incident I was given a commendation for my outstanding performance, and told that I was on the fast-track to success," droned Wethers.

"I see," said Wendy, smoothing over her impatience with a forced smile.

"That was one of the high points of my early career," he clucked.

"But just to be clear, you're still referring to your time as a newspaper delivery boy?" asked Wendy.

"Yes," said Wetherblain, with a dramatic show of impatience unique to those higher beings who must occasionally interact with lower ones.

"Right. So when are we going to reach your time on the force?" Wendy ventured, conscious that the interview had started almost two hours ago and that the murder had barely been mentioned.

"Oh I'm coming to that young lady; a little patience, if you please," he gobbled. "My young career as a newspaper delivery facilitator was very important to my later career as a police constable, which in turn proved crucial to my career as Head Porter of Midsummer College."

Inwardly Wendy groaned. She knew that a job at a local newspaper was hardly worth moving away from Bath for, but with graduate journalism programmes in London being virtually unobtainable, her new job at The Cambridge Clarion was the best she could get until the job market recovered. She was determined to work her way into a national daily, but on days like this her enthusiasm for journalism took a severe beating.

"Perhaps you'd like a short break?" she asked hopefully. "It's coming on for lunch, after all."

"No, young lady, that will not be necessary," said Wetherblaine, his eyes closed in annoyance. "Perhaps you should have prepared yourself better by having a larger breakfast. A professional journalist should be prepared to put in the hours."

Wendy gritted her teeth.

"Okay no problem, Mr Wetherblaine. We'll carry on until you're ready for a break."

"I won't be needing one."

Wethers was as good as his word, and for Wendy the next four hours were an excruciating experience. The worst, however, came when the conversation turned to Wetherblaine's discovery of the body. She was forced to listen as every exaggerated fact was recounted in graphic detail. As it turned out, her job of heroising the wretched man amounted to little more than accurately transcribing his own account of his actions, which he portrayed as little short of superhuman. All that was needed was for her to swallow her pride and pamper to an already grossly over-inflated ego.

"And so I sprinted across the grass at a terrific speed. It was really something to watch. A younger man certainly couldn't have done it."

"Amazing," Wendy forced herself to say. "How did you know where to look?"

"Oh I knew instinctively. When you've as much experience as I have of crime you just know. Well Dr Palic pointed me in the direction of the body, but essentially I already had a strong feeling about where it lay without his help."

"How clever."

"Yes, I really took control of the situation until the police arrived. And even after they came I was still really the one in charge. The police officers may have been taking directions from their senior officers, but it was clear that my presence there was what held everything together."

"How remarkable."

"I am, aren't I? I really find that's the case."

"So do you feel that you've made a real difference, Mr Wetherblaine?" asked Wendy.

"Oh absolutely. If I hadn't found the body and called the police, who knows what would have happened. It was the first step towards justice being done, really. I'm the one who started the police on the road to catching the killer, and in that respect I'm actually the most important cog in the justice machine that brings him down. I hope you make that perfectly clear in your article."

"Oh yes, don't worry Mr Wetherblaine, everything you say is going in," she said, unable to suppress a small sigh. "I expect there will be a lot of interest in this case, and in you personally."

"I should jolly well expect so, young lady!"

Eventually the agonising interview was concluded, and Wetherblaine clucked off back home to preen. Shortly after he had left, Dave Blithe poked his head round the door and nodded to her.

"Nice one, Wendy. That came off even better than I expected. I think you can take on this case exclusively for the moment. Start sniffing around and see what you can find."

"Thanks Dave," she said at the unexpected compliment.

Constrained as she was by Blithe's agenda, she had felt the interview a complete waste of time. Surely no reader would believe all that nonsense about Wetherblaine's heroism? Frankly she was embarrassed to put her name to it. Now, however, being offered the chance to do an investigative project on the case was grist to her mill. She smiled at her scruffy editor as she left the interview room, and went to her desk to prepare.

*****

Over in Professor Fringe's office a very different sort of meeting was taking place.

Dr Alan Tanning, Senior Lecturer in Roman Wall Painting and Dr Eliot Norther, Senior Lecturer in Ancient Greek Navigation Techniques, were in conference with Fringe.

"Things are going from bad to worse," growled the head of the Faculty. "Harriet's death was manageable, but now that Wildencrust has died the eyes of the police may well fall hard on the Faculty. Really, how often do two classicists peg it in so short a space of time and in such freakish circumstances?"

"Well, quite, but it's nonetheless been rather shocking," said Norther. "Harriet's death was only a few days ago, and even after that my wife was urging me not to venture out after dark. Now she's virtually taken to bed with fear herself."

"Indeed," said Tanning. "It won't be long before the fact that Harriet and Penton are… were… both classicists will be seized upon by the local papers. There'll be all sorts of comparisons with Greek tragedy I should think."

"Don't be stupid, Tanning," growled Fringe. "Only chavs read the locals. They won't know what a Greek tragedy is, and in any case what they may or may not think is of no consequence."

"But what about the nationals?" asked Norther. "I don't want to sound like a wet weekend, but we'd better be careful. Once it gets beyond local interest…"

"Look, will you two stop whingeing on about the bloody media reaction," Fringe snarled, concealing his own concern at the idea of nationwide headlines. "We'll have to take it as it comes. Harriet's unfortunate death shook things up a great deal, but now that that idiot Wildencrust has got himself killed things are really looking shaky."

"Indeed," said Norther, with Tanning nodding his head in agreement. "So where do we stand, all three of us?"

Fringe leant back in his chair and looked at each in turn.

"It means that the stakes are much higher than before," he said with earnest. "It means that the risk of being caught is that much greater than it was when there were five of us."

Norther and Tanning cast a nervous glance at each other. This was immediately noticed by Fringe, who leant forward again in his chair and glowered at them, menacingly.

"I hope you're not getting second thoughts about this, gentlemen." His tone was cold and threatening. "Because if either of you so much as think about backtracking you'll find yourselves in very, very hot water."

Tanning and Norther shrank submissively into their chairs.

"You see if I come to have any doubts about either of you, I might have to take some very drastic action. If such a situation were to arise I might have to release some information to the newspapers, anonymously of course, about the somewhat controversial dealings that each of you have had with some of the more voluptuous undergraduates."

Tanning and Norther looked horrified.

"You mean…? No you can't…?" gulped Tanning.

"Surely you don't…? But that's just an accepted part of academic life!" spluttered Norther.

"Yes, perks! Surely nobody would question that?" said Tanning.

"Oh I think you'll find that plebs have a rather different view of such things, as do the University authorities," chuckled Fringe. "And in case you're wondering, I have more than enough evidence. Pictures speak a thousand words, after all."

"You mean…? Oh God…" mumbled Norther.

Each shot nervous glances at the other. Friends for many years, the two had graduated together and spent their entire working lives at Cambridge. Few knew, however, that their camaraderie extended as far as a taste for the same female students. Their gentlemen's agreement to share and share alike was something that required a discerning eye and refined instincts when scouting for potential new flings. Sometimes entire terms would pass before a young woman could be found who was willing to spend her nights in bed with the two senior lecturers and keep her mouth firmly shut about it.

As beads of perspiration formed, Alan Tanning wiped his brow with his hand. How was it possible that Fringe had pictures? They had always been so careful in their handling of student romps. Each year they would carry out introductory lectures to freshers, which were used as a chance to reconnoitre those females with the requisite balance of slaggish propensity and tight-lipped discretion. He could scarcely believe that they had been caught in the act.

"How do we know we can we believe you?" enquired Norther, hesitantly but bravely. "We've always been absolutely discreet about this, and the girls we've chosen were always absolutely sound."

"That's right," agreed Tanning. "We were never as careless as Wildencrust. What proof could you possibly have?"

Fringe's expression did not change, his face moved not a muscle. He simply placed his hand on his computer screen and swivelled it round to face the two senior lecturers.

There, set as his wallpaper on an empty desktop, was a photograph of Margo Goyle, a former classics student who had graduated last year. Her immense mane of frizzy, ginger hair was almost luminous in the dim light of the bedroom in which she stood. She was facing the camera full-on, displaying, though she did not know it, the entirety of her naked form. Her figure was such that, in silhouette, one might have mistaken it for a sack of bricks, though in the weak light of the bedroom it was more akin to a pile of wet concrete. Her prematurely dangly breasts lolled under her armpits, vast, pale and globulous, like huge dollops of royal icing sliding slowly from the spoon. Though her face was slightly blurred, her teeth could be clearly made out. They had all the grisly disorder of a collection of lichen-covered tombstones, set at dreadful odds in sinking, marshy ground, two or three to a grave. Behind her were Tanning and Norther, both also naked. Tanning was caught mid-sentence, his hands a blur of gesticulation as he addressed his colleague. Norther was sitting on the bed and looking up at him, his sage countenance of rapt attention somewhat at odds with his baby bonnet and huge man-nappy.

The jaws of the senior lecturers dropped.

"How did you…?" stammered Norther.

"I can't believe…" stuttered Tanning.

"Yes, you'll find there's a camera set up amongst the books on the shelf in your bedroom," explained Fringe, with more than a little glee in his voice. "I won't go into the logistics of it, but suffice to say it did the job. There are plenty more where that came from, too. So how are we feeling about keeping our mouths shut and following orders?"

"I… I think we can all agree on a common resolve," said Tanning, looking shamefaced. Norther simply nodded demurely.

"Good," said Fringe, settling back in his chair and adopting a smug air. "Now then, lets get an overview of the situation and rethink our plans."

CHAPTER FOURTEEN

As the assembled deities who ruled the universe sat in council, deep in recesses of James's nervous system, emotions were running high.

"This has been the biggest fucking cock-up that I have ever seen!" yelled Hera. "I don't know where to start with how badly that went!"

"Now, Hera, the meeting hasn't been formerly announced yet," said Dionysos. He felt utterly shameful about his dire performance the previous evening, and had even thought twice about appearing in council. Eventually, however, he had swallowed his pride and decided to face the public. The voice with which he answered Hera's bellow, however, conveyed not a shred of the authority he felt he had lost. "If you'll just let me announce the proceedings I'll…"

"Shut your mouth you little pipsqueak!" spat Hera. "If it wasn't for your meddling we wouldn't be in this situation! I could fucking well wring you clean! What the hell made you think of stepping in and pissing things up? Why did you think that plying mortals with divinely charged alcohol would be a good way to carry our plan forward? Look at the mess you created! The poxy man got beaten to death by mistake and we watched like a bunch of idiots! You complete, effing moron!"

Hera was screeching uncontrollably, and though Dionysos opened his mouth to speak, he could think of no comeback. He was meekly silenced.

Suddenly Hera whirled round and pointed a milky-white finger at Aphrodite, who was sitting in her usual spot at the front of the assembly. She was composed and dignified, though clearly self-conscious, and her eyes avoided those of everyone else. She knew that she would have to suffer one of Hera's onslaughts. She had known since the moment Wildencrust had fled his room and run into the arms of the rowing team. She winced inwardly and cursed the failure of her plan. She had aimed too high, and now would have to deploy a great deal of skill not to get roasted.

"It's you I blame," hissed Hera slowly. "You're the one who deviated from the plan. You're the one who secretly took it on yourself to kill Wildencrust and gain all the glory." The Queen of the Gods was staring directly at the Goddess of Desire, hatred smouldering in her eyes. The gods on either side of Aphrodite shrank back as if fearful that Hera would lash out like a snake.

Aphrodite, however, held her head aloft and returned Hera's stare, her face expressionless.

"Tell me why we shouldn't kick you off the council and send you packing! Tell me!" yelled Hera, almost frothing at the mouth. Even Athena, always one to jump onto her heroine's bandwagon, was silent. She simply looked awkwardly from one goddess to the other, holding the same hope as all the other deities: that a second clash of the Titans was not about to erupt.

By temporarily clothing herself in Harriet Mason's form and attempting to bring about the death of Wildencrust, Aphrodite had breached the cardinal rule of the gods: no direct involvement in the death of those on the Cambridge List. In the last meeting she had used the threat of Zeus's wrath as a means of stealing a march on Hera, but by carrying out her own plan for Wildencrust's death and, worse, by failing, she had left herself extremely vulnerable. Nevertheless she was damned if she was going to let a cock-up like this scupper her standing in council.

With a subtle shrug Aphrodite allowed her hair to tumble over her shoulder. She looked away from Hera and took a little sigh. Every movement was calculated to express a casual nonchalance.

"Oh Hera," she said, as if to a mildly annoying child. "Things are hardly as bad as all that. The wretched man is dead and really that's all there is to it. So what if the mortal, James Connor, cocked up and didn't kill Wildencrust himself. I for one don't hold it against the little bag of flesh and bone."

Hera's face was a picture of outrage. Being spoken down to was something that no other deity would dare to do, and for such patronising words to fall from Aphrodite's lips was too much.

"Bullshit!" she bellowed. "This has nothing to do with the mortal. It was you who cocked up our plan. You're responsible. When the mortal arrived in Wildencrust's room he found him on the floor almost dead. We know that you'd been interfering because the mortal's nasal receptors detected the perfume of Fatty Mason. I was aware of it, even if he wasn't. I knew at that instant that you had been meddling. I knew when I saw Wildencrust's near-lifeless body on the floor and smelt that pungent scent that you'd had a go at robbing us, the immortal gods, of our collective honour. Do you think I wasn't able to put two and two together?"

Aphrodite had remained inscrutable throughout the tirade. Now she replied calmly.

"Your abilities at arithmetic are of no concern to me. Yes, as it happens, I did visit Wildencrust beforehand and, yes, I came as Harriet Mason. That hardly constitutes a breach of protocol. After all, Mason had already been eliminated. Therefore if I interfered directly it was with a past rather than a prospective victim, which breaks no rule that I'm aware of."

"Sophistry!" yelled Hera. "Your direct interference with Mason, which you admit," she said, looking around the council dramatically, "constituted direct interference with Wildencrust."

The council murmured approvingly at this. Aphrodite looked about James's hippocampus at the ripple of agreement coming from the assembled deities. This was precarious. She would have to change tack if she was to win them round.

"Let me remind you of Zeus's words on the matter Hera," she said. "He ordered that there must be no interference with prospective victims but through the vessel of our divine wrath. True?"

"True," said Hera, her voice tinged with suspicion.

"Did he mention James Connor?"

"What does that matter? The important thing is…"

"Did he mention Connor?" repeated Aphrodite, adopting the inflated air of confidence necessary to interrupt Hera.

"Well no, not specifically," conceded the Queen of the Gods.

"That's right. He said 'vessel of our wrath.' So let me ask you this: what made James Connor our vessel? I mean in the practical sense."

The other gods were rapt. Before the council session they had all heard of Hera's plans to savage Aphrodite over her personal attempt on Wildencrust's life. No one, not even Hera, had actually witnessed it directly, and none had the perceptive powers of the Muse. All, however, had drawn the same conclusions as Hera when they saw through James's eyes the body of Wildencrust lying on the floor of his room.

"Flanoxiride," said Hera. "That was the means by which he was actually 'made' our vessel. But what of it?" She was feeling a touch of anxiety now as she began to perceive Aphrodite's line of reasoning.

Aphrodite was not blind to the look on her opponent's face. She almost smiled as she saw Hera catch up with her argument. Nevertheless she remained poised and aloof as she spoke.

"That's right, Hera. Flanoxiride made James Connor the vessel of our wrath. Through him we exercise our plans. Yes?"

"Yes," said Hera, through gritted teeth.

"Well it just so happens that Mason herself also ingested Flanoxiride, since it was used to poison her doughnuts."

Gasps arose from the assembled deities, and Aphrodite seized the moment.

"That's right, Hera. Fatty, dead though she may be, was just as legitimate a vessel through which to act as James. And all thanks to the poisoned doughnuts, which were, by the way, your idea. If you remember I opposed the whole thing, and when I confronted you about it you punched my precious boob. I told you the doughnut plan would lead to trouble, that rabid guinea pigs were the way forward, but you wouldn't listen. You can hardly blame me now for enacting a plan for divine wrath through means that you created and which were agreed by the council."

Aphrodite had delivered a winning blow: through her riposte she had implicated the entire council, including Hera, in the cock-up; legitimated her own part in it, and, better still, had drawn attention to her boobs.

Hera could only smoulder. This should have been an easy victory and now it had been snatched from her. She could hardly let it go without some sort of resistance, though.

"That still doesn't excuse the fact that you attempted to kill Wildencrust after the council explicitly designated James as the killer," said Hera, clutching at the only straw she could find.

"But I didn't kill him, Hera," parried Aphrodite. "Nor did I intend to. I simply used the body of Mason, temporarily, in order to soften Wildencrust up so that James could deal the killing blows when he arrived. After all, there was hardly a guarantee that that feeble little mortal would have been able to overpower Wildencrust on his own."

This was stretching the truth but there was no way that her word could be disproved, and now the other gods were nodding and murmuring in open agreement.

"Furthermore," said Aphrodite, eager to capitalise, "I couldn't help noticing that when the mortal raised Wildencrust's head aloft to break it against the bedpost, he shouted something. What was it, now?" she pondered, dramatically posing her question to the assembly.

"Well... I... I don't remember him shouting anything," stuttered Hera.

"Oh yes," insisted Aphrodite. "There was definitely something said. What was it? I think it may have been..."

"All glory to... someone!" piped up an anonymous god from the back row. Everyone turned in their seats, glancing this way and that as they scoured the hippocampus for the speaker. Hera shot a filthy glance towards the back seats, but there was no way to know which toe rag had spoken.

"Oh yes, that's right," said Aphrodite. "It was 'all glory to... 'someone' wasn't it?"

"Er, well yes I believe it was, but I don't think he managed to finish before Wildencrust leapt back up," said Hera, quickly.

"True," said Aphrodite, "though I believe there is a strong chance that he may have been about to say 'Hera.'"

The suggestion was so cogent that only the most shameless soul would have attempted to deny it.

"Absolutely not, Aphrodite, I resolutely contest that," blustered Hera. "There's no proof that he was about to say my name. And even if he was, that hardly constitutes interference or deviation from the plan."

"True, Hera, but it does suggest that you are more than willing to cast aspersions about others exerting undue influence whilst being quite happy to exercise it yourself."

This was the trump card and Hera knew it.

"Well I... Yes, but..." The Queen of the Gods could not think how to respond. The other gods were muttering openly, and it became clear that the only thing to do now was to implement damage control. Hera closed her eyes and grimaced. "Very well. On balance I'm quite happy to say that the Wildencrust affair was a complete cock-up. Lessons have to be learnt and all that shit. I propose that we just forget the matter and move on."

The gods turned as one to Aphrodite, who gently nodded her head.

"Agreed," she said, before turning to Dionysos. The god had been keeping a low profile throughout, preferring to let the entire matter pass by without mention of his embarrassing behaviour.

"Oh, er right. Yes, well if there are no objections I think we can all agree to put this behind us, then. In the interest of future concord I think we should make it clear that James is the singular vessel of our wrath and that no one else may be used in that role."

The gods murmured approvingly.

"Right then," he continued. "Let's get down to the real business here: the third death."

*****

Wendy Pipford's first day as The Cambridge Clarion's official correspondent on the Wildencrust murder was turning out to be rather anti-climactic. Earlier that morning she had entered Midsummer College, thrilling slightly as she slipped through the police cordon with her press pass, which the local constables had examined with perplexity and baffled acquiescence. The college had been quiet, and a white tent marked the place where the body still lay, forensic specialists providing the only evidence of human life in Great Court. Having made her enquiries amongst the staff, students and any fellows that she could find, it became clear that the place was on lock-down. Anyone willing to talk knew nothing worth recording, and all those who had attended the feast were unwilling to say a word. There had been, however, one chink of light in this information blackout: a certain Dr Palic.

148

Wendy had found him squatting in a corridor, rocking gently and muttering to himself. Having engaged him in a stilted, somewhat one-sided conversation, it had become clear that the poor man was so traumatised that he had become an emotional wreck. She had listened to the tail of Hector being dragged "thrice round the walls of Troy" until her patience ran out. After fifteen minutes of garbled nothings she had prepared to excuse herself when Dr Palic, until now babbling and incoherent, became suddenly lucid.

"The boy. He saw it all. He saw the entire thing from the doorway. I saw him standing there," he said. His eyes stared into space, though his words were clear and carefully composed.

"What did he see?" asked Wendy. As she glanced at her watch she became suddenly aware that her presence in college might not be as inoffensive to the police inspectors as it had been to the constables at the college gates. Pressed for time, she decided to acquit herself of the broken man.

"James Connor!" shouted Dr Palic, just as she placed her notebook in her bag and stood to leave.

"I'm sorry?" she said. This was the first name he had mentioned that seemed to belong to someone other than a Greek hero.

"The boy, James Connor. It was he, he who saw. He saw but could not act. He… He…"

Now, once again Dr Palic slumped down on his elbows and descended into a fit of mumbles. There was clearly nothing more than this to be gained from the conversation, but as she departed Wendy was determined to find out who James Connor was.

Back at the grotty offices on St Andrew's Street, she took not twenty minutes to produce an address and a skeleton profile. Thus, armed with little more than the knowledge that her target had been a student at Midsummer, had studied a humanities subject and was now living just off Jesus Green,

149

she set out to give her first proper interview. As far as she was concerned, Wetherblaine didn't count because he was so patently full of codswallop, and Dr Palic was invalidated as he was full of drool and little else.

*****

James woke with a start. Easing himself up, he looked about his room with eyes veiled in grogginess. Glancing at his clock and noting that it was 10:20am on Wednesday, he swore under his breath.

"Fuck me. I can't have been asleep for that long. Thirty two hours!"

Having watched Wildencrust being beaten to death by his unsuspecting colleagues, James had retuned home and collapsed, fatigued, onto the bed. The horrors of that night seemed like weeks ago, though as he recalled them he did not feel the same cold panic that he had experienced the morning after slaying Fatty. Instead he felt nothing at all; nothing more than a compelling hunger and the need for a comprehensive scrub.

Without waiting for feelings of remorse to catch up with him he made a leisurely tour of the bathroom and kitchen, before returning to his bedroom, washed and sated. Having cranked-up his ancient laptop it suddenly occurred to him that it had been almost a week since he had been to work. Presumably Abigail had long since written him off. Checking his emails he found a small cache of missives from his former boss, which he read with mounting amusement.

October 18th
Dear James

I hope all is well with you. I note that you didn't turn up for work today, and am writing to ask if everything is okay. I got David to cover your lesson with Mischka as well as your afternoon group tutorial with the Bulgarians. Please come to work (on time!) tomorrow.

Best wishes
Abigail

October 19th
Dear James
Since you did not have the courtesy to reply to my email yesterday I am writing to let you know how disappointed I am with your commitment to the job. I am seriously considering your future with Elite Learners English Language School. Please contact me to let me know what your position is.

Abigail

October 20th
James
Since this is the third day that you have failed to turn up for work or account for your absence, I am writing to let you know that I have decided to terminate your contract with immediate effect. Please do not contact me again, since I have no wish to deal with you and am absolutely furious with the discourteous and disloyal way that you have treated both me and the company. I would prefer it if you did not use us as a reference as I don't, in all honesty, have a good word to say about you.

Abigail

October 22nd
Dear James
A Croatian student has arrived, and both David and Camilla are off sick. Would you by any chance be free to take over their slots?
Please reply
Abigail

October 23rd
James
Since you have once again failed to reply, and have quite clearly snubbed me, I am writing to let you know that this is absolutely definitely the last contact we will ever have, and that you are completely sacked and that I absolutely mean it.
Abigail

October 24th
Dear James
Camilla and David have unexpectedly left to go travelling around Thailand together. Would you mind doing me a huge favour and taking over their slots for the next week until I can rearrange the schedules? It would be a huge favour to me.
Please consider it. Please.
Abigail

James chuckled to himself. Just then a vibration from his phone alerted him to a new email. Logging on, his smile fell.

"hey babe. hope u slept well- it's the only rest u'll be getting for a while. lol. seriously though, prepare to get to work. u got killin to get on wiv, innit. x"

James's groan was followed immediately by another message.

"stop huffing and puffing. a reporter is on her way here now & has heard your name in connection with Wildencrust. but before u shit yourself just listen: if u balls up the next murder u'll be dead meat. i thought u could do it by urself, but it turns out you're shit at killin people. i know it sounds nuts, but your're gonna need her later. trust me."

"Are you serious?" asked James aloud.

"yep, for real," came the responding message.

"But how do you know? How can she help me? And what about the risks? She's a journalist for Christ's sake."

"babe just trust me. i've seen enough murders in my time to know wot i'm on about. sooner or later the police are gonna get wise to the pattern of murders, and that'll happen a lot sooner if u don't get more effective. u need someone on ya team."

"You must be joking, Muesli. How the bloody hell do you expect me to persuade this girl to become a killer? I can't even ask girls out on dates, never mind recruit them into a death squad. Besides, I can't exactly tell them about you lot in my head, can I?"

"obviously not. look, leave the thinking to me. the gods r gonna come up with their demands for the next death soon, and if u don't get it bang on they'll snuff u out. they're not gonna care if u get caught in the end or not, but i do."

James sank back into chair and sighed.

153

"Fine. I've been destroying people's lives left and right, so why not. But on your head be it when all this goes pear-shaped. At least I don't have to kill her."

"that's the spirit!" came the responding message.

Suddenly the doorbell rang. James stilled himself and waited to hear if anyone else would answer. The silence indicated an otherwise empty house. Another ring. James rose and, creeping downstairs, gingerly answered the door.

"Yes?" he said nervously, opening it only a fraction.

"Hello. My name's Wendy Pipford. I'm a correspondent with The Cambridge Clarion and I'm looking for James Connor."

"Oh," muttered James in a voice laden with anxiety. "I suppose you'd better come in then." He inched the door open with evident reluctance.

"You mean you're…"

"Yes, yes, I'm James. Sorry, pleased to met you," he said, offering her his hand.

"How do you do," said Wendy, James's awkward body language putting her uncomfortably in mind of Dr Palic.

"Shall we go upstairs? Sorry about the mess, it's been quite a hectic week."

"Oh no problem," said Wendy as cheerily as she could. As they entered the bedroom she was confronted with a scene that resembled a cross between an overstocked charity shop and a prison laundry room. "Quite a collection of clothes you have here," she ventured light-heartedly.

"Oh yeah, I've been meaning to get all this sorted out," said James, who had long since grown accustomed to eking out an existence amongst the piles of unwashed pants and dirty t-shirts. "So how can I help you?"

Wendy perched on the swivel chair at his desk.

154

"Well I'm reporting on the death of Dr Wildencrust, and I heard from one of the classicists at Midsummer that you knew him." Wendy knew that this was stretching the truth but pressed ahead all the same.

"Oh yes," said James, shifting uncomfortably. "He marked my thesis in the final year. I didn't know him well."

"I see. So you've graduated now, then?" Wendy had begun making notes on a small pad that she produced from her bag. It was virtually identical to the little flip-pads that police officers use in cheap crime shows, and the sight of it caused a nervous ripple to run down James's back.

"Er, yes... well what I mean is," he stammered. "Look I haven't graduated... yet, but..." he trailed off awkwardly.

Sensing his embarrassment Wendy skipped ahead.

"So you did know him then? It must have been hard to read about his passing away," she gently suggested.

"A little," said James. He was beginning to regret opening the door to her. Perhaps he was paranoid but he sensed that she would not be happy with mumbled half-answers. Fear began to cloud his mind. "She's probably the sort who smiles and asks really incisive questions that you can't dodge without looking like a tosser," he thought to himself. "Damn her sweetness." He was beginning to feel trapped, and looked to his computer screen in the hope that the Muse might have thrown him a helpful message about how to play it.

Wendy shook her biro and frowned.

"Bloody thing," she muttered as she leaned over and rummaged in her bag for another.

Whilst she was occupied James seized his chance and casually turned his computer screen to face away from her. As surreptitiously as he could he tapped quietly with one hand on his keyboard. If he could just get a few words of advice he'd be okay.

"Not disturbing you am I?" said Wendy suddenly. James jumped. She was sitting up and looking straight at him, pen in hand.

"Oh, er… oh no, not at all. Well actually I was sort of in the middle of something. I teach academic English to mature foreign students and I was just giving a lesson when you arrived. Hard at it today," he said, trying to sound light-hearted.

'I see." The politeness of Wendy's tone now conveyed a suggestion of scepticism.

"Oh yes," laughed James nervously, looking at his computer. "I was giving it online."

"Online?"

"Yes, I'm on the, er, learning, e-forum, language… thing, right now, actually."

"You're looking at your email," she said flatly.

James went red. His thoughts about her perceptiveness were confirmed. She must have noticed the screen as soon as she entered the room.

"Y-Yes, I am," he stuttered. "I am aren't I? You see that's actually the forum itself."

"I don't think I understand what you…"

"Oh I'm giving a lesson through email."

Her face was a picture of disbelief, though her silence compelled James to continue.

"Yes, er, I'm teaching this particular student through email because that's the sort of thing everyone wants to learn these days. Kids today," he nervously chuckled.

"I thought you said they were mature students," said Wendy.

"W-Well, they are. You know, relatively. I suppose."

"And academic English?"

"Yes that's… I mean… Well in many countries today, email is used by students… mature students… instead of classrooms." He wanted the ground to swallow him up. "Fuck," he thought. "I sound like a tool. Fuck!"

He leant on the desk in an instinctive show of nonchalance. As he did so, however, he knocked a mug of water onto his lap.

"Shit!" he yelled. Leaping from the chair, he inadvertently flung his arm across the desk, catching the computer screen and twirling it full tilt towards Wendy. "Oh bollocks!" He hastily bent over and span it back to face him again. "Sorry, sorry," he stammered.

Wendy could not have scrutinised the messages if she had tried, such was the speed of James's reaction. All she had been able to observe was a single sentence, which flitted into her line of vision faster than James could reach the screen:

"u got killin to do, innit."

This was more than enough to electrify her. A tight knot of suspicion formed in her stomach as it dawned on her that James was more than just a socially awkward young man. He was hiding something.

"Look I'm sorry, but would you go now?" asked James. He vainly tried to compose himself. He had to get rid of her and he didn't care how.

"Oh. Right, okay. I mean, if you're sure you don't want to answer any more questions," she said. She didn't move from the chair, however. If she had learnt anything from her journalism degree at Bath it was that the person who could impose the highest level social awkwardness on the other controlled the interview. Wendy felt certain that this damp squib of a man wouldn't be bold enough to insist on her departure.

"Yes, quite sure. Please leave," said James.

Wendy was taken aback. Never mind, she was trained for this. It was time to ramp up the level of social awkwardness.

"I understand," she said with a crisp, professional air. "I can see I'm making you uncomfortable. It's okay that you feel threatened by me. Not all men are bold enough to face a few simple questions."

"That's right," said James. He perceived her tactic, but Wendy was not a patch on Hera when it came to manipulation. "What an amateur," he thought smugly. "If she thinks I've got any self-respect left to exploit she's sorely mistaken."

"Blast!" thought Wendy. "Time to change tack."

She fixed him with a firm look of suspicion.

"What's the hurry, James? Do you have something to hide?"

James felt himself becoming flustered again.

"Shit, she's not bloody well moving. What am I supposed to say?" He glanced despairingly at the screen, and there, to his immense relief, he saw a new message from the Muse.

"babe, it's time to get her out of here now. nice work, by the way."

"Just tell me what I should say!" he thought, almost mumbling the words aloud.

"she's becoming very suspicious of u now, and she's slippery, she won't leave easily. there's only one sure way to make her leave the house running…"

Wendy refused to take her eyes off James. If his squirming and awkwardly long silence were anything to go by he was about to crack. In a few seconds she would simply resume her questions. She didn't know why he had suddenly started staring at his screen but she was determined to stay her ground.

"You can't be serious! It's just not in me!" thought James in response to another of the Muse's rapid-fire missives.

"do it. there's no other way," urged the Muse.

"I can't do it! I just can't!" he thought.

"don't fuck anything else up! do as I say and you'll be fine. just swallow it. If she won't get out then you've gotta do wot needs to be done."

Wendy noted that James's expression was becoming increasingly contorted, almost as if he were resisting the urge to be sick. The time to resume the questioning had arrived.

"James, I…"

"Wendy, please!" he said, desperately, his eyes flicking back and forth between her and the screen.

"Look James, I'm not going to bite, I just…"

"Wendy I don't want to have to tell you this, but if you don't go…"

"Look, I just want to ask…"

"Get out! Get out now!" he screamed.

Wendy jumped at the sudden outburst.

"James! What on earth…?"

"Just fuck off! Fuck off right now!"

She scrambled up and nervously grabbed her bag from the floor.

"Look, I'm… I'm sorry if…" she stammered, not quite knowing what to say.

"Get the fuck out of my house! Now!"

Despite the fact that they were shouted so forcefully, and in obvious evidence of a disordered personality, something about the delivery of the words seemed contrived. With his eyes screwed tight and his reddened face turned away from her, it seemed almost as if he were reciting them from memory. But she was certainly not going to linger to dwell on it. Without another word she ran down the stairs, leaving the front door wide open as she bolted into the street.

CHAPTER FIFTEEN

The last council meeting had left the gods shaken. All across James's brain Olympians were gathering in corners, whispering of a new mood in the air; of how Aphrodite had trumped Hera so spectacularly and against all the odds, and that this was the biggest political turn-around for as long as anyone could remember. The Greek deities, all of whom had been cowed for millennia by the bullying of Zeus's wife, had scores to settle with the alpha goddess. Not one, however, had either the means or the backbone to effect rebellion. Now, with the Wildencrust murder having gone so spectacularly wrong, the strain was beginning to show. As fickle as mortals, the gods had seized Aphrodite's stunning rhetorical triumph as more than simply a striking act of self-preservation in a desperate moment. In the light of its extreme novelty it was cast as an indication that the Queen of the Gods had at last met her match. It was, ran the whisper through the chambers and private places of the immortals, a sign of change.

Dionysos was not deaf to these whisperings. Still smarting from Hera's verbal attack at the last meeting, and stunned by Aphrodite's brilliant performance, he had listened with keen interest to the gossip that could be heard at the junction of every nerve cluster and across every synaptic pathway of James's brain. Not that he cared about what it may or may not have portended for the divine balance of power. His concern remained the very same that had caused him to manipulate the chemical balance of the wine at the Founder's Feast; the same that had set in motion Wildencrust's botched murder. His concern, as it had been from the start, was that sack of flesh and bone, James Connor. Thus, amongst this conflagration of rumour and speculation, Dionysos was the only immortal whose mind was at all focused on the mortal vessel of the gods' divine wrath. The lust that Aphrodite had

160

cast over him continued to burn, and he had no mind at all other than to act upon it.

To this end he made his way across James's brain to the fragrant chamber of Aphrodite. Now that she appeared to have gained (even to her own surprise) the upper horn in the divine rut, Dionysos felt that it was the time for her to make good her promise. He had decided that enough was enough, and that if she should refuse he would take matters into his own hands.

"Dion, my darling," smiled Aphrodite as she admitted him into her sanctum.

"Hello Aphro," nodded Dionysos, the thin veneer of politeness indicating that this was not merely a social call.

"Now what can I do for you?" asked the goddess, knowing that he would make his way to her sooner rather than later. "It's been a while since…"

"Aphro!" he cried, giving vent to his pent-up feeling. "I can't go on pussyfooting around anymore. After Hera laid into me at the meeting I thought she'd figure out that I was after James. She figured out that I had enchanted the wine, but thankfully she was so concerned with having your guts for garters that she didn't follow through with me. It's a mercy she hates you so much and that you were such an easy target. Otherwise she'd have put two and two together and I'd have been roasted.

"Not such an easy target as it turned out," said Aphrodite pointedly. "If you hadn't taken it upon yourself to go against my advice and pursue the mortal then the whole cock-up would never have happened."

"Oh, I know, I know!" moaned Dionysos, running his hands through his hair in despair. "It's just that… Look, I know I went against your advice, and it was stupid. I can see that, really I can. But I'm absolutely desperate. I haven't felt so strongly attracted to a mortal for centuries. I know you said that you could fix up a liaison between us if I were to wait, but really I've done about as much waiting as I can bear. Honestly

Aphro, if you don't make it happen I'm just going to take it on myself, consequences be damned."

As she listened, Aphrodite intently observed the god's demeanour. It was clear that the effects of her enchantment and the savaging from Hera were causing him to think irrationally. She did not want to be cornered into honouring her promise, but if Dionysos took matters into his own hands her manipulation would certainly be discovered.

She sighed.

"Very well, Dionysos. I accept what you say. I did make you a promise."

His eyes lit up.

"But remember what you promised me," she continued.

"I don't, but whatever the hell it is you can have it!" he gasped, delighted.

"Primacy in council," said Aphrodite.

"You've got it, no problem! Yes!" he yelled, punching the air.

"Before you carve that notch on your bedpost," said Aphrodite, clearly less than overjoyed at the arrangement, "you must understand my terms. I told you before that I couldn't alter James's brain chemistry directly. It would be too obvious an infringement and would leave me open to accusations of jeopardising the mission. In order to get around that I'll have to think of something else…"

She bit her lip, and a frown of concentration flickered elegantly across her porcelain skin.

"Oh come on. Aphro! Think! Think!" nagged Dionysos desperately.

"Right…" said Aphrodite, still half lost in thought. "Okay, I think I've got it." She turned to him. "This is what I'm going to do. I'm going to alter the quality of *your* appearance. Not in a way that anyone can actually see, but in a way that corresponds to some quality that James, deep-down, already finds attractive. In essence I'll give you a certain *je ne sais quoi* that he'll find irresistible."

"Wonderful. Everyone's a winner!" exclaimed Dionysos, riding the wave of elation.

"Well perhaps. It's still a hell of a risk. But now listen to my terms. This enchantment will only be temporary. Once you've had your way with him it will be over. Enough will have to be enough.

"Don't worry, once is all I'll need," said Dionysos chasing his own train of thought.

"And it will only begin after the next death. Once you've given me primacy to force through my plans and they've been carried out I'll cast the spell."

"But Aphro, I…"

A milky-white finger held prohibitively before his face was enough to silence him.

"Okay, fine. We have a deal."

*****

The gossiping and whispering that echoed across the neural pathways of James's brain did not go unheard by the Queen of the Gods. Hera had left the council meeting as stunned as the others by Aphrodite's performance, and furious that her initial advantage had been reversed. That fury had turned to horror, however, as the murmuring began. To hear herself spoken of as a diminishing force was galling to the goddess, who had secured her reign through naked aggression and force of will. She well knew the power of gossip. It had after all been she who had started the rumour, millennia ago, that Zeus's first wife, Metis, was destined to give birth to a son greater than him. It had been this scare story that had prompted Zeus to swallow his unfortunate spouse and pave the way for Hera to muscle her way into his marriage bed. Now, after consolidating a dominance that had lasted for thousands of years, she was not prepared for it to be swept away by a lot of talk. Conceptions of her fall from power on the back of Aphrodite's surprise performance may have been overstated, but such stories could all too easily provide the impetus for future challenges. The Queen of the Gods was damned if she was going to let the Goddess of Desire trump her. She had to be stopped.

Thus Hera had called Athena, her closest and most loyal ally, to her chamber to discuss a plan of battle. But for the fact that she was the daughter of Zeus, Athena would never have been of the slightest interest to Hera. Now that salacious gossip was spreading like wildfire, however, a devoted ally was worth her weight in rhetoric.

Sitting in private, the goddesses were hatching a plan to remove Aphrodite as a force on the council so that the good of the entire divine collective might be better served.

"How the hell the other gods can have so easily fallen onto the side of that whore is beyond me. They're bastards, every one of them. I'd happily wipe them all out and be the sole deity in the universe," fumed Hera.

"And a fine ruler of the universe you'd be too," said Athena sycophantically.

"Oh shut up, moron. I didn't call you here to be my echo," spat Hera.

"No of course not. Terribly sorry."

"What do you think of this gossiping that's been happening behind my back?"

"Oh it's absolutely awful, Hera. To think that after all these millennia of having you as a role model the others should turn on you simply because Aphrodite got the better of you in…"

"She did not get the better of me!" yelled Hera, causing Athena to jump.

"Oh, er, no, sorry. What I meant was 'after Aphrodite tricked the others into thinking that she got the better of you.' It's just awful that they should be so short-sighted."

"So you agree that we need to act."

"Absolutely. Have you formed a plan?"

"Yes and it's pretty damn simple. At the next meeting we'll be deciding the mode of death for the third member of the Cambridge List. During the proceedings I'm going to launch such a scathing attack on that bitch that she won't know Monday from Sunday."

Well, yes, that does sound like a fine plan, but..." said Athena, nervously.

"But, what?" hissed Hera.

"Well... I think it might need a little padding out. You attacked her last time and she managed to wiggle out of it. I think, with absolutely heaps of respect and all that, that you might need to offer some wonderful plan for the death of the third don. If... If you see what I mean..." She trailed off as Hera's eyes shot daggers.

"Did you think that I hadn't thought of that?" she said darkly. "I'm going to propose that the mortal kill Elliot Norther by means of an arson attack. I'll deliver it in terms of 'the flames of divine wrath,' or some such nonsense. Once the oratory is sorted out those bastards always toe the line."

"Oh Hera, they'll love it! They'll simply lap it up!" gasped Athena in obsequious tones. "What a plan!"

"Yes, isn't it," agreed Hera. "All I need you to do is to provide a link between your father and the council, like before. Except this time you'll run off to tell Zeus of the meeting shortly before we all convene. When you return, tell the council that Zeus has heard of a special plan developed by Hera, and that I am to be given a special position, centre stage, to extol it. When the others hear that Zeus is behind me they'll change their ways. And once the third death has been carried out on my terms, and my position has been consolidated again, I'll smack down those who dared to speak against me."

Oh yes! What a genius you are!" squealed Athena, delighted. She then hesitated, a hint of uncertainty in her voice. "But... It's just that. Well, I don't mean to be rude, but haven't *all* the gods been speaking against you since the last meeting."

"Exactly so," muttered Hera, darkly.

*****

"Order! Let the council of Olympus come to order!" intoned Dionysos, as the crowds of omnipotents assembled in James's hippocampus. His voice had a steadiness that hitherto it had lacked, charged as it was with the expectation of reward. The god glanced at Aphrodite, serene amongst the divine mob. The Goddess of Desire caught his eye, and in the merest of glints confirmed the pact between them.

"Order, I say!" he now yelled, impatiently. The gods fell silent, and more than a few noted his sense of self-command (which, had they but known it, was on this occasion the very expression of desperation).

"Now then," Dionysos began. "We gather today to determine the death of the third blasphemous lecturer, Elliot Norther. I urge the council to note that time is of the essence and that suggestions are to be kept brief. Who would like to propose a means of divine retribution for the next victim?"

"Thank fuck for that," shouted Hera dramatically. "I thought you'd never get down to business." Straightening her back, she prepared to launch into an aggressive pitch.

Dionysos, however, simply raised his hand.

"Thank you, Hera, I think your disrespect for the position of Chair has been well established. I repeat: are there any suggestions?"

Hera's mouth opened and closed in disbelief, and she was momentarily silenced. The other gods, equally stunned, looked at her, awaiting the torrent that must surely issue forth against such a blatant, though thrilling, transgression of the accepted pecking order.

In the moment of silence that Dionysos's retort had bought him he seized on the chance to put his plan into action.

"Aphrodite," he said, nodding in her direction. "I believe you twitched your eyebrows. Perhaps you have something to suggest?"

All eyes, including Hera's, swivelled towards the goddess, who nodded at Dionysos demurely.

"Thank you, Chairman," she purred. "Indeed I do have a suggestion to make."

"Now just a moment! I damn well spoke out first. If you think that…"

"That's enough of that, Hera!" boomed Dionysos sternly.

The assembled crowd gasped. Whatever had gotten into the God of Wine had certainly made him bolder than he had been before. So unexpected was the outburst that Hera once again gasped wordlessly.

"Carry on, Aphrodite," urged Dionysos, taking advantage of the silence once again.

"Thank you," smiled the goddess, who then raised her voice to address the assembly. "I think we can all agree that the last death was a complete cock-up and reflected very badly on our divine glory."

Murmurs of assent filled the hippocampus.

"Moreover, I think we can all assume a collective responsibility for the disaster," she said quickly, as she saw Hera about to leap in. "As a result, I have decided to put forward a plan that will deliver divine wrath and mortal destruction in the most satisfying portions. Elliot Norther will rue the day that he acted against the immortal gods!"

The crowd, ever susceptible to such fiery talk, loudly expressed their approval.

Hera, however, was not about to allow Aphrodite to hog the floor.

"Oh what a load of old codswallop! We went through all this at the last meeting, you stupid cow."

Dionysos once again stepped in.

"Any more disruptions to the proceedings and I shall have to take stern measures, Hera," he warned, casting a dark glance her way.

Hera laughed mockingly.

"Oh really? 'Stern measures?' And just what would they comprise? Stamping your little foot? Throwing a tantrum, perhaps? Don't make me laugh, you little drip!"

"I think you'll find that as Chairman I have the power, vested in me by Zeus himself, to take any measures necessary to maintain order at the meetings."

"I most certainly will not be quiet!" spat Hera, savagely. "If you think that I'm going to kowtow to a little snot like you, you're very much mistaken."

"You're bloody well going to have to," said Dionysos. Every word was calculated to bait the Queen of the Gods, to stir her to greater anger.

"You just try and make me!" she roared.

"Are you saying that you refuse to recognise my authority? That the authority vested in me by Zeus carries no weight with you?"

"Precisely," said Hera, head held defiantly.

Dionysos paused, and a thick silence filled the hippocampus. The gods sat rapt, every breath held, caught in suspense.

The God of Wine rose, turned to face the assembled mass and spoke in a low and august tone.

"Deities of Olympus. I ask you, as Chairman of the council, to make it known as to whether Hera, Queen of the

Gods, shall be allowed to remain. She has not only defied my authority, but failed to recognise it altogether. Until such time as she revokes what she has said, I recommend that you cast her out. Make clear your intentions."

The silence continued, and now the atmosphere was electric. Though all had whispered of her worthy trumping in the last session, who would now openly speak out against her? Seconds ticked by.

Then a single voice spoke out.

"Begone," said Aphrodite.

"What?" mouthed Hera, shocked, her voice barely audible even in the silence.

"Begone," said another god from the back row.

"Begone," said another, and then another. Suddenly the chant was taken up by a whole row, and within seconds had gained momentum.

"Begone! Begone! Begone!" it ran, as it swept the mass, gathering force and volume.

Hera could not believe her ears. She had never witnessed an expulsion in all her millennia on the council. That she should be the subject of the only one in her lifetime was galling. She looked into the crowd. How could they have turned so suddenly? Before, not a single one of them would have dared raise a voice against her, particularly Dionysos. Now, with her trumping in the last meeting and the rumours about her decline, some latent strength of feeling was being lent to the collective voice of the downtrodden masses.

"How dare you all! How dare...!"

"Begone! Begone! Begone!"

"Silence! I order you all to... I command...!"

But it was no use. They had sensed weakness. She could hardly wade against the raging torrent directed at her.

"Begone! Begone! Begone!"

She rose to her feet, visibly shaken. This seemed only to increase the volume and ferocity of the chant.

She could see that she had no choice. Turning on her heels, she stalked out of the hippocampus. The only sound audible through the din was a barking command to Athena to follow her.

The sight of the Queen of the Gods leaving the council, beaten by that most unlikely of forces, the expression of popular will, caused an instantaneous outburst of elation. Gods and goddesses leapt from their seats, shouting and waving with delight.

After indulging them for a few moments, Dionysos spoke up.

"Now, everyone, calm please. That's right, calm down. We must resume the meeting."

As the crowd settled, he turned to Aphrodite, whose knowing look conveyed all the assurance he needed that his part of the bargain had been fulfilled.

*****

The meeting of the council surpassed Aphrodite's hopes. As she put forward plans for an 'erotic death,' the audience's initial scepticism had turned to delight. When she had proposed an 'insurance policy' against collective shame, should the enterprise go awry as before, delight turned to glee. She herself would take on responsibility for the plan, she had told the assembled mass. If there were any mistakes they would be down to her, though of course any glory would be held collectively by the council.

She had known that such words were of only rhetorical value. Without Hera, there was no one else who could have posed a credible threat to her, no one to propose a better idea. Nor, if the plan were successful, would there be any doubt as to who was really responsible.

As the vote had been taken and unanimous support registered for the erotic murder, the thought of getting one over on her great enemy left Aphrodite tingling.

*****

Whenever Elliot Norther's wife was nervous she baked. With the murder of Harriet Mason, her husband's close colleague at the Faculty, she had been unable to resist a couple of Victoria sponges. During the frenzied press speculation about the identity of the murderer, a Dundee cake had appeared, followed swiftly by a Battenberg and a Lemon Drizzle. Since news of the Wildencrust murder broke, the kitchen, dining room and study had come to resemble the storerooms of an industrial bakery, every surface heaving with the weight of sponge and cream. Yesterday, having at last been overwhelmed by the fear and rumour that swept the town, she had taken herself off to her mother's house in Hampstead, leaving her husband to soldier on alone. When he had last seen his wife, Elliot Norther noticed that she had been putting the finishing touches to an impressive, triple-tiered wedding cake, beating a batch of royal icing into a sickly paste.

Lying on the sofa in his study, Norther smiled as he observed the vast, voluptuous globule. It was wonderfully thick, sliding down at a glacial pace, almost translucently pale. He watched with great satisfaction.

"You look like you're in another world, old thing," said Margo Goyle, as she leant over and allowed her pasty, globulous breasts to smother Eliot Norther's face.

"Mmm… thmnn… mmrn…" came the futile reply from beneath the depths of the pale flesh.

"What I believe my colleague is trying to say is, 'oh yes, that was rather fucking fantastic,'" said Alan Tanning, from the opposite *chez long*. "Considering we used to get this for

171

free, I can't think why we decided to start paying you," he continued. It was the only hint of dissatisfaction that had made itself known that evening.

"Well, chaps, you get what you pay for these days. Seeing the motley state of the latest crop of undergrads you should jolly well count yourselves lucky that I'm charitable enough not to have doubled the bill. Besides, last year you were my supervisors. It would have been most improper of me to demand money from you."

"Then in that case I most thoroughly regret that you didn't decide to continue into postgraduate research," said Norther, now emancipated from the pile of breast.

"Why bother? There's so much dosh to be made as a Cambridge Consort," replied Margo. "Frankly, I can't think why I bothered with three years of classics at all."

A year ago, having graduated with a starred first, awarded for her intricate understanding of the ancient past, Margo Goyle had found herself having to consider her future. With her impeccable academic credentials and superb family connections, her ears rang with the jingle-jangle of golden handcuffs: city law firms winked at her; banks beckoned seductively, and even a certain hedge fund sent out tender feelers. Having surveyed this glittering world of professional prospects that had opened up before her, Margo had chosen what was quite clearly the most lucrative career of all: high class prostitution.

The Cambridge Consorts was a group 'stock market traders,' headquartered at a discreet farmhouse in the Fens, and an open secret amongst Cambridge's elite. The 'stock' comprised a group of socially and physically illustrious young women. Their 'market' was formed of the large group of affluent Cambridge-dwellers whose sex-lives could only be fulfilled at great expense and with little romantic attachment. There was, in truth, only one trader: the legendary Mrs Featherstoneshaw, known to all, including the long-frustrated vice-squad, as 'The Madame.' The firm's slogan and ethos had remained the same since day one: *Rather Better than Your Wife*. When Margo had applied to the Consorts for their internship, The Madame had been sceptical, an attitude justified by the applicant's appearance ('absolutely, bloody hideous,' was the verdict recorded in the preliminary interview notes). Any doubts about Margo's value to the company, however, were soon dispelled when the firm's social intelligence-gathering machine was put into operation. It found that here was a girl whose capabilities in the bedroom were second to none, and whose sexual profligacy in the her final year went some way towards explaining the firm's lower-than-expected profit margins during that period. Thus, she was hired, and had continued to generate a steady stream of income ever since.

"Oh I think classics made its mark on you, my dear," said Tanning. "Having Ovid whispered in one's ear in the original Latin whilst you carry out that... well, whatever that extraordinary performance is called, is an experience that only a classicist could deliver."

"And one that only a rather well-moneyed academic could pay for," said Margo, her breasts lolling over her sagging stomach as she rummaged around in her handbag. "Right," she said, hoisting herself upright again. "That'll be seven hundred and twenty five pounds, please." She brandished a portable chip-and-pin device. "Which of you is paying this time?"

Tanning glanced at Norther, who rolled his eyes and grabbed his wallet from the table.

"Tell the Madame she's robbing us blind," he said irritably as he punched his numbers into the keypad.

"Oh I can quite assure you she knows. She, however, refers to it as her 'business model.' Awfully effective, I'd say."

"Yes, rather too much," scowled Tanning.

173

Margo handed Norther his credit card and a receipt for 'financial consultancy services rendered.'

"Right, better be off," she said, slipping on an overcoat and stilettos.

"Would you like to use the dining room to get dressed?" asked Norther.

"I am dressed," she smiled. "Or at least as dressed as I need to be for my next engagement. My driver pulled up outside whilst you were paying. He's been with the firm for years, so I don't worry about sparing his blushes. Or, indeed, yours." As she spoke she seductively licked her yellowing, tombstone-like teeth at the two men, then turned on her heels and walked out into the night.

"Ravishing creature," breathed Tanning.

"Leaves a damn hole in the credit card, though," muttered Norther. "And that, if I may say, brings me to concerns rather more pressing than pretty girls. I feel bound to tell you, Tanning, that I'm having doubts about the Fund."

Tanning's eyes narrowed, and he took a nervous breath.

"Doubts? About carrying it through?"

"About the deaths of Mason and Wildencrust."

Tanning looked almost relieved.

"Shocking, but we can't let that divert us. Fringe has got enough to ruin us, and if we don't get it through in the next few days he'll have no qualms about doing just that."

"Don't you feel riled by it all, though?"

"How do you mean?"

"Well, after Wildencrust was killed I couldn't help wondering if there wasn't something… targeted about it."

"Targeted?"

"Perhaps one of the ambassador's enemies…"

"Now Norther, get that nonsense out of your head! I must admit that such thoughts crossed my mind, but they do one no good. We have to get on with this for the sake of our careers. There's no use getting flustered by what is almost certainly just a horrid coincidence."

"Yes, yes, you're right, of course," Norther replied quickly. "I think I just need to pull myself together."

"That's right. Now have a large drink and get yourself to bed. We've got to get this thing tied up, and only then can we afford ourselves the luxury of worrying about nonsense," said Tanning, resolutely. He looked at his watch. "Goodness, I must be off too. See you tomorrow, old boy."

The door slammed behind him.

Alone in his study, however, Norther's doubts remained, lingering in the air with Margo's perfume.

*****

Athena winced. She had never seen Hera so incensed in all the millennia she had known her. This second trumping in council had been stunning, and now, back in her chambers and with the uproar still fresh in her mind, the Queen of the Gods had every excuse to vent her spleen. In the confines of her boudoir, Hera's torrent of abuse was almost more than Athena could bear, and the yelling risked piercing her divine eardrums.

Or at least it would have done, had there been any abuse or yelling.

Through the silence Athena winced in pained expectation.

Hera's face, however, remained a picture of calm. Staring into the middle-distance, her beautiful lips slightly parted, she appeared to be occupied with some other thought.

"Er... I say, Hera. I, er... I don't suppose you'd like to talk about what happened back there would you?" dared Athena timidly. Surely the torrent would have to rage sooner or later and, trusty doormat that she was, Athena would be there to receive the brunt of it.

"No," murmured Hera through a haze of thought. "But I would like to talk about something else. Something that explains what happened."

"What's that," whispered Athena, drawing closer. Though she was mildly scared, the thought that Hera was about to confide in her was thrilling enough to entice her to within punching distance.

"It's about Aphrodite and Dionysos. And the mortal."

"What about them?"

"I can't believe I didn't see it before. It was happening all along and I never saw."

"Saw what, Hera? What's been happening?" Athena could scarcely contain her excitement.

"Aphrodite. Dionysos. The mortal. They're…"

"What? What?"

Suddenly Hera gazed straight into Athena's grey eyes. "Rumbled."

*****

The microwave timer beeped, and as James opened the door to reveal the steaming meal his stomach rumbled loudly. It had been ten hours since food had passed his lips, and the looming prospect of another killing had prompted him down to the kitchen to seek nourishment. As luck would have it a more than usually thorough search through Greg's kitchen cupboard had revealed James's favoured Thursday evening delicacy: a tin of beans and sausages.

"Perfect murder food," he had thought to himself as he emptied the pale orange slop into a bowl. The sausages would provide protein, which, as everyone knows, is essential for the cultivation of strong, murder-capable muscles, whilst the baked beans would provide the carbs necessary to fuel the impending killing spree. As he carried his meal upstairs to his room he ruminated on the method that the next death might take. Soon there would only be two targets left and then he would be free. That was assuming, of course, that he could evade detection by the police and that the gods vacated his head once he was done.

He rarely turned his mind to life after the Cambridge List. It was easier to focus on the immediacy of murder than the bleak, grey future that he felt awaited him again once his mission was complete. Though he wanted nothing more than to be free from the dangers of divinely sanctioned killing, he felt little nostalgia for the dreary life he had led in the months preceding his first encounter with the Olympians.

As he sat down at his rickety desk to his comfortable and familiar student food, James pushed away these thoughts. Self-examination was dangerous, whereas beans and sausages were safe. You could probe a bowlful of beans and sausages to your heart's content, only to be met with the same mulchy texture, the same pale orange colour and very same sweet, malty flavour all the way through. Beans and sausages were perfectly consistent, perfectly comforting. In fact they were perfect in every way. Unlike life, which is shit.

"Absolutely, fucking shit," James mumbled to himself as he shovelled in another mouthful. "Still, there'll always be beans and sausages, thank God."

"Gods," corrected Aphrodite.

James coughed and nearly spat out his mulch.

Sitting on his bed, the Goddess of Desire, a model of graceful comportment, smiled alluringly.

"Oh do turn around, my darling. I know you're making love to that bowl of shite, but I'm dying to know that I can still attract your attention.

A swift glance at his groin confirmed to her that, as ever, his attention was undivided.

"Hello Aphrodite," James ventured cautiously. "What an unexpected pleasure."

"I can see that," she said, without lifting her eyes from the bulge in his trousers. "But know that this is only a flying visit."

"Oh really. Well don't feel that you have to," he said, attempting to avoid broadcasting his sense of relief.

"Oh I wouldn't linger in this dump for a moment longer than necessary." Her disdain was visible as she cast her eyes about the room. "I simply came to tell you that your next victim is to be Elliot Norther."

"Right, sounds good to me," said James, shifting uncomfortably as the ache from his groin intensified. "What do you want me to do?"

Aphrodite sighed impatiently. "I'm not lingering to explain the ins and outs. We've downloaded detailed instructions onto your mobile.

James squirmed as an awkward thought that had begun to nag at him surfaced. Steeling himself for a telling off, he summoned the courage to voice his concern.

"I don't want to sound rude, honestly I don't," he said deferentially. "But since I stopped working I've had no income, and... well, things are getting pretty tight."

Aphrodite was unmoved.

"Tough. You'll just have to continue ferreting around your housemates' cupboards for food. You seem to have got by that way so far," she said, grimacing at the rapidly cooling beans and sausages.

"Oh yes. Sorry, I suppose I shouldn't have assumed ..."

"What, that you'd be paid? No."

She had risen and walked over to the door, but now paused and turned to him again.

"One more thing. Your last attempt at murder was a complete cock-up. I think you'll find us less than forgiving if it should be repeated."

"Oh, no, no, of course not," said James nervously. "I can absolutely assure you that I'll be on top form. I won't let you down again, I swear."

"Good," she said, casting one last glance about the room. "Your little life depends on it."

*****

Only one week ago Wendy Pipford would barely have thought it possible, but here before her eyes the creepiest employee of The Cambridge Clarion was smiling sweetly at the most ghoulish employee of Cambridge University.

"Oh yeah, that's right Mr Wetherblaine. Hold it right there, that's perfect. You're a natural," said Ken the photographer.

"Well I should've been surprised if my excellent posture hadn't shown through," said Martin Wetherblain with a delighted gobble. "It must be quite a relief to work with someone who responds so well to the camera."

"Yes that's right, it's great. You're doing really well, Martin. Can I call you Martin?"

"No," drawled Wethers.

"Oh. Well that's fine Mr Wetherblaine. Now, I wonder if we can't get a picture of you smiling."

"Why on earth would you want that?" asked Wetherblaine, his voice tinged with scepticism.

"Oh the readers love it. It won't necessarily go in, it's just that we need as many different shots as possible."

"Oh very well."

"That's the spirit. Now just give us a nice, big... Uurrgh!"

"What's wrong?" demanded Wetherblaine, snapping back into his usual grimace.

179

"Oh, er, nothing Mr Wetherblain, nothing at all," said Ken, smiling unconvincingly from behind the camera. "I just got a... a static shock from the equipment, that's all."

The shock that Ken received had in fact been caused by the sight of Wetherblaine's seldom-seen grin. Legend had it amongst the undergraduates at Midsummer that the head porter would smile at female students whom he suspected of having fallen pregnant in order to artificially induce labour and thus furnish himself with an excuse for reporting them to the dean. 'Wetherblaine's smile' had long since entered Cambridge jargon as a euphemism for the termination of an unwanted conception.

"Let's pick up where we left off and have you looking stern and authoritative, shall we?"

Throughout the photo shoot Wendy had been distracted. As image after hideous image of Martin Wetherblaine was burned into the camera's memory card, her thoughts drifted to what had become the single object of her concern: James Connor. Since her encounter with him the day before, she had been unable to remove from her mind those words that she had seen on his computer screen:

"u got killin to get on wiv, innit."

She was sure that this was no joke from a friend. For one thing, her journalistic instincts had tingled at the sight of it. For another, the idea that such a socially awkward creep should have friends was frankly ridiculous.

Notebook in hand, she doodled absently as speculation piled upon speculation about whether she had chanced upon a suspect. Perhaps he was linked to the Wildencrust murder. If so, it could be the find that made her career. She would be known as the reporter who busted the case wide open, and before the police had even got a look in too. Perhaps it would propel her out of this dive and onto one of the nationals. Perhaps it might even lead to...

"Watcha darling," leered Ken the photographer.

Wendy closed her eyes impatiently. He had interrupted her daydream just at the point when she was making an acceptance speech at the British Press Awards amidst the glitter of the Dorchester Hotel.

"Hello," she muttered, coldly. "Nearly finished?"

"Oh yeah, nearly done," said Ken, his body slightly too close to hers for comfort. "The crypt keeper over there has just nipped out for a quick toilet break. Probably has to empty his catheter or something."

Wendy stifled a smile. He was such a letch that to laugh at one of his remarks would have been to elicit unwanted attention, of which she had already received the requisite dose upon joining The Clarion a year ago. Like every new recruit, she had been subject to his clumsy advances in the pub after work, at the first office party and during every fire drill. His eyes seemed magnetically drawn to her chest, and were so expressive of a sweaty lust that they made her feel positively clammy. Wendy was determined: nothing Ken said could ever be funny.

"Fine, just round it off quickly, I don't want this dragging on the rest of the afternoon."

"No worries, babe, we're nearly done. And speaking of the rest of the afternoon, I was wondering if you fancied grabbing a pint with me down the Sceptre afterwards. Since both of us are…"

"No thank you," interrupted Wendy sharply. The sense of finality in her voice, however, was lost on Ken, who flashed a lecherous smile.

"Come on, darling. Just come for a pint. You know you want to."

Wendy stepped forward and leaned to speak softly into his ear. He was momentarily thrilled at the proximity.

"Look, would you mind awfully just getting lost? I've told you I'm not interested. I've got big things to do tonight and you most certainly aren't one of them."

In a momentary lapse into sensitivity, Ken deflated.

"Fine, don't bother then. Doesn't fuss me. Got some other bloke on the go I shouldn't wonder."

"No actually," said Wendy, slightly riled. "I've got work tonight. Potentially the biggest story I've seen since I've been here."

"Really? What is it?"

"Mind your own business. All I'm saying is that I'll be focusing on something big and important, which doesn't revolve around taking pictures of jumped up little creeps in porters' uniforms. Got it?"

"Are you referring to me, young lady?"

Wendy span round and came face to face with Wetherblaine. His cold eyes met hers and she blushed.

"Oh, no, no, Mr Wetherblaine, of course not. We were just talking about…"

"You were both quite clearly talking about me." In the artificial light of the studio his scowl was etched deep into his forehead.

"No, Mr Wetherblaine, no." She was flustered. "We were just… well, we were referring to someone who…"

"Of course you were referring to me. I'm not an idiot, young lady."

"Look I'm really sorry, Mr Wetherblaine, I honestly didn't…"

"When I heard the words 'big and important' I knew at once that you were discussing me. And why shouldn't you be? I'm sure I'm the most significant personality that you've had the privilege of working with. After all, someone in my position wouldn't usually stoop to being interviewed, much less photographed, by a local rag."

He rocked on his heels and gobbled with satisfaction. It was only natural that these little people should be admiring him. A little celebrity worship was to be expected.

"Well if you're ready Mr Wetherblaine, shall we get back to the shoot?" asked Ken, with strained politeness.

"Immediately," drawled Wetherblaine. "I do have other, more important things to do."

Wendy, having watched them resume, glanced at her watch. Her words with Ken had been bluff, she had had no plans for this evening. Now, though, her mind was made up. If she was to get anywhere in this industry she would have to learn to follow her instincts, all of which told her that James Connor was a prime lead. Intel was the key, and as she doodled on her pad her determination hardened: tonight after work she would trail him and find out exactly what this strange young man was up to.

*****

James lay back on his bed and whistled through his teeth. He had just finished reading the lengthy message the gods had sent to his phone, providing instructions on how he was to kill Elliot Norther. Ringing clear in every one of the twenty-eight points was the sense that that their faith in his abilities as a serial killer was abysmally low. His brow had furrowed as he read the patronising text.

'Point 22: You'll know that the victim is dead when *both* moving and breathing cease.'

'Point 23: As a murderer, it *your* responsibility to make sure the victim dies.'

'Point 24: Do not attempt mouth-to-mouth resuscitation.'

He was sick to the back teeth of their snide remarks about his incompetence. For a complete beginner he thought he'd done rather well at unlawful killings with malice aforethought. In fact he'd like to see any of them do better in his place. If they gave up hiding behind the skirts of divinity and lived a day or two in his shoes they'd probably be hopeless cock-ups too.

"No, better not start thinking that way, Connor," he said to himself. "They're bound to be listening. Save it till after they've fucked off."

He glanced at his phone and scanned their instructions again. There was only one point of detail that they had omitted, and it was troubling him. Without it, failure was guaranteed.

As his mind turned over the problem, he flicked through his list of messages. After failing his degree he had become increasingly isolated, and his contact with old friends had long since dwindled to virtually nothing. In fact the only person other than the Muse to have texted him at all since the gods had appeared had been Bumrash. His housemate had been messaging him continuously, and every one had been left unread and unacknowledged.

James propped himself up and began to open them.

"mate have you started taking the pills? remember: 1 pill twice per day. let's start u off easy. Bumrash."

James skipped forward two days.

"jimmy where have u been. I gotta go away 4 a few days, but if u started taking the pills remember u mustn't drink. also clean the bathroom. it stinks."

Four days later.

"mate where the fuck are u? have u not got my missed calls? why have u started locking your room? call me."

Yesterday, and the last message.

"seriously james, where are u??? if you've taken the pills and there have been side effects i need to know! please mate, i'm really concerned now."

James smiled as he typed a reply to his anxious friend. Here, perhaps, was an opportunity.

*****

184

"Jimmy you bloody idiot! You stupid, bloody idiot!" yelled Bumrash, throwing his arms around James and laughing. "I'm so fucking relieved, I can't tell you! I thought you'd died or something!"

James laughed.

"You never did."

"I swear. Honestly, I swear to God. I was gonna call the police."

"After you'd emptied my room and found my wallet!"

"Nah, I'd wait till they took me to identify your body before slipping it out of your pocket. No rooky mistakes for Bumrash, master criminal," he said, tapping his nose and winking.

James laughed with relief at the warmth of feeling between them. He could still feel warmth it seemed, despite everything. Bumrash slapped him on the back like no time had passed, and James smiled with mirth. He smiled as though two killings had not taken place, as though one would not take place this evening and that coming here did not bring it one step closer.

They were standing in the lobby of the Macmillan Building, a low-level glass and steel structure owned by the Faculty of Natural Sciences and used as a base for teams of biomedical researchers. Light and air flooded the place, lending it sense of professional tranquillity.

"Quiet today" said James.

"Yeah there aren't many people here at the moment. One of the second floor managers is leaving and she's treating everyone to lunch."

"Didn't fancy it yourself?"

"You know me," said Bumrash. "Look Jimmy, I can't tell you how relieved I am to see you, and later on I want to hear all about how Flanoxiride has been working for you. But like I said in my text, I'm rushed off my feet today; running around like a blue arsed fly."

"Aren't we all."

"Exactly. Do you mind if we grab a coffee and take it up to my lab on the first floor? We'll have to make this a 'working reunion.'"

"No problem, mate."

Amongst the bright, clean rooms of the Macmillan building Bumrash's lab was an oasis of chaos. The two other members of his team were perfectly congenial to his slobbish habits, and together the three were known to other workers as 'Team Cess-Pit."

Standing amidst the mess and waiting for Bumrash to return with the coffees, James scanned the surfaces. They heaved with innumerable glass implements and bottles of liquid. He couldn't see what he was looking for though, and wandered purposefully from one counter to the next. Despite the lab itself being small, the sheer quantity of scientific detritus made an item-by-item inspection impossible. As he moved about the room his criminal instinct, conditioned entirely by snatched episodes of Morse and The Bill, urged him to move nothing, so as not to arouse suspicion. As he scanned the surfaces for a third time, however, desperation mounted. This was his only chance to get what he had come for. If Bumrash came back before he found it he'd be screwed. Glass vessels now clinked as he began to probe the crowded workspaces.

Suddenly he saw it. The bottle was much smaller than he had expected, and as he slipped it into his pocket the door opened and Bumrash entered the room backwards, carrying a pair of steaming paper cups.

"Here we go, Jimmy. Fresh from the knackered coffee machine."

He looked about the surfaces for somewhere to put them, and James winced as he placed one in the space the bottle had occupied.

"You okay, Jimmy? You look a bit white."

"Oh yeah I'm fine, I'm fine." James hated thinking on his feet. His ferret-like instinct to shuffle into the nearest dark corner was beginning to rise. "It's… It's just that…"

As concern appeared on Bumrash's face James realised that the question had been off-the-cuff. By stuttering he had dug a hole for himself, and to climb out would necessitate a carefully delivered ad hoc fib.

"It's just that I've been having anxiety attacks lately. I never told you about them before, but they come on when I'm in unfamiliar environments."

"Oh my God, Jimmy. Did these come on after you started taking the pills. Man, if they're causing you to have these attacks you better leave off them."

"No, no, they'd been happening for months before. Actually they've calmed down since I started taking Flanoxiride."

"Really? Well that's great, that's exactly the sort of effect I was hoping for. It means they're displaying some of the antidepressant effects that we observed in the lab."

"Great," said James. His anxiety was steadily mounting as he could feel the outline of the bottle in his pocket.

"Jimmy you really don't look well, mate. Did you take one of the pills this morning?"

"No I didn't. It slipped my mind."

"Shit. Have you got any with you?"

"No."

"Well you'd better get yourself back home and pop one. Quick!"

"Bummers I don't want to cut this short. We haven't see each other for ages."

"Mate, your health comes first."

"Yeah I suppose you're right. I'm really sorry."

"Don't be silly. Go on, go."

"Cheers, Bumrash."

"Don't you go disappearing again, Jimmy. I'm gonna be looking out for you now I know you're alive," he smiled. "You keep in touch. "

"Will do, Bummers," he lied.

CHAPTER SIXTEEN

Appointments with Mr Haberdasher were extremely expensive, but Elliot Norther was happy to pay. His efforts to push through the Classics Outreach Fund were progressing at breakneck speed, and the stress was taking its toll. In the past forty-eight hours he had experienced the dreaded heart flutters, and several attempts with his blood-pressure home testing kit had stoked his fears.

Earlier that day he had called the office of the illustrious practitioner.

"Mr Haberdasher's, how can I help you?" the clipped female voice had answered.

"Hello, this is Elliot Norther. I'm calling to make an appointment."

"Hello Dr Norther. Yes of course. Would you like to come into the office, or would a home visit be preferable?"

"A home visit, please."

"Certainly. The usual premium will be charged. You know the price, of course."

"Oh yes."

"And when would you like it to be?"

"Well I know it's short notice, but I was rather hoping for this evening."

"This evening? Dr Norther, you know that Mr Haberdasher is the most in-demand practitioner in Cambridge. You can't possibly expect that he could fit you in this evening."

"I know, I know. It's just that my blood pressure has been through the roof. It's my work, you see. It's been more stressful in these past few days than ever before, and I really need to have a treatment. My health depends on it. I'm willing to pay extra if you could make a space in his diary."

"Well… I suppose we could move some things around. But you must understand that this is most irregular, and would not even be considered if you weren't a long-standing patient. There will, of course, be an additional charge."

"No problem, no problem at all. Shall we say ten o'clock this evening?"

"He'll see you then. Goodbye."

Having waited in eager anticipation all day, the appointed hour had now arrived, and Elliot Norther stood expectantly in the front hall. His ears pricked as he detected the sound of car wheels crunching the gravel of the drive, followed by the clunk of a car door. The bell had barely completed its chime when Norther rushed to answer it.

"Nurse!" he exclaimed at the woman standing in the doorway. "You've brought Mr Haberdasher with you?"

"Of course, Dr Norther," she replied coolly.

"Good. Come in, both of you. A pleasant journey I trust?"

"Yes thank you. Mr Haberdasher is not, of course, at liberty to dawdle. Where would you like the treatment to take place?" she enquired, stepping into the hall and looking through the door that led to the sitting room.

"Upstairs in the bedroom," said Norther. "Follow me."

The nurse nodded and instinctively smoothed her pale blue uniform, as was her habit when arriving on home visits. She was barely twenty-three years old, though she might have passed for forty. Attending patients in their home was her favourite part of the job. Since she had been a little girl her purpose in life had been to work in the caring profession. Giving aid to the needy and vulnerable was her joy, though any outward expression of it was mediated by a carefully crafted professional demeanour. She had worked hard to get to where she was today, building a relationship of trust with patients who relied on her to deliver first class treatments. Studious good form on a suitable course at university had rewarded her with a position at a firm of professional care-providers, and now she carried out her work with diligence and satisfaction.

As run of the mill as her life story sounds when rendered in the abstract, this young woman was far from ordinary. For the university at which she had studied so hard was Cambridge, the course at which she had excelled was Classics and her name was Margo Goyle.

After the pair of them had ascended the stairs and entered the bedroom, she shut the door and removed her coat. There she turned to Norther, arms folded.

"Tell me the problem."

"Well, nurse, it's the usual symptoms I'm afraid. They've been getting worse too. To tell you the truth I've been quite out of my mind with worry."

"Calm yourself, Dr Norther," commanded Nurse Goyle. "There's no sense in getting hysterical. These things have to be treated calmly and rationally. Now, it's my professional opinion that the problem lies with your tonsils."

"Oh yes, tricky things, tonsils. That was my very conclusion," concurred Norther with an excited nod.

"Quite. If there's an infection there it can play merry hell with the rest of the body. I suspect that Mr Haberdasher will want to perform a full oral examination."

"I thought he might," said Norther. "In fact, I set up the equipment especially."

Margo Goyle glanced over at the bed and noted with professional approval an elaborate network of ropes and leather straps.

"Good," she assented. "You see, the examination can be rather uncomfortable, and in an entirely uncharacteristic slip in my professional standards I've forgotten to bring any gas to help relax you. You'll have to brave it, Dr Norther."

"Oh not to worry, not to worry," he said quickly. "You shall strap me in so that if I were to move about or gag I shouldn't disrupt the examination."

"A prescient move."

"And once Mr Haberdasher has finished the examination you can simply release me," he said.

"Naturally. If you're not too disruptive, that is."

Norther could barely contain his eagerness, and rubbed his hands together. At this point Nurse Goyle deftly slipped out of her crisply ironed uniform and stood with nothing but a pair of vast, beige granny-knickers to conceal her modesty.

"So is the great man to show himself?" asked Norther. "I should like to greet Mr Haberdasher before he sets to work."

"Certainly, Dr Norther. Here he is."

And with that, Margo Goyle dropped her knickers.

Elliot Norther gasped and feasted his eyes upon the sight.

"I say! Has Mr Haberdasher paid a visit to the barbers? He's looking quite the dandy!"

"Indeed he has, Dr Norther. His last patient had both the inclination and the money for a session with the clippers. Of course Mr Haberdasher insisted that his sideburns be left intact." As she spoke she combed her fingers through the long, tufty hair that lined her inner thighs. "I've always thought a pair of mutton chops looks most distinguished on a gentleman."

"Most distinguished indeed!" exclaimed Norther.

"Rather like Gladstone in my opinion," said Goyle. "Now then, since Mr Haberdasher has other clients to see I'm sure you won't mind if he supervises whilst I strip you down and tie you up. The sooner we expedite the examination, the better for your tonsils."

"Oh the better indeed!" yelped Norther with glee.

Had Nurse Goyle and her patient not been so preoccupied with the medical examination upstairs, they might have heard a pane of glass in the kitchen door shatter, and an intruder enter the house.

Since returning home from his meeting with Bumrash, James had spent the rest of the afternoon preparing himself for his murderous expedition to Norther's dwelling. After the sun had set and the appointed hour approached, he had made his way on foot through the fields on the outskirts of town to his victim's residence, a large Victorian house in the village of Newnham. Following the gods' instructions he had dressed for the deed. The requisite inconspicuous clothes were amply provided by a wardrobe that had long contained nothing but grey and black attire, and all of a baggy and ill-fitting cut. Only the black woollen hat and pair of gloves that he had purchased especially for the occasion indicated any deviation from his usual dress.

Standing in the darkness of the kitchen, with a scattering of glass glinting in the moonlight, James was frozen in anticipation. He had had to steel himself to shatter the pane and reach in to release the lock. If the gods' instructions had been even slightly off, and Norther had been downstairs at the time, he would have been caught red-handed. The coast, however, had been clear, and despite straining he could hear no signs of life.

He pulled out his phone and re-read the gods' email.

"When you enter the house the victim will be upstairs with his lover. Enter the property by stealth and make your way to the bedchamber. If there is a guard dog, neutralise it. If there is a guest, kill him or her too."

He had noted with apprehension the worrying implication of the text: that the gods did not know whether or not there would be dogs or guests when he entered. The limits of their divine prescience were hardly reassuring. As he listened in the darkness, however, hardly daring to move for fear of making his presence known, he was met only with silence.

"Okay Connor," he thought. "There's no one else here. Let's just get on with this."

Painfully slowly, he crept forwards, relieved to find that the wooden floorboards did not creak. He paused as he entered the hall. A light on the first floor landing was on, illuminating the stairwell. Now he could hear voices coming from one of the bedrooms. He recognised Norther's at once, though the other seemed to belong to a woman. From its tone James guessed her to be around forty.

He gulped. In order to sneak into the bedroom he would have to turn off the landing light, or else give himself away immediately upon entering. Creeping forward he flicked the switch and winced at the subsequent wave of adrenaline.

James breathed a sigh of relief as the chatter from upstairs continued. Creeping up to the first floor landing, he pressed his ear against the bedroom door, attempting to gauge the sense of space from the voices, trying to place them in the room before he entered. He could hear them clearly now. Norther appeared to be in a reclining position, his voice directed upwards. The woman, who was definitely closer to fifty than forty, was standing near to the don. It sounded like they were both facing the far wall. Looking down, James saw that the light entering the landing from under the door was faint, probably that of a bedside lamp.

Tentatively, he opened the door by half an inch and peered in.

Suddenly, he flinched and looked away. Illuminated by the light of a small reading lamp, Norther was indeed lying down. In fact there was no possibility of his rising or sitting up. There upon the bed he was naked, bound with an elaborate set of straps. They encompassed his entire body, with his hands and feet tied separately to the bedposts with taut lengths of rope. His saggy skin, held tight by the bindings, oozed over the rope and leather. The sickness that James felt at such a sight, however, was compounded by the fleeting impression he had gleaned of Norther's companion. She was on the bed too, but squatting over him, her feet either side of his head and her nether regions positioned just above his face. With her squab form, ludicrously coloured hair and rolling hillocks of back fat, even a brief glance had revealed more than he had wished to see. Despite the fact that she was facing away from him, it was immediately clear to James that he had misjudged the don's female companion: she was at least sixty. Would she have to be killed too? Being in such atrocious physical condition she could hardly be expected to put up much of a fight. Murdering a pensioner seemed a bit much, though, even under divine imperative.

After a moment's contemplation of the gods' instructions, James determined that if he could carry out his plan without making himself known to her, then he would leave her be.

Steeling himself for the next step he peered round the door once again. Neither of them could see him, and conditions were as favourable as they were likely to get. With a silent breath he entered the bedroom, slipping inside unseen by either of the occupants, observed only by the walls, the silence… and Wendy Pipford.

At the foot of the stairs the intrepid young reporter for The Cambridge Clarion was dumbstruck. This evening had brought one surprise after another since she had arrived outside James's house and tailed him all the way to Newnham. Given his shifty demeanour and gait, she had been surprised that his movements hadn't aroused suspicion in others. When she observed him breaking in through the kitchen her suspicions were all but confirmed. The resulting thrill, compounded by her carefully delayed entry into the residence, was tempered only by the implications of the evidence: that she was entering a house with a murderer and was about to encroach on what would quite possibly become a killing.

Standing in the darkness, one foot on the bottom step, she had resisted the instinct to gasp aloud as she saw James slowly enter the bedroom. Every action of his that she had observed reinforced her impression that he was about to commit murder. His movements, though awkward, conveyed a sense of determination, of mission. His body language bore a sinister resolve. Perhaps now was the time to call the police. She had seen him go through the door into the room where she could hear two other people. He carried with him a bag, and who knows what implements it contained? The very fact that he had homed in on the one room in the house that contained signs of life was evidence that he was there to extinguish it, and told against any flimsy hypothesis that he was a petty thief.

Now was her chance to call the police. Turning the idea over in her mind, as she felt she was duty bound to do, she found that the instinct to dial 999 was weaker than that which compelled her to follow, observe and record. Wendy Pipford was ever the journalist and only incidentally the citizen. Having chosen the vague comfort of ignoring the idea of calling the police, rather than completely dismissing it, she reached into her pocket for her mobile phone. Activating the camera, she placed it at head height and gingerly made up the stairs to the bedroom door. She had already taken a brief film of the house's exterior, her entry into the kitchen and her progress to the hall. Good journalistic standards had to be maintained even when dodging the call for civic responsibility.

Reaching the door, she too observed the dim light visible from under it. Now was her chance. She had counted her way up the stairwell and the number of steps from the top of the stairs to the bedroom. If need be she could beat a hasty retreat to the hall and out the front door even in the darkness. With a sharp breath she pushed the bedroom door open a crack and slowly inched her phone through. Actual entry was beyond the limits of her courage, and instead she looked at the screen, which captured almost the entire interior.

In what was otherwise pitch blackness, broken only by the weak light of the reading lamp, she observed the bed, the shackles, the naked, tightly-bound lecturer, his female lover and her highly compromising position above the revolting man's head, which was completely obscured by her grotesque form.

There was, however, no sign of anyone else. Squinting at her phone, she could just make out the other furniture in the room: the easy chair, the bookcase against the rear wall, the carpet. Probing the shadows, however, she could see nothing else.

How long would she wait? She carefully took another breath. She was consciously aware of each inhalation, and now, in her state of high concentration, she felt a bead of sweat on a slow, itchy course down her forehead.

Perhaps another view would reveal more? Should she pan the phone around? No, any movement would compromise the view. The bed was in the centre of the shot, a detailed mass of pixels, the only colour in a room of shadows.

She gently exhaled into the silence.

Suddenly the screen was filled with the image of a man. Wendy clasped her hand over her mouth and stifled a cry. Appearing from the side of the shot, he ran towards the bed, hunched over in rushed stealth. He must have been crouched against the wall beside the door, watching the bed and its occupants from the same angle as Wendy, unaware of the phone as he focused on his victims. He hadn't been in the shadows, he had been right there. She gasped with shock, and a tear involuntarily sprang from her eye. She managed to hold the camera still, though. She saw the man reach the bed and grab the woman roughly by the head, gripping her face tightly with his hands. Wendy looked on in horror, and from beyond

197

the camera lens heard the muffled scream of the female and the confused shout of the man on the bed.

What had she done? What should she do? Paralysing fear rose up in her. She found that she could not take her eyes from the screen. If she were to look beyond the pixels she would surely scream. Strange, unfamiliar feelings of terror and self-preservation combined, rooting her to the spot and transfixing her on the image of the woman struggling and the man on the bed beginning to thrash against his bonds.

At that moment nausea swept over her stomach, unlocking her. She flinched and ducked out into the hallway, throwing herself against the wall next to the door and gasping for breath.

She gulped the air and winced. She had to leave, to run. Now.

She fled breakneck down the stairs and into the hallway. Behind her she could still hear the muffled sounds of killing. She heard them all the way to the kitchen and down the side path of the old house. She could hear them still as she ran through the fields from Newnham, as they chased her through the silent outskirts of the town. Those gasping, stifled screams were there when finally, panting, she entered the darkness of her own flat, frantically double locking the door and flinging on every light before collapsing hysterically on the living room floor.

*****

Before leaping into action James had fumbled silently in his bag. Having fished out the bottle of chloroform, spirited from Bumrash's lab, he had doused his handkerchief in the liquid. Watching the pair on the bed and hearing the pleasured moans of Norther as his lover gyrated over his face, waves of adrenaline pulsed through James's body as he formulated his plan of attack.

198

"Right, here we go. Norther's tied up nicely, and with that woman straddling his face he won't see a thing. Thank God she's got her back to me."

The woman's identity was unknown to him, and he had yet to glimpse her face. Only her red hair and appalling physique could be made out in the weak light of the lamp. He did not know what prompted him to rush forward when he did, but clutching the sodden handkerchief and fighting the panic that threatened to overwhelm him he had sprung with a speed unknown even to himself.

In a mere moment he had reached the bed and grabbed the woman's head. She did not have time to turn around, but against her instinctive flinch he took hold of her neck and wrapped the handkerchief tightly around her face, pressing it down hard. He barely heard her mumbled cries as he waited for her to lose consciousness, but within seconds her body slackened and became limp.

As her arms fell to her sides he moved forward and steadied her. Below, Norther's movements were frantic. As soon as the don had sensed the struggle he had cried out, though the mountains of flesh bearing down on his face soon muffled his screams. James, holding the woman steady from behind, looked down over her shoulder and noticed with relief that Norther's movements were still constrained by the ropes. As he forced the weight of the woman down as hard as he could on Norther's face, he attempted to distract himself from the spasms that could be felt from below with the thought that at least suffocation did not involve blood. With his head encompassed by his escort's flabby nether-regions and his lungs deprived of air, Norther began to thrash with such violence, however, that James feared he would snap the straps. But they held firm. Clinging onto the woman's body and pressing down even harder, he made certain that Norther's head was buried fully beneath the mounds of flesh.

James could smell the woman's expensive perfume. Her hair, immense, frizzy and outrageously red, was pushed into his face, half obscuring his vision of the struggle below. He felt certain that she had not seen him. She could be spared. No need for another death tonight.

A minute passed, and Norther's desperate thrashings gave way to involuntary convulsions. Peering through the red foliage and over the woman's shoulder, James felt sickened but dared not look away. He had to make sure that Norther died or else the gods would seek retribution against him. Just one more minute.

Instinctively he began to count. Slowly, methodically he intoned aloud over the awful sound of leather being drawn tight and buckles clinking. As he reached twenty-three he noticed that the force of the spasmodic shudders was diminishing. Norther was beginning to die. One of the five people who had cast his life into such blackness was expiring on the bed before him.

As James looked on he found himself thinking back on his life, just as he expected the don would be doing as he lay struggling, failing to breathe. Casting his mind back across the years, he found his thoughts settling on his first classics lecture at Cambridge. Sitting in a cold, musty lecture-hall amongst two hundred young classicists ready to embark upon their degrees, he had observed Elliot Norther himself step forward to the podium and deliver those opening lines that now rang out in his head.

"Classics is the study of sex and death."

The audience had been instantly captivated, and an awed silence prevailed. Norther had proceeded to hold forth upon the virtues of the field and the offerings it held in store for those who dedicated themselves to it.

James looked down at the body flailing in asphyxiation upon the bed before casting his glance about the bedchamber. How many sordid acts had been performed in this room, with shelf after shelf lining the walls and each groaning under the weight of classical scholarship? How many hours had Norther spent with those books at the desk or even upon the bed itself, before his life, an existence dedicated to classics, was extinguished under the weight of his lover?

With every shudder that was cast upwards from the bed, James felt a pounding of adrenaline wrack his own body. There was a rhythm to the convulsions, a forceful urgency. As he steadied the unconscious woman in his arms he recalled the exhilarating climax of that first lecture, the moment that Norther recited from memory his favourite Latin expression, casting it out like a spell across the audience, challenging them to translate.

"*Pedicabo ego vos et irrumabo, Aureli pathice et cinaede Furi, qui me ex versiculis meis putastis, quod sunt molliculi, parum pudicum.*"

It was met with silence. Two hundred students cast stunned glances at their neighbours, though none dared the attempt.

Then a movement was heard near the back of the room, and all heads turned. A girl had risen and was making her way to the front. Climbing the steps, she stood before the podium and surveyed the audience. Her hair was outrageously red and her well-stuffed dress dropped heavy hints at the chubby frame contained within it. In the charged atmosphere of expectation she opened her mouth, cleared her throat and in deep-voiced, horsey tones delivered a translation.

Gasps filled the lecture hall. Such was the unadulterated filth of the verse that it left the audience agog. Her delivery was perfect, her eloquence cutting right through to the seedy heart of the poem, which cast the sexual licence of the students' twenty-first century upbringings in a distinctly Victorian aspect.

'Who is this girl?' was the question on everyone's lips, as the collective gasp gave way to thunderous applause and frenzied speculation.

"Thanks everyone. Awfully good of you," said the girl, turning red at the podium in response to the raucous acclaim. "I know we're all still getting to know one another, and I'm jolly excited to meet you all. My name's..."

"Margo Goyle!" cried James. "Oh my God, it's Margo Goyle!" Memory washed over him, and in shock he dropped her limp form. She slumped over Norther. The lecture's convulsions had ceased, and now his rapidly cooling corpse lay still on the bed, unresponsive as Margo's fat, lumpy frame fell upon him and her red hair splayed across his thighs and knees.

As James took a step forward his hands began to shake. He stepped round the bed to where Margo's head had slumped, and gently moved her face into view. It was definitely her, there was no doubt.

Suddenly he felt sick. She was not simply an anonymous prostitute but a former classicist in his year. He had known her, he had spoken to her. She would wink conspiratorially at him when they passed in the library. Now here she lay, naked upon the corpse of Elliot Norther. Every shred of dignity gone, robbed not only by her own actions but by James himself. He winced at the thought, and tears of shock and self-loathing pooled rapidly in his eyes. What had he done? He had to escape; the sudden urge to run away was overwhelming.

He bolted. Grabbing his bag, he sprinted out of the room and down the stairs. He would leave by the front door and he didn't care if anyone saw him. He careered through the hallway, slammed into the door and began fumbling with the handle. Just as he turned it to reveal the street beyond, he noticed a small black object lying on the welcome mat: a mobile phone. Without thinking, he picked it up, shoved it into his pocket and ran for his life through the empty streets of Newnham and towards the fields that led to Cambridge.

He did not stop to look back, he simply ran. His heartbeat was deafening in his ears, and he fell repeatedly in the darkness. Eventually, however, he reached his house. He tried vainly to stifle his gasps for breath as he opened the front door, though when he entered he could hold himself back no longer. He bolted upstairs to the bathroom and vomited.

*****

As James retched in his bathroom, Wendy Pipford picked herself up from the floor of her living room and walked over to her desk. She had just witnessed a murder. That evil bastard, James Connor, had strangled that poor prostitute before her very eyes, and was no doubt about to finish off the man on the bed.

She wiped her eyes, which were still streaming, sat down in her chair and began fidgeting with her trembling hands. Her instinct to call the police welled up again. What if she had dialled 999 when she saw James break into the house? Or when he entered the bedroom? Instead she had been happy to stand and indulge her journalistic bent. She winced as feelings of guilt turned her stomach in knots.

Now though, through the tears and the regret that threatened to overwhelm her, one thought rose to the surface of her mind.

"I've just got the biggest scoop The Clarion has ever had," she whispered to herself, even as salty moisture flowed over lips.

Another pang of guilt.

"Oh God I can't think like this!" she cried. "No. I've got to do the right thing, even if it's too late. I've got to call the police and tell them what just happened. They don't need to know how I know, I'll just leave an anonymous tip-off. I just need to make it right somehow."

Having resolved to do her civic duty, Wendy reached into her coat pocket for her mobile. Finding it empty, she searched the pockets of her trousers; then her bag; then her coat again.

Nothing.

Now her feelings of guilt turned to panic. Her phone was gone. She must have dropped it when she fled the house. In that case it would still be there, sitting in the middle of a crime scene. Not only was it full of her personal details, but it contained the film she had taken of the murder itself.

Wendy winced as she recalled the images on the phone, but let out a despairing gasp as the consequences of her actions dawned on her. She had watched a murder as it happened. She had been there at the time of the killing, and not only had she failed to call the police, but had filmed it whilst it took place.

If anyone found her phone, she would be inextricably linked to the crime, an accomplice in a savage act of murder.

She began to tremble violently. Moving from room to room, her movements became frenzied as she reeled at the force of her panic. She had messed it all up, everything. Why did she follow that psychopath into the house? And why the hell didn't she call the police like she knew she should have?

Suddenly images of prison flashed vividly into her mind. She slumped to the floor as she imagined her future laid bare before her, incarceration and gross negligence leaving her career in ruins, her dreams of journalism destroyed.

She was ruined.

As realisation chilled her, however, and she sat upon the cold floor of her kitchen, her tears ceased. So too, by degrees, her trembling gave way to calmness. As she stared into space and her emotions began to subside, she started to take stock. Wendy Pipford had always been an excellent stock-taker, having a resilient determination that was the wonder of all who had observed it.

Though her face was drained of colour and she felt weak, she picked herself up off the floor and walked into her living room. Resuming her place at her desk, she stared at the screen of her laptop and made a resolution.

"Wendy, you've done a bloody stupid thing today, and all in the name of journalism. If it comes back to bite you, as it probably will, then you've only yourself to blame. Until then you're going to keep your chin up, keep your mouth shut and carry on."

She looked at her watch. It was late, and the morning's newspapers had long since gone to print. She would simply have to wait until tomorrow to make her report. Focus and self-control were the key.

Wendy Pipford was damned if she was going to let a little criminal responsibility get in the way of her doing her job.

*****

Over in Newnham, Margo Goyle's eyes flickered open. With her mass of red hair piled on top of her face her field of vision was a blur.

"What on earth?" she mumbled.

Pressing forward with her hands, she began to hoist herself upright. Beneath her palms she felt a pair of male legs.

It came back to her: Elliot Norther, her client.

But had she fallen asleep? Surely not. Such a thing had never happened before, and was surely impossible.

What about Elliot Norther though? That, she thought to herself, was even less likely. She didn't charge the rates she did simply for clients to doze off in the middle of her performances. Her sex was far too significant for that. She

205

tapped him roughly on the leg, but there was no response. Her slaps to his upper thigh elicited no reaction either.

Confused, she eased herself up, and as she did so she found that she had been lying at a very odd angle. Her legs were tucked awkwardly underneath her.

She shifted her weight to move off of him entirely, and in doing so realised the precise location of his head.

As she rose up onto her knees, she looked down between her legs. There lay Elliot Norther's face. It was contorted and his eyes were still open. Deep red marks lined his neck, where it had made fierce contact with the leather straps. Dark blue tinged the tops of his lips, lending them a deathly hue.

"Oh God!" she whimpered in horror, instinctively reaching down and touching her stubbly groin. The dead, unseeing eyes of her client stared into her own, and panic overcame her.

"Mr Haberdasher, what have you done?!" she screamed. "Oh mercy God, Mr Haberdasher, what the fuck have you done?!"

CHAPTER SEVENTEEN

"CAMBRIDGE KILLER STRIKES AGAIN! SEX DEATH SCANDAL OF THE DECADE!" declared The Echo.

"LECTURER 'BITES OFF' MORE THAN HE CAN CHEW! WHAT NEXT IN THE BANQUET OF DEATH FOR CAMBRIDGE DONS?!" shouted The Reporter.

"SEX-FIEND CLASSICIST CHOKES ON 'MAIDEN'S MODESTY'! THIRD DEATH IN A WEEK!" screamed The Clarion.

In the grotty offices on St Andrew's Street, excitement had reached fever pitch. From the overflowing desk in his tip of an office, editor Dave Blithe was holding forth in a stream of rapid-fire meetings with his staff. Summoned to his lair one after the other, they ran the obstacle course to his desk, dodging the ancient PC that propped open his door, leaping over the undergrowth of wiring, and weaving through the mounds of old newspapers and memos.

The telephone had been pressed to his ear since he had arrived at work, and conversations were awkwardly divided between the disembodied voice at the end of the line and the staff member on the receiving end of his dictates.

"Simon!" he yelled at the young man who had dutifully appeared in front of his desk. "Contact the Old Bill again. Get them to confirm that statement, it's full of holes. What? No don't give me that, I told you to... Yeah, yeah. I said hold the tomato. Lots of salad cream, but no tomatoes whatsoever, got it? Jesus, what's so difficult about that? Do you want me to call the police myself or what? Get moving!"

Simon the journalist was less than entirely clear about what he was to do. Having been a member of staff on The Clarion for less than a year, he had yet to decipher the nuances of Dave Blithe's multitasking.

The editor winced as his phone conversation turned sour. He pressed the handset to his head with his shoulder and waved angrily at Simon, who had failed to notice the menu for Jeff's Bang-Up Bakery on the desk.

"Go on then, Simon! And send Wendy in after you! Yes *without* tomato! God, you call this service?"

Two minutes later Wendy appeared at the door.

"You wanted me, Dave?"

For the first time that morning the handset was replaced.

"Yes, Wendy. Come on in."

His voice was unreadable, making Wendy uncertain as to what mood she had caught him in. Of the two dozen people who had been called to his office since she had arrived for work, all had left in a state of excited nervousness, but no one had repeated their conversation with him.

"Sit down, Wendy," he said, gesturing to an old swivel chair with an arm missing.

She eased herself down, as much in fear of Blithe's notorious mood swings as of the chair itself.

"Now then, Wendy. Your headline on the latest murder.

"Yes, Dave?"

"It was great, and the article was top notch."

She breathed a sigh of relief, but could not relax. She sensed a caveat.

"But," he continued, pressing his hands together and furrowing his brow, "we didn't get the scoop, did we?"

"No, Dave. I got the same call as all the others. When I arrived on the scene every journo in town was on their way."

His expression did not change.

"I did get that juicy piece of info from my contact on the investigation team, though," she added quickly. "You know, that bit about exactly *how* Norther was asphyxiated?"

"So did The Reporter," Blithe muttered, unmoved.

"I know but, Dave, what was I supposed to do? I couldn't barge through the police cordon and start poking around? At least we got one up on The Echo."

Blithe sighed and rubbed his hand across his jaw.

"Yeah I know, Wendy. But this is the biggest story to break in Cambridge since... well, ever, and I need you to be on top form. Who knows whether this creep will strike again. If he doesn't then we've missed our last chance for a scoop. Like I said, you've done well up to now and I'm keeping you on the case. But I want a scoop. Even if you have to work miracles, I want a bloody scoop. I know Simon's been angling for a chance at your place on the murders." His gaze remained neutral as he spoke. "I talked to him just now, and we chewed this whole business over," he lied. "I told him that if you weren't up to working miracles then I'd give him a go. You've been warned."

Wendy felt pang of tension in her stomach.

"Okay, Dave. Don't worry, I won't let you down."

"Good. Now get out there and find me some dirt."

Wendy left the filthy office and fetched her coat. She had no choice but to strike out into town and fish for information. Reflecting on the meeting, she pondered on what she had told Blithe. As she had sat before him constructing the lie about not being able to report more on the murder, the horrific scene she had witnessed the night before did not enter her mind. She had almost believed what she had said. Now, walking down St Andrew's Street, she mulled over the issue of her mobile phone and its incriminating film. Surely if it had been left in the house the police would have found it and viewed the contents by now, in which case they would already have dragged her to the station.

Perhaps she had not dropped it at the scene at all, then. Perhaps it was lying in the fields between Cambridge and Newnham, or on the pavement of one of the streets she had run down on the way to her flat. Even if that were the case, a member of the public would likely find it and hand it in, and an official knock on the door would soon follow.

Despite the dire consequences that this would bring, and the hysteria that she had experienced the previous night, she did not feel panicked. For when she arrived back at the house, now cordoned off with police tape, and began to gather information from the officers present, an interesting fact had emerged: the young prostitute that James had appeared to attack had not died, but had survived unharmed. It turned out that she had only filmed the beginning of what would become a killing, and had not recorded the moment of the murder. A court, though, would have little truck with such niceties, and time in prison would be guaranteed nonetheless. Despite the prospect of criminal liability, however, her resolve was growing. She had made her vow to dismiss thoughts about her actions that night as fruitless worry and to get on with her life as best she could, and she was damned certain that silly, emotional behaviour was not the way forward. Murder was murder and if she had acted inappropriately in the heat of the moment then she would just have to buck up and get on with her life.

Amidst her new found calm at the possible consequences of filming the grittiest crime the town had ever seen, a single preoccupation filled her mind: the scoop. Though she could not reveal the details, juicy as they were, she alone knew the culprit. No one else was aware of James's identity, neither the police nor her rival journalists.

Wendy could hardly approach him as she had before, though. Even if he had seemed like a socially awkward dolt, it was now quite clear that he was in fact a hardened killer. By the time she had returned to her flat later that afternoon, however, she had decided her course of action. She would make contact with the brute, tell him that she knew everything and use the threat of informing the police to squeeze as much information from him as possible.

Blithe would have his scoop.

*****

Aphrodite's beautiful face was a picture of unmitigated glee. As the council exploded into thunderous applause, she could see from the jubilation on the face of every one of the Olympians that her stock was at an all-time high. Not even after her victory in the Judgment of Paris had she felt so elated. And the best of it was that this time there was no Hera to start a Trojan hissy fit. Since the Queen of the Gods had been expelled from the council neither she nor Athena had been seen or heard by any of the other gods.

Aphrodite looked across to Dionysos, who was also beaming.

"Soon," she mouthed subtly to the God of Wine, before turning to the crowd. "Gods and Goddesses, deities of the Earth, the seas and the great heavens of Olympus, hear me!" she cried. "Today is a great and glorious day, a testament to our divine power in this mortal realm. Elliot Norther, he who would dare to insult our glory, has been wiped out, his soul despatched in ignominy to the Hall of Hades!"

The cheering redoubled into an immense roar, its force sweeping the length of James's Hippocampus, deafening even to the assembled deities though unheard by the mortal himself, who was quietly eating a sandwich in his kitchen.

"Hail, Goddess!" cried Hebe, wife of the divine Herakles. "All glory to your cunning!"

"Glory to you, Goddess!" yelled Hephaestus, God of Craftsmanship.

"Aphrodite, we honour your greatness!" shouted Artemis, her frenzied clapping compromising her usually crisp and virginal demeanour.

The recipient of such praise could have stood listening to her magnificence being extolled for hours, but prudence required her to grasp the nettle. Though Hera was lying low for now, her absence would surely be only temporary, and strategic imperative required that this tactical advantage be capitalised.

"Now, my fellow deities. Pray be silent."

After a prolonged round of applause, the crowd eventually settled down to listen to the words of their new heroine, who smiled charmingly.

"Gods and Goddesses," she began. "Though our victory here has been glorious we must look to the future."

"*Respice finem*," nodded Mnemosyne, Goddess of Memory.

"Precisely so," concurred Aphrodite. "Let us take stock. Though we have one way or another managed to eliminate three of the five members of the Cambridge List, we still have two targets left to extinguish: the mortals known as Alan Tanning and Paul Fringe."

A collective murmur of hatred rippled across the crowd.

"Bastards," muttered Ares under his breath.

"Those filthy flesh-bags," Demeter whispered angrily to Hebe.

"And we must not rest on our laurels," continued Aphrodite. "Let us take this session of the council to determine their fate, striking whilst the iron's hot."

In the electrified atmosphere, approval for her proposal was unanimous. Almost.

Dionysos had other thoughts on his mind. Though he applauded with the others and raised a cheer at the appropriate junctures, he was waiting for his moment. As soon as Aphrodite declared her intention to proceed with the other murders, he pounced.

The Goddess of Desire stood basking in the roars of approval.

"Very well, deities of Olympus. If we are agreed that haste is best, then let us…"

212

"Stop, Aphrodite!" came a commanding voice. The gods and goddesses turned in surprise. Dionysos had seized the attention of the assembly. "As the Chairman of the council I decree that there is no basis for advancing the cause precipitously, and every reason for a cautioned approach."

"But Dionysos, what on earth are you…?" began Aphrodite, angry that a shadow should be cast over her warm glow of popular acclaim.

"No, Aphrodite. As Chair it's my responsibility to ensure that orderly proceedings are followed and that we do not endanger the mission by rushing through hasty decrees."

Mumblings of disappointment could now be heard. The deities had been whipped into a frenzy, and only the pursuit of revenge that Aphrodite offered would satisfy them. Amongst the Olympians anticlimaxes were treated with the greatest disdain.

The Goddess of Desire registered the mood with satisfaction, and turned to Dionysos smugly.

"Will you deny the masses what they want, Chairman?"

Dionysos, however, was not to be swayed.

"I couldn't possibly deny the masses what they want, Aphrodite, since the masses are not here in their entirety."

Aphrodite raised her eyebrows in suspicion. The God of Wine could be devious when required, and the tone of his voice urged caution.

"Meaning what?" she asked warily.

"Meaning that Hera and Athena are not present among us. Without them I hardly think it fair that major votes are taken."

"But they were cast out from the council. They can't just saunter back in as if nothing happened," retorted Aphrodite angrily.

"I think not. They were cast out for failing to acknowledge the primacy of the Chair. I believe it right that a period of time should be given for Hera to realise the error of her ways and return with an apology. We needn't rush through hasty decrees. Of course, if you were to declare your opposition to the Chair then you would suffer the same fate. Perhaps you two could swap places?"

Aphrodite narrowed her eyes as silent fury rose in her. It was not worth embroiling herself in a needless row in council, especially with one who was supposedly her ally. It was clear that Dionysos was pushing his desire to bed James, and that he was now willing to cause public complications for her if she obstructed him. Best, from a tactical perspective, to acquiesce if only for the sake of a smooth ride in the longer term. Her plans, after all, depended on Hera's absence.

"Very well, Dionysos," she declared with a show of earnest. "I agree that we should allow a brief adjournment in proceedings to give Hera a chance to change her mind and repent." Her voice was calm but inwardly she was livid. Groans could be heard from the assembly. They would be made to wait before the excitement resumed.

As the deities reluctantly made their way out of the hippocampus, Aphrodite held back. As the last of the gods departed, her calm demeanour shattered. She grabbed Dionysos by the arm and hissed in his ear.

"Don't make trouble for me, you little shit. If I think you're becoming a pest I'll knock you off your perch without a second thought."

"Don't worry, Aphrodite. You know what I want and as soon as I get it I'll be as good as gold. I promise."

At this she drew away from him slowly, looked into his eyes and addressed him in a cold, hateful voice.

"Then go forth and claim him, and I will have you at your word when you return."

*****

"Come on babe, just get on with it will ya?"

The Muse sighed and flicked back her greasy ponytail irritably. Sitting on the bed in the middle of James's clothes-strewn bedroom, she kicked her feet out in mounting frustration at his hesitancy.

"I know, I know I need to get it done. It's just that..." He trailed off as he flicked at the phone in his hand and replayed the video for what might have been the hundredth time since last night.

Arriving back at his flat after the killing, James had found the Muse waiting for him with a smile on her face.

"Well done, darling," she had said to him after he emerged from the bathroom, having thrown up.

"I managed it, I... I managed it Muesli," he had gasped.

She had laughed sweetly and drawn near to him.

"Yes you did, and I congratulate you on it... and on this."

She had reached into his pocket and withdrawn Wendy Pipford's mobile phone, deftly flicking to the recently recorded video and handing it to him.

Horror had gripped him as he watched it, and sickness welled up in him once again. Despite this, however, it had exercised a curious hold over him, and he had replayed it again and again until every moment was memorised. Now, at ten o'clock the next day, after countless tinny renditions of Wendy Pipford's muffled dash down the stairs and the clatter of the phone as it fell to the floor, the Muse's patience was wearing thin.

"How many more times do I have to explain it to you?" she asked, rolling her eyes.

James inhaled anxiously.

"I just... I know that I have to do it. I'm just still not sure why.

"I'm sorry mate, but I just don't think the chances of you successfully finishing off the last two dons are good without some help. In fact I think it's a dead cert that you'll balls it up."

"Well I managed this one just fine," he retorted.

The Muse grated her teeth.

"Yes darling, you did, and I congratulated you on it. But after Wildencrust you can't afford to slip up even one more time. They really will do you in if you don't get these next two killings picture perfect. It's not just an idle threat. And I can tell you exactly how, too."

She paused to observe fear silently freeze James's face.

"They'll flood the council Chamber. Which to you, of course, is the Hippocampus. They'll tear down the walls of the chamber in their rage and the whole place will be drowned in blood. In modern, medical terms that means they'll cause you a massive fucking brain haemorrhage. You'll be carried off to Hades' Hall before you know what's hit you."

"Shit," breathed James before shaking his head. "Okay I know what you say is true. I could do with all the help I can get. I mean, even you didn't know that circumstances would combine the way they did to fuck up the Wildencrust killing, did you?"

The Muse looked at him darkly.

"No, guess not," she muttered with irritation. "But I did know enough to make you speak to Pipford when she came knocking, and to make you rouse her suspicions about your dubious character. Not that you needed much help with that."

James nodded and slapped his hand on the desk decisively.

"Okay then, I'll do it. Right now. No more messing about."

"Good, finally."

"I think I've got the script covered."

"I should bloody well hope so, the number of times I had to explain it!"

216

"Look Muesli, I'm not an actor. I don't have a memory for things like that."

"Obviously. Just remember this: the exact words you use don't matter, as long as you sound threatening."

"Yes I see," said James uncertainly.

"It's easy, just summon up all your charisma and pour it down the phone line," said the Muse, gesticulating expressively.

"Charisma you say? Now, don't get me wrong, but if we're relying on my charisma are you sure that we're not absolutely screwed?"

She laughed and, to his surprise, leaned over and kissed him on the cheek.

"Of course not, babe," she said smiling. "I'm immortal, remember? The only one who might be 'absolutely screwed' is you."

"How could I forget," said James, rolling his eyes. "Okay then, let's just get this over with."

With a deep breath he picked up the phone again and scrolled through the address book until he found an entry labelled 'home.'

"Mean and threatening, mean and threatening, mean and threatening," he muttered to himself as he counted down the rings.

*****

Sitting in the living room of her flat, Wendy Pipford was deep in thought. Having dug out a copy of the telephone directory and discovered that James's house was not listed, she was slightly at a loss. How might she contact the brute without knowing his number and being quite unwilling to visit his home in person?

Perhaps the University would be willing to give her his number? She dismissed the thought at once. All her dealings with the University authorities had been painfully slow and almost invariably fruitless.

Was there anyone else she knew who might have some way of contacting him? With another shake of her head she cast away the idea. James was clearly a loner, and the thought of a third party acting as an intermediary was preposterous.

As she sat pondering the problem, solution after solution was proposed, examined and swiftly rejected. Without her mobile phone and its address book stuffed with the numbers of people who were adept at tracking, she was stuck. Annoyed, she cast an irritated glance at the bookshelf, in the recesses of which lay her diary, a thick, leather volume with copious room for names and contact details. It had been an expensive present from an ex-boyfriend, and every page remained blank. How un-twenty-first century of him, she had thought when presented with it. What a caveman.

As she grated at the irony, she realised that she was becoming distracted, and angrily shook herself back into her train of thought. How the hell was she to get in touch with him? And what kind of a journalist was she if she wasn't even up to such a simple task?

Self doubt, though, had no place in her mind, and she reassured herself that if James was the cold, calculating killer that he seemed to be then pinning him down would be difficult for even the most accomplished investigator. After all, it seemed that he had thus far evaded the attention of the police, who were devoting all of their resources to catching the murderer.

With this thought she allowed herself to relax slightly. She was clearly up against the most sophisticated serial killer the town had ever seen; one who was doubtless ten steps ahead in the game and who would stop at nothing to remain hidden from prying eyes. Such was his confidence in his own abilities that he had allowed her to interview him in his own home. It would clearly take every ounce of her skill as an investigative journalist to trap him.

Suddenly her house phone rang.

She walked into the hall and lifted the receiver.

"Hello?"

"Hello," said a man's voice.

There was an awkward pause.

"Hello?" said Wendy again. "Do you have the right number?"

"Oh definitely. At least I think I do. Is this Wendy?"

"Yes."

"Wendy Pipford?"

"Yes, who is this?" asked Wendy. The voice sounded vaguely familiar, and she mentally ran through the men in the office, trying to identify it.

"Right... *Miss* Wendy Pipford?"

"Stop stalling!" came a faint female voice in the background.

"Who the hell is this? Is that you, Rick? Is that Sandra with you?" Wendy was about to slam the phone down.

"No, no it's me, James."

The penny dropped and Wendy Pipford froze. Now she recognised his voice. It was him. He had actually called her. He knew her house number. Was she his next victim? She had clearly underestimated him. He was more calculating than she had imagined.

"What the... What the hell do you want?" she tried to remain calm.

"I just wanted to phone you to let you know that... Well if I'm being frank, the reason is that there's a matter of particular import that you and I need to... Ooof!"

Wendy jumped. It sounded as if someone had elbowed him in the ribs, and the slightly pained tone of voice that followed seemed to lend weight to her suspicion.

"Okay, right, I've got your phone."

219

For a moment Wendy did not speak as her confusion mounted.

"You've got my phone? What do you…? Oh God, My Phone! You've got my mobile phone!"

"Yeah, you dropped it on your way out," said James. His voice now contained a note of confidence, and as he continued it rose in volume, becoming increasingly threatening. "You know you really should be more careful when you sneak up on people. Perhaps I should have finished you off as I did Norther. Maybe next time I see you I'll…"

"Shut up you little runt!" snarled Wendy. "I'll finish *you* off when I see you! I'll tear you limb from limb!" Her fear had gone, instantly swept away by rage.

"But I… Oh sorry, I was just trying to…"

"To scare me? Was that it? Try harder you little dimwit!"

"Hang on though, I'm a serial killer. Aren't you scared?"

"Too right I'm not! But you will be when I wrap my hands around your throat!"

"Oh, but I…"

"Shut up! I've been worried sick all this time and then you call telling me you've got it? I'll kill you!"

"But… Well… Okay, but bear in mind that I've got a certain little film of yours."

"You can take your film and shove it up your…" Suddenly she stopped short. "What did you say?"

Now James's confidence was renewed.

"That's right, Wendy," he replied smugly, sensing the fact that despite her anger she had realised the implications of the situation. "I've got the video. It's fascinating, it really is. Although I think the police might be more interested than I am."

Panic washed over her.

"You can't be serious! That video shows you initiating a murder. You'd have to be brain dead to hand it in to the police!"

"Actually it shows an unidentifiable man in a dark room. The only identifiable person other than the girl and the victim is you, the person holding the camera."

"But... But, they'll know I didn't do it," she cried desperately. "My DNA. It's nowhere on the body."

"You still filmed it. What's a jury going to think?"

Wendy began to shake. Even in her worst-case scenario she hadn't imagined this.

"What do you want?" she asked, her voice trembling.

"To put it bluntly there's going to be another killing and I want your help."

"You want..."

"Your help, Wendy.

Tears began to stream down her face.

"You want me to help you kill another person? Are you out of your mind? You're sick! You're absolutely sick! I'm not doing that. Give the phone to the police if you want, you sick freak!"

James's tone was calm.

"I thought you might say that, so you've got three hours to decide. Let me know within three hours if you're on board or the police will be knocking on your door. Your choice."

"You've got my answer right now, you freak. You can get lost!" She was sobbing furiously, and her voice was unrecognisable even to herself.

But James was not to be moved.

"Give yourself some time to decide. If I don't hear from you by three o'clock I'll hand it in."

"Wait!"

But Wendy's plea was made into the ether, as the dialling tone rang in her ear.

*****

Paul Fringe stalked through the Classics Faculty with a fearsome gait. Since news broke that a third member of his inner circle had been murdered, his mood had been black. The little creatures who populated the building over which he ruled were ill advised to cross his path today. The show of pleasantness he had adopted at the staff meeting after the death of Wildencrust had proven momentary. The Classics Outreach Fund, the final hurdle before his dream of becoming Vice Chancellor of the University could be realised, was days from completion, and the pressure was mounting. There was no time left for exchanging pleasantries with the underlings.

As he walked through the dark corridors of the Faculty Fringe reflected angrily on this new turn of events. Now that Norther had idiotically managed to get himself murdered whilst *in flagrante delicto* with a brazen hussy, it would fall upon Alan Tanning to push through the final round of paperwork by himself. The urgency of the situation would have to be brought to bear on the Senior Lecturer in Roman Wall Painting. If he didn't pull out all the stops to have the Outreach Fund finalised and the money ready for transfer to Sir Malcolm soon, Fringe's dreams would lie in ruins. Without that final payment, the last and greatest gesture of loyalty, the ambassador would not hesitate to express his displeasure in the most ruthless manner. Fringe had seen it happen before. There was no doubt in his mind that if the ambassador had not received his payment within the next three days, he would drop Fringe like a hot stone and throw his weight behind some other candidate.

The ruler of the Classics Faculty felt his blood pressure rise as he contemplated the fact that all his hopes now rested with Alan Tanning. Norther might have been just as much a philandering moron, but at least two blithering idiots could divide the workload between them. If Fringe had possessed even the slightest inclination towards financial paperwork he would have undertaken the task himself rather than delegate it to lesser mortals. Still, if there was one thing he had learnt during his slippery ascent of Cambridge's greasy pole, it was that the more aggressively one's underlings were bullied, the more effectively they performed.

A brief visit to Tanning's office to deliver a dose of gut-wrenching intimidation would have been just the thing to hurry the dolt along, and would surely have been a tonic to Fringe's mounting blood pressure. Upon bursting, unannounced, into Tanning's den, however, he had found it empty. A brief glance at the desk, with its papers untouched and the paper calendar still displaying yesterday's date, had told of an occupant yet to sit down to his work. It was midday, and Tanning had no lectures scheduled. Fringe knew this because in the past two weeks he had successively relieved his minions of their teaching duties, the better that they might focus their efforts on the Outreach Fund.

As he slammed the door and the noise echoed down the hallway, he growled inwardly, and set about finding the wretch. Skiving was akin to the sin whose appearance would not be tolerated at any cost: disobedience.

Thus far the corridors of the Faculty had been empty. Students did not venture into this part of the building as it housed only staff offices, and since the news of Norther's murder had broken, most of the non-essential staff had remained at home. Fringe's brisk pace increased, the sound of his footsteps rebounding off the walls.

Suddenly a female figure could be seen ahead, at the end of the hall. Fringe squinted but could not make out her identity. With his predatory instincts piqued, however, he strode ahead, ready to intercept. Within a few steps he had identified her. Though she was still too distant for her face to be visible, by her denim kaftan, orange leggings and lurid green shoes he readily placed her as Dr Glynys Leverton.

The toothy Roman historian was famous amongst staff and students alike for both her scatterbrained timidity and her appalling taste in clothes. It was widely speculated that the former disposition explained the latter, and that her shocking ensembles acted as a defence mechanism, much like that of a forest beetle whose violently colourful shell dissuades hungry lizards from making a meal of it.

If this was her intention, however, today her impressive visage failed to live up to the task. Realising that the Faculty's top predator was almost upon her, Glynys Leverton issued a squeal. Caught in the beam of his terrible gaze, she was too slow to escape, and stood rooted to the spot.

"Good morrow to you, Professor Fringe," she mumbled nervously, clumsily offering him a half curtsey.

Fringe screwed his face up in distaste at her hideous get up. Stepping in close, he loomed over her. When he spoke, his voice was threateningly subdued.

"Leverton, what the hell were you thinking when you decided to come to work today dressed like that?"

"Oh I... Well, Professor Fringe, I suppose I wasn't really thinking about my attire so much as the tragic news that..."

"The tragic news that Farmer Brown has decided to employ a less hideous scarecrow to frighten the birds from his cornfield?" he spat sarcastically.

Glynys went pale, averted her eyes and mumbled subserviently. After enjoying her pained stammering for a few moments, Fringe leaned down and spoke into her ear.

"Tell me, scarecrow, have you seen Alan Tanning? I can't help but notice that his office hasn't been occupied today.

"Oh, I... That is to say I thought that..." she murmured. Her fear of Fringe was such that she could hardly form words to articulate her thoughts.

"Speak!"

"I... I saw him earlier I believe," she jabbered. "Yes... Yes I'm certain I saw him in..."

"Where?"

"In the stationery cupboard."

Upon hearing this, Fringe terminated the conversation by abruptly turning and sweeping down the corridor at an even brisker pace than before, leaving Glynys to scurry away, thankful that her encounter with the predator had been so brief.

Within moments he had reached his destination, and flung open the cupboard door. There, sure enough, sitting cross-legged on the floor was Tanning. At the sound of the intrusion he looked up, startled and betraying a red, puffy face fresh with tears.

"Professor Fringe?"

"What the hell do you think you're doing here?" asked Fringe, quietly and with menace.

"I just... I can't do this, Professor Fringe. First Harriet, then Penton and now Elliot. What's going on? It's as though we're being picked off one at a time." The tears continued to flow down his face as he looked pleadingly up at his master. "I don't think I can go through with it anymore."

Fringe stepped inside and gently closed the door. Kneeling down slowly, his movements were careful and deliberate. He smiled and placed a hand on Tanning's shoulder, addressing him in a gentle and forgiving voice.

"Now, now, Tanning old boy. There's no need for all that. Come on, let's get up off the floor and we'll talk it all through, shall we?"

He raised himself up and leant down to offer his hand.

Tanning was visibly surprised at this show of affection and responded by smiling feebly, grasping Fringe's hand and tenderly hoisting himself up.

"There now, Tanning. Let's sort this out shall we?"

A sniffling nod was the response.

"You're feeling a little upset, aren't you? Well let me show you just how to deal with it," said Fringe softly. He then raised his hand into the air and brought it down with an almighty smack into the side of Tanning's face.

Tanning flinched and cried out.

"What on earth? What do you..."

"Shut up you little runt!" snarled Fringe, grabbing Tanning by the collar and drawing him to within millimetres of his face. "Now pull yourself together and listen to me. The others are dead. Dead. It doesn't matter who killed them, or how, or why. All you need to know is that you're the only one left who can complete work on the Fund and you've got three days to do so. I don't care about your bloody feelings. All I know is that if you don't get right round to that office of yours and resume work I'll kill you myself! And if I hear the words 'I can't go through with it' even once more I'll rip your throat out! Understand?"

With every word the volume and shrillness of his voice increased, and his eyes were wild and unblinking. Tanning shrank back in terror.

"But Professor Fringe, I..."

Fringe's hand slammed into his face again.

"Understand!?"

Tanning spluttered at the raw pain that spread through his cheek.

"Please, Professor..."

Another smack, harder this time, and Tanning's head was jolted to one side.

"Do you understand?!"

"Yes, yes... Please Professor Fringe, I'll... I'll do it! I'll do it at once!"

"Good. Then get to it."

With this, Fringe released his grip on Tanning's collar and instead grabbed his ear. He then proceeded to kick open the door and drag the hapless lecturer squealing to his office.

Upon entering, Fringe threw his minion to the floor and strode over to the door, before turning and uttering a last threatening reminder.

"Three days, Tanning. Three days is all you have to make it happen. If you fail I'll make sure you're dead anyway."

*****

That afternoon the skies closed in, and as they did so a cold wind blew gently across the Fens and through the little city of Cambridge. It has travelled this vacant land since long before the spires of churches and the turrets of towers pierced the vast East Anglian Sky. The wind, though, did not bring with it droplets of rain. Instead it meandered feebly through the spokes of bicycles and skimmed gently the surface of the river. There was precious little to nourish it today.

Then, as all the clocks in Cambridge struck three and the bells pealed out across the town, something changed. Suddenly, after three hours of chilly calm a piece of dangerous gossip was thrown to the wind, and it grew strong. Whipping up into a ferocious squall, it blew hard. For at precisely three o'clock in a house on Jesus Green, a certain young man, having heard nothing from a certain young lady, and fearful that she had revealed his secret, released a certain recording onto the internet. Thrown into the ether, the video was snatched by the wind, which now blew hard all through the town. Onwards it travelled, casting itself out into the open countryside, gathering force and whipping into a fierce tempest. Soon it reached that vast metropolis on the horizon, the fulcrum of humanity whose name is known even to the wind itself: London. There it scattered the video across every household and every workplace, pouring it into every computer and every mobile phone, and electrifying all who watched it.

At 4:00pm the storm broke. The national media, in their vast convoys hastily packed with reporters and newsreaders, television crews and producers, descended on the little city of Cambridge. The national press had taken only a passing interest in the spate of deaths that had occurred in this quiet corner of East Anglia. A combination of major news developing in the Middle East and the relatively small amount of information released by the Cambridgeshire Constabulary had combined to relegate the murders to the middle pages. Now an anonymous video of a man attacking a woman in the prelude to a third murder had been posted onto a website that contained only the words 'Elliot Norther,' and within minutes it had gone viral. Editors, unable to take their eyes from their screens, salivated at the mystery of the person who had posted it up. Was it the same person that had recorded it? Why had it been filmed on a mobile? Was there more to come? Few had been able to contain their excitement as they stopped the presses and dispatched squadrons of their finest journalists to the Fens.

*****

Sitting in her living room, Wendy Pipford checked her watch again.

4:00pm.

She was an hour over James's deadline, and anxiety was beginning to get the better of her. Many times she had walked determinedly out into the hall, lifted the receiver on her phone and prepared to dial the police. Every time, however, fear had overwhelmed her. She could no more bear the thought of explaining her presence at a murder scene now than she had been able to before, and images of prison had burned themselves into her mind.

Her last attempt to conquer her terror had been at 2:59pm, spurred by the thought that it was her final chance to

228

act of her own accord. Now, an hour later, she had given up attempting to muster courage, and had decided to wait and see what fate would bring.

Picking up the remote control that lay next to her, she switched on the television. She had grown tired of constantly checking her watch, and any relief that could be found in background noise was to be welcomed.

Flicking through the channels, Wendy was greeted by the usual array of mid-week, mid-afternoon pap. After quickly dismissing two home renovation programmes, a gardening show and a lengthy advert asking if she had been injured at work and needed lawyers on a no-win-no-fee basis, she settled for a game show in which contestants purchased items at car-boot sales and sold them at provincial auction houses.

She lay back and watched. Minute after minute ticked by, though the inane programme provided her with little relief. Somehow she could not share in the ecstasy of discovering a dented, early twentieth-century frying pan at a stall in a field near Scunthorpe, nor in the thrill of doubling its price at auction to £2.50. For the first time since receiving James's phone call she closed her eyes, allowing the vulgar tones of the show's insidious antiques expert to pass over her unheard.

Suddenly the excited chatter exchanged between Pauline and Stacey from the blue team was terminated by the sound of the familiar news gong, and the measured tones of Caroline Hamilton, the BBC newsreader.

"We interrupt this broadcast to bring you breaking news. A recent murder in Cambridge has triggered national interest after a video, taken on a mobile phone minutes before the killing, has been released on the internet."

Wendy sat bolt upright and hurriedly turned up the volume on the television.

"Elliot Norther, a classics lecturer at Cambridge University, was killed at home yesterday evening during an encounter with a sex worker, in an attack that police have called 'callous and unprovoked.' The woman, who is not a suspect and whose identity has not been revealed, has been taken into police protection. The video shows a male attacking the woman whilst she is engaged in sexual activity with Dr Norther. It does not show the murder itself, though this is believed by police to have taken place just minutes later. The woman remembers nothing of the incident and is understood to have been drugged. The video itself is too graphic to be broadcast, though it can be found on our website. The killing is the third to have taken place in Cambridge during the last…"

The remote control slipped from Wendy's hand and the blood drained from her face. Barely aware of her movements, she rose from the chair, stumbled to her desk and punched in the web address for BBC News. Immediately a link to the video appeared, accompanied by a warning of graphic content. As she watched James leap out from the side of the shot and heard her own recorded gasp, she felt numb.

"Oh Jesus Christ. Oh God Almighty," she said to herself as she began to tremble. Every ounce of fear and anxiety she had felt since yesterday returned to her, sweeping through her body.

What had he done? This was worse than going to the police, worse than the threat of investigation. He had exposed her video to the world, and in so doing had dragged her into the savage and fickle consciousness of the British media.

As adrenaline surged, she began to feel her heart pounding in her ears. Amidst the terror that gripped her, a cold fury rose up and began to claw at her. She had to speak to him, to shout at him. She had to know why he had done it and when he would present her with the first opportunity to tear him limb from limb.

Leaping from the chair she rushed to the phone and dialled her own mobile number. After a mere two rings it was answered by the man himself.

"Oh hello Wendy, I see you've been watching the..."

"Shut up! Just shut your mouth you little toad!" she roared. "What the hell did you think you were doing releasing that video? Tell me what the hell you hoped to achieve by doing that?"

"It's quite simple, Wendy. Now if you go to the police, you go to the nation. Or rather the nation's faithful mouthpiece, the media. But then you should be on good terms with them, shouldn't you, being a journalist yourself?" James's voice was calm. This time he was not riled by her outburst.

There was little in the way of sensible counterargument that she could make against this, for she knew it to be true. If she claimed ownership of the phone, the story would be plastered across every newspaper and news channel in the country. Her rage became all the worse for the fact that he was right.

"I'll... I'll kill you, you scumbag!" she ranted.

"Look, Wendy," he replied almost consolingly. "It's not as bad as all that. Remember it's all anonymous, no one can make any connection between you and the video. And they never need to, either. All you need to do to ensure that is to agree to help me with another couple of killings. How hard is that?"

"Never!" she screamed. "Go to hell."

James could be heard sighing down the line.

"Look Wendy, it's nothing personal. I just need to get this done. And despite what I said before, you don't need to make up your mind right now. I'll give you a little time, and I'm sure you'll come to the right decision."

The dialling tone sounded in her ear as the grizzly details of Norther's death were recounted in measured tones from the living room.

*****

231

Midsummer Common is a broad stretch of public land lying in the shadow of the college after which it is named. Every year it is host to such festivities as the fireworks display on Bonfire Night, the circuses that occasionally come to town and other sundry events. By day it is a peaceful place, where cows can be found relaxing on the grass and dogs may be seen running across its broad, open stretches. Of all the regular occupants of the common there is one who may be seen at precisely the same time seven days of the week: the Prime Turkey of Midsummer College.

Each day at 4:30pm Martin Wetherblaine would come gobbling from the porters' lodge and strut about the length of the common, in a walk that had long comprised his afternoon constitutional. This ritual was sacrosanct to Wethers, as indeed were all the many rituals that dictated the rhythms of his life. After taking afternoon tea at 4.05pm precisely, which would unfailingly consist of a milky cup of Assam and one and a half Digestives, he would rise from his porterly chair and proceed on his promenade. With his head forward and his finest scowl assumed, he would advance at a brisk pace with his bony hands clasped firmly behind his back (only to be unclasped once the constitutional was complete, or if a student required telling-off and a pointed finger were needed for extra emphasis).

Today, as he rounded the corner that led from the lodge to the common, Wetherblaine breathed in the crisp air with a sense of supreme self-assurance. Only two days ago he had featured on the front page of The Cambridge Clarion, being dubbed 'the Hero Porter' alongside a dramatic account of his discovery of Wildencrust's body. This had been a boon to what was already an immense ego, and since the issue had gone to press he had been more than usually insufferable. The fact that he had now been swept from the news by the death of Norther mattered not a jot to his sense of well-being. For this had been reinforced each morning since the issue had gone to press by the many copies that now lay scattered about his house, and which he re-read each day in lieu of the morning paper.

Turning onto the common, and clucking as he did so at his greatness, he was suddenly stopped in his tracks by a most unexpected sight. There, scattered across the grass was a positive regiment of trucks, tents and temporary platforms. Lying in between each of these monstrosities was equipment of all kinds: wiring, chairs, lights and heaven knows what else. What on earth could all this be? And who the devil were all these people in suits milling about and shouting instructions to each other?

Outrage instantly ruffled Wethers' plume, and he gobbled indignantly. Though Midsummer Common was public land, the fact that it was next to his college meant that *de facto* it belonged to him. Woe betide any group of hippies who dared to make use of it without his knowledge.

He marched into the middle of the scrum and looked about him for someone to become pompous at. People didn't seem to be taking much notice of him. It appeared that they were all too engrossed in their own work, whatever that was, to register his presence. Had they no idea who he was? It seemed very unlikely that none of them had seen his picture in the local paper.

Suddenly an expensively dressed man in shirtsleeves and a look of high agitation approached.

"Excuse me sir, we're trying to set up some sound equipment and we do ask that members of the pubic try to steer clear."

"And just who do you think you're talking to, young man?" asked Wethers, shrilly.

"I'm awfully sorry, but we've got a broadcast to do in less than fifteen minutes and we really need to get…"

"And what is your name, young man?" Wethers interrupted.

"What? My name's Paul."

"And are you a mature student? Which college are you with? I'll have you reported to the dean, that's what I'll do. All this commotion on the common."

Paul looked slightly taken aback.

"No sir, I'm not a student. I'm an assistant producer. We're the BBC. We're here to cover the story of the serial killer. Now if I might ask you to make a little room…"

"The BBC? Assistant producer?" clucked Wethers in surprise. "You mean you're the media?"

"Yes sir, that's right," sighed Paul, whose patience was beginning to fray. These provincial towns were the worst for filming with members of the public lurking around. Why couldn't the story have broken in London, where no one gives a damn about film crews?

"Well then, young man, I'm just the official you need to speak to!"

"Look sir…" sighed Paul, who heard the same thing from every member of the public who strayed into the midst of a set-up.

"Oh I really am, young man. I can assure you."

"And why would that be?"

"Because I've been personally involved in the case myself. I discovered the body of Wildencrust, who was murdered only days ago."

At this, Wetherblaine produced from his pocket a copy of the front page of The Clarion, bearing an image of his grisly face glaring into the camera. He handed it to Paul, who looked at it with surprise.

"You mean this is you?"

"It certainly is, young man," said Wethers, beaming.

Paul was most interested.

"Come with me."

*****

As Wendy Pipford's eyes flickered open she realised that she had been asleep. Glancing at her watch and noting that an hour had passed since her conversation with James, she rose from the sofa and stretched. She ached all over, and the inside of her head felt like it had been lacerated. Her skull still buzzed, and as memories of the last few hours rose in her mind once again, she clenched her fists and forced them back down.

She rose and rubbed her eyes. Despite the rawness of events, she found that her nap had done her good. With some relief she realised that she no longer felt overwhelmed, and a peculiar sense of equilibrium prevailed. She would try to hold on to this for as long as she could.

Walking into the hall, she glanced at her phone and saw the answering machine indicating a new message.

She swallowed, and closed her eyes as she pressed the replay button.

"Alright Wendy, it's Dave," came the gruff voice of her editor. She exhaled with relief. "I'm just phoning to say that you've got a new mobile here waiting for you. Do us a favour and try not to flush this one down the toilet."

She smiled as she deleted the message. A new phone, a sign of normal life continuing. Who could say how long it would last, but at least it was better than a call from the police. Perhaps it was best to pick up where she had left off and resume her policy of 'carry on as normal?' Perhaps getting back to work and leaving events to play themselves out without attempting to interfere was the wisest policy?

Wendy nodded to herself, and decided that the only resolution a sensible girl like her could make was to buck up and get on with things. If that creep wanted to make trouble for her by calling the police, he'd be cutting his nose to spite

235

his face. Surely he knew she'd give a full account of who and what she saw if she was dragged down to the station? Anyway, it was best not to dwell on the internal machinations of a sociopath. She would continue her course of normal life for as long as it lasted and let fate play out as it might.

With her determination set, she turned her mind to her job and to the media circus that had arrived in town. The television was still on in the living room, and it seemed that the reporters had been broadcasting continuously on every channel since their arrival. Wendy could not help but think about the convoy parked on Midsummer Common, and as she did so a sense of envy rose in her. She should have been out there amongst the broadsheet journalists and correspondents. Instead she was one of the local hacks whom those from the national papers sneeringly looked down on. Now she would be reminded of her unfulfilled aspirations for as long as the story was dragged out. And dragged out she knew it would be. For had James not said that there would be another killing? She chafed at the fact that she, with more inside knowledge than any of those high-flying career journalists on the common, not to mention the police, was relegated to the position of lowly new-girl at The Clarion.

Suddenly the phone rang, interrupting her train of thought and making her jump. She could not help but feel a tinge of fear. After a few moments, however, she reaffirmed her decision that the pretence of normality should take precedence, and tentatively lifted the receiver.

"Hello?"

The voice on the other end of the phone was that of a woman. She spoke with a refined accent, with warm tones but the firm suggestion that her intention was business.

"Hello, am I speaking to Ms Wendy Pipford?"

"Yes, speaking."

"Hello Ms Pipford, my name is Margaret Hunter. I'm the Managing Director at Core News Inc."

"I see," said Wendy, unable to conceal her surprise. She had never heard of Core News, but a call from someone in the news industry was a pleasant novelty. "How can I help you?"

Margaret Hunter explained that Core News was a new online venture being established by a consortium of business leaders based in London. Yet to go live, it was intended as a high-quality news outlet set in competition with the national broadsheets. Miss Hunter had been working to create a team of correspondents, and was particularly interested in young talent. It was the company's aim that the body of journalists should be divided equally between men and women.

When Wendy heard the words 'on the lookout for new, young talent' her heart raced. When she heard that her name had been shortlisted as a potential candidate for East of England correspondent she almost leapt for joy. What could she do to secure her place?

Well, explained Margaret Hunter, the reason that she had been chosen as a potential candidate for the job was her impressive reporting on the Wildencrust murder, which the team at Core News, unlike most of the media up until now, had been following with interest. If she could produce reporting that was as effective as that then she would be placed at the top of the list.

Wendy excitedly reassured her that she was more than up to such a task, which consisted merely of maintaining the high standard to which she always held herself.

That was all well and good, said Margaret Hunter, though things were not as simple as that. The Core News website was to go live very soon, and correspondents had to be selected within the next two weeks. That meant, in effect, that successful members of the shortlist would be selected on the basis of scoops that they achieved within the next few days. If Wendy could deliver a knock-out exclusive in that time then, given the calibre of her previous work, she would be guaranteed the place. If not then it would almost certainly go to one of the other candidates, all of whom were of outstanding ability.

Wendy could scarcely believe her ears. Here she was being offered her dream job, a sure stepping-stone to the career she had always longed for. All she had to do was deliver a scoop. Who cares how she did it, she would think of something.

She breathlessly accepted the offer and profusely thanked Margaret Hunter for her interest. As she replaced the receiver she could scarcely keep her balance for the giddy rush of joy. Now all she had to do was find a way to guarantee a scoop. Everything rode on it.

*****

Having said goodbye and good luck to the ecstatic Wendy Pipford, Margaret Hunter put the phone down and turned to her colleague. Rolling back her shoulders and letting out a little sigh, she smiled at him.

"We done it, babe. I told you all this would be worth it."

"You mean she bought it? Oh Muesli, you're brilliant!" said James, with delight.

CHAPTER EIGHTEEN

Nearly twenty minutes passed, and James and the Muse sat in silence, he in mild anxiety and she in a calm furnished by long experience.

Suddenly, from his desk Wendy Pipford's mobile phone rang.

"Hello?"

"Hello, James, it's Wendy."

"What a pleasant surprise."

"Spare me the false courtesy. I'm not going to have a long, drawn-out conversation about this or anything. You know you said you were going to kill again soon?"

"Yes."

"How soon will that be, exactly?"

James glanced at the Muse, who mouthed a guess.

"Let's say tomorrow evening," he said.

"Great. I'm in," said Wendy without hesitation.

"Wonderful. Meet me this afternoon. My place."

"Done."

CHAPTER NINETEEN

Sitting at his desk in his room, James was in a self-congratulatory mood. Having slain Elliot Norther and brought Wendy Pipford on side for the next killing, and both within the space of forty-eight hours, he was feeling rather pleased with himself. Now all that remained was to receive his orders for the next murder, and until then he might consider his time his own.

Leaning back on his chair he grabbed the remote control and flicked on the small television that sat on his window sill. The media scrum that had descended on the town had not escaped his notice, and he had taken more than a passing interest in the continuous stream of news reports regarding his handiwork. Margo Goyle's police-sanctioned anonymity, the subject of frantic discussion, had yet to be breached, though it was surely only a matter of time before an enterprising investigator struck lucky.

Currently being shown, to James's mild surprise, was an interview with the Head Porter of Midsummer College, which was being shot on location on the common. The detestable creature was being questioned about his thoughts on the latest murder by one of the Corporation's most seasoned field journalists, Marion Carlton, a distinguished woman of at least fifty-five whom Wetherblain insisted on addressing as 'young lady.'

James cringed as he watched the spectacle unfold.

"So Mr Wetherblaine, tell us your thoughts on the latest killing."

"I think it's utterly appalling," clucked Wethers. "An indictment against our society, and strong evidence of the laxity in modern values. If people were able to control their urges there would be far less suffering in the world. Yes, in my day if a man had strong sexual desires he'd simply spend

240

an hour or two reading Whittaker's Almanac. That'd sort him out, let me tell you. I've not the slightest doubt that if Elliot Norther had shown prudence, instead of engaging in disgraceful behaviour, he'd still be alive today."

Marion Carlton had been patiently nodding, though with visible perplexity. What on earth was this man prattling on about?

"Do you mean that Elliot Norther was murdered because of his relationship with the sex worker?" she asked, attempting to find some strain of rationality in Wetherblaine's hypothesis.

"Well in a manner of speaking, yes," came the drawled response. "Elliot Norther was clearly a sexual profligate, and as a result of that he was killed. Now, I believe that like comes to like, and that when one moves in Cambridge's sordid underworld, seeking the most vulgar pleasure from the most deranged souls, one places oneself in the company of such unbalanced people as thieves and killers."

"If you'll pardon my saying so, that hardly seems like a fitting analysis of…"

"Silence young lady," said Wetherblaine, closing his eyes and calmly raising his hand. "I'll have you know that before I became Head Porter of Midsummer I was with the Cambridgeshire Constabulary. I know all about the criminal mind, and I would advise you to defer to my expert opinion."

At the sight of Wetherblaine's hand and the condescending note in his voice, Marion Carlton's cheeks reddened.

"I'll have *you* know, Mr Wetherblaine," she said with a calm composure that belied furious indignation, "that formerly I was chief political correspondent with the Financial Times. I'm quite familiar with the process of reasoned analysis, I can assure you."

"I'm not talking about 'who's top of the pops,' or 'who's the latest heart-throb at the cinema,' or whatever your line of work is," gobbled Wethers. "My mind is used to

241

dealing with more important things, and my judgment on such matters as this is absolutely to be relied upon. Just ask your husband, he'll tell you that I'm right. Men are always right when it comes to the big questions in life."

Marion Carlton could hardly prevent herself from trembling with fury. Never had she encountered an interviewee so stridently willing to express views of such staggering chauvinism.

"Now look here," she said, with rather more feeling that she had wished to show.

"Hold on a moment, my dear, I'm not finished yet," said Wetherblaine, calmly raising the hand once again. "I think you'll find that a few words on the benefits of staunch moral cogency will be most nourishing for your viewers. Yes, most nourishing indeed."

James chuckled as he watched Marion Carlton desperately attempting to terminate the disastrous interview, battling against the combined might of Wetherblaine's infinite wisdom and the frequent appearances of the hand.

Suddenly a tone from his computer indicated an email.

"Isn't it a relief now that she's gone?" it said.

James read it with confusion. The sender's name was not listed. It was as if it had come from nowhere. As he scrutinised the page another tone indicated an email.

"I'm glad she was cast out. Let's hope it's permanent."

This was also anonymous, and was immediately followed by another.

"I finally feel free after all this time!"

Suddenly his phone beeped and a text message appeared on the screen.

"At last. I've never felt so free."

As he read, more beeps rang out from both phone and laptop, and a flurry of anonymous missives flew in.

"This is the best thing that's ever happened!"

"Freedom tastes sweeter than I remembered!"

"Long may she remain absent!"

James could barely keep up with the deluge, and as he flicked between screens, panic began to rise. What was going on?

Then, across the room the radio switched on. Voices rang out, both male and female, though each was different and delivered but a single line.

"Glad to see the back of that monster."

"It's the beginning of a new age."

"This is a chance to start again."

"I'd felt oppressed for so long."

James jumped to his feet. His phone and laptop continued to beep over the mounting cacophony. At that instant he became aware that the dialogue between Marion Carlton and Wetherblaine had changed. Both were staring, pale faced, into the camera and taking turns to speak.

"She's truly got her comeuppance now," said Wetherblaine.

"At last I can look forward without fear," said Marion Carlton.

"I'm just so happy now that she's gone."

"I hope it stays this way."

James covered his ears as the volume of the voices and the beeping rapidly increased. It was becoming deafening, and his scrabbling attempts to turn off the radio and television proved futile.

"That ogre can just…"

"I'm glad that she's…"

"She was always such a…"

"What's happening?!" he cried, though barely able to hear his own voice.

Suddenly it all ceased, and the room was plunged into silence.

"Oh thank God," he gasped after a few seconds.

He nervously looked over at his television, which was now off, as were his laptop and phone.

"Did you enjoy that, mortal?" whispered Hera into his ear.

James yelped and span round. There, standing behind him, was the Queen of the Gods.

"Hera! I'm... I'm so sorry, I didn't hear you come in. I was just..."

"You were just listening to gossip."

"No, no, there was some sort of..."

"Oh indeed you were. I let you have a little taste. The voices you heard were those of the almighty Olympians. They're what I've had to listen to. They're chattering right now, all across your brain. They're talking about how I'm a spent force now that I've been thrown off the council." As she spoke she walked right up to him and leaned into his face.

James could feel his heart pumping furiously, but dared not move.

"I don't understand," he whispered. Events in council were of course entirely unknown to him, though Hera had no concern to explain.

"They think that they've seen the last of me, and that they can pick up and carry on with a new order, a new *ruler*." She spat the word with hatred. Though she looked into James's eyes it seemed that she was speaking aloud to herself. "She thinks that she can take up my mantle. She and her little lapdog. She is, of course, greatly mistaken, and you, my little mortal, are going to help me demonstrate how."

"But I..."

Before he could finish she grabbed him by the collar and lifted him clean off the ground, holding him just above her head.

James cried out and struggled instinctively against her grip.

Hera's arm did not flinch. She simply raised her free hand aloft, clenched a milky-white fist and slammed it into the side of his head.

*****

Dionysos hadn't been this excited in millennia. Finally he was about to obtain the prize that had been denied him all this time: the ravishing mortal, James Connor. After the turbulence surrounding Hera's expulsion from council and the chronic case of Aphrodite-worship that currently seemed to be afflicting the entire divine population, he was more than pleased to remove himself from the fray and strike out in pursuit of his target. It had been a positive relief that the third murder had gone so well and that Aphrodite had finally given him leave to indulge his passion. Frankly it had been rather a cheek of her to place strictures on his sexual licence at all. In the old days he would have had whichever mortal he liked without so much as a second thought.

Still, none of that mattered now. Not when he was standing at James's front door, having rung the bell, and was eagerly awaiting the scrumptious mortal to come and answer it. As he shuffled impatiently he considered his options. It might be the case that he would be met with some resistance, and if so then an old-style abduction would have to be endeavoured. Perhaps it might be easier simply to clobber the mortal over the head and then do the deed to his unconscious body. Yes, that might furnish a pleasantly pliant subject. None of that irritating kicking and screaming that so stimulated some of the other gods.

As Dionysos pondered, a figure appeared behind the frosted glass. The door opened, and there, as glorious as ever, stood James.

Dionysos gasped.

"Gosh you're looking good! Of all the sacks of flesh and bone, I think I've chosen rather well."

"You certainly have, Dionysos," said James. "And may I say that of all the deities to have conceived a passion for me I'm delighted to have been the object of such a looker as yourself. Come on in."

What a bonus! No kicking, screaming or begging for mercy. Not even an attempt to flee. The mortal was positively furnishing himself for a divine seeing-to.

As he stepped into the hallway, however, Dionysos noted there was a confidence in James's bearing that he had not observed before. This was coupled with a self-assured note to his voice which, though unexpected, added a delicious ring to his words and electrified the god.

"You… You mean you're up for it?" he replied with obvious surprise, as James closed and bolted the front door. "You've actually come round to the obviously brilliant idea of sleeping with me?"

"Of course I have, how could I refuse? Who am I to deny myself such an honour? After all, few 'sacks of flesh and bone' get to experience something as transcendent as sex with a god," smiled James.

"Well I must say I'm delighted to hear you speak such sense! Initially you didn't strike me as the sort to indulge in carnal desire, but now I can see you've made a very enlightened about-face."

"Under your irresistible influence, of course," said James flatteringly. "Though I'm curious, how long have you actually had this passion for me?"

"Oh ever since I walked in and saw you in that gods-forsaken little café."

"Really?" said James with mock surprise.

"Oh yes," said Dionysos. "I can't tell you how glad I am that Aphrodite persuaded me that day to go and inform you that Wildencrust was to be the next victim. If she hadn't then

246

I'd never have met you there, and perhaps we'd never have ended up where we are now."

"Imagine that," said James almost to himself. "But she didn't push you to inform me of the third victim, did she?"

"No she didn't. Strange, I didn't think anything of it at the time either," he said, before shrugging. "Oh well, who can divine the thoughts of a goddess?"

"Did she encourage you to pursue me today?" asked James disingenuously.

"Well she kept promising me that I could have you, but then kept holding back. It's all to do with council politics, nothing that you need bother your little head with."

"Council politics?"

"Yes. I don't know if you know this, but Aphrodite's had a long-running spat with Hera that's been going on for millennia now. Well she and I are old acquaintances, and she didn't want me to come and claim you for myself until she'd been given a controlling position in council. That's why I've had to wait. But I'm here now and that's the most important thing, isn't it."

"Absolutely."

Dionysos smiled good-naturedly, and with a look that unmistakably conveyed his intention to commence with the proceedings.

"Shall we?" he said, inclining his head towards the stairs. "I assume your bedroom is up there?"

"Indeed it is," said James, patting Dionysos on the shoulder and leaning in close to the god's face. "Let's begin."

*****

Two hours later, the God of Wine lay back and whistled with satisfaction. Though his physical engagement with James had been such a long time coming, the event itself had more than lived up to expectations. Aphrodite's spell had now run its course, though in its final moments it had spurred Dionysos to feats of carnal outrage that even he had never attempted before. The entire event had been vastly satisfying.

The god's mind, however, was not untroubled. The good grace with which James had accepted him into his bed had come as quite a surprise. More so, however, was the fact that the mortal's composed demeanour had been unwaveringly maintained throughout the proceedings. Not once had James resisted or raised objection to Dionysos's demands in the bedroom. Even the most obscene of the god's tastes had been indulged with almost supernatural serenity. Not once had James cried out or expressed pain during any of the many instances when the god felt sure that his assault would breach the limits of its object's tolerance. Throughout, the mortal had worn an expression of transcendent detachment.

As Dionysos lay on the bed contemplating the two-hour marathon, he turned this over in his mind. Might not the fact that this mortal had been so serene throughout suggest something deficient in the god's abilities? Could it be that the reason for James's seemingly impenetrable calm was that Dionysos himself had actually failed to deliver the divine throw-down?

The god smiled and shook his head. The thought was ridiculous. Perhaps the bag of flesh and bone had been *so* traumatised by it all that he had become catatonic, and unable to express anything but the smile of a simpleton. A much more likely explanation.

Having thus dismissed the nagging threat to his divine virility, Dionysos prepared to return to Olympian headquarters. He had carried out his conquest, and now it was time to get back to the serious business of the Cambridge List. Thanks to his obsession with James he had let things slip in his role as Chairman of the council, but now that he had had his fill the mortal was no longer of any interest to him. With a

248

clear head he would devote himself to his duties wholeheartedly. No more slacking.

"Right," he said, throwing off the covers, "time to get back. Thanks for that, mortal. For an oversized sack of blood and guts you were okay."

There was no response. Glancing over, Dionysos saw that James had buried himself under the covers. It seemed the poor creature couldn't bear to look at him. Perhaps he was crying? The god smiled to himself.

"Wonderful!" he whispered. "I knew I'd made an impact!"

The temptation to confirm his suspicions was too great to resist, and he leaned over, reaching for the bundle of bedclothes.

"Come, come, mortal. Don't be shy, it's okay to admit how traumatic that was."

He peeled away the sheet, smiling expectantly as he did so.

"Now let's have a look at your…"

"My what?" said Hera.

Dionysos jumped out of bed with a cry.

"What the…? Hera!"

In his shock he had involuntarily dragged the sheets clear from the bed, exposing the superb, naked form of the Queen of the Gods. Her golden hair tumbled over the pillow, covering her exquisite shoulders, and her cruel enjoyment of the god's terror cast a flattering glint in her eyes.

"You… When did you…?" stammered Dionysos. "How did…?"

"Oh I've been here the whole time."

"The whole time? You mean you saw…?"

"Oh yes," she said, rolling her head back and laughing. "Saw. Heard. Felt. Everything."

Colour drained from the god's face as the realisation struck him.

"You couldn't have… Surely you couldn't have?" he murmured.

"Oh I did, and it was ever such an honour to be bedded by one of the gods themselves." Her words were said not in her own voice, but that of James.

"But… But why?" asked Dionysos in horror.

At this she rose to her knees on the bed, looking him directly in the face. Her smile vanished.

"Because now I know your sordid pact with Aphrodite. I know how you plotted at my expense, and believe me the suffering I'm going to inflict upon the pair of you will make the Trojan War seem like a teddy bears' picnic."

"But Hera please, I didn't mean to…"

"Silence!"

As she saw Dionysos flinch and shrink back she narrowed her eyes and smouldered with fury.

"Oh Hera, I'm so sorry. Please, please don't be so angry!" he begged.

She made no reply, but continued to stare.

"What… What are you going to do?" ventured Dionysos timidly.

"Well," said Hera, slowly. "I'm going to go to the council and turn you in. But first, you and I have some business to settle."

"Please, Hera… Please, no…" he whimpered.

"Oh yes, I'm going to teach you a lesson about what happens to those who try to deceive me."

"Please, Hera. I'll do anything, I'll…"

She lunged, and her delicate fingers clamped round the god's throat. Lifting him into the air, she threw him down onto the bed.

The wooden frame cracked under the impact, and the old house shuddered.

*****

250

James suddenly became aware of tapping. It was coming from very near his head, and sounded like someone knocking on wood. As he tenderly opened his eyes he found that he was slumped in a dark, enclosed space, with objects, fabrics, hanging close to his face. They were so close that he felt almost buried under them. Raising his arms and hearing the clattering of coat hangers above, he realised to his consternation that he was in the wardrobe.

With a groan, he attempted to raise himself up, but as his body leaned forward a splitting pain shot across his head, and he slumped back again.

More knocks, and this time a muffled sound. Was it a voice? Now the pain came in waves, and he instinctively reached for the side of his face, which stung to touch.

It was definitely a voice on the outside, but whose? It was so high pitched that it must surely be a woman's, though the throbbing ache made it difficult to hear.

Suddenly the wardrobe door opened a crack and light flooded in, causing him to squint gingerly.

"Babe? Are you okay?"

"Muesli? Is that you?" asked James cautiously.

"Yep. You had a run-in with Hera. Do you remember what happened?"

He instantly recalled the sensation of being lifted from the floor, and the brief sound of the impact of the goddess's knuckles against his skull.

"Yeah I remember," he groaned.

"Good. Well no major damage then. Come on, it's time for you to get up and start preparing yourself. You've got murdering to do later. Heave-ho."

She reached in and grabbed his arm, attempting to hoist him up.

"Careful, careful. Bloody hell, I feel like shit!"

251

James stumbled out of the wardrobe, and having gained an upright bearing, instantly felt sick. He squinted as he attempted to adjust his eyes to the light.

"Quite a shiner you've got there, mate," said Muesli, with a smile.

"What? Oh fuck!" he cried as he stumbled over to the mirror, which revealed an enormous, blue bruise on the side of his face. "Bloody hell, I look like I've been in a fight!"

"Yeah, and a pretty one-sided fight at that," she chuckled.

But he was not to dwell on his injury for long. Another look in the glass revealed the state of the bed behind him, and he span round.

"My bed! What the hell's happened to my bed?"

The entire frame had been shattered, and now lay in two pieces. Every leg had buckled and the sheets were torn into rags, scattered over the splintered pieces of wood. The foam from the pillows was lying in clumps and the pillow-cases were strewn about like old sausage skins amidst the wreckage.

The Muse took a deep breath.

"Okay mate, it's like this. Hera discovered that Aphrodite and Dionysos were working together to undermine her in council. She was recently cast out, you see, and she decided to take revenge. She came here, knocked you out, assumed your form and slept with Dionysos, thus confirming her suspicions and giving herself all the evidence she needed to turf out Aphrodite. Understand?"

James hadn't moved, and was still standing with his mouth open.

"My... My bed!" he cried.

"Did you hear me," asked the Muse, impatiently. "Are you listening to…"

"What the hell happened to my…"

"Oh for fuck's sake!" she snapped. "Hera battered Dionysos and broke your stupid bed in the process, okay?

252

Explained? Happy? Bloody hell, deal with it. It's not like you don't have bigger things to worry about. She returned to Olympian headquarters with him in tow just before you woke up, and now you need to get yourself prepared for the next murder."

"She battered Dionysos?" repeated James. "On my bed?"

"Yes, on your poxy bed!"

"So really I got off quite lightly," said James, looking at the wreckage and suddenly feeling that his bruise did not seem quite so dreadful.

"This time, yeah."

At that moment there was a knock at the door. From the other side James heard Greg's voice.

"Jimmy, you there?"

The Muse turned to James and whispered hurriedly.

"You were having sex!"

"What? I was having sex? But...?"

"Answer him!" she rasped.

"Oh, hey Greg. Are you okay?" he called out awkwardly.

"Yeah, mate. Can I come in?"

"Sure."

James reluctantly stepped over and opened the door. Greg was standing on the landing in his t-shirt and jogging bottoms, and was sporting a pair of large, fluffy, dinosaur feet slippers.

"Jimmy, you okay? We came back from lectures to hear the house shaking. What the hell's been going on in..."

As he spoke he caught sight of the wreckage that had been James's bed.

"Jesus! What happened here?" he gasped.

James inhaled in preparation for the lie.

"Well the thing is, I was... Well, I was having... sex."

"You were having sex?" repeated Greg in disbelief. "With who?"

"With me," said the Muse from behind him.

"But…" Greg pointed at the bed. "You mean you... in the… with…"

He paused, his face dumbstruck. Then, slowly and triumphantly he raised his hand in front of James's face.

"Nice one, mate, nicely done! High five!" he yelled gleefully.

James made feeble contact with Greg's palm, sending his housemate running from the room and shouting down the stairs.

"Maisy! Maisy, guess what! It was Jimmy! He was shagging!"

"No way!" called up Maisy from the kitchen. "Who was he shagging? Bumrash?"

The reciprocal cackling began, and James slammed his bedroom door.

"Happy now?" he asked Muesli with irritation.

"Sure am, lover," she winked.

CHAPTER TWENTY

Having been assembled in the council chamber for several minutes, and with proceedings still yet to begin, the gods were becoming restless. Amidst the impatient fidgeting, however, the mood was ebullient. In her usual position at the front sat Aphrodite, whose smiles to the crowd when she entered had caused a stir of excitement. Now, though, as she looked at the empty speaker's chair, a knot of concern appeared on her brow.

Where on earth was Dionysos? He had never turned up late for council before. The minutes continued to tick by, and with no sign of the god her concern began to grow. His absence surely had to have something to do with his excursion to see James earlier that day, and the thought that his amorous advances might somehow have rendered the mortal unfit for duty nagged at her. Even more concerning, though, was the possibility that any misconduct on the god's part would leave a trail of evidence pointing firmly at her manipulation. She swallowed and tried to assume a placid countenance.

Another five minutes passed, and now the crowd's restlessness was growing. Dionysos's name could be heard throughout the chamber, and all of the assembled deities cast expectant glances at the doors.

Suddenly, from the middle row Ares, God of War, stood up.

"Does anyone know the whereabouts of Dionysos?" he asked in a booming voice.

"No, no one," replied Demeter, Goddess of Natural Fertility, from the other side of the chamber.

"What shall we do then?" piped up Hephaestus, God of Craftsmanship, from the back. "We can't carry on without a speaker."

The chamber echoed to the sound of concerned muttering.

Ares, sensing the mood, took a deep breath and prepared to offer his own services. At that moment, however, the doors of the council chamber were flung open with a clattering boom. Conversation was instantly silenced, and every head turned. Suddenly Dionysos came flying through the air. With a great bodily tumble he hit the floor and skidded to a halt at the foot of the first row. The gods and goddesses closest to his crumpled form instinctively stood and stepped backwards, and gasps could be heard around the room.

Aphrodite, mere feet away, remained seated. Only a short intake of breath betrayed the shock that coursed beneath an otherwise calm countenance. At the sight of Dionysos's unmoving body her fears were confirmed. But it was too late to make plans for damage limitation, nor would she be afforded the chance to escape what she knew was coming. For at that moment a familiar voice from the doorway echoed across the length of the chamber, making all inside flinch at its force.

"Hello my snivelling little wretches. I'm back," said the Queen of the Gods.

Hera momentarily surveyed the crowd, which stared in stunned silence. Striding into the room, she walked up to Dionysos, who was still lying where he had landed, grabbed him by the neck and hoisted him to his feet. She then frogmarched him to the Speaker's chair and threw him down. He slumped over its arms and groaned.

The gods and goddesses were rapt. All shrank in their seats as Hera turned, placed her hands on her hips and allowed her blistering gaze to sweep the room. She surveyed each of the deities in turn, and her satisfaction grew as every one of them averted their eyes. Lastly and with heavy emphasis she turned to Aphrodite, who alone and with her head raised in defiance returned her stare.

256

The Queen of the Gods smiled coldly.

"Well now, everyone" she said, without removing her eyes from Aphrodite's. "I suppose you're all wondering what I'm doing here? Allow me to explain. If you remember, I was expelled on a technicality for failing to respect the authority of the Chairman." As she spoke she raised her hand and indicated to Dionysos. He was still slumped over, and winced in pain as he tried vainly to lift himself up. "As you can see though," she continued, "I've now placed him back in his chair, where he so rightfully belongs, and I dutifully acknowledge his authority. As a result I humbly beg his leave to return to council."

With this she stepped over to Dionysos and grabbed a fistful of his dark hair, with which she wrenched his head upwards to face her. The crowd gasped at the cry of pain that issued from the god's bloodied mouth.

"Am I welcome back?" she spat, looking into his swollen eyes and shaking his head emphatically with each syllable.

Pained though inarticulate sounds emerged from his mouth as he attempted to answer.

"Well?" she snarled with another violent shake.

"Y… Yes," came the broken reply.

She immediately dropped his head and turned back to the crowd.

"Wonderful. Such a relief to be back in the game. And now that I'm restored to my old place in council there is an order of business that I would humbly submit for the consideration of the assembly.

Now her eyes fell once again on Aphrodite. The Goddess of Desire knew what was coming, but was damned if she would give Hera the satisfaction of seeing her countenance break. She continued to return the smouldering stare.

"Before we can resume our work on the destruction of those wretches on the Cambridge List," continued the Queen of the Gods, undeterred by Aphrodite's defiant composure, "I must make a revelation about a plot that has been taking place under our very noses, and which casts dishonour on the very spirit of the assembly itself."

With this she swept the room with her eyes once again, and observed the submissive and pale faces of the gods and goddesses. Her dramatic entrance had had exactly the effect she had hoped for, stunning the wretches into meek silence. For all their chattering and vain hopes about a new order, complacently made when she was not present, none would dare mount a challenge to her power when it was on full display. The fact that Aphrodite had not said a word was surely the strongest indication that she knew the game was up. Enthused by the effect that could be read in expressions of the audience, she continued.

"Aphrodite, the Goddess of Desire, who sits in our midst and makes the pretence of debate at the meetings of this great council, has been engaged in a conspiracy."

Now, for the first time since Hera had entered the room, the eyes of the audience turned to the front row. Aphrodite could feel them upon her neck, though she did not allow her gaze to waver.

"She," continued the Queen of the Gods, "has been plotting to manipulate the assembly's decisions by attacking the very heart of the institution itself: the Chairman." She raised her hand and a slender finger directed the eyes of the crowd to Dionysos. The god had succeeded in propping himself up on one elbow. "Isn't that right, Chairman?" said Hera with a sharp glance.

"That's... That's right," came the pained response.

Now the silence was broken and the gods and goddesses began muttering to each other. What on earth could Aphrodite have done? She had brought them all glory by engineering the death of Elliot Norther. What manipulation could be involved in that?

Hera allowed the confusion to mount for a few more moments, whetting the appetite for the revelation that was to come. The atmosphere was perfect.

"Allow me to reveal all," she said, raising her hands for silence. "Aphrodite cast a spell upon Dionysos, a grievous enchantment that was done not in the rightful exercise of her power, but in full opposition to the spirit of our great endeavour to destroy the five members of the Cambridge List."

At once the conversation increased in volume, and Hera's own excitement grew accordingly. Only a few more moments, a few more carefully chosen words of revelation, and the crowd would be calling for blood. Doubtless when she told them of how the Goddess of Fucking Everyone had manipulated the passions of Dionysos and placed the mission in peril they would demand her permanent expulsion. She could wait no longer to deliver the killing blow.

"For she, acting only for concern of her own ambition, made the Chairman of this mighty assembly lust uncontrollably for James Connor, promising him that she would deliver the mortal into his arms in exchange for influence in council."

There was silence.

Hera scanned the assembly. All eyes were on her, but now they only expressed passive surprise. Where was the shock, the outrage? Perhaps she had not spelled things out clearly enough.

"Aphrodite," she continued, resuming her booming tone, "was willing to gamble the entire mission on her bid for power. The desire that she placed in the heart of Dionysos was so strong that even she could not control it. Why, this very afternoon the Chairman, helpless against the conspirator's spell, and acting under its irresistible imperative, visited the mortal to satiate his desire. I know this because I dutifully put James Connor out of harm's way and assumed his form myself. Having donned this disguise, which was overlooked by the god on account of his manic lust, I nobly accepted the sexual punishment that he dished out in his attempt to satisfy himself. Though the performance was pitiful for a god it would surely have been fatal for a mortal." She then turned to the god himself, who winced under the force of her gaze. "As you can see I doled out a plateful of Olympian punishment for his part in the plot, even though he did act against his will." She then turned back to the audience, intoning with severity. "Had I not intervened as I did, the mortal would have been killed and the mission ruined. And all because of the vaunting ambition of Aphrodite."

There. That was the winning blow.

Silence.

Scanning the chamber, Hera noted with mounting anger that the faces of the gods merely exhibited the same, bland look of idiotic surprise that they had worn before. Why weren't the morons hissing at Aphrodite?

"Didn't you hear what I just told you?" she shouted incredulously. "It was a shocking revelation! Shocking! Aren't you all shocked?"

Now the murmuring resumed. Gods and goddesses spoke in hushed voices to each other, and as snippets of conversations reached Hera her fury mounted.

"It's a bit naughty to manipulate the Chairman like that, but Aphrodite did do jolly well with the third murder," said Ares to his neighbour.

"Nobody's perfect," muttered Demeter, leaning across to Hephaestus.

"Frankly, it's been a bloody relief to have Aphrodite steering the council. I say good luck to her," whispered Poseidon to the gods either side of him, who nodded in agreement.

"No, no, no!" yelled Hera. "This is all wrong! You idiots are not supposed to sit back and meekly accept that the wool has been pulled over your eyes. Don't you know the significance of what I've revealed to you? Don't you realise that I've brought you proof positive of that bitch's manipulation? Tell them that what I've said is the truth!" she barked at the broken Dionysos, who nodded acquiescently. "There! See that? What more do you morons want?"

Now it was for Aphrodite to smile.

"I think they want what I gave them, Hera," she said smugly. "They want the self respect that I delivered." As she spoke she turned to the assembled masses behind her, emboldening several individuals to voice their support.

"That's right Aphrodite!" came a cry from the back.

"We forgive you! You're the People's Goddess!" came another.

"The assembly seems to be of one mind," said Aphrodite.

"But... but...!" spluttered Hera. This was impossible. She had played her trump card, but all she had achieved by way of victory was a severely pounded Dionysos and her old place on the council.

"She must be punished!" she bellowed. "She must be cast out as I was! How can she be allowed to abuse this great institution in such a way and get away with it?"

Aphrodite seized her chance. Walking over to Dionysos she placed her arms around his shoulders and stroked his back consolingly.

"There, there, Chairman. Don't concern yourself with it all now. You're back where you belong. Let none of this unpleasantness sway you from your duty. If I have pained you I apologise solemnly."

Now the audience applauded loudly.

"She's made frank admission and apologised! What a great heart she has!" yelled a god from amongst the crowd.

"See how she comforts him! What compassion!" cried a goddess.

"I hate you, you fucking bitch," whispered Dionysos in Aphrodite's ear, before descending into a fit of pained coughs.

His rasping voice was heard only by her, and as she leaned in with her ear near to his lips she smiled beatifically.

"Oh Dionysos!" she said loudly, for the sake of the crowd. "How gracious of you to forgive me. And indeed you're right, I did it all for the sake of the council."

At this the applause increased and shouts of approval rang out.

In the middle of the chamber Hera stood shaking with rage. This was not the overwhelming victory that she had planned. In fact she had barely leveraged herself back to the position that she had held before she was expelled. She cast a baleful glance at Athena, who alone amongst the cheering crowd sat meekly.

"My chambers. Now," she mouthed.

CHAPTER TWENTY ONE

The sound of the doorbell heralded the visitor that James had been waiting for. As he walked briskly down the hallway, he thanked his luck that Greg and Maisy had departed for the pub half an hour earlier. This was the sort of meeting that ought to take place undisturbed.

"Hello Wendy," he smiled as he opened the door.

Standing on the step, her hands shoved into the pockets of her tweed jacket and her neck swaddled in a thick cashmere scarf, Wendy Pipford wore an expression that brooked no social niceties. She cast a fleeting grimace at the bruise on the side of his face before barging past him into the hallway.

"Oh yes, do come in," said James hurriedly.

"Don't talk to me like that," she snapped, marching into the kitchen.

"Like what?"

"You know like what. Like we're on civil terms."

"Oh but there's nothing wrong with a polite..."

"Oh be quiet! Don't think you and I can be friends, James. I'm here for reasons that I have no intention of explaining to you, so don't bother asking. But rest assured it's nothing to do with your attempt at blackmail, so you can put that right out of your mind."

She had sat down on a bar stool, and addressed him in a clipped tone.

"Well I suppose that's fair enough. Would you like a cup of tea?" he ventured.

"Please." She did not look at him, but fished out a pen and notepad from her bag. "So now that I'm here, why don't you fill me in on what's going on."

"Right," said James.

"You're planning on carrying out another murder."

He nodded.

263

"And you want me to help you."

"That's right."

"And you're responsible for all three murders to date?"

"Yes."

She paused. Her face betrayed a curious mixture of disgust and fascination. She looked him up and down before continuing.

"And why exactly did you start killing people?" she asked, her pen hovering over the pad.

"Look Wendy," sighed James, "I know you're a journalist and all that, but before we start this we need some ground rules. This isn't an interview, this is an operation. Anything I tell you has to be confidential."

She raised her eyebrows as if to dismiss a bad joke.

"I'm serious," he continued. "You can't just take down what I say like you're making a record. You're in this the same as I am. It's for that reason that I'm keeping your phone."

"You're keeping my…? No you're not!" she yelled, rising from the stool.

"Calm down, it's okay. Look, sit down and let me finish. I'm keeping it until after we're done. You have to understand that I can't take you on your word about this. If I give it back to you there's nothing to stop you from shopping me to the police. You must understand that I can't let that happen."

"Fine," said Wendy, resuming her seat. "But you need to understand something too. I'm not just going to follow orders blindly. I'm going to have to have some information first."

"Naturally, but only what I can afford to let you know."

Slowly she replaced her pen and paper in her bag, before turning and looking at him calmly.

"Fine, James. So why *have* you taken to killing people? A nice young man like you?" the irony in her voice was palpable.

"It's all about grievances. Partly mine, but mostly those of another group of people."

"They're the ones who are directing you?"

"In a manner of speaking, yes."

"And do they take part in the killings themselves, or is it just you?"

"No, just me. They direct from behind the scenes."

Wendy narrowed her eyes.

"I don't suppose you'll tell me who they are?"

"No."

"And the nature of the grievances?"

"It's personal."

"And academic," she ventured.

"Well... yes, but..."

"Three classicists die and a former classics student is responsible. Sounds pretty academic to me."

"There's more to it than that," he said, sitting down next to her. "Look Wendy, I'm involved both personally and academically, as you say. But the people I work for are very, very dangerous, and some of the guys at the Faculty have crossed them."

"So they've got you to do their bidding and bump off a string of lecturers one by one."

"Right."

"But what leverage do they have over you?"

"I can't tell you."

She sighed impatiently and looked away.

"I'm sorry Wendy, I've told you all I can."

"So what do you want me for?" she asked, turning to him again.

"I need someone on board for the next murder."

"And the one after," she said, raising her eyebrows.

"Well, yes. But that's it, no more after that."

"And why can't you get someone else to do it? What made you pick on me?"

He looked into her eyes but didn't answer.

"Oh I suppose you can't talk about it?" she said with irritation. "Well don't worry, I get the picture. I'm not talking about my reasons for accepting your offer either, I suppose we can leave it at that."

James smiled and Wendy, quite against her mood, did likewise.

"So what do you want me to do, James? You can't tell me the ins and outs, you won't give me my phone back, but you need me to help you kill. Twice. Throw me a bone here and tell me who, at least. Or am I to stab at random and hope to hit the right target?"

"I wouldn't fancy your chances," laughed James.

"Well I know who I'd go for first," she said with a reluctant chuckle.

"Okay, okay," he said, holding his hands up. "I'll confess that, as of yet, I don't know the details. All I know is it's almost certainly going to take place tomorrow."

Wendy's face suddenly fell.

"Right," she said, swallowing hard.

"You are up for this aren't you? I mean, you know what's involved?"

"I've seen you at it haven't I?" she said darkly. "Of course I'm up for it. You don't ask a girl if she's up for murder having blackmailed her first."

The mood had suddenly changed, and James sensed her disdain for him reassert itself.

"Okay what's your new number?" he asked.

She retrieved her pad and scribbled it down.

"Thanks," he said, slipping it into his pocket. "I'll call you later and give you the details. Just be ready, because we won't necessarily have a lot of time to prepare."

"Of course." She stood up and slipped her bag onto her shoulder.

"Oh and remember, once we're done you'll need to get rid of that new mobile too."

"I'm not an idiot you know," she sighed, before walking down the hall and opening the front door. She winced at the cold air, which blew against her face and flushed her cheeks red.

"See you tomorrow," called James, as the clunk of the door signalled that he was alone once again.

*****

"There, there, my darling," Alan Tanning's wife had said as he had read the morning papers. "Elliot was a good friend, I know, but you'll get over it in time."

"There, there, Dr Tanning," Glynys Leverton had said in plummy sympathy when she passed him in the hallway earlier that day. "We're all awfully sorry."

"There, there," had been the sympathetic mantra following him since the death of his comrade, and now as he cycled through town the words chased him along the frozen streets.

"There, there," he said to himself vacantly. Mechanically following his usual midday route between the University Library and the Faculty, he barely noticed himself turn corners or glide across pathways. The tears that fell freely down his cheeks were unnoticed too, as he was unable to detach his thoughts from the calamity that had befallen him.

"There," he repeated. "There one minute and gone the next. Oh Elliot, how could it happen to you?"

In his distraught state pedestrians and cars alike were phantoms to him, and a student stepping into the road cried out as he clipped her with his handlebars.

"Bloody hell, watch out!" she yelled, as he raced ahead unhearing.

267

"There one minute and gone the next," he whimpered as he blindly turned another corner.

Since Fringe had discovered him in the stationery cupboard and dragged him back to his desk, he had buried himself in his work. Every moment had been dedicated to finishing the Fund, which, thanks to the desperate flight from grief that it afforded him, he had virtually completed. Now, on his way back from the library and without the prospect of more work waiting on his desk, sorrow overwhelmed him.

"There," he sobbed as the Classics Faculty loomed ahead. "There it is." The sombre bricks and dark windows were forbidding on even the brightest of days, but now under the dead hand of winter the place conveyed an air of doom.

Tanning slowed as he passed. A sudden impulse, perhaps a wave of sadness or a repugnance at the thought of running into Fringe again, caused him to drift past the bike racks. Looking into the windows he saw the outline of figures in the offices, engaging mime-like in the routines of academic life.

He shuddered and carried on riding. Never before had he dodged the Faculty, but in his present mood nothing could have been less appealing to him than walking back inside and facing his desk. As memories of Norther swept over him he suddenly found that being inside that building was not a step that he could take. He drifted back onto the road and began peddling down Silver Street and into the city centre.

Now as he glided along, he turned his attention outwards and noticed the faces of the people on the streets. Every countenance conveyed the same emotion, the same feeling was written on the expression of every person who passed him: fear. Though all were huddled into their jackets against the cold, their steps were faster than the wind dictated, their eyes cast to the ground. They did not want to be outside on the streets. They were exposed, vulnerable. Tanning continued to look about him. The pavements were emptier than usual, and even the cars on the roads were fewer in number. The atmosphere echoed the very emotions that he himself felt as he cycled onwards.

But where would he go? What other purpose had he than work? Peddling ahead, the image of his friend fixed in his mind, he cared nothing for such concerns. All he wished to do was to ride on. Only tiredness or hunger could call him back, though under the rawness that he carried with him on his bike they were entirely subdued.

*****

Several streets away Wendy Pipford was making her way back to her office. Despite the excitement there was still work to be done, and even her shabby office with its mouldy central heating was preferable to being out on the streets. Why the hell hadn't she brought her bike?

She cursed under her breath at her lack of foresight, though immediately clenched her teeth as a sharp gust of wind whipped her hair across her face.

"Bloody hell, I hate this beastly town," she muttered angrily, sweeping it back behind her ears and pulling her woollen hat down further.

She had been walking for ten minutes and had now reached the centre of town. The place was almost entirely empty. Shops, their windows lit against the encroaching gloom, contained but one or two individuals, whose demeanour suggested a desire to seek shelter rather than to purchase. Those who did pass her had their coats pulled about them and had bundled scarves around their necks. The colours of the colleges could be seen here and there, though every young body that was contained beneath the otherwise dull layers of fabric marched stiffly, almost militantly, ahead. No one made eye contact with her, and indeed seemed to speed up at the sight of a fellow pedestrian.

Wendy looked about her and perceived for the first time a city in the grip of terror. But who could blame the townspeople, ignorant as they were of who was carrying out the killings, and being subject to the uninterrupted stream of fear-mongering emerging from the media circus on Midsummer Common. The savage wind was almost the very manifestation of the threat hanging over the town, reaching out from darkened alleyways and lurking round shadowy corners.

If only they knew.

"Soon, Wendy. Soon you'll blow this story open," she muttered. "And when you do you'll be out of this wretched place."

She smiled as she remembered the voice of Margaret Hunter from Core News. Even against the chill Wendy felt a warm ripple at the thought of the career dangled before her. She would have to get a scoop in, and soon. Still, once James contacted her about the details of the murder, she would feel secure. She would just have to cross her fingers and hope that the police didn't catch him first. In the meantime a news story had to be concocted about the current state of affairs in town. Perhaps a piece about the invasion of Cambridge by the national media? Or perhaps something about the mood of fear and how it was affecting the lives of ordinary people?

She was only a few minutes away from her office now. Turning her face into her scarf, she picked up speed. Nearing the corner that would lead her onto St Andrew's Street, the thought of a steaming hot cup of tea drove her on, and her pace increased to a half-skip.

Clutching the security pass in her pocket, she turned the corner, and as she did so marched straight into a young woman who had been travelling in the opposite direction. They bumped heads, and each staggered backwards a few steps.

"Gosh! Sorry, my fault," said Wendy quickly.

"This is fine," came the heavy, Slavic accent from beneath a veritable mountain of brightly coloured garments. A little cave-like opening betrayed a pair of striking blue eyes and the upper half of a pretty face.

Suddenly Wendy had an idea.

"Excuse me," she said, smiling. "I'm a reporter, and I'm writing a piece about how people are coping with a murderer being loose in town." She had chosen her theme that very instant. "Do you mind if I ask you a few questions."

"Yes. You can ask me what is questions," nodded the girl with her eyes closed.

"Thanks very much," said Wendy, awkwardly fishing her pen and paper out of her bag. "Right, can I start by asking your name?"

"Mischka."

"And your age?"

"You ask me 'how are you old'?" said Mischka, opening her eyes and arching an eyebrow.

"Er… yes."

"I am nine and teen."

"Right, nineteen," said Wendy, scribbling. "And how do you feel about the murders? Are you afraid to go onto the streets?"

"On streets? No, no."

"No fear at all?"

"No."

"Why not?" asked Wendy.

"In Russia, we have always murder. There is murderer here, murderer there, murderer all over." Raising her hand in the manner of a shotgun, Mischka then made a little popping sound as she pretended to shoot Wendy in the face.

"Right, I see." Wendy was slightly taken aback. Lifting her pen, she prepared for the next question, but Mischka was in full flow, and not to be stopped easily.

"He murder you, he murder me, he murder everyone. In Russia, murderer is everywhere."

"Well what do you think of the fear that people feel here in England? Can you understand why they're afraid?"

After a moment's internal translation Mischka shook her head.

"No."

"Really? You can't understand why people are afraid of the murderer."

"No. You have word for this."

"A word for what? What word?" Wendy's confusion was mounting. Perhaps the interview was not such a good idea after all.

"Murderer is *bollocks*." Mischka enunciated the word slowly, and with the polish of hours of practice. "Murderer is bollocks," she repeated. Then she furrowed her brow and closed her eyes in preparation for another much-practiced though more complex rendition. Removing a glove, she licked her finger, held it up as if to test the wind and solemnly intoned: "I freeze my bollocks."

"You what?" gasped Wendy.

"I freeze my bollocks. Goodbye."

With that, Mischka tugged the cords of her hood, scurried round the corner, and there ended the interview.

CHAPTER TWENTY TWO

Once upon a time, far away across the seas, three goddesses assembled for a trial of womanhood. The first was supernaturally beautiful, the second awe-inspiringly attractive, whilst the third, though passable in most respects, was simply there to make up the numbers. Most mortals would not have had the privilege to observe these prime examples of female divinity at close quarters, never mind all at once. Three thousand BC, however, was an unusual time, and Paris was no ordinary warrior.

One day, having been lounging about his palace, toying with the idea of a pillaging expedition to an Aegean island, the strapping specimen of Ancient Greek masculinity was suddenly transported. In a flash of light and a strange popping of the ears he found himself standing in a vast and sumptuously appointed chamber. Beside him was a table decked with fruits, and before him a pool of water rippled gently. The sun's rays, falling through a skylight above, were cast, glittering onto its surface and a little bird perched on its edge.

"Where am I?" exclaimed the warrior. "What happened?"

"Welcome, Paris, to the home of the gods. You are on Mount Olympus, in our divine abode." The smooth, heavenly voice was that of a female. Though its point of origin was uncertain, it was exotic and caused a conspicuous rustling amongst the lower folds of his toga.

"Crikey! Well I certainly didn't expect to end up here! I thought that when a chap died his soul made its way to the house of Hades, deep beneath the earth."

"It does," came another voice, also female, though deeper and with a disturbing authority. "So obviously you're not dead." She sounded put-out.

"Well what am I doing here? Does this have something to do with that ox I sacrificed to the gods last week? Now look, I'm awfully sorry about that. I know the old boy was rather lame and only had one horn, and it probably was rather cheeky of me to use it as an offering. Asking that you grant me fifty sons was probably going a bit far, too. The wife certainly didn't look too pleased, let me tell you!" With his arms folded across his broad chest he chuckled thoughtfully. Greek heroes, being rather used to supernatural exploits, tended to take such occurrences in their stride.

"This has nothing to do with your ox, decrepit though it was," said the first voice. "You have been chosen to preside over one of the most important contests that has ever taken place amongst the deities of heaven."

"How can I be of service, my goddesses?"

"There has been discord amongst the Olympians, Paris," came the authoritative boom of the second voice. "Strife and disharmony have racked the assembly of the gods. Even Zeus himself knows not how order might be restored. Such has been the level of disunity that god has turned against god, goddess has fought with goddess. Factions have emerged and threaten to break the heavenly order apart."

Paris was taken aback.

"Tell me what I must do, mistresses. I am at your command."

"You must be the arbitrator," said the first voice. "You, a mere mortal, must stand in judgment over us."

"But what is the nature of the dispute? What am I to decide?"

The second voice answered.

"The division that has rent the divine family in two rests on this question: which of the goddesses is the most beautiful?"

"But surely I couldn't possibly choose? I'm a mere human!" he gasped.

274

"Here," continued the booming tone, "are assembled the prime candidates. The two most beautiful goddesses in the heavens, plus Athena. We didn't realise she was in the room with us when we transported you here, but never mind."

"Hello Paris!" came the disembodied voice of Athena, who sounded delighted to be included.

"My lady," nodded the warrior respectfully. "Who am I to judge?"

Suddenly a shower of sparks shot up from the floor at the other end of the room. The warrior raised his hand to his eyes and squinted against the brilliant flash of light. As it faded he beheld the most beautiful female he had ever seen in his life.

"I, Hera," she said with the now familiar tone of power.

Another shower of sparks and there appeared a woman whose exotic eyes sent shivers across his skin.

"And I, Aphrodite," she said seductively.

At that moment a side door opened and another woman walked in, perfectly pretty, but without the sense of animal magnetism possessed in obvious abundance by the other two. Athena walked self-consciously across the room and stood next to Hera, who wore a look of mild irritation and refused to meet her gaze.

"Blimey!" gasped Paris as he looked repeatedly from the first goddess to the second, whilst making the occasional polite glance at the third. "How am I to choose?"

"Just get on with it. I'm the most beautiful and you know it, so hurry up and vindicate me," said Hera. Her voice betrayed impatience but also a tone of anxiety. What was she to do if Aphrodite won? She'd lose standing in council without doubt, especially since the debate had been raging for over four hundred years now.

Aphrodite, for her part, took a nervous glance at Hera. The Queen of the Gods had never worn *that* dress to council meetings, and annoyingly she happened to look rather gorgeous in it. The bitch. Despite usually possessing an unassailable confidence in her own sense of attractiveness, now the Goddess of Desire felt nagging self-doubt. She could hardly use her powers to make Paris fall in love with her, though, not right in front of Hera. But then again she couldn't guarantee victory without a bit of undue influence.

After a few moments' careful thought, in which Paris could be seen agonising in painful deliberation, Aphrodite hit upon an idea.

"Athena that's horrible!" she yelled, staring across with a shocked expression.

Athena looked at her in surprise.

"What have I done?"

"Pulling a face at Hera like that. How rude! I saw you look her dress up and down."

"What?" boomed Hera, casting a dark glance at Athena.

"Oh Aphrodite, what nonsense!" she laughed nervously, before turning to Hera. "I didn't, Hera. Honestly I didn't. You look great! Astounding! In fact I withdraw. See? Nothing to worry about."

"You little shit. I bet you thought you could upstage me, didn't you? Well I accept your withdrawal and will give you a little helping hand on your way." With that she grabbed Athena roughly by the arm and dragged her towards the door.

Paris's understandable shock at the sight of this divine bickering left him mute. Rooted to the spot, he merely averted his eyes and prayed that the whole episode be over. They all looked stunning, but what if he were to choose the wrong goddess? Would he be killed by the angry loser? Perhaps he would be stripped of his heroic status and sent back to Earth as an enfeebled nobody?

As he pondered these thoughts with a rising sense of panic he became aware of a fluttering. Looking to his left, he saw that the bird which had formerly occupied the edge of the pool was perched on his shoulder. Opening his mouth in surprise, he was about to speak, when the little creature interrupted him.

"Ssshh. Don't say a word, Paris."

He was startled. Its voice was that of Aphrodite. Glancing across the room he saw her wink. Behind her, Hera had opened the door and was hissing inaudible words into Athena's ear, presumably as a prelude to kicking her out.

"I must be quick or we will be spotted. If you choose me as the most beautiful goddess you will be amply rewarded."

"How?" he whispered.

"With a beauty that will be all your own."

"What beauty?" He was intrigued.

"Look to the pool."

As he did so he saw ripples disturb the surface of the water. The light that fell upon it distorted, colours appeared and after a moment the image of a woman could be seen. There was no comparison between her and the goddesses, but for a mortal she was exquisite.

Paris's delighted silence told Aphrodite all she needed to know.

"Think quickly, noble warrior. For she is Helen of Troy, and she can be yours."

With that, the bird flew over to the pool, and as it plunged into the shallow water, shaking its feathers vigorously, the image of the entrancing woman was broken up.

Hera had now returned and once again stood next to Aphrodite, whose countenance was nonchalant.

"This has gone on long enough, mortal," she said sternly. "Let's have your decision."

With a deep intake of breath, Paris closed his eyes.

"My ladies," he said solemnly. "I have not without difficulty reached my decision."

The goddesses were silent. Each knew that precious standing in council rested on the outcome, and that loss of face would be a PR disaster.

"It is Aphrodite," he said, exhaling tensely.

With those fateful words the judgment of Paris was rendered, and the greatest division that had yet been seen was unleashed amongst the gods. Shortly afterwards Hera, convinced of foul-play though without proof, gathered her supporters about her. Aphrodite, adamant that the decision was fair, drew together her own entourage and, with that, both sides joined in battle. The conflict between these, the greatest of goddesses, was waged not on the heights of Olympus, but on Earth below, amongst mortal men. Through the competing sides of the Trojan War, in which countless warriors met their end, the political manoeuvrings of Aphrodite and Hera were played out as the world looked on in horror.

Now, three thousand years later, a sense that history was repeating itself had settled over the Olympians, who now resided in the rather less glamorous setting of James's brain.

Since Hera's dramatic return to council and Aphrodite's refusal to be evicted, gods and goddesses had begun to form factions as grave divisions emerged. The Queen of the Gods, though unable to oust Aphrodite from her place on the assembly, had used the time-tested tactics of bullying and coercion to draw deities into her orbit. Aphrodite deployed a tactical bombardment of charm and persuasion to create a substantial entourage of her own. Between them they carved up the Olympian family into rival teams and made ready for the conflict that would surely follow.

Dionysos, after his humiliating treatment at Hera's hands and the long-overdue realisation that Aphrodite had used him as her pawn, had detached himself from this atmosphere of intrigue. Since the high drama of the last assembly meeting he had taken to venturing out of his chambers only when absolutely necessary, though even with

278

excursions kept to a minimum, he had ample opportunity to observe the deterioration in relations between the gods. For at the junction of every nerve cluster deities gathered in nervous gossip.

'Which team are you on?' was the common mantra. 'Who do you support?' 'How am I to decide who to join?' Olympians everywhere grappled with these questions feverishly. Aphrodite had proven herself a credible opponent to Hera, perhaps she was the safest bet? Then again the Queen of the Gods had proven her staying power over the millennia. And did she not always come out on top in the end?

The clock was ticking. The meeting to decide the death of the next don was approaching fast, and the goddess with the most significant following would force through her proposals and bask in the glow of unchallengeable influence. Whichever goddess won would dole out vicarious glory to her supporters, and to the loser and her team she would bring ruin in council.

Surrounded by fervent speculation and the rapid formulation of alliances, Dionysos closed himself off to the sights and sounds of a divine family drawing itself into two camps. He refused to be pulled into either one. For him the occupation of James's brain had been a complete disaster, and now he was quite happy to keep his head down and wait until the wretched task of eliminating the members of the Cambridge List was over. Unfortunately he still had to attend assembly meetings. His role as speaker demanded that he be present to preside over the proceedings, though other than carrying out his constitutional duty he wanted nothing to do with the political scene whatsoever.

The assembly meeting was imminent, and the decisive moment approached.

CHAPTER TWENTY THREE

The kitchen cupboards were virtually empty and James's frustration was mounting. Apart from a highly unappetising bag of dried lentils, Bumrash's shelves offered nothing. Maisy's pantry was similarly bare, save for a box of assorted dried herbs, and Greg's cupboard, which had always been the last resort, was filled only with pots and pans. It was the second desperate inspection of the kitchen that James had made that day.

"Why the hell can't people replenish their food supplies?" he muttered to himself angrily.

Suddenly the door bell rang. Kicking the cupboard door closed, he made his way down the hall.

"Thought you might be hungry, babe," said the Muse, holding up a pizza box.

James's heart skipped a beat. He had long since frittered away the last of his money, and under the compulsion of extreme hunger had spent the past hour scouring the house for sustenance.

"Muesli you genius!" he said, flipping open the cardboard lid. "Anchovy and baked bean special! My favourite!"

"Delightful," she grimaced, at the sight of what closely resembled the wreckage of a car crash. "Only, let's not eat it here on the doorstep, eh?"

"Oh right. Sorry," he mumbled through a mouthful of pizza. He threw down the greasy slice which, in his haste, he had already begun stuffing into his mouth, and nudged open the door with his foot. "Come on in."

Once in the kitchen the Muse propped herself up onto a stool and surveyed the turned-out cupboards.

"Been on a treasure hunt, have we?"

"Yeah," chomped James, already into his second slice. "You don't want any do you?" he asked, holding it up. It was clear from his defensive posture that the question was asked in the hope of a polite refusal.

"No babe, I'm fine," she smiled.

"So did you just come round here to feed me, or was there something else?"

"Oh charming, I'm sure." She rose from the chair in mock outrage. "I'll just be off, then." Grabbing her fake leather handbag she marched dramatically towards the hall.

"No, no, no," said James, nudging her back to her seat with the pizza box whilst taking a bite out of his third slice. "I'm joking, I'm joking. All I meant was 'what's the news?'"

"Oh big things are going down." She had settled back onto the stool and now started picking at her black fishnet stockings.

"What, to do with the murder?" He was scooping up his fourth slice.

"Only indirectly. The gods are about to start the debate to decide on the death of the fourth victim."

"Alan Tanning?"

"That's right."

"I don't know why you bother meeting to decide things like that," he said, chomping loudly. "You might as well say 'James, get on with it. Just get it done any way you like.' I mean why bother deliberating?"

"These things matter a great deal to us," said the Muse sternly. "And it's that very thing that I've come here to talk to you about. The fact is that there are deep divisions amongst the gods."

"Aren't there always?"

"No, not like this. You remember I told you that Hera got kicked out of council?"

"Yeah."

281

"Well now she's back. And not only did she make an eye-popping re-entry, but she revealed that Aphrodite had been manipulating Dionysos in order to marginalise her and dominate the proceedings. Quite successfully for a while, I might add." The Muse said this almost admiringly.

"So what does that have to do with me?" asked James, tenderly lifting the last slice of pizza to his lips.

"Well Hera tried to have Aphrodite kicked out, but Aphro's popularity is sky-high at the moment on account of Norther's successful murder, and so…"

"Thanks to me," interrupted James through a mouthful of crust.

"Yes thanks to you. And anyway, so Aphrodite dug her heels in. Well that meant there was a stalemate. Both goddesses found themselves secure in council and neither could get the upper hand. As a result they've each been gathering followers to support them in this meeting. The problem is that in doing so they've literally divided the gods in two. Half have stuck with Aphrodite and the other half have gone over to Hera."

"Why would anyone go with Hera?"

"Partly through fear and partly because they think that, when it comes to the crunch, she'll come out on top. It's a question of self-preservation."

"And this whole conflict rests on who has the last word in council about the nature of the next murder?" asked James incredulously.

"Yep."

"Isn't that a bit trivial"

"No James. Whoever gains the upper hand in council is the top dog, and whoever loses is confined to the doldrums of the divine pecking order. This is serious."

James threw the now empty pizza box onto the counter and rubbed his hands together with satisfaction.

"If you say so. Either way I'm sure they'll let me know what they want me to do."

"Oh don't worry James, I'm sure that... Wait."

She rose from the stool and looked ahead vacantly.

"What is it?"

"They've just started the meeting."

"Why do you look so concerned?"

"I've never seen the chamber like this before."

"Like what?"

"Well the gods and goddesses are sitting at opposite ends of the hippocampus. Dozens of them, all clumped on two sides. It's as if neither group wants to be near the other. Hera's sitting with her followers and Aphrodite's sitting with hers. They're really eyeballing each other too. I've never seen them with faces like that. There's a lot of noise."

There was concern in her voice, and James shuddered with a sudden awareness that what she described was taking place in his head at that very moment.

"So what do you think it'll..."

"Sshhh! James, don't say anything. I'm trying to... Okay, Hera's stood up. The crowd have gone silent. She's making a few rude remarks about Aphrodite, saying her team is smaller, pathetic, blah, blah. Right, now she's getting down to it." The Muse squinted, as if straining to hear a distant sound. "Hera wants the death to be slow. Really slow. She says that none of the deaths so far have given enough satisfaction, and that the anguish of the fourth victim must be drawn out for as long as possible. She's sat down again."

"What do the other gods think?" asked James.

"There's loud applause from Hera's team, but Aphrodite's are keeping quiet. Okay, Aphrodite herself has just stood up. She's saying that Hera's plan is a waste of time. She says that the only thing that will satisfy divine honour is a death that humiliates the victim. She's saying that the speed at which he dies is neither here not there. She's calling Hera an amateur."

"Bet she doesn't like that," said James almost to himself.

"Too right. Gods from each side are calling out now. There's hissing and some are shouting names at each other across the floor. Hera's piped up again. Bloody hell she looks pissed off. She's saying humiliating deaths are timid and that Aphrodite should stick to putting on make-up and arranging her hair. Hang on, some of her followers are shouting something at Aphrodite. Now Aphrodite's are responding. It's really getting loud in there."

Now, as he observed the Muse's face, James began to perceive the first traces of fear creeping across her brow.

"There's a real clamour in there," she continued. "Gods on each side are starting to get personal with the insults. They're getting carried away with the emotion. Ares has just stood up and called Demeter a filthy coward for joining Hera."

James drew a long breath. The Muse's mouth was tightening as the tension in her voice mounted.

"Deities are leaving their seats now. They're actually getting up from either side and approaching each other." She shook her head slowly and blew through her teeth. "They're starting to get in each other's faces. James this is getting really bad. They're beginning to get violent. They're…"

Suddenly she looked directly into his eyes.

"James watch out!"

"Watch out for what? What do you… Aaarrggh!"

A sharp pain pierced his head and shot down into his eyes. It was immediately followed by another volley, which cascaded across his neck. His legs gave way at once and he sank to his knees.

"James!" shouted the Muse, rushing to his side.

But before he could respond, agonising waves swept across his head, as if a shower of hot coals were falling onto him from above. His attempt to cry out was futile. Though he opened his mouth, no noise issued forth. Collapsing onto his side, his body contorted in silence.

"James it's the gods," yelled the Muse. "They're attacking each other, Hera's people against Aphrodite's. They're tearing up the place. They're tearing up the inside of your head."

James could hardly hear her as he lay there, his body wracked with convulsions.

"Okay mate, I'm gonna try and help you. If I don't do something you're a gonner. Hold on James!"

*****

All across the council chamber the clamour of screaming and pounding fists echoed deafeningly, as Olympians turned upon each other in rage. Under the compulsion of mass hysteria they fought, gods and goddesses against each other, every one swept away by the bitter struggle between Hera and Aphrodite. Friendships that had endured for millennia were shattered in the violence of divine hands laid upon divine bodies, and furious curses thrown in anger. As the clamour rose and waves of fury swept the chamber, all was chaos.

At either end of the room the two great goddesses searched for each other. Suddenly Hera caught sight of Aphrodite, who likewise turned and saw her enemy. They were separated by the great mass of deities, who fell upon one another with roaring violence and presented a churning barrier of divine flesh. This was not to deter them, however. Caught in a storm of their own making, they had tired of cloak and dagger politics and would fight it out here and now.

"I'll destroy you Hera! I'll wipe you out!" screamed Aphrodite over the tumult.

"I'll kill you! I'll bring mortal death upon you!" bellowed Hera, nearly losing sight of her enemy as the mob surged.

285

Both goddesses advanced through the swell of combatants, forcing their way through in their urge to destroy. Closer they came, moving by degrees through the tide of bodies. Within seconds they had come almost within touching distance of one another. Hera reached out and Aphrodite lunged forwards.

At that moment a cry rang out across the hippocampus. "Everybody stop!"

The voice was of such a penetrating tone that it pierced the ears of every deity in the room. All stopped and turned towards the speaker.

"What the fuck do you all think you're doing?" gasped the Muse, panting at the exertion of raising her voice to such a volume.

The effect upon the gods of this interruption was pronounced, and the violent mood that had animated them against each other suddenly changed to one of surprise. In the immediate silence all were still.

"What the hell are you doing here?" demanded Hera in fury.

The Muse noted with relief that Hera and Aphrodite had not yet started to trade blows. She had made it in time. Holding up her head and meeting Hera's eye, she spoke with as much gravity as she could summon.

"I think you'll find that I'm a goddess too, same as you, and as such I've got every right to attend the assembly."

"Rubbish," said Aphrodite in obvious outrage at this unexpected interruption to her imminent attack on Hera. "You've never come before. You've always looked in from the outside like a creepy little peeping Tom. And besides, you're interrupting the most important debate since the Trojan War." She spoke with not the slightest sense of irony. Both she and Hera had known that open and physical conflict was inevitable, and had come ready for the fight.

286

"I'm not interested in the meeting, I've come here cos I have to," returned the Muse. "If this fight goes on, and you two start smacking each other up," she looked earnestly from Aphrodite to Hera, "then James Connor will die. And if that happens the mission'll die too."

Murmurs suddenly swept across the chamber, and gods and goddesses looked at each other in shock.

"It really is that bad," said the Muse, catching the mood. "This might be just another day at the office for you lot, but remember that this war council is convened inside the head of a mortal."

Aphrodite and Hera smouldered at each other. The hatred that each harboured for the other flickered in their eyes, but this moment of imposed calm had tempered the urge for immediate satisfaction of their fury. They stepped back and looked about themselves. Their followers were intermingled. All around, pairs of deities who had battled in anger were now regarding each other with looks of exhausted bemusement.

"You know I'm right," continued the Muse.

"But how can this be resolved?" said Hera, without taking her eyes from Aphrodite.

"Indeed," said the Goddess of Desire. "The mode of the fourth death has yet to be decided, and that's the contentious issue."

"Look, I'm not asking you both to kiss and make up. All I'm saying is that you need to recognise that the limits of the mortal's endurance must condition the limits of your disagreement."

At this, deities across the hippocampus nodded in agreement and muttered to each other.

"Perhaps so," said Hera grudgingly. "But I'm not backing down and giving way to *her* plan."

"Nor I to hers," retorted Aphrodite.

"I'm not saying either of you two should give way. Look, if Hera's dead set on a slow death and Aphrodite's intent on a humiliating death, then it makes sense for you both to combine them. A slow, humiliating death sounds pretty good to me."

"You mean join together?" gasped Aphrodite.

"You must be joking!" spat Hera.

The mood, however, had swung decisively in favour of concord, as the growing talk amongst the gods and goddesses across the chamber revealed. There was little chance now of violence reasserting itself. As they looked around the hippocampus and saw that their respective teams had begun to merge back into each other, both Aphrodite and Hera could not but conclude the impossibility of either gaining the upper hand.

Thus, for the first time in perhaps three thousand years, and under the duress of extreme reluctance, divine violence was settled by truce.

*****

James tenderly opened his eyes. Slowly registering his surroundings, he became aware of a throbbing pain across his body. The kitchen floor was cold and hard beneath him, and he let out an involuntary cry.

"A slow and humiliating death," said a familiar voice. It was Muesli.

"Oh God," he groaned. "Can't you stop it? You've got to help me!" he rolled over and exhaled sharply.

"No babe, not you. You're fine. I've saved you. And just in the nick of time too. A slow and humiliating death is what you have to deliver tonight."

"What?" he wheezed, half turning.

"That's right, James," she said with a sense of achievement that was lost on him. "I saved you, and now you've got to get on with your work. Heave yourself up and let's get cracking. I need to get you up to speed on what needs to be done. Come on."

"But I'm… I'm," James protested feebly.

"Yes I know, babe. You're only mortal."

CHAPTER TWENTY FOUR

In the grotty offices on St Andrew's Street the buzz of excitement that had been unleashed by the death of Elliot Norther continued unabated. David Blythe continued to summon journalists to his office to receive barked sets of instructions and reporters continued to run between desks with frantic enquiries about the latest developments. A bank of televisions suspended high above the vast open-plan room displayed the major news channels, from which the measured tones of correspondents competed in vain with the noise rising from the office floor below. At The Cambridge Clarion all was hectic activity.

Wendy Pipford, however, was serene. Clad in her fluffy slippers and jogging bottoms, and grasping an over-sized mug of milky tea, her thoughts were uninterrupted by the sound of the reporters shouting to each other across the office. Sitting in front of her laptop in her warm living room, she was glad to have left The Clarion early in favour of working the rest of the day at home. One more summons by Blythe to be asked whether she had cracked the case yet would have pushed her over the edge, and on the pretence of writing a piece about the mood of a town in lockdown she had departed for the comfort of her sofa. Here in her flat the only sound came from Radio 4 and its professionally cool reporter:

"We turn, now, to the story that continues to dominate headlines: the multiple killings that have taken place in Cambridge."

This was what Wendy had been waiting for. Putting her feet up and taking a sip of tea, she listened intently.

"Since the death of Dr Elliot Norther," announced the smooth-voiced correspondent, "the police have still given no clues as to the possible identity of the killer, and have yet to issue a list of suspects. Though it has been revealed that a woman was present at the time of the death, and it has been confirmed that she was a sex worker, her anonymity has been closely guarded. The previous victims, Harriet Mason and Penton Wildencrust were, like Elliot Norther, lecturers at the Classics Faculty. As experts have pointed out, this fact, along with the short time between each death, suggests that this is the work of a serial killer. The police, however, have neither confirmed nor denied that they are linking the murders."

Wendy took another sip and jotted a few notes onto the pad that lay next to her on the sofa.

"Must try and dig up something on the relationship between the three victims," she whispered absently to herself as she continued to listen.

"Few have come forward with information about the case," continued the reporter, "though, earlier today, we spoke to two students who shared their memories of Harriet Mason and their thoughts on the possible identity of her killer."

Wendy listened carefully as the extract played. It was brief, and comprised two rather well-spoken girls answering a question from the interviewer about Mason's personality.

"Oh yah, well as to her character I'd say she was a bit of a brute. Clarissa and I both thought so, didn't we Clarissa?"

"Absolutely Jessica," said the other girl. The noise in the background suggested that the interview had been carried out on the street.

"Too frightful that she was murdered though, isn't it?" said Jessica.

"Totally, yah."

"We both think that whoever did it was probably a drug dealer from one of those council estate places, don't we Clarissa?"

"Totally agree, Jessica. Probably from somewhere up in Chesterton. Oh my God, I hear they deal drugs in the school canteens up there!" she gasped.

"Oh my God, that's awful!" squealed the other.

At this point the voice of the correspondent resumed.

"You can hear the full interview on the BBC Radio 4 website. In other news…"

Wendy rose and switched off the radio. Though it was only late afternoon it had already begun to get dark, and a brief look through the window at the greying sky prompted her to complete her half-finished article. She sat down again and opened her laptop, but before she could put her fingers to the keyboard the house phone rang.

"I bet that's Blythe," she muttered as she rose and walked out into the hall and lifted the receiver. "Hello?"

Almost at once her face tightened.

"Oh it's you."

Having unconsciously slipped her pad and paper into her pocket when she had gone to turn off the radio, she now retrieved them and placed them on the little table next to the phone.

"Yes I'm fine, thank you. How are you? Good, good. So what's happening? Have you…? Oh…"

She started nodding, and jotted notes on a fresh page.

"Tonight? No, no, I'm not having second thoughts, nothing of the kind. No I'm absolutely up for it. What do you want me to do?"

She continued to scribble.

"Yes I can pick up some things. You mean supplies?"

Her frown indicated that the answer was negative.

"Then what? You want me to… What? A gimp mask? What the…?"

She frowned and rolled her eyes at the response.

"Okay, okay, you can tell me later. I don't know where you expect me to get one though. Very funny. Look, just leave it to me, I'll manage it."

She tapped her pen absently on the paper.

"What else? Rope? Yes that's fine. Easier than the gimp mask."

Another volley of instructions followed. Now her notes became detailed, and she narrowed her eyes intently.

"That's more like it," she said at length, still scribbling. "I can definitely do that. Don't worry about that, I'm totally fine with it. You concentrate on getting the rest of the stuff and I'll make sure he's there at the right time. No don't worry, I'm not going to say his name over the phone."

Two further minutes of conspiratorial exchange followed, after which Wendy Pipford replaced the receiver and made her way to the bedroom to prepare for the evening.

*****

In the endless corridors and gloomy rooms of the Classics Faculty a mood of dread pervaded. Since the death of a third classicist in less than two weeks, both students and staff alike had found themselves more than usually subject to the depressive effects of the hideous building. Undergraduates who passed each other on their way to lectures no longer offered greetings, and staff had begun to steer clear of one another in the common room. Exhaustion at the sole topic of conversation, and the impossibility raising a subject other than the killings, combined to stoke a sense of despair that clung to the very walls.

As Paul Fringe sat at his desk he smiled in the knowledge that his many underlings in the Faculty, helpless to escape that oppressive atmosphere, were sagging under the weight of their workloads. For after a long and leisurely lunch in his office, he had decided to let himself off at 3 o'clock in order to spend the rest of the afternoon at his home in Grantchester. As the entrance door to the Faculty had closed behind him, the sound of the great iron portal clunking shut might have been that of a workhouse gate, sealing the wretched occupants inside. Fringe had delighted in it.

Sitting at his desk in his sumptuously appointed study, pleasant thoughts about the suffering of his minions turned to his imminent appointment as Vice Chancellor. How happy he would be finally to sit at the apex of the University's ruling elite. The prospect of a new and greater set of creatures to terrorise was a boon to his already glowing mood. Having paid a suitably threatening visit to Alan Tanning earlier in the day and discovered that the blubbering idiot had completed the final arrangements for the Outreach Fund, Fringe felt brighter than he had done in all his life. It was this that had led to his decision to leave work early. As soon as he had arrived back at home he had changed into his most informal and relaxing attire, and proceeded to play the most jolly and upbeat record in his collection. A grey smoking jacket and the dour tones of Queen Mary's Funeral Music were a rare and frivolous departure indeed. That his starched collar was left to fend for his neck's modesty without the assistance of a tie pointed to a carefree mood that was quite unheard of. Here, ensconced in the grand surroundings of his Victorian house, and with the familiar view of its large grounds to delight his eye, Fringe allowed himself to relax.

A knock at the door, usually a dangerous provocation on the part of a hapless visitor, was met with nothing more than a cheerful, "Come in Miss MacAfree!"

Fringe's housekeeper, a family retainer of seventy-three, entered. There was no need for severity with her. She had served his father whilst he was alive, though for twenty years since the late Eustace Fringe had passed on she had dedicated herself with loyal zeal to his son.

"Welcome home, sir," she uttered imperiously. "Rather early for you."

"Indeed Miss MacAfree. Thought I'd take the time to savour my last few days as a mere mortal."

"Before you're elevation to Vice Chancellor. Glorious to think you'll be following in your great-great grandfather's footsteps."

Her voice was utterly devoid of emotion, though her sense of pride was real enough. Fringe and his servant understood each other entirely, as only two beings of an equally cruel temper might. It was not for nothing that Miss MacAfree enjoyed the title 'Fringe's Goon' amongst those poor tradesmen and jobbing gardeners who had the misfortune of having to deal with her.

"Glorious indeed," agreed Fringe. "Let us savour these days before my apotheosis."

"Shall I bring you tea, sir?" she enquired dryly.

"No, Miss MacAfree. Bring me champagne," he whispered through a bloodless smile.

CHAPTER TWENTY FIVE

In the first week of November Cambridge is a violently bleak place. Throughout this dread month the town is pierced by a wind that residents insist blows from Siberia. It chases them through the streets in the daytime, angrily snapping at their ankles and clawing at the back of their necks. When darkness falls and the streets are empty it lingers menacingly, whistling through doorways and rattling locked windows, searching for cracks.

It was late in the evening, and the feeble sun had long since gasped its last against the encroaching gloom. The centre of Cambridge was deserted, not a person was to be seen on any of the streets between King's Parade and Magdalene Bridge. The chill had chased them all away, and they had hurried home all the faster for fear of whom they might meet in the dark alleys and winding roads. A murderer was loose, and terror skulked with the wind.

Had any brave soul ventured back out into the cold as the clock of Great St Mary's Church struck nine, they might have seen a figure turn onto Queen's Road, walk its length and pass into Garrett Hostel Lane. Amongst the many layers of cotton cladding wrapped hard against the cold, and the muffling hood pulled tight about the head, this lone personage was carefully anonymous. The gait, however, was that of a woman. Down she walked, over the little bridge that led into the centre of town. At its end she stopped and looked about her. Here at the back of Trinity Hall was the river, silent and black. Skirting it was a shadowed lane that led past a warren of walled college courts. It was into these depths that the woman stared.

As she squinted, another figure emerged from the darkness, only yards away.

"James?" whispered Wendy Pipford.

"Yeah it's me. Hi Wendy." He shuffled up to her and smiled. It was colder than either had expected, and they stood with their arms tightly folded.

"Did you bring the gear?" asked James in a subdued voice. He cast a quick glance at the windows high up in the walls that lined the lane. Though they were all dark, caution was paramount.

"Yes, here they are," said Wendy, nodding to the black sports bag on her shoulder.

"No trouble with the gimp mask then?" he smiled.

"Actually no." She stepped closer to him and looked cautiously about. "I didn't want to go out and buy one, and I remembered someone at work once telling me about an office party a few years back, before I joined. He said that there had been a really wild Halloween do, and that someone had turned up as a gimp. Anyway I managed to find a box in an old storage cupboard which contained some of the costumes, and *voila!*" As she spoke, she reached into her bag and pulled out the mask triumphantly.

"Very industrious," said James. "Let's have a look."

It was made of cheap, black leather, and had narrow slits at eye level. He smiled as he noted the crucial details: a thick band of material that completely covered the mouth, and a series of straps at the back.

"Once we've put it on him we can seal it with this," said Wendy, pulling a small padlock from her pocket.

"Brilliant. And there's no chance he'll be able to cry out with it on?"

"Well I haven't exactly tried it on myself," said Wendy, rolling her eyes. "But it looks pretty restrictive to me."

"Well in that case I guess all we have to do now is wait. You know what to do?"

"Yes James, I know exactly what we're doing. I mean with two of us working together and the element of surprise on

297

our side it can't be that difficult, surely? We just have to be cool, calm and collected."

Her crisp, 'roll-up-one's-sleeves-and-get-on-with-it' tone caused mild consternation in James, who suspected this was precisely the attitude that Shire girls, such as he presumed Wendy to be, took to bottling jam for the village fete. Wendy, being from Bath, had never made jam, though this was precisely the approach that she took to managing her Christmas card list each year, and it had never gone wrong yet. To her, James's scruffy attire spoke volumes about his lack of practicality. Had he not committed three murders prior to this she would have strongly questioned his ability to carry out an execution. In all events he was doubtless one of those people who paid utility bills late and never set an alarm.

There was silence as each scrutinised the other.

"Have you contacted Tanning like we discussed?" James said at length.

"I certainly did," she replied, looking at her watch. "He should be here any minute now."

"Great. So tell me what you said to him."

*****

Earlier that day Alan Tanning had reached one of the great milestones of his career: he had finally completed the arrangements for the Classics Outreach Fund. Now that his task had been completed Sir Malcolm would guarantee that Fringe became the ruler of the University, and Tanning, in reward for his slavish service to his academic master, would be elevated to a senior professorship. The pile of paperwork on his desk before him represented the glorious culmination of his many years as a loyal minion.

Gazing at the evidence of his handiwork, however, at the letters, balance sheets and forms all laid out before him, he felt not the slightest hint of jubilation. Each document signified his

298

part in a grand scheme of financial embezzlement, his role in a project of criminal corruption designed to consolidate the power of an already mighty academic clique. As he looked down at the mass of paperwork on his desk, the physical manifestation of the vast, criminal deceit, he quaked. Now that the arrangements for the Outreach Fund were complete and his role was fulfilled, the implications of what he had done filled his mind. He was a criminal. His part in one of the greatest acts of fraud the University had ever seen was set in stone. Even if no one else knew of the Fund's existence, the thought of his criminal liability, of the police one day knocking at his door, made him wince with fear.

Why did he ever agree to join Fringe's group of lackeys? How could the prospect of a professorship ever have lured him into this? His mind turned to his murdered colleagues, and any lingering sense of sadness or pity was washed away by clammy waves of anxiety. Beyond the grave, they were outside the reach of the law. He would have to answer for all of their crimes. He was the one whose life would be lived in fear of discovery, of imprisonment. Whilst they were free from worry and care, he would never be free to rest again.

He wiped a trembling hand over his brow and turned away from his desk. He could not look at the papers. All the evidence needed for a life sentence was there before him, and as he contemplated the thought, sickness rose in his stomach.

Suddenly the phone rang.

He winced. He couldn't speak to anyone, not in this state. But what if it were Fringe demanding the papers be brought over? He swallowed hard and reached for the receiver. His voice, when he spoke, was hoarse.

"Hello?" he rasped.

"Hello is that Dr Tanning?" asked the female caller.

"Yes, this is Tanning. Who is this?"

"Good afternoon Dr Tanning, my name is Inspector Emma Knight from the Cambridgeshire Constabulary. Would this be a good time to talk?"

Tanning stifled a cry. What on earth could the police be calling about? They must have discovered the Outreach Fund. They had been digging into the lives of Mason, Wildencrust and Norther and had found out.

"W-Well, it's… I mean…" He gulped a mouthful of air and paused. Despite his panic he had to steady himself. "Yes it's fine to talk. What can I do for you?"

"Well Dr Tanning, during our investigations we turned up some interesting facts about Harriet Mason, Penton Wildencrust and Elliot Norther, and we wanted to question you about their relationships with each other. And yours with them."

Tanning could hear his heartbeat in his ears as he heard the words. There was no doubt in his mind: the police knew. He could no longer keep the fear from his voice.

"Inspector Knight, I really can't… I mean I don't know anything that would…" He was stumbling.

"It's okay, Dr Tanning," said the inspector reassuringly. She could sense his panic, and spoke in a soft voice that seemed to offer understanding. "Let me say first of all that there's no reason for you to be worried. You're not linked in any way to the investigation other than being in a position to offer us some background information."

Tanning's breathing had become heavy, and he gasped into the receiver.

"I see. Do I have to go to the… the police station?"

"Not if you'd rather we spoke somewhere else. Look, I can appreciate that you must be under terrible stress at the moment, and that a trip to the station isn't going to help your nerves; neither will us turning up at your place of work with all your colleagues present. I was going to suggest meeting you this evening after work in town. That way I can put some

300

questions to you, informally of course, and we needn't trouble you further. How about that?"

The thought of travelling down to the station filled Tanning's mind with dread, and he felt his heart thumping harder at the very mention of the idea. With the possibility of a discreet and informal meeting on offer, he gladly accepted.

"Oh yes, that would be much preferable! Much preferable indeed!"

"Good. Now I've got a lot of work on with the investigation, and I won't be able to meet you until nine."

"Very well, Inspector."

"We'll say at the end of the bridge on Garrett Hostel Lane, on the Trinity Hall side."

"Yes Inspector. I… I just wanted to add…"

"What?"

"That I had nothing to do with the financial arrangements at the Faculty. That was all down to Mason, Wildencrust and Norther."

Despite his relief in not having to visit the station, a nervous impulse had caused him to speak out, to deny any part in what he still felt sure the police now suspected.

There was a pause before the inspector replied.

"Yes, Dr Tanning. I've noted that down. See you this evening."

*****

"That's amazing!" whispered James, excitedly, his breath steaming in the cold night air. "And he didn't suspect a thing?"

"Apparently not," said Wendy.

"What did he say after you told him to meet you on the Trinity Hall side of the Bridge?"

"He didn't say anything. I just ended the call."

"Well congratulations to you!"

"Thanks," she smiled.

"Right, so we've definitely got everything? And you know exactly what to do?"

"Yes, James," she said, rolling her eyes. "We've been through it twice already. We'll force him to the ground and put the gimp mask over his head. Then we'll drag him to that corner and… finish him off."

"Yes but slowly, we have to strangle him slowly. And after that we'll strip him off, save for the mask, and drag him into the middle of the street."

"Can I just ask, James, did you think of that or was it the ones whose orders you follow?"

"Oh that was their idea. They wanted a slow, humiliating death," said James.

"That's pretty sick you know."

He made no reply, but simply shrugged his shoulders in the manner of one who has long since learnt that his protests bear no fruit.

At that moment a bicycle could be heard on the other side of the bridge. He and Wendy both turned at once.

"He's coming!" she whispered. "Get into position!"

*****

Tanning's breath made clouds of steam in the chill of the night air, and as he puffed his way up the notoriously steep bridge, it came in sharp bursts. His lungs were not as young as they used to be, and this was a route that he usually avoided precisely on that account. If a trip to the dreaded police station could be avoided, however, then an exception would gladly be made.

As he reached the crest of the bridge, he squinted into the dark depths of Garrett Hostel Lane. Save for the trickling river below he could hear nothing, and no one appeared to be waiting for him. He frowned as he leaned forward and allowed gravity to propel him on the downward journey.

Reaching the other side, he slowed his bike to a halt and paused. Still no sign of anyone making their way up the road. He checked his watch and noted that it was exactly nine o'clock. He would wait for a few more minutes. It was so cold that any longer and he would freeze.

Still sitting on his bike he blew into his gloved hands and rubbed them together. What would he say to her when she arrived? What if it turned out that she was not so accommodating as she had been on the phone, and started to ask him difficult questions? He would have to prepare himself for that. A pang of nerves shot through him at the thought of having to think on his feet. Surely she would know immediately if he lied to her? Her training must have prepared her to spot dissimulation and subterfuge? Perhaps he could...

Before the thought could form fully in his mind an impact knocked him sidewards and sent him tumbling to the ground. He tried to cry out but was winded, and could only gasp noiselessly. Had it been a car? Surely he would have heard it coming?

At that moment a new fear swelled in his stomach, as a hand reached down and grabbed his hair, yanking him upwards, whilst another pushed a cold, leathery mask over his head. This was an attack. Despite his disorientation Tanning's immediate realisation of this made him cry out in terror. He had to alert someone. But the mask was instantly tightened around his face, and his cry was released as a muffled choke. With his head wrapped in the darkness of the vile-smelling leather, his vision was severely constrained. Unable to see his attackers, he felt another pair of hands joining the first in wrenching him upwards and dragging him across the cold tarmac.

What the hell was happening? Who could they be? He struggled but found that one of the attackers had pinned his

303

arms behind his back, and as soon as he was brought to a halt a piece of rope was tied tightly about his wrists. With a sharp jolt he was thrown to the floor again.

"Please don't hurt me!" he tried to cry out. "Please, I'm just a lecturer, I've nothing of value! Just take my wallet, it's in my pocket!" But his pleas were merely distorted gasps from beneath the mask.

"I can't die!" he thought to himself. "I can't! Oh God, let Inspector Knight get here before they do whatever they're planning to do." Suddenly he paused and drew a sharp breath. His assailants were still outside his field of vision, but now he could hear the attackers talking. One of them had whispered the word 'cord' to the other. The word had a sinister resonance that made him shudder. "Oh Lord, what are they going to do to me?" he gasped inwardly. "I can't end up like Elliot. I have to escape. I have to get out of these bindings. I… I need to run…"

*****

"Pass me the cord, Wendy," said James, without taking his eyes from Tanning. The latter had fallen onto his side, and lay visibly shaking next to the wall. "Hold him still while I tie his neck with it."

"Right," said Wendy, kneeling down behind the lecturer and heaving him up. As she did so Tanning convulsed in his futile struggle against the ropes that held him, and a constrained mumbling could be heard from beneath his mask.

"Hold still!" she rasped in his ear.

Though, to her victim, her voice conveyed the animal brutality of an indiscriminate killer, her angry command was born entirely of professional urgency. He had something she needed, and she was determined to find it whilst James was fishing the cord from her bag. Her nimble fingers ran across

304

his body, searching for pockets until a chinking indicated her target.

Moments later James appeared. He held the length of material in his hand, and brandished it as he knelt down behind Tanning and next to Wendy.

"Ready?" he whispered.

"Yes."

"Remember Wendy, this needs to happen slowly, so make sure you hold him still."

"Will do."

With that, James reached round from behind the lecturer and sealed the cord around his neck. He shook as he prepared to tighten it. This was the first time that he had murdered someone with his bare hands. Even in Norther's case, Margo Goyle had been the means by which his victim was choked; it was she who had been in contact with his skin. Now, for the first time, James was to commit an act of classic murder and the thought weakened him.

He swallowed hard, closed his eyes and began to tighten the cord. Kneeling next to him, Wendy Pipford had averted her eyes and now focused on the dark shadows on the other side of the street. This was merely an event, a grand scoop that would be a boon to her career, nothing more than that. Once it was over and done with she would just have to forget it. She drew in a deep breath as she attempted to steady herself.

At that moment, just as Wendy exhaled and the cord was drawn taut in James's hands, Tanning jolted. His body lurched backwards so unexpectedly and with such force that Wendy was taken completely by surprise and thrown off balance. She stumbled backwards, and as she did so she instinctively grabbed James's coat, pulling him down with her. Both cried out in surprise, and their voices echoed down the empty street.

Instantly thrashing to get up, James's hand flailed in Tanning's direction, catching the rope that bound the lecturer's hands. The rough, sinewy material was hard against

305

his fingertips, and he noted the firmness of the knot. In that same instant, however, the solid construction of the knot changed. Suddenly the curves of rope, which had twisted around and upon themselves, slackened and fell away from each other. He gasped as he felt Tanning's bindings loosen.

Now James's shock turned to horror. He gritted his teeth and fought down the urge to yell in frustration. After a few desperate seconds he scrambled furiously to his feet and looked frantically about him. Tanning was no longer crouching on the floor, and the rope lay where it had been shed. James frantically turned and peered down the street into the darkness. His heart thumped in his ears and a prickly nausea rose in his stomach.

"Where the fuck has he gone?" he whispered to himself. "Wendy, where is he? He must have run into town! He's going to find someone on the street and tell them! We've got to…"

"There he is!" hissed Wendy, who had by now also clambered to her feet.

James followed the direction of her gloved finger and looked towards the river. There, thirty yards away near an old wall that skirted the grounds of Trinity College was Tanning. He had clambered into one of a pair of old punts that lay unused on the riverbank. Standing at one end of the little vessel, he was now pushing out into the black water with a punting pole.

For a moment James and Wendy stood in mute horror at the scene before them. Their masked victim was escaping, albeit at extremely low velocity. They bolted towards the river, though in the seconds it took them to reach the bank Tanning had made it too far out for either of them to get to him. Attempting to swim out was unthinkable in the biting cold, and the pair stood looking at each other in disbelief.

"What do we do?" whispered James urgently. "How are we going to…"

"There's another punt!" said Wendy, looking over his shoulder to the base of the wall. "Come on!"

She ran over and pushed the wooden craft into the river, wincing as it clattered over dry stone before rolling into the water. She jumped in and was immediately joined by James, who held in his hand a discarded pole that had been lying nearby.

"After him!" she hissed.

James hesitated.

"What's wrong?" she demanded.

"It's just that... I'm not really that good at punting," he replied sheepishly. "I only did it the once and my pole got stuck. I had to be rescued by a couple of girls in a kayak. Wouldn't you rather?"

"No!" she rasped. "You're the one who went to Cambridge! So punt! It's punt or prison! Make your choice!" She furiously indicated upstream with her outstretched hand.

James closed his eyes and inhaled determinedly.

"Okay I'll do it. Here we go! We're gonna catch that bastard!"

With that he dashed to the rear end of the boat and began repeatedly lunging his pole into the water. For several seconds nothing happened, and it took half a minute before the punt began to inch forward. Wendy's blood pressure mounted with each agonising second.

Looking up the river she suddenly noticed that Tanning was only twenty feet ahead. Turning to James her countenance was hopeful.

"James he's only just ahead of us!" she whispered, as loudly as she dared. "If you pick up the pace we can catch him!" She took another glance up the river. "Oh my God, he's almost as slow as you are. We're still in with a chance. Hurry!"

"I'm trying, Wendy! This is as fast as I can go!" he gasped, heaving the pole out of the water. Even in the gloom his cheeks shone red from the exertion.

Another minute passed, and the gap between the punts remained the same. Wendy was growing angry.

"James," she said, pointing emphatically. "The chap in that punt is a middle aged man who's just been violently assaulted, and you're slower than him! What's wrong with you?"

"Look I don't get much exercise, okay?" he snapped. "Don't be such a shrew!"

"A shrew?" she gasped in outrage. "How dare you!"

"Look, if you think you can do better, you take over."

"Fine, give me that pole!"

Wendy rose and they awkwardly changed places. Standing at the end of the punt, she began a furious exertion which, despite her efforts, produced not the slightest increase in their speed.

James could not resist a triumphant gloat.

"I notice he's still ahead of us, Miss Pipford. How's my punting looking now?"

"Oh shut up, James, we're going much faster," she hissed back. Her vigorous response was somewhat undermined, however, by the moorhen that gently paddled past them, offering a curious glance at the humans who were on the river at this time of night. With a dismissive chirp it proceeded to overtake them, and within moments had done the same to Tanning.

"Look, that duck's just overtaken us," whispered James. "That's how slow you are."

"That isn't a duck, it's a moorhen. That's how slow *you* are!" retorted Wendy.

"Whatever. I can see him now," said James, turning and noticing that the back of Tanning's gimp mask was clearly visible. The little padlock that had been used to seal it glinted in the moonlight.

"Great, throw something at him," commanded Wendy, who now cleaved the water with renewed enthusiasm.

James rummaged in her bag with a frown.

"There's nothing in here but more rope."

"Then use that."

"Okay," said James, reaching in. Gripping the rope in his hand he waved it over his head and threw it in the direction of the other punt. On the third attempt it landed with a feeble tap on Tanning's ankle.

"What the hell are you doing?" hissed Wendy incredulously.

"Well I'm, you know… whipping him," said James. He flung the rope again, though this time it missed the punt altogether and slopped into the water.

"Well stop it, you just look weird!"

"What am I supposed to do then?" asked James, sheepishly.

"For God's sake, make a loop and try to hook it onto him. Pull him off balance."

At this point the moorhen returned, gently bobbing alongside the punt as it floated inch by inch on its furious chase down the river. The bird immediately began chirping at James, militantly.

"Oh shit, that duck's back," he whispered nervously to Wendy. "It's making a bloody racket, too. Someone'll hear us at this rate."

"It a bloody moorhen, you idiot! And forget it. Just get on with that rope."

James hastily fashioned a rudimentary loop and proceeded to fling it girlishly at Tanning. Inevitably it missed its mark, though it caused Tanning to turn his head and frantically attempt to push his vessel more quickly through the water. Wendy's efforts were beginning to pay off, and the space between the two punts had started to diminish.

Perceiving this she whispered to James.

"Can you jump across that space?"

Tanning heard her and turned once again. Though his mask prevented scrutiny of his features, his posture suggested terror.

"I'll never make that," said James.

Wendy sighed angrily.

"Leave it to a woman," she whispered to herself, before lifting the pole out of the water and forcing it down with all her strength. After repeating the action twice the gap between the punts was reduced to three feet.

"How about now?" she panted.

"I'll try," said James. He rose and stepped to the end of the wooden craft. The water below was dark and forbidding, but with a deep intake of air he summoned his courage and leapt.

His landing was a hard one, and Tanning's punt shook violently at the impact. James immediately sank to his knees to avoid falling overboard, but a loud splash indicated that Tanning had not been able to steady himself in time. Rising at once, James looked over the side. There, thrashing in the darkness was the Senior Lecturer in Roman Wall Painting. The noise made James wince, though to his relief the gimp mask continued to prevent the don from giving voice to his terror.

"Yes!" he whispered to himself, punching the air. "He's dead, he's as good as..."

His elation turned at once to shock as he saw Tanning turn himself around and begin doggy-paddling to the grassy bank at the edge of the river. It was only fifteen feet away, and if he reached it he would be able to make his getaway across the lawns of Clare College.

"Fuck!" James hissed desperately. "What the fuck am I supposed to do? I can't get in myself."

"Hey, take this!"

His thoughts were interrupted by Wendy. She had manoeuvred the punt alongside Tanning's, and as James turned he saw that she was extending the pole to him. He grabbed it without hesitation.

Tanning had now proceeded four feet further towards the bank, silently shimmying through the water with clumsy strokes. Reaching out with the pole, its end tipped with a metal hook, James began to make equally clumsy prodding movements at the lecturer's back, prompting the latter to do all he could to speed up. After a few attempts, however, James caught the hook on a fold of clothing and pulled back, dragging Tanning towards the punt.

"Do it!" rasped Wendy from the other vessel.

James plunged the pole into the water, applying all his weight as he did so. Instantly, and with a silent gasp, Tanning was pushed down into the cold blackness. As soon as he disappeared under the surface the sound of thrashing vanished. James held firm against the struggles that could be felt through the pole until, after what seemed like hours, a series of bubbles broke against the surface. Moments later, the struggling began to diminish, until finally it ceased altogether.

Looking over his shoulder, James's smile was met with a knowing nod from Wendy and a familiar vibration from the pocket containing his phone.

CHAPTER TWENTY SIX

After a careful manoeuvring of their punt and some deft work with the wooden pole, Wendy and James dragged Tanning's body to the grassy riverbank. It was now a question of waiting for the corpse to be discovered, and as they punted downstream to a point where they could safely disembark, James turned over the killing in his mind. A slower and more humiliating death could not have been asked for. He glanced over at his companion as she exerted herself once more in pushing the little craft forward. She had been an asset. Who knows how things would have gone without her?

Having travelled a hundred yards up the river, the water dripping from the pole the only accompaniment to their silence, they found a spot. As James clambered out, Wendy rummaged in her bag. Producing a bottle, she sprinkled its contents around the inside of the punt, reached over for James's hand and stepped onto the grass.

She glanced at him as she fished a box of matches out of her coat pocket.

"Ready?"

He nodded.

At a stroke the little craft that had delivered death to the fourth victim was set ablaze.

*****

"Well, I'll say goodnight, then," said Wendy.

"Okay. But make sure you head straight home. I mean, you look like you're holding up pretty well, considering, but what we've just done will hit you soon. Trust me. You'll need some time to gather your nerves for the next one."

"I know, James. And thank you."

"You were... well, rather brilliant actually," he said sheepishly. "I don't know if it's the adrenaline making me say this, but I... well, I don't think I could have done it without you. You know, not quite as easily I mean," he added quickly.

This sudden warmth of feeling alarmed her, and she dismissively patted him on the shoulder in a display of chumminess so emphatic as to verge on hammy.

"Er, right, well let's get going then," James responded, straightening his back and adopting an awkward, business-like tone. "Remember: straight home."

"Of course James," she replied.

The words were fresh in her mind as she walked alone down Queen's Road. She purposefully made her way to Sidgwick Avenue, where a cluster of academic buildings were located. Amongst them a great looming hulk of forbidding presence was her target. Standing before it and noting that none of the windows were lit, she prepared herself for the foray.

She reached into her pocket and produced the key-ring that she had spirited from Tanning's coat in the moments after the ambush. It contained only three keys. One was marked 'Room 1.07,' the other 'Main Door' and the last, unmarked, appeared to be domestic.

With a muffled clunk Wendy unlocked the entrance to the Classics Faculty and slipped inside.

In the hall it was dark and silent, and despite an acute awareness that time was of the essence, she paused. The atmosphere of the empty building was more chilling than she had expected. Its bleak, bare-brick walls lent a sinister countenance to the plaster casts of Ancient Roman busts that lined them. Set deep within white, bloodless faces, the eyes of the dead men seemed to gape at her. She suppressed a shudder at the prospect of venturing through the corridors.
Straightening her back, however, she set about finding Tanning's office.

313

Prudence made her loath to turn on the lights, and instead she relied on the feeble illumination of the emergency exit signs. As she advanced through the Faculty her determined level-headedness began to give way. Several times as she turned corners or crept down long, windowless passages she was frozen by the same, sudden sound: a low arrhythmic whistling, each time seeming to move a little closer. With ever more strained attempts, however, she continued on her way. Once, having passed an inconspicuous stairwell, curiosity had diverted her from her search. Grasping the banisters and squinting, she had peered upwards, her eyes piercing the gloom to distinguish three upper levels. They were empty, though on the first-floor landing she caught sight of a shape, blacker than the surrounding darkness and outlined against the banister. A shiver ran across her shoulders. Suddenly it moved, darting towards the stairs, and in a rush of terror Wendy bolted. Running blindly through the corridors, she worked herself into breathlessness before she stopped and regained her composure. After further seemingly interminable searching, all the while looking over her shoulder and with nervous gasps before every turn, she eventually found Room 1.07 and unlocked the door to Tanning's office. Slamming it shut behind her, she leant against it and inhaled deeply.

"For God's sake Wendy, get a hold of yourself," she said aloud. "There was nothing there, nothing at all, so take yourself in hand."

Relieved at this self-administered dose of sensible advice, she flicked the light switch. To hell with stealth, she wanted be out of this place as soon as possible. The nagging doubt that it might all have been a waste of time, that there was nothing to find, was ruthlessly squashed.

Squinting against the instant brightness, Wendy surveyed the room. The walls, also of the same, dreadful bare-brick, were unadorned. Long shelves were lined with books and tatty periodicals, with not an ornament amongst them to enliven the deadening space. Conspicuous on the desk was an ancient computer, which played tenant to teetering piles of bureaucratic detritus. The mountains of paper that spanned the desk formed an uninterrupted range encompassing the computer's tower and its immense monitor. Only the keyboard was bare, each otherwise dirty key bearing an incongruous clean slick in place of a letter.

Something was amongst them. Wendy could feel it. And if she had to excavate, then so be it. Her watch said quarter to ten. If she hurried she could still get to the office for midnight and get her exclusive on the murder out for the morning run.

She rolled up her sleeves and set to work. Alone she laboured, searching for the secrets of Alan Tanning, whilst out in the silence of the night the darkness clung to the dead man's body as it lay on the grass by the river, discarded but waiting to be found.

CHAPTER TWENTY SEVEN

Whoever it was at the door, they were persistent. Three rings on the bell had gone unanswered, and now they were holding their finger on the buzzer with ear-splitting determination.

"Bloody hell," thought James. "It's 3am, who could it possibly be?" He had returned home from the killing hours before, but had yet to go to bed. Still in his dark, deliberately anonymous clothes, he sat at his desk and ran his fingers across his brow. The piercing sound unnerved him. He had never been any good with buzzing, high frequency noises. Until the age of twelve he had fled to his room whenever his parents' ancient washing machine reached full spin.

He could take it no longer. Replacing his mug of tea on his desk, he hesitantly rose and made his way downstairs, during which time the noise had splintered into a series of rapid bursts.

"Wendy!" he exclaimed upon opening the door. "What are you doing here? It's…"

"3am. Yes, I know." She bundled past him into the hall. "Sorry, but I need to speak to you, it's important."

With a tentative glance up and down the street, James retreated inside.

"What's happened? Is something wrong? We weren't seen were we? Oh God, we can't have been seen! Surely someone…"

"Get a grip, we weren't seen. Goodness, you're like a wet hen. Look, are your housemates in?"

"No but…"

"Good, let's go to your room. This hallway's nearly as cold as the street."

"Well I don't really think we…"

But she was already bounding up the stairs.

316

Striding through his open door, she began to undo her coat when, with a gasp of surprise, she spotted someone standing by the desk. It was a young woman, not more than nineteen, and of an appearance that Wendy had only ever seen in passing during forays into the less salubrious parts of town. Tight, violently bleached hair was torturously scraped back into a ponytail, giving full display to neon-coloured slatherings that coated her lips and eyelids. She was appallingly dressed, with a dirty hoody hanging over a micro skirt, and laddering in her tights forming so extensive a system of canals across her scrawny legs that Wendy wondered if it wasn't part of a design. A brief glance at the shocking pink trainers, however, indicated that cogency of dress held little sway with this striking personage. Around her neck she sported a large, sparkling necklace composed of fake diamonds. Together they formed a single word which, amongst her blisteringly colourful collage of rags, doubled as both a mark of ironic subtlety and the young lady's bombastic description of herself: 'BABE-A-LICIOUS!'

"Oh... Awfully sorry," said Wendy, flustered. "I didn't realise that..."

James suddenly appeared behind her, his face flushed with panic.

"Wendy.... This is, er... I mean it's..."

"I'm James's girlfriend, Leticia," said the Muse in her melodic twang.

"Golly," thought Wendy. "That's his girlfriend? Surely not? She's a complete wreck. And who on earth calls their child Leticia?" She was certain that restraint had prevented her face from expressing her surprise, but as the thoughts formed in her mind she shuddered to see the young woman's eyes suddenly darken.

"Oh damn," she said inwardly. "Have I just grimaced by mistake? But I'm pretty sure that... Oh God, she looks angry!"

Leticia's overcrowded lashes bristled against one another as she suddenly scowled threateningly.

Wendy was plunged into a fit of middle-class fluster. Her cheeks reddened and she looked about her, desperately searching for a place to settle her gaze, only to be drawn by the sparkle of the fake diamonds. Realising that she was staring, she hastily looked away, only for her eyes to fall upon the irresistible glare of the neon trainers.

She flinched, and panic set in.

"Oh God, I'm staring! Now she'll think I'm trying to look down on her. Oh Lord!"

She winced at the thought of provoking such a creature of the streets. Her nerves, however, increased as she considered her own sudden appearance.

"Crikey, I've barged into her boyfriend's house at 3am and come straight up to his bedroom. She probably thinks I'm here to try it on with him!"

She forced herself to breath normally. Any conspicuous signs of fear would confirm what this Leticia woman surely thought.

"Okay Wendy, just give her a smile," she thought, desperately. "Give her a nice smile to show that you're not a threat to her."

But mounting tension proved too strong, and thwarted her attempts to tease her facial muscles into a friendly countenance.

"Oh blast, this isn't a smile!" she winced. "I look like I'm sneering at her! I've walked into her boyfriend's room, looked her up and down and sneered at her like a man-eating, chav-hating bitch!"

"Don't worry, darling," said Leticia, whose countenance suddenly softened. "I know you don't mean no harm."

Her assurance, being entirely unexpected, was so welcome that Wendy visibly breathed a sigh of relief.

"Oh yes, that's... that's right. Of course I don't," she said, exhaling deeply. "Wait, how did you...?"

"Sorry darling, gotta go. Lovely meeting you," said the Muse with a knowing smile.

She made her way to the door in the type of shoulder-swinging swagger necessary to command respect on a youth-infested shop corner. As she passed James she ran her bright talons lightly across his chest and smiled, it seemed to Wendy, more in amusement that affection.

"Gotta go, babe. We'll finish what we were talking about later."

After she made her way down the stairs, several moments of awkward silence followed, terminated by the sound of the front door clunking shut.

"Sorry Wendy, I should've mentioned that..."

"No really, I'm sorry, I... I didn't have the right to just barge..."

"Oh that's fine, fine..."

"And Leticia is... she's just... lovely..."

"Oh thanks, thanks, I... So shall we, er... You wanted to tell me something?"

"Yes I did."

With an end to the painful exchange of half-finished pleasantries at last forthcoming, Wendy began to reveal to James the secrets she had unearthed in Tanning's office.

CHAPTER TWENTY EIGHT

"Calm down everyone, calm down!" yelled Dionysos. Though his plea was barely heard over the jubilant cries of the packed council chamber, the god was unmoved. Sitting in the speaker's chair, he could scarcely be bothered to keep order, and was almost content to allow the furore to continue until it had run its course. Since his misuse at the hands of Aphrodite and his public humiliation by Hera, his commitment had withered. In truth he was bored with the mission to wipe out the members of the Cambridge List, and couldn't wait until the project was over and done with.

The same could not be said for the Goddess of Desire. In her usual spot in the front row, Aphrodite smouldered with delight as she heard her name on immortal lips around the hippocampus.

"Glory be to you, beautiful one!" cried Helios, God of the Sun.

"Hail, Mistress of Seduction! Hail!" yelled Hephaestus, divine ruler of craftsmanship.

Even Herakles, a sour goat at the best of times, was on his feet, stamping his approval and saluting Aphrodite from the back row.

Amidst the clamour of success, Aphrodite could scarcely suppress a smile of satisfaction. The death of Tanning had gone fabulously and the prevailing feeling of the council was that she the one responsible. There was political capital to be made of this, and as she glanced around the chamber, absorbing the sound of raucous applause, her eyes eventually fell upon the one deity other than Dionysos who remained seated.

Hera was unmoved by the success of the fourth murder. Around her, gods and goddesses had risen and were waving and shouting. Her face, however, remained an image of sour dissatisfaction. With every cry of Aphrodite's name her eyes darkened, and each congratulatory remark thrown across the floor was a wound to Hera's pride. How had the council come to associate the killing with the Goddess of Desire? Why did none of them call Hera's name aloud? As the moments passed, her temper increased until she could no longer exercise restraint.

Slamming her fists onto the bench, the sound echoed even above the jubilant roar, and as she rose the noise dulled to a hushed silence.

"You wish to speak, Hera?" ventured Dionysos. His resigned countenance gave way to concern as he recognised the body language of the predator.

"Yes, chairman." Her reply was subdued, though as she cast her hateful gaze around the room, the sense of threat was palpable. "I would first like to remark on what a well-executed killing that was."

A long pause greeted this unexpectedly moderate opening, followed by a nervous murmur of approval.

"I would like to think that the final act of vengeance will be carried out just as effectively," she continued. "There is, however, something that I would like to discuss before we determine how the fifth murder will be enacted."

"And... And what's that, Hera?" Dionysos was apprehensive as he saw her stare meet that of Aphrodite.

"I wish to know why so many in this chamber should give credit for this killing to *her*." A slender, milky-white finger was raised and pointed menacingly at the Goddess of Desire, whose only response was a polite smile. "Why is it," continued Hera, her voice beginning to rise, "that *she* should be praised for this enterprise when it came as a result of... of... *compromise* between us?" She balked as she spoke the offensive word.

Now it was Aphrodite's turn to stand and command the attention of the council. She rose slowly and purposefully, gathering about her the eyes and ears of the assembled immortals, who leaned forward on the benches in eager anticipation.

"Well Hera, I can only say that I'm sorry if you feel you've been left out. I can't imagine how awful that must be." Her patronising tone was calculated for provocative effect. If Hera's temper could be piqued, her self-control would diminish, and then she could be tripped up. "I think you'll find, however, that I have *taken* none of the credit for this. It is simply that credit," she paused, looking slowly around the room and smiling as if in conspiracy with the audience, "has generously been *given* to me."

Laughter rippled across the benches, jabbing at Hera's veneer of moderation.

"I was not *left out*," came the reply through clenched teeth. "Everyone knows the truth."

"Which is?"

"That I am just as responsible as you are for the success of the murder."

At this, Aphrodite placed her hands on her hips and turned dramatically to the rows behind, eyebrows arched in comic surprise.

"Well Hera," she said to the sound of delighted laughter from across the chamber, "if you say so."

"Yes I bloody well do say so!" bellowed Hera. "As a matter of fact…"

"Yes?" smiled Aphrodite, with heavy condescension.

"As a matter of fact it's more my success than yours. That's right, my fucking success!"

This was all that Aphrodite had waited to hear, and she went in for the kill. The smile fell from her face and she adopted a serious air, raising her hand and wordlessly ending the continuing laughter.

"I thought that this great success was enjoyed by all the gods, Hera."

The Queen of the Gods saw the trap too late, and flustered.

"Well I... That's not what I..."

"I had thought," continued Aphrodite, "that this great murder, this lawful vengeance, was the shared glory of all the immortals in this great chamber? Is that not the case?"

"Well yes, but look here!"

"Very well then," cried Aphrodite. As Hera stammered to regain her footing the Goddess of Desire spoke over her head and addressed the assembled deities. "You have all been so kind as to credit me with this victory, when it is you who should be thanked for it!"

At this, approving voices began to make themselves heard.

"For a victory of mine is a victory of yours, and I declare that the next victory will be even greater than the last. I propose a murder in fire!"

This came out of the blue. To propose a new method of killing in the midst of a victory speech was unheard of, and gasps resonated around the chamber.

"Just what do you think you're playing at?!" yelled Hera, still reeling at being wrong-footed.

"What say you, gods and goddesses?" continued Aphrodite, cutting her off once again. "Will you accept my proposal for death in fire and consolidate our collective glory yet further?"

The roar of triumph that had filled the chamber at the beginning of the session now returned as a cry of approving bloodlust.

"Yes, yes! Let the mortal sinner burn! Glory to us all! Glory to Aphrodite!" shouted Demeter.

"Death in flame! Aphrodite shall bring glory to the immortals! Hail! Hail!" roared Ares.

Hera looked about her in horror. The crowds had swallowed that bitch's rhetoric about democracy *and* her plan for the next death! This was too much. This could not be tolerated.

Aphrodite read the machinations on her enemy's face as if they were put into script. Now the final move had to be made before the game could be played out and her great adversary brought low once and for all.

"Hera," she yelled over the noise. "Will you join us? Will you accept my plan, my great formulation? Will you accept that the glory shared through me will bring glory to us all?"

"She honours all the gods alike!" cried Hephaestus.

"What a democratic attitude she has!" yelled Herakles, forgetting himself. "Her success with Tanning proved it, and her plan for death in fire will do so again! Glory be!"

"She mocks me! She's openly mocking me!" raged Hera inwardly, as she turned and stared in rage at the rejoicing masses. "Accept *her* formulation? *Her* plan?" Formerly she might have turned the situation on its head. Once she might have used wile and rhetoric, brash and bullying to rally the chamber to her own cause, but now humiliation had been poured upon humiliation. She gave vent to her fury and it overcame her.

"Never!" she cried above the deafening roar. "I will never accept your plan!"

"Then you do not accept that glory is for the council to share." Aphrodite's reply was barely audible, but in those words the Goddess of Desire delivered such a blow as she had never struck before, and one whose force would not truly be felt until the flames had consumed the fifth victim of the Cambridge List.

She turned and nodded commandingly at Dionysos, whose shock at this sudden outburst was visible.

"M-Motion passed!" he yelled above the deafening noise.

324

CHAPTER TWENTY NINE

"KILLER STILL AT LARGE AS NEW VICTIM
DISCOVERED! UNDERTAKERS REPORT BUMPER
PROFITS!" bellowed The Chronicle.

"LECTURER'S CORPSE FOUND DUMPED BY
RIVER BANK: NO 'DUCK-SPECTS' HAVE BEEN
NAMED," screamed The Echo.

"LETCHY LECTURER FOUND DEAD! RESIDENTS
FEAR FOR SAFETY! FEMALE UNDERGRADS
RELIEVED!" gasped The Clarion.

In the domestic opulence of his study, Paul Fringe
scowled at the papers laid out on his desk. Every one of them
was a rag, a disgusting local rag written for the pathetic little
specimens that populated the town. As he read and re-read the
headlines, irritation rose in his stomach and the sound of his
heartbeat thudded in his ears. It had been doing so ever since
Miss MacAfree had knocked on his bedroom door early that
morning. She had been out on an errand, and had noticed the
first editions of the papers in the local newsagents.

What on earth had she been thinking, bothering him with
local gossip?

Urgent news, Miss MacAfree had replied, breathlessly.
Alan Tanning had been murdered; his body discovered by the
river on the grounds of Clare College.

Fringe had momentarily been rendered mute. If Tanning
were dead and it had already been reported in the papers, then
the police…

Within minutes he had dressed, and in the company of
Miss MacAfree was speeding down the lanes in his motorcar
into town. Through Newnham they hurtled, down Sidgwick
Avenue and onwards to the Faculty. In those early hours it
was still locked up, and Fringe had let out an audible gasp of
relief at the sight of the darkened windows. The police had not

yet arrived. There was still time. But it would not be long before officers appeared, drawn to investigate the circumstances surrounding the wretched man's murder. Soon detectives would want to search his office to retrace his movements. And when they opened the doors and saw the papers on his desk, all the evidence of the great fraud would be there before them, waiting to be read. Fringe had winced at the thought. If a police officer so much as glimpsed the contents of Tanning's office he could kiss goodbye to his freedom, never mind the Vice Chancellorship.

They proceeded with unprecedented speed to Room 1.07, from which they systematically removed every scrap of evidence pertaining to the scheme. Even the computer was taken, its immense screen clasped between the sturdy, gardening-hardened arms of Miss MacAfree. There had been, of course, no need to explain to her the great fraud; she who had helped Fringe perpetrate many a crime before. It was enough that he required her service for her to act upon his whim, and if it be in a cause whose dark intent separated her from the weak specimens of humanity whom she detested with a vehemence equal to her master's, then so much the better.

Thus, with the boot of the car filled, Fringe and Miss MacAfree had proceeded home in haste.

From the knock at his bedroom door that morning, the throbbing pressure in Fringe's head had exerted itself with dreadful urgency. Now, sitting at his desk, his bloodless hands clasped together and the incessant sound of shredding coming from one of the upstairs rooms, the throb continued unabated.

"That moron," whispered Fringe, his voice hoarse with fury. "That little streak of spittle. Killed. Killed, like all the others."

The shredding momentarily stopped as an exhausted motor made a grinding protest, before the rhythmic drone resumed once again.

"No matter, though, no matter. With that idiot dead and out the way, and the evidence being dealt with by Miss MacAfree, the scheme will never become known."

He closed his eyes and the flickers of a dreamlike smile animated his tight lips.

"In mere days I shall become Vice Chancellor. Vice Chancellor of the University! And then nothing can touch me, nothing. Let them die, all of them. If the deaths of those worthless insects have been sent to test me, then I've shown myself more than worthy. Soon I shall take my rightful place..."

At this moment Miss MacAfree entered the room. She was covered in sweat, and her demeanour was one of high tension.

"Excuse me, sir," she said, wiping her brow with her substantial forearm. "I've disposed of the offending papers. How should I proceed with the computer?"

"Any way you like, Miss MacAfree," whispered Fringe, whose eyes remained closed. "I suggest burial in the garden."

"Very good, sir." She turned, before hesitating. "Excuse me, sir, but with regard to the computer..."

"Yes?"

"What might the police think when they find it missing from the office? No one else knows the existence of the papers, but surely it will be assumed that he used a computer. What is..."

"That's enough speculation!" spat Fringe as his eyes flickered open. "What the police suspect or do not suspect about the computer is of no concern. The only concern I have is getting through the next two days and taking my place as Vice Chancellor." His voice was strained and his gaze unfocused. Miss MacAfree had never before seen him like this. His self-control, always worn about him like a mantle, was slipping.

"Very well, sir. I'll prepare to burn and bury it."

"No, Miss MacAfree. You will first bring me some champagne."

"But, sir…"

His eyes were wide and his face a sickly pale.

"To toast my impending elevation."

"Very good, sir."

*****

"Excellent stuff, this," mumbled Dave through a mouthful of cheese and pickled onion sandwich.

"Thanks, Dave," said Wendy, wincing as she observed a fresh sprinkling of crumbs coat his filthy desk. The editor's office was even more of a pigsty today than usual; the result of another night of excited activity prompted by the discovery of Tanning's body.

"I was talking about the fact that this nutter is still out there getting down to business on every don who sticks his head out the front door."

"Charming," muttered Wendy under her breath. The pulverised contents of Blythe's mouth were exposed as he spoke, as if to exaggerate the coarse, unformed character of the man himself. She turned her head away in distaste.

"Now listen, every paper in town has got this story tied up. Basically, right now we're all level pegging. What I want from you is an exclusive. A bloody great scoop that'll put us way ahead in the game. Tell me what you can… mmwf fmrw mmwr…"

Another mouthful of soon-to-be-demolished sandwich had been shovelled into his mouth mid-sentence. Wendy noted with relief that there were only a few bites left, and found herself instinctively willing him to finish.

"Well, Dave, there is something I've got that might just…"

She trailed off. Blythe leant forward with the contents of his mouth once again exposed, though this time in silent curiosity.

"What is it, Wendy? You've got something? Well spit it out."

She hesitated. If she took the next step there would be no going back. Awkward questions would be inevitable.

"Come on, Wendy, if you've got something show me."

"Okay, Dave. It's like this. You know the dons that have been killed?"

"What about them?"

"They were all senior members of the Classics Faculty at the University, weren't they?"

Blythe rolled his eyes and bit down again on his sandwich irritably.

"That had better not be your juicy little bit of gossip!" he snapped.

"Of course not, Dave, what I'm trying to…"

"Spit it out, girl!" he said in another shower of crumbs.

She paused, and for a moment held his gaze.

"They were all part of a large-scale fraud operation."

Blythe stopped chewing.

"They were…?"

"Part of a fraud ring. A big one. Together they were siphoning off Faculty funds to an off-shore account."

"What sort of funds? How much are we talking?"

"Millions," said Wendy. "

Blythe remained silent, and fixed her with a look of scepticism.

"How do you know?" he asked in a hushed voice.

At this she looked away. If she played her hand badly here the implications might be severe. No one could know that she had been in Tanning's office. If they discovered it then she would be undone.

329

"I was…" she swallowed again and steadied herself. Looking up, she met his gaze. "I was informed by an insider in the Faculty. A source whose anonymity I've guaranteed."

"A source? Well have you got proof that what they've told you is legit?"

"Yes I've got it right here."

A look of predatory anticipation manifested itself on Blythe's blotchy face. He leaned over and looked instinctively at Wendy's bag.

Ignoring his stare, she rummaged in her pocket and produced a USB drive.

"It's on here."

"Well plug it in, quick!" said Blythe, gesturing impatiently at his computer.

Moments later, photographs of the documents she had seen only hours before had been uploaded, and they flicked through them together. With Blythe's revolting pickle breath filling her nostrils she leant beside him and led him through the trail of fraud.

As she pointed out the records of transactions, the complex manoeuvrings of money from one fund to another and the details of the numbered Swiss bank account, the editor of The Cambridge Clarion remained in mute shock. This was his story. This was what would put him ahead. He could see it now. The other editors at the rival papers would choke when they picked up the headline. It would run something like "Great Big Fraud in Faculty," or maybe "Massive Con Discovered," or… well, something snappy. He'd always been crap at headlines, but one of the monkeys in the newsroom could come up with that. Anyway, who cares about the wording, it'd be the scoop of the year.

Wendy, glancing at his face, perceived his greedy approval and guessed rightly what he was thinking. Her lips tightened as she prepared for him to ask her to explain everything she had just been through.

"So where does the money come from, then?"

"Well, Dave, as I've just mentioned, it's from the Classics Outreach Fund."

"Which is…?"

"A pot of money made up of corporate and private donations solicited for the purpose of promoting the study of classics both in the UK and abroad. It's actually one of the largest funds of its kind in the country."

"And who's the money ultimately going to?"

"Impossible to say. Whoever it is, these documents don't name them. Chances are it's meant to be that way. Whoever it is, they're very powerful."

"And all four of the murdered dons were involved?"

"Well it's clear that Tanning and Norther were responsible for most of what you might call the 'administrative' aspect of the scheme. Their names can be found in the correspondence with several of the parties listed in these documents. Mason and Wildencrust are mentioned, but mainly in emails that refer to meetings with contacts. It seems clear, though, when you read between the lines that someone was giving them orders."

"Who was it?" Blythe was enthralled.

Wendy shook her head.

"I don't know. Whoever it is, they were very careful to avoid doing anything that might have left a paper trail."

"And your source handed you these pictures?"

"Yes. They said they'd known about the scheme for a long time and couldn't stand by any longer."

Blythe leaned back and whistled through his teeth.

"So the four murdered dons were killed for their involvement."

"I guess so," said Wendy, hoping she sounded more convincing to Blythe than she did to herself.

"Well you've really pulled a rabbit out of the hat with this one, my girl. We're gonna clean up with this one. When this hits the shelves later on we're gonna cause a storm."

"You mean…?"

"Yep, I'm pulling the morning headline and putting this up for the afternoon issue. So go on, girl, get back to your desk. You've got two hours before we go to print."

CHAPTER THIRTY

Miss MacAfree had been waiting outside the door for twenty minutes, knowing that she would be needed again soon. Listening to the noises coming from Fringe's study, she strained to hear his voice. The seconds ticked loudly by on the grandfather clock on the opposite wall, but still nothing. Finally deciding that action really ought to be taken, she tentatively pushed open the door and peered round.

"Sir?" she ventured. "Sir? Are you alright?"

But her master was not to be seen. The room, with its well-ordered sense of luxury, might have been empty. But he was in there somewhere. Walking over to the desk, she saw the copy of the local rag that she had brought him twenty minutes before. As she re-read the headline her face once again darkened with anger.

"MURDERED DONS IN MULTI-MILLION POUND FRAUD RING! MASSIVE CORRUPTION AT CLASSICS FACULTY! MILLIONS SIPHONED TO SWISS ACCOUNTS!"

"How dare they," she whispered under her breath. "Filthy gutter press."

Peering around the room, she still could not see Fringe.

The television, set within its antique cabinet, was on and the volume of the BBC news reporter's voice competed with that of the radio, where a commentator was announcing the latest development reported in The Clarion. Miss MacAfree winced as the voices merged into each other, knowing that each syllable was a knife to her master's hopes.

"You're here with me, Emily Crawford, on BBC Radio 4, and if you've just joined us we're discussing breaking news from Cambridge. A local newspaper has reported the existence of documents detailing a massive fraud operation carried out by the highest members of the Cambridge Classics Faculty and involving the four murdered academics. Speculation is rife that…"

"I'm on the scene at the Classics Faculty in Cambridge where, as you can see behind me, there is a heavy police presence. Since the story broke that a massive fraud operation has been uncovered involving all four of the murdered academics, many have wondered not only whether the murderer will strike again, but who is behind the plot. Suspicion is falling on…"

"The head of the Faculty, Professor Paul Fringe, has not been available for comment since the story hit headlines, though police will doubtless want to speak to him about what is becoming one of the biggest scandals that Cambridge has seen since…"

"…turning into a scandal of national significance, compounded by the fact that Professor Paul Fringe, head of the Faculty, has been unavailable for comment…."

"… is not in his office and has been unavailable to comment on the situation. Police have not confirmed the existence of such documents, and questions are being asked as to how copies fell into the hands of a local paper, prompting suspicions that…"

"…speculation of a mole inside the Faculty. We'll be providing constant coverage of the…"

"…round-the-clock reporting from the Faculty itself, which will be available on the BBC News website."

Miss MacAfree stormed over to the cabinet and angrily silenced the television and radio. Where on earth was Professor Fringe? He couldn't possibly have left the room without her seeing. After delivering the paper to him she had waited outside, knowing the effect it would have on him. She couldn't bear to think of his reaction as he read it, and the fact that he was nowhere to be seen filled her with dread.

Suddenly a small movement in the corner of her eye caught her attention. It came from beside a large, heavily embroidered chair near the window. She marched over, and there cowering behind it was Fringe.

"Oh, sir!" she gasped with relief. "I didn't know where you were! I thought perhaps you…" But she stopped herself. Fringe had not looked up at her. He was crouching, his knees pulled up to his chest and his eyes staring into space. "Sir? Are you alright?"

Seconds passed, and in the silence the ticking of the great clock in the hall could still be heard. Miss MacAfree was about to ask again when, without warning, Fringe spoke. His voice was hoarse and his speech seemed laboured.

"It has happened."

Miss MacAfree looked at him concerned.

"What has happened, sir?"

"*It* has happened, Miss MacAfree."

"Sir, I know that this has happened very suddenly but you mustn't assume that the worst will…"

"It has happened. He has called. It is over." Fringe's voice was stilted and his frame trembled as he spoke. Still he did not look up at her. "The ambassador has called. I am… I am *not* to be made Vice Chancellor."

"But Sir!"

"I am… *not*… to be made Vice Chancellor. The scheme has been uncovered and I am a… he called me… a liability. He said that I was… a…"

His voice was increasing in volume as he spoke, though with anger, shock or some other emotion Miss MacAfree could not tell. His trembling was growing stronger.

"Sir, I don't think you should…"

"A liability!" Now he screamed, and Miss MacAfree stepped backwards.

"Sir, please!"

"Everything I've done! Everything! And now this! Everything taken from me at a stroke!"

335

Slowly he rose from the floor, with a countenance so fierce that Miss MacAfree backed instinctively towards the door.

"A liability!" Suddenly he grabbed a substantial china vase from the table closest at hand and threw it at his housekeeper. It missed by inches, and Miss MacAfree ran from the room and up the stairs. Behind her she could hear the dreaded word repeated again and again as Fringe stormed into the hall and back into the study again. She had seen her master's fury erupt before, and had learned not to be present when it did so. She ran to her room at the top of the house and locked the door behind her. In the past, such outbursts, usually provoked by a minion who had failed to perform adequately, had abated. Now that his lifelong hopes lay in ruins, however, she feared his present instability would not die down so readily.

"No good end will come of this," she said to herself, pacing her room as the noises from two floors below became increasingly savage.

CHAPTER THIRTY ONE

"Knock, knock," said Muesli as she pushed open the door to James's bedroom. "Anyone at home?"

The room, as usual, was a pigsty, and the Muse tutted lightly as she scanned the debris. James was sitting on the bed, staring into space. She carefully picked her way over to his side.

"You okay, Jimmy? You don't look yourself."

"No I'm not okay actually, Muesli." His voice was distant. Though calm it betrayed a tinge of emotion that the Muse detected at once.

"What's happened," she said, kneeling and looking into his face.

"Wendy. She told me everything. Everything that went on in that... fucking... faculty."

"When did she tell you this? You mean after I was last here? But babe, that was hours ago. You mean to tell me you've been up here this whole time getting stewed-up over that?"

"Yes I've been bloody well getting *stewed-up* over that!" he snapped.

"Okay, sorry, don't bite my head off. Bloody hell."

"You knew?"

"Of course I did, babe. All the gods knew. But that fraud business was irrelevant mortal shit. We were only concerned about how the actions of the dons towards your thesis affected our honour. And since all five of them were involved in marking it we decided..."

"Why the hell didn't you tell me?"

"What difference would it have made? Like I said, it was all background shit. Besides, you've been killing them off one-by-one, so what's the problem? You've been getting your revenge, we've been getting ours."

337

At this James stood up and walked across the room. For a few moments he said nothing, but then turned to face the Muse.

"I can't exactly... It's just that... When I was killing them, even though I was reluctant at first, I came round to the idea. I remembered what they had done to me and... well it was still a form of revenge. Even though you made me," he said, shooting her a firm glance. "But now I know that chucking me out was just one part of some elaborate fraud; just a means of getting something else that had nothing to do with me..." He breathed in heavily. "It just means that I was even less significant to them than I thought when they failed me."

The Muse looked pityingly at him.

"Oh, darlin. What do you care? They obviously didn't give a shit about you either way, so what difference does this make? No offence, but come on, babe."

"I can't explain it!" said James, suddenly angry. "But... well what with being failed by the Faculty and then commandeered as your murder weapon, I felt like I was a punch-bag for everyone else. And now I discover just how true that was. It just... It just makes me fucking angry!"

He clenched his fists tightly.

"Well if you like I can leave you alone for a few hours? But I can't give you any more time than that because the gods have made a decision on how Fringe will be..."

"How I get to murder him?" James looked at her with violent eagerness.

"Well yes, that's right. The council have just..."

"How? Tell me how!"

"By fire. You're gonna burn his house down with him inside." She spoke with suspicion as she looked him up and down. "Jimmy, don't take this the wrong way but I've never seen you like this before. You seem to have suddenly acquired a sort of... blood lust."

James shook his head and looked away.

"You don't understand."

"Oh I understand. And to be honest babe, I'm just a little bit impressed," she said, smiling.

"You'll be even more impressed when you see those flames consuming that bastard," whispered James under his breath.

"Oh stop it, you cold blooded killer, you!" Muesli looked away and laughed bashfully. "Although, seriously, if you want it to go as well as last time I'd get your girlfriend, sorry, 'girl-who-is-a-friend,' to help you." She winked, and chuckled as his cheeks reddened.

"Muesli I'm not even going to dignify that with a response, except to say that…"

"Yeah, yeah, I'm only kidding. Is she on board for the final death?"

"I don't know. I'm not sure how she's coping after the last one. You know, 'morning-after-the-night-before' syndrome? She knows it's taking place but I don't know if she's up for it or not."

"Well there's one way to make sure. Pass me your phone."

*****

At The Cambridge Clarion, the office floor was a frenzy of excitement. When the scoop on the fraud broke, the national media's fickle attention momentarily focused on the grotty offices in St Andrew's Street, and phone lines and inboxes alike were swamped with requests to look at the evidence.

David Blythe, with characteristic concern for his colleagues, had hogged most of the attention, and the barked commands from his office had stirred up wild activity amongst his legion of journalists. At her desk, Wendy's head was spinning. One phone call after another left her with little time to think, and the hour since the headline had been released had passed in a fast-action blur.

Over the din of the office yet another ring blasted next to her, and she instinctively thrust her arm out to the phone on her desk, slamming the receiver to her ear.

"Wendy Pipford. Talk to me."

The ringing continued.

After a moment's confusion she smiled as she realised that it was coming from her mobile. As she answered she noticed the number was withheld.

"Hello Miss Pipford, this is Margaret Hunter of Core News. How are you?"

Almost before she realised what she was doing, Wendy ducked and reduced her voice to a whisper.

"Miss Hunter! How delightful to hear from you again." She looked around cautiously. No one in the office could possibly have known that she was talking to an editor from another, better, news outlet, but her professional fear could not be ignored.

"Is this a good time to talk, Miss Pipford? I hear a lot of noise in the background."

"Oh yes Miss Hunter, it's absolutely fine."

"Good. Well to cut to the chase, we've seen your exclusive on this fraud business, and let me tell you we are extremely impressed. This bodes very well for the job offer." The clipped tone oozed professional self-assurance, and Wendy could not help but picture the sleek London office from where the call was probably being made.

"Thank you so much, Miss Hunter! Does that mean that I'm being offered…"

"Not quite, Wendy. You see, as impressive as your scoop was, it hasn't persuaded everyone on the selection committee. I oughtn't even to be calling you up personally like this, but…"

"Yes, Miss Hunter?" Wendy's voice betrayed her eagerness, and on the other end of the line, a mile-and-a-half away in James's bedroom, the Muse smiled.

"To be perfectly honest I really think you're the one, and I've been trying to persuade my colleagues so. If you were to deliver another headline I think I'd manage to swing things your way."

Wendy could not contain her excitement, and the volume of her voice momentarily increased. "Oh thank you, Miss Hunter. I'm absolutely sure I could do it. Honestly, I won't let you down!"

"Good to hear, Miss Pipford. It's all down to you now."

With that the line went dead.

For a few moments Wendy held it in her hand and looked at the screen contemplatively. Then with a nod she scrolled through her address book and put the phone back to her ear.

"Come on, come on…. Oh James, is that you? It's me. Yes, yes, I'm good. Look, I need to know when the, er…" she reduced her voice to a barely audible whisper, "the you-know-what is going to take place. Yes James, the *you-know-what*. For God's sake, do I have to shout for the whole town to hear? Yes that. Tonight? Brilliant, can I come? Good. What time and where? I'll be there."

CHAPTER THIRTY TWO

Across Cambridge the shadows had gathered in. Fleeing before them, the people of the town had long since hurried home to their dwellings in fear of who might follow them on the wind. As the church bells of Great St Mary's tolled nine times, the sound echoed across the ancient city and out into the countryside. It made its way over the roofs of the ancient buildings and the lone trees that dotted the landscape, until eventually, faintly, it hit upon the grey, flinty stones of a great house. Standing by itself in grounds that were all its own, the mighty building stood firm against the wind.

As the sound of the bells faded away, two figures stirred in the shadows on the lawn.

"So this is where Fringe lives?" whispered Wendy admiringly. "Not bad."

"I wouldn't get too attached if I were you," said James. "It won't be here for long. Did you bring the stuff?"

"Of course." She opened her bag to reveal boxes of matches and a bottle of paraffin.

"Good. Remember what we said?"

"Yes, quick and quiet. So how do we get in?"

"This way."

They crept through the garden to the back of the building, where an old door led to the kitchen.

It looked insubstantial, but as Wendy inspected it a puzzled look came over her face.

"So how are we going to get in? It's locked."

"We're gonna break the glass, obviously," said James.

"What? You must be joking, we can't just…!"

"Sshhh! Wendy keep it down!"

"But we can't smash the glass! We'll be heard!"

"Well if you've got a better way?"

She didn't reply.

"Thought not. Now stand back."

Wendy turned in irritation and winced at the sound of the glass shattering. For several seconds neither she nor James dared to move, but in the ensuing silence only the whistling of the wind through the cedar trees could be heard. James reached in and turned the key that had been left in the lock, and moments later they found themselves standing on the flagstone floor of an old kitchen. Inside, the house was dark and silent. Sensing the vast, empty rooms surrounding them, Wendy felt even colder. The atmosphere within the ancient dwelling set her on edge, and she recalled the sinister figure darting on the stairwell in the Faculty.

"James, my heart's pumping so hard!" she whispered. "This is awful, it's not a bit like last time. Let's just light the fire and get the hell out of here. James?"

But he was no longer at her side. Wandering through the kitchen, he had found his way into the entrance hall, a grandly proportioned chamber dominated by an immense oak staircase. Wendy ran after him.

"James! Where are you going?"

He didn't reply.

"James, what are you doing? What's going on?"

Slowly he turned, and Wendy caught her breath at the sight of his face in the pale light of the hall. His skin was colourless, glistening with a film of sweat. His eyes, though, glinted with startling force. His presence was no longer that of the weak young man she had known. For the first time she felt afraid of him.

"Please James, what's going on?"

"I think you'd better go, Wendy. It's not going to be an in-and-out job after all."

"But James, I…"

"Just go. This is for your own good. I've got something to take care of."

343

"What can you possibly have to take care of here? Look let's just stick to the plan. Start the fire and go!"

"I'm sorry, Wendy."

Suddenly he turned and walked up the stairs.

"James!" she rasped. She followed him to the first step, but fear prevented her from going further. After he had disappeared out of sight she strained into the darkness. What was she supposed to do now? She couldn't just leave him, and she certainly couldn't start the fire whilst he was upstairs. Looking about her she realised that her bag was missing. Walking back into the kitchen it was nowhere to be seen. James must have taken it with him upstairs. But surely he couldn't be so stupid as to start a fire whilst he was on an upper floor?

*****

James advanced slowly across the landing. Fringe was presumably asleep in bed, though the location of his room would have to be determined by trial and error. At the end of the hall he saw another staircase and he crept towards it, wincing at every creak in the ancient floorboards. Suddenly a different noise froze him in place. It was a voice, a word spoken aloud. Turning, he saw that at the end of a small passage leading off from his right a light was shining beneath a door.

Could it be Fringe?

He advanced, and within moments he was close enough to press his ear to the wood. Inside he could hear a man speaking, posing questions and responding to answers, though there seemed to be no one else there.

*****

"How many years? Tell me! How many years?" yelled Fringe, to the ambassador. The latter, not being present to hear the conversation, was in no position to answer. His silence, though, was more than enough provocation to enrage his accuser.

"Oh I'll tell you how many. Thirteen. We've helped each other for thirteen years! As equals! That's right, equals! I was always your equal, whatever you may have thought. You looked down your nose at me but I was always at least your equal! Is it not true?!"

The empty chair that Fringe, in his rage, had nominated as a substitute for the man who had swept away his life's ambition remained unmoved against the torrent of abuse. Fringe, whose countenance was that of a drunk though he had imbibed not a drop, was not to be deterred by this frosty response.

"I should never have listened to you! Never! Judas! Didn't I give you everything? Didn't I risk everything for you? And this is how you repay me? You abandon me! You and all the others! All those good-for-nothing corpses! Well I don't need you! Any of you!"

This one-sided fight had been carried on for hours, commencing the instant Fringe had thrown the vase at Miss MacAfree. Now every hatred and injustice he harboured, every slight accumulated over a lifetime at Cambridge, was cast against the absent ambassador. The bitterness and savagery that had gathered in his mind was levelled against his former patron who, in the space of mere moments that afternoon, had become his undoer.

Through this act of abandonment his anger was exposed in all its fullness. Fury such as Fringe was capable of could not be abated simply through burning itself out. Bitterness, which swells with time and remains after all else is gone, fed his anger. It began to drip into his blood and sting his eyes.

345

Looking over at the empty chair, Fringe could see the ambassador as clearly as if he were really there.

Walking up to the phantasmal figure, whose condescending smile was still attached to its face and whose chin was thrust arrogantly up, he leaned in and whispered in its ear.

"I'm going to kill you. One day you'll return to this place and I'll be waiting."

He leaned back to look at the ambassador's face, only to be met with the same haughty expression, the same unchanging look of superiority. And at this his self-control crumbled once again.

"I'll kill you! I'll kill you, you dog! You hear me I'll…"

"… kill you," came a voice from the doorway. "My thoughts exactly."

Startled out of his frenzy, Fringe span round. There, standing and looking at him was a young man. In the artificial light of the room his palour was almost ghostly, though his eyes had an intensity that was unnerving.

"Who the hell are you?" asked Fringe after a moment's hesitation. "What are you doing in my house?"

The young man slowly advanced until he was but a yard from the professor. Despite the intensity of his gaze, his voice was calm.

"Don't you remember me?"

"No, I don't think so. Should I?"

"Perhaps my name will ring a bell."

"Well… perhaps. What is it?"

"My name is James…" A moment's pause, and the young man leaned forward emphatically. "James Connor."

Fringe's slightly bewildered expression remained firmly in place.

"Right. Can't say it rings a bell."

"What?"

"Sorry, I just don't remember."

"What the…? What do you mean you don't fucking remember? Think!"

"Look I don't know who you are or what you're doing in my house!"

James stepped closer, his eyes narrowing.

"I'm the one you scammed out of his degree; the one whose exams and thesis you failed."

The confusion on Fringe's face did not abate.

"The one who was pushed out to make way for someone else."

"Make way for…?"

"For the ambassador's son!"

At this a spark of recognition lit Fringe's eyes, and his mouth twisted into a cruel smile.

"You! I remember now. Oh yes, you were a step on the way to my becoming Vice Chancellor. You were part of the scheme. The ambassador's scheme. The one in which I was abandoned. You mean you've come here after all this time because…? Ha! Oh I see! Ha ha! That you should think yourself ill-used compared to me! How pathetic!"

He began to laugh, a malicious jabbing that pricked James in the pit of his stomach.

"Ha! James Connor! I'm surprised you even have a name. You're nothing! You never were! Oh dear God, this has been sent to me as a sweet relief!"

The laughter continued, and with each rasping inhalation James's heart pumped bile into his veins.

As evil mirth overcame him, Fringe doubled over, gasping for air.

"You think you were hard done by, is that it! Ha! You think the Faculty misused you? Oh you pathetic little wretch! If I had my way now that Faculty would be wiped from the face of the Earth, along with its occupants. But even if I could I wouldn't undo what I did to you!

Then James struck. Lashing out, he caught Fringe on the side of the head and sent him tumbling to the floor.

"Dear God!" spluttered the professor in shock. "What do you think you're…?"

But James set upon him, his fists pummelling the man where he lay. Each strike was both a burning relief and a stern encouragement to strike again. And for the first time he struck in anger, in hatred. Though he had taken life after life, soliciting death to visit his enemies, it was only now that he struck with the wish to kill. Only now did the desire to end the life of another come full into his heart, growing stronger through his thrashing, accelerating punches against the prone form before him. He would not stop. He could not. Never mind the law, or morality, or the gods themselves, he would strike until he dealt silent, unspeaking death to Paul Fringe.

Suddenly the professor kicked out with his foot and sent James tumbling to the floor. Another instinctive lash and James himself was caught in the head.

He struggled to his feet and looked down as Fringe, wheezing, began to clamber up. The savage rhythm of the attack was broken, and all the invisible constraints of civilised conduct clamped themselves around James once again. He could not resume the attack. As he saw Fringe struggle to his feet he ran to the bag that he had left in the middle of the room. Grabbing the bottle of paraffin, he ripped the top off and threw the container at the professor's head, catching him by surprise and sending him tumbling back to the ground with a cry. Liquid burst out, and droplets of the chemical spattered across the floor. James, however, was untouched, and he began fumbling with the matches.

"Come on, come on!" he growled as one after the other broke in his trembling hands.

"Connor, you pathetic little runt! You're nothing!" cried Fringe as he struggled to regain his footing.

Suddenly a spark, and a flame flickered into life between James's fingers. There was no need for words now. Hatred had expended his voice. He flicked the match at Fringe, and in the same instant blistering heat came into being.

James stepped backwards against the sudden light, and covered his eyes. But as he did so he tripped on his bag and landed hard on the floorboards. For several long moments he was dazed and could not focus, but as his vision re-established itself he gasped in fear.

The room was already engulfed. Flames raced up the walls like a glowing liquid flowing backwards against itself, whilst the heat that surrounded him seemed to suck the very air from his lungs. He had to get out.

Scrabbling up, he ran for the door, which was barely visible through the thickening smoke. As he reached it, however, he heard a cry above the roar. It was Fringe. He looked back, and through the blaze could see him, a mere collection of limbs dripping fire. He could not perceive where the professor ended and the flames began, and in that moment they seemed almost one.

Not a thought or feeling crossed his mind as he looked on at the man being devoured. He stepped through the door and shut it behind him.

The corridor itself was burning now, and amidst the choking fumes his sense of direction began to falter. With sickening urgency he managed to retrace his steps. Amidst the chaos around him he could see the stairs that would lead him back to the great hall.

James pressed ahead. As he reached the top step, however, something slammed into him, and he spluttered as he was knocked sideways against the wall. Gasping for breath, he looked up to see a figure running away from him and down the corridor to the room where he had left Fringe.

"Who the hell was that? That can't have been Wendy, surely?"

But the thought alone made him call out her name as he ran down the stairs.

"Wendy! Wendy are you there?!"

The oak staircase was beginning to burn now, delivering destruction up the spine of the great house. He staggered through the entrance hall towards the kitchen, when suddenly he felt himself grabbed by the shoulders.

"James! What the hell have you been doing up there? I've been scared out of my wits! What did you do? How has the fire spread so quickly?"

"Wendy, I…" he gasped.

"Don't speak! We don't have much time, we need to go now! Here, lean on me."

With that she bundled him through the kitchen and out the door. In the coldness of the night they gasped, and James convulsed with a fit of coughs.

"James, we need to go. The firemen will be here any minute."

Without waiting for a reply she hoisted his weight against her small frame and dragged him into the road and down a footpath leading away from the house.

Behind them the great edifice was savagely illuminated against the black sky, with the wind snapping eagerly at the leaping flames. Had they looked back, the pair might have wondered at the terminal countenance of that noble building. Lit from within, its grand façade looked defiant against the flames. As the heat began to burst the windows, however, its desperation grew evident.

CHAPTER THIRTY THREE

In the packed council chamber of the immortals there was silence. All the gods of Olympus were gathered in unspoken excitement there in the nerve-centre of their democracy. All had assembled on the great benches and now leaned forward in strained anticipation, waiting.

All, that is, but one.

Moments passed, and in the mounting tension immortals began looking to their neighbours with urgent glances.

Suddenly the door to the chamber opened and a goddess entered. Her beauty, in its eternal immediacy, would have elicited gasps, but silence remained. With slow dignity she walked to the centre of the chamber and stopped. Raising her hand, she looked about the room and strung the assembled masses on moments more of charged silence. When finally she spoke, a spark jolted through the listeners.

"Immortal gods and goddesses. I give formal announcement of the news that we have long awaited. The five wretches of the Cambridge List have been destroyed!"

The eruption was thunderous. Places were cast aside as immortals across the hippocampus flooded onto the floor in a riot of cheering and applause. They surrounded the Goddess of Desire, pressing inwards in an immense surge from all sides.

"Hail Aphrodite! It is you who brought us this glory!" came an anonymous cry from amongst the throng.

"Glorious one, you have honoured us all! What victory!" said the voice of a god whose identity was lost amongst the crush.

"Hail Aphrodite, defender of our greatness!" cried others.

"My divine comrades!" yelled Aphrodite. "I am humbled by your praises, but I beseech you not to give credit for this great day to me, but to yourselves. For you are the ones to whom this glory is owed. It was you who graciously listened to my proposal and carried it through. Now it is *your* day that you celebrate, and collective glory for us all!"

The cheering intensified and a hysterical chant emerged.

"All glory to Aphrodite! All glory to Aphrodite!"

The Goddess of Desire smiled graciously, and in perfect concealment of her triumphal feeling. The last word had belonged to her in the council's war plan, and her proposal had led to final victory.

She had won. Almost. For her ultimate plan was yet to be carried through, and in order for that to happen the democratic sentiment that saturated the council would have to be mobilised yet further.

Looking past the crowd, she scanned the benches. They were empty, as their former occupants danced about her. Narrowing her eyes she peered through the swell of deities, and there she spotted a lone figure on the front row at the far side of the room.

Hera.

The Queen of the Gods was staring at her, and though her eyes shot penetrating needles of hatred, her face and demeanour were composed.

"You've lost," mouthed Aphrodite silently through the jubilant roar.

Hera made no reply, and her composure remained unchanged.

Aphrodite, after giving her enemy a moment to rise to the bait, impatiently raised her hands and called for silence.

"Gods and Goddesses, quiet please!"

Within moments the chamber had fallen back into hushed anticipation, though an excited whisper could still be heard from a large group at the back.

"As we all know, there has been discord amongst the gods of late. Strife that has cut at the heart of our divine unity."

The murmur intensified.

"And I believe we all know the quarter from which it came."

At this the crowd, as even crowds of gods are wont to do, parted to reveal the known agitator. In a great shuffling of feet a clear line of sight was formed between Hera and Aphrodite. The gods and goddesses lining it looked back and forth between the two excitedly, whilst those deeper in the crowd stood on tiptoes, angling for a better view.

"Hera," intoned Aphrodite. "We have achieved collective glory. An honour we all share through my democratic plan. Will you renounce hostilities and share in it with us? Will you acknowledge the wonder of my plan, its success in bringing what we share today?"

Finally Hera rose. The most feared of all the immortals drew herself up in command of her awful power, which had been used to level her enemies, mortal and Olympian alike, throughout the aeons.

The deities closest to her, however, did not shrink back. This time no one moved. No eyes were averted. All gazed steadily at her.

Hera saw none of them. When she spoke, her voice was low, for there was no one else in the chamber, no one she wished to address. No one but her enemy.

"I will never accept your part in this, Aphrodite. Never."

"Even if it means denying the collective glory that we all share? The glory of the council?"

"Yes."

"Then I think," said the Goddess of Desire with a long awaited sense of thrill fluttering in her chest, "that you can no longer be part of this council."

Gasps arose, and the crowd's composure was broken. Immortals looked at one another with expressions of shock. Could such a thing be possible? Could Hera really be permanently expelled from the ruling body of the gods? Surely not without open war?

Amidst the flurry of whispers, however, Hera did not move. Across her face a smile crept.

Even Aphrodite was taken aback. Why was she not putting up a fight?

"I believe, Goddess of Desire, that you are right. I can sit on the council no longer. I will leave."

With that she stepped down from the benches and began to cross the floor. Despite standing their ground as she had risen to speak, the great crowd of immortals now scrambled to part before her. Reaching the door to the chamber, she stopped and turned. When she spoke it was in the same low voice with which she had addressed Aphrodite. But now she did not speak to her enemy. Nor as her eyes glinted, darting across every face and in a voice reduced to a whisper, did she address the crowd. Somehow, with words of calm, unassuming hatred she spoke to each and every god on their own. In that moment every individual in the silent chamber was alone with their fallen Queen.

"Be sure that I will find you here again. Be certain of it."

Then she turned and was gone.

Silence remained. A coldness had cast itself across the chamber and a strange fear hung over the heads of the gods and goddesses. Was this really the end? The question lingered unspoken in the mind of every deity. Each knew it must not be answered; that to do so would be to repeat Hera's words. Her promise.

At length the singing and dancing were once again struck up, though with an urgency borne as much of this strange fear as of victory itself.

As the first voices and sounds of movement rose in the silence, Aphrodite closed her eyes. She had felt the same chill, the same momentary dread whose echo is heard only in the quiet moments of solitude.

No matter. What happens in the great beyond of forever is of no importance to an immortal god. In the council of the Olympians, where schemes are played out across infinity, the only victories that truly matter are those of the very moment. With a shake of her head Aphrodite looked out across the crowds, smiling as the thronging celebration mounted around her.

CHAPTER THIRTY FOUR

The blackness was all about him, and as he grew aware of it, it became palpable. It was enveloping. A thick, dark mass that floated, coursing over him like smoke. Every so often a spark of light could be seen through it. Then several at once, accompanied by heat. But as soon as they appeared they were enveloped by the blackness.

Suddenly a burst of burning light flashed close against him and he jolted.

"James!"

"What… where… where am I? What's happening?"

"James, it's me. Can you see me?"

He blinked, and blurred shapes slowly converged.

"Wendy?" he whispered. He heard his voice as if for the first time, and it sounded distinctly different. "What's going on?"

"Oh hang on, I'll draw the curtains a little. I think the light's hurting your eyes."

The room suddenly dimmed, and there standing over him was Wendy Pipford. Though she was surrounded by haze, he sensed from the sound of their voices that they were alone in a small room.

"Wendy," he croaked.

"Don't worry James, you're fine. You're in Addenbrooke's Hospital. You've been here for about thirty-six hours. Don't worry, everything's absolutely alright, you'll be able to leave soon. Do you remember what happened?"

James winced as memories flooded back, and as he blinked the flames reared up before him again, forcing him to catch his breath.

"Did we… Did we get it done?"

"Absolutely, James," beamed Wendy. The police have found a body. It's burnt beyond belief apparently, but it's there. We did it." She was cheerful, and not simply for the sake of reassurance.

"What about the other body?"

"What other body? You told me that Fringe was the only one in there."

"I thought he was, but… but when I was running out someone passed me on the stairs. I couldn't see who it was, but they ran into the room Fringe was in when I left him."

Wendy looked sceptical.

"I think perhaps you imagined it, James. They only found one body, and trust me there's no way anyone else could have survived. You and I were lucky to make it out in one piece ourselves."

"Perhaps," said James, momentarily pushing doubt beneath the surface. "But what about the police. Do they suspect anything?"

"They don't suspect us, if that's what you mean. I managed to drag you to the A&E myself. Nearly killed me," she chuckled. "I told them you were smoking pot in a shed at a friend's house and that whilst you were high you managed to set fire to it and burn it down."

"They believed you?"

"There were more than a few raised eyebrows, and I got a hell of a talking to from one of the surgeons. He warned me about the dangers of drugs and matches and all that rot. He said that because no one else was seriously hurt he'd forgo calling the police this time."

"Nice one, Wendy. Thank you. For everything."

"Not at all, James. I should really be thanking you. I managed to turn the fire into another scoop for The Clarion. Haven't had a wink of sleep since it all happened, but never mind."

"I'm sure it was all worth it," he whispered hoarsely.

"Well between you and me" she said, leaning close to him and lowering her voice. "An editor from a start-up news outlet has been in contact with me in the last few days. She says they've been very impressed with my work and that I'm a prime candidate for a job opening. I think this might be the one to clinch it."

"Fingers crossed."

"Thanks, James. Anyway I'd better shoot off. The town's gone absolutely wild since the news broke. The national press are having a field day. Almost everyone thinks, rightly as you and I know, that Fringe was behind the fraud, but…"

"What is it?"

"There's also wide-spread speculation that he was behind the murders, too."

"You mean…? Wow!" murmured James, whistling feebly through his teeth.

"I know, isn't it great? Everyone's saying he killed himself once the net began to close in. The police are saying it's yet to be established and all that, but at least it puts us in the clear."

"I'll say!"

"There is one thing I was curious about, though."

"What?" he croaked.

"I know you probably can't talk about it, but ever since I discovered the fraud I haven't been able to stop thinking about it. The people who made you kill the five victims; were they involved in that Outreach Fund business? Are they the ones giving you orders?"

James closed his eyes and smiled.

"No, Wendy. And I think it's best if you don't ask any more questions. For your own good, you know?"

"I thought not," she said understandingly as she looked at her watch. "Anyway James, I really must be off."

She walked to the door, but before opening it she turned and smiled again. "I think perhaps it's best if we don't, you know, contact each other again. I'm sure you understand."

"Of course. Goodbye. And thank you again."

As the door closed behind her he exhaled, and winced at the pain. With the sudden realisation that he had lost a day and a half, the outside world seemed to beckon. Hopefully a doctor would be along soon to discharge him.

"Don't worry babe, you won't be here much longer. You're fine, really. Which is more than I can say for her chances with that 'editor.'"

James started, and looking to his side saw a nurse. Her uniform was far too tight, her neckline open and exposing a wealth of fake gold jewellery. Her hair, scraped back in a greasy, bleach-blonde bun, revealed two immense hoop earrings that would have broken the dress code of even the slackest establishment.

"Muesli! What are you doing here? And as... that?"

"I'm here to say goodbye, darling. I would say so on behalf of all the gods too, but the others are having a bit of a celebratory shindig at the moment. In your head as it happens."

"Were you not invited?"

Shaking her head, she wrinkled her nose in an unconvincing display of nonchalance.

"Oh, but you might be interested to know that Hera has been kicked off the council."

"Really? Ha! Good riddance!" he laughed.

"I know, good innit? Still babe, you've done it. You've carried out the mission we set for you, and somehow you survived. So fair's fair, it's time we left you in peace."

"You mean... for good?"

Despite his aching body James hoisted himself up in the bed.

"Yep. I'm here in my official capacity as nurse at the noble establishment of Addenbrooke's Hospital to administer a little treatment of my own." As she spoke she smiled and adopted an air of comic officiousness.

"What treatment?" he asked.

"Well as you must know by now, the Flanoxiride in your system is what's allowed us to commune with you all this time. I'm going to give you the antidote."

"The… The antidote? But what…?"

"Morphine, babe. It neutralises Flanoxiride." Reaching out, she took from the tray beside the bed a syringe.

"Well, okay, whilst that's bloody amazing news, will I ever see you again?"

"Oh darlin," laughed the Muse. "What are you like? Bit of a softy really, ain't ya."

"But Muesli, I've got something to tell you."

"Tell me in a second, babe. Just a second."

A sudden pinch in his arm was followed by a surge of warmth throughout his body. He blinked in surprise at the sudden pleasure.

"Muesli? Muesli, I… I need to tell you… something. I just wanted to say…" He looked to his side, but there was no one there. He was alone.

"Bollocks."

EPILOGUE

A cold wind whipped across the Fens and through the little city of Cambridge. It has travelled this vacant land since long before the spires of churches and the turrets of towers pierced the vast East Anglian sky. It will continue to journey here long after grass has covered the untilled earth, and the square-cut stones are buried deep beneath. On this cold morning, the wind brought with it droplets of rain. Miles they fell, until the curve of the Earth became the sharp line of the horizon. Landing across the city they covered it in a fine film, imparting a fluidic, slippery beauty to the ancient colleges and narrow streets.

From across the barren fens, hidden by the mist, a man looked upon the city. No one saw him there, that lone figure. No one looked upon him and saw the scars written on his face, the twisted contortion of his lips. But from his mouth came a single choked utterance, spoken with a force to rival the wind and the rain.

"Revenge!"

If you would like to find out more about Robert Clear and his writing, visit his blog:

www.the-cambridge-list.blogspot.com